Quicksilver Soul

Also in the Shadow Guild Series

Gilded Hearts

Quicksilver Soul

Book Two in the
Shadow Guild Series

CHRISTINE D'ABO

New York Boston

Copyright © 2014 by Christine Arsenault
Excerpt from *Gilded Hearts* copyright © 2014 by Christine Arsenault
Cover design by Christine Foltzer
Cover art by Dominick Finelle
Cover copyright © 2014 by Hachette Book Group

Forever Yours
Hachette Book Group
237 Park Avenue, New York, NY 10017
hachettebookgroup.com
twitter.com/foreverromance

First ebook and print on demand edition: April 2014

Forever Yours is an imprint of Grand Central Publishing.
The Forever Yours name and logo are trademarks of Hachette Book Group, Inc.

The publisher is not responsible for websites (or their content) that are not owned by the publisher.

The Hachette Speakers Bureau provides a wide range of authors for speaking events. To find out more, go to www.hachettespeakersbureau.com or call (866) 376-6591.

ISBN 978-1-4555-5054-8 (ebook edition)
ISBN 978-1-4555-5055-5 (print on demand edition)

Acknowledgments

I've been fortunate in my writing career to have gained so many wonderful friends who have been there to lend a hand and offer their support. As always, I want to thank my writing buddies Kristina, Paula, Amy, and Kimber. Your emails make me smile and keep me going when I want to stop.

A special thank you to my partner in crime, Delphine Dryden. Ever single IM we had while I was writing this book helped me so much. You're fantastic, darling; never forget.

To my wonderful agent, Courtney Miller-Callihan. You got me from day one and that has always meant so much. Your support is amazing.

To my editor, Latoya Smith. I can't tell you how exciting it has been to work with you on this project. Thank you for helping me make these books awesome.

And finally to my husband, Mark. Dude…love you always.

Quicksilver Soul

Prologue

Keegan O'Connor stayed huddled in the corner of his cell, his forehead pressed to the tops of his knees, and muddled through prayers he didn't believe in. The man hadn't been by to visit him for so long that he'd lost track of the time. It couldn't have been more than a few hours, yeah? Surely not more than a day. The other Underlings would have noticed he hadn't been seen in a while. They might even start to poke around, see if they could find his sorry arse. They'd assumed he'd been pinched by the Sentry if he didn't show by midnight. Glyn would be pissed, and he'd catch an earful when he got back.

If he got back.

No one would miss him though. Not really. His mat in the abandoned house they used at night would be filled by another quick as could be. If Keegan was gone long enough that boy or girl would be put to work on Keegan's streets to pull in the marks, though no one was as good as him. He was the best there was at parting them upper crust from their purses because he was *special*.

He'd lived longer on the streets than most. That first night all alone after his parents had been taken by the Clockwerker Guild had nearly killed him. It didn't matter to their landlord that he was five and essentially an orphan. *Ye can't pay the rent then get the fuck out!* His fingers turned purple from the cold, his cheeks forever scarred from the frostbite. If he hadn't found the steam grate in the alley when he had, it would have been the end of poor little Keegs.

That had been the first time his special abilities showed. The one item he'd managed to take from his home before being cast out.

Without needing to look, Keegan reached into the pocket of his trousers and touched the small fob watch nestled between the thinning fabrics. His rising apprehension started to fade, making it easier for him to breathe once more.

It was only luck that the man hadn't taken his one prized possession away from him. Yes, it was broken and comprised of worthless metals, but Keegan had seen boys killed for far less out on the streets by men who didn't look a thing like killers. The man had even seemed pleased when Keegan showed him the trick that never failed to bring him coins from the muckety-mucks who pranced around the streets. They always liked him, liked the way he reminded them of their son, nephew, grandchild, and would step closer. He could make the metal sing, dance, do what he wanted, all with a single touch, pulling his marks in as they tried to figure out what he was doing.

Not that they ever could.

This bloke hadn't been much different from the rest. He knew the man was American from the way he spoke his words, long and stretched out. There weren't many tourists who came to New London these days, but when they did they were easy for him to pick clean. He'd be the poor starving waif, needing money for his mum. Oh, and look what I can do! It would be simple enough to show him the trick with his watch, spin a bit of a yarn about how the watch was magic, and when he was focused on the ticking of the hands, Keegan would reach into the bloke's pocket and pinch his purse. Easy peasy.

What he hadn't expected was for the man to wrap his hand around Keegan's wrist, his fingers tighter than any metal band he'd ever felt. He'd thought he would surely be dragged off to the King's Sentry and thrown into the prison in the guts of the Tower. Instead, the man made him perform the trick again and again until Keegan's mind throbbed from the pressure. It was too much, made his brain hurt and his skin itch, like bugs beneath the surface trying to get free.

"I have a better place where you can show me, son." The man smiled in a way that made him feel worse than his crawling skin. "Someplace quiet."

Keegan's weakened state made it easy for the man to haul him into the back of a hackney, that and the two men he had with him. Keegan had fought, kicked, and punched, called out for help, but no one cared. He was nothing more than an Underling, a street rat who was going to get his what for. That had been the last time Keegan had seen daylight.

Hours? It couldn't be days, could it? Maybe. It was so hard to tell here in the dark. He shifted so his eye socket was covered by his kneecap. The pressure served as a short distraction for him, though he knew he'd adjust to the small pain soon enough. It was then that his stomach chose to rumble, reminding him of the thin soup he'd swallowed down for his breakfast...whenever that had been.

Approaching footsteps made him release his grasp on the watch and curl further into himself. It was a pointless act on his part; there was no place for him to hide in the empty cell. The bastard hadn't even put him in one with a steam pipe for warmth against the cold winter's air. With the sound of each approaching step, Keegan tried to make his brain work, to come up with an idea, some sort of plan to get out of here. But it had been far too long since he'd had a proper meal, and the chill in his bones made it hard to concentrate.

Not that he was going to give up. Fuck that and fuck the man if he thought Keegan would simply roll over and die. He'd survived the streets of New London up to this point, and he'd find a way to survive this, too.

The footfalls stopped with a soft shuffling of soles on stone. Keegan could feel the weight of the man's stare on him through the cell bars, but refused to lift his face from his knees. He might be small and weaker than most, but he wouldn't make it easy for the bloke. The second someone touched him, he'd launch himself at them, clawing at their eyes. Let's see how much they like that.

"Well, that doesn't look comfortable." The click and grind of the gears of the locking mechanism that held this cell door closed filled the room. "And I'm sure you must be starving."

The thought of food had Keegan turn his face so he could peer at the man. He was wearing a well-pressed suit, though the top hat and radiation goggles he'd possessed upon their first acquaintance were now missing. The man was smiling, his eyes crinkling at the sides, as he stepped into the small cell.

"I'm sorry I couldn't offer you better accommodations, but this warehouse was the best location I could find to suit my needs. With all of my equipment scattered about, I didn't want you wandering away and getting hurt. Not until I have the opportunity to set up proper living accommodations. I promise that your stay here will be more pleasant in the future."

Keegan knew every nook and cranny of New London's darker sides. They hadn't been in the hackney long enough to have gone out of the city. If they were actually in a warehouse, then it was likely they were down by the Thames. There weren't many places they could be…

"Why'd ja bring me to Southwark, sir? There ain't much down here. Or is ya planning to off me?"

The man grinned. "I knew you were a smart one. I could tell by that look in your eyes when you asked me if I wanted to see a trick. No, my boy, I'm not planning to *off* you. We'll have to work on your vernacular if you're going to stay here. You'll need to speak proper English so I may understand you." Reaching into his pocket, he pulled out a small bag. "Sweet?"

Keegan's mouth began to water. Sweets were a temptation he'd rarely been faced with. He'd only had one or two before in his life, a stolen joy. "What I need to do for 'em? No one gives away things for free."

"No, they don't. I can tell you've got a shrewd business sense to go along with your special skills. I like that." He tossed the bag so it landed by Keegan's feet. "You are correct. I do need you to do something for me. But I believe in paying my employees up front, as a sign of good faith."

Pay? He'd never earned a wage before. Even if he had, Glyn, the leader of the Underlings, would have taken every copper. Eyeing the bag, he let his hand slip from its resting place on his leg until it touched the cold stone floor. When the man made no attempt to stop him, he risked reaching out, brushing his fingers along the paper.

"Go on. They're yours, and no one will take them. What's your name again, son?"

"Keegan, sir." He knew he shouldn't take them, that nothing

good ever came from accepting charity from strangers. But the smell had set his stomach rumbling once more and he knew he couldn't resist. With one final look toward the man, Keegan took the bag and stretched his legs out.

The bag was still stiff, fresh from the confectionary where the man must have purchased the treats. Keegan opened the bag, revealing small squares coated in a white powder that stuck to his fingers, even after he placed one in his mouth. The sugar was a rare and precious delight as it melted away upon his tongue, pulling a smile from Keegan. "S'good, sir."

"I've yet to meet a young lad who didn't appreciate the taste of sweets." The man cocked his head to the side. "And you should have said, 'These are good, sir.'"

"Mmm." His stomach rumbled in earnest as the treats filled the void. "These are good, sir." His tongue stumbled over the speech, but he managed to mimic the man's words.

"Well, Keegan, there are a lot more where those came from. I'm sure we can include the occasional bag as a part of your fee. I would expect a bright lad such as yourself to be able to deliver on your promises." The man dusted off his hands before sliding them into his pocket. "How would you like to come work for me?"

Work? Keegan snorted. "I ain't done a decent day's work in me life, sir."

"I find that hard to believe. An enterprising boy has to work hard to keep out of the grasp of the various guilds that plague this city. I imagine with your skills the clockwerkers would love to put you to work in one of their factories. Set you to toil away building some contraption or another for the king."

He'd come close to being caught by them on a number of occasions. If it hadn't been for the help of the Underlings,

Keegan would have been buried deep in the guts of a machine long before now. No matter how harsh Glyn was, Keegan owed him for getting him off the street.

"I'm too quick for 'em, sir. They won't catch me."

"But you do like to work with the machines. Like your watch."

Keegan shoved the last of the sugary treats into his mouth, holding them in his cheeks as long as he could before he gave in to the temptation to swallow. "That's just a trick. Something to keep the dandies still so I can lighten their load."

The man stepped farther into the cell, his smile widening slightly. "I'd like to see your trick again. You can consider it your first task, earning your treats."

The throbbing in his head had lightened as the sweets worked their way through his body. "Sir? It's just a stupid trick."

"No, my boy." The Man's gaze narrowed. "Not stupid. From the beginning. The whole thing as though you've just met me."

He supposed it was only fair. The man had paid up front, and Keegan enjoyed making people wonder. Ignoring the way his legs ached and his head spun, he slowly got to his feet. The metal of the watch was warm from his body, giving it a comforting feel against his cold hands. Keegan held it up, showing the unmoving hands of the watch.

"'Ello, sir. Wanna see a trick? This watch is special. It doesn't work, but it does wot I tell it te do."

He placed the convex back in the middle of his palm, presenting the cracked glass face for the man to see before Keegan closed his eyes. He thought it might be harder to find the quiet place in his head where he could see and feel the cogs of the watch, given how he currently felt. But the connection was easy enough to find. The spark of life that flowed through the metal, the soft hum as it vibrated against him, was still there, calling to him.

The muscles in his shoulders and back relaxed as his awareness spread out.

Keegan could feel the man's fascination, knew without looking that he was now three and three-quarters feet from him, approaching two and a third inches with each subsequent step. In his front jacket pocket was a second bag of sweets. Keegan would ask for those after. He knew that the man honestly had no intention of harming him, but there was something *wrong*. As though a dark stain had stretched across the man's soul.

The first cog, the largest in the watch, the one that always got things started, clicked forward. It was getting impatient to play, wanting Keegan to help it dance. Fine. They would do this, and then he'd get his reward.

The slip and click of gear against gear became the beat of their tune. Keegan picked up the invisible thread and pushed it forward until the wire wound tight. Then a breath, a beat, and a simple nudge sent the cog flying forward. *There it was!* The rhythm and beat that made the metal slide together, a perfect instrument in an orchestra of motion.

Keegan took a breath and opened his eyes to stare at the now moving second hand. The soft *tick, tick, tick* was the only sound beyond their breathing. It wouldn't last long. There was a gear deep inside the works that needed repair. It would grind on every second turn, slowing the dance until it stopped dead.

The man closed the distance between them. Once again his iron grip was around Keegan's wrist, preventing him from moving. "I want you to make the minute hand move as well."

There was a note in his voice that made Keegan shiver. It didn't feel right next to the smile he still wore. It was *off*. Yet in this moment he was his boss, and Keegan could tell he meant what he said about the food and the room. It would be better than being on the streets, away from Glyn and his heavy hand. Maybe, if the man could actually be trusted, he'd finally be safe from the guilds and the coppers. Given the recent dealings with Jack the Ripper, Keegan wasn't ready to trust a stranger.

"Now, please."

Keegan didn't need to close his eyes again, now that the connection was locked in place. The watch was still clear in his head, still listening to what he had to say. It only took a heartbeat to find the right path, the right gear, and give it a little push. It was simple to have it move, not a challenge at all. Easy, easy, easy to dance with them.

Keegan watched as the man's eyes widened.

"Can I have that other bag of sweets now, sir?"

The grip around his wrist was now a painful brand, squeezing deep into his bones. Nails dug into his flesh, sending a bolt of pain up his arm and into a spot on his back. The man met his gaze. Keegan had come face to face with one of them zombies once, the archivists. He'd hated the way their white eyes looked as they hooked up their memory box to the dead body. While his eyes were blue, there was something else there, something that made Keegan's stomach turn. Something that scared him in a way the zombies never did.

This man was a killer.

"Make it do something else." The man's voice was low and seeped into Keegan's body. "Something special."

He'd never tried to do anything beyond making the cogs spin. It was a bloody broken watch, not a clockwerker's automaton. "No."

"Come now, I thought you wanted that second bag of sweets." The man patted the outside of his pocket. "This is nothing more than a distraction, a ruse. Show me what you can really do."

"Fine." But he wouldn't do it for sweets. There was something about the man, a feeling Keegan couldn't quite put a name to. A darkness, a hidden danger that Keegan knew he'd need to protect himself from. And yet he couldn't turn down this opportunity to change his life. But Keegan had to proceed with caution. If Keegan had learned nothing else during his time on the streets, it was to gather as much information as possible. You never knew when you'd need it to save your neck.

It took him several moments to trace the spinning metal down to its center, but once he found the spot it was clear what he needed to do. With a thought, he *pushed* the metal, bending it in such a way that the tension broke. The second it snapped Keegan laughed and opened his eyes.

"Yes." He grinned, watching the result of his handiwork. "How's that for ya?"

The minute hand was spinning backward, opposite of the second hand, while the hour hand stood straight at the twelve. Each would cross over the stuck fast hour hand, giving the illusion of a man circling his arms in an effort to regain his balance.

"That's perfect." The man's smile became a full-on grin. "You are a very special boy." He released his hold on Keegan's wrist and dropped the second bag of sweets on top of the watch. "Very special indeed."

The temptation to eat the sugary treats was nearly blinding, but Keegan tucked them away in his pocket. "Can I leave?"

"Leave?" He crossed his arms, shaking his head. "I offered you a job. A position with my corporation, one of great importance, I might add. I don't make such commitments lightly, and I'm always true to my word."

"I don't wanna work in no factory." That was what had killed his parents. The night before their door was busted in and his parents were pulled out, kicking and screaming, he'd promised him mum he'd do what he could to stay out of the grip of the guilds. *I'll run away. I'll die first.* "I'd rather be out on the streets."

"A factory?" He snorted, cutting the air with his hand. "Nothing of the sort. Do you think a man such as myself would be allowed to run a business here? An American living this close to the French? The guilds would just as soon see me dead as risk me getting a foothold on their business. No, this won't be that sort of work."

"Then what?"

"Why don't you eat your sweets and we'll discuss it?"

"I dunno." It would be awfully good to have another taste of that sweetness. But he'd learned the hard way to save any extra food for the times when it was scarce.

The man's gaze narrowed. He wasn't expecting Keegan to say no to him. Well, he was an idiot if he thought someone would simply trust him. Respect and fear were the only two ways an Underling would pay attention, and Keegan was still an Underling, so he was afraid of nothing.

"What if I told you the job would entail working with a very special machine? And your payment would be room, food, and all the sweets you would ever want. If you're concerned about this cell, I promise improvements will be forthcoming." The man put his hand on Keegan's shoulder and gave it a squeeze. "You see, I dislike the guilds as much as you do, though that's not the only reason why I'm here. I have a...special project that could only be accomplished here in New London. There aren't many people I can trust to help me with a task this delicate."

Keegan could appreciate that. "And you trust a street rat?"

It had been years since anyone had shown him any kindness, let alone trust. Not since his parents had been taken away by the guilds. They'd been able to make machines do special things too, though not in the way he could. They would work longer and longer hours, leaving him home alone to fend for himself. He still didn't know why the guild took them the way they did, but he knew they were dead.

God, he'd been lonely, despite having fallen in with the Underlings. On the nights when he couldn't sleep, Keegan would dream that his mum was still there, that she'd wrap her arms around him and kiss his cheek. His dad would pick him up and carry him around on his shoulder, so high that Keegan could touch the ceiling. Those were the nights he'd wake up with tears on his face, wishing someone, anyone, would hold him, take care of him.

This might be his chance to find a new family. Maybe the man could be a father for him. Keegan squirmed, not wanting to let the warm feeling growing in his chest show.

"What kinda machine is it, sir?"

He laughed and clapped him on the shoulder. "Oh, none of that *sir* stuff with me. Come along and I'll show you what I started to build. You can tell me what you think of it. I bet you'll be able to make it do amazing things, maybe even offer suggestions on how to make it better. Even more than what you can with your watch."

The hallway outside of his cell wasn't in much better shape. The air was cool and damp, making it hard for Keegan to warm up.

"Thanks, sir. Ah, what should I call ya if not sir?" As they walked away, Keegan took the bag of sweets out of his pocket and shoved more of them into his mouth. *I could get used ta this.*

"In America it's customary to refer to your employer by his name." He reached down and ruffled Keegan's hair. "You can call me Mr. Edison."

Chapter 1

Emmet Dennison stood outside the Ministry of Guild Relations building and let the bitter winter wind slam against him. The freezing temperatures were a welcomed change from the stagnant air of the minister's office. The steam heat had been turned too high in the small space, which was filled with more bureaucrats than legally should have been allowed in one location. For seven hours he'd been forced to sit and listen to the demands of the government, the changes they expected the Archivist Guild to make in the wake of the recent tragedies that had gripped New London, all while being forced to suffer the stench of their sweat.

"We expect the archivists to do their duty, to extract the memories of the dead," the minister said with such disdain it was nearly palpable. "Jack the Ripper was your guild's doing. Your arrogance unleashed a monster upon this city, and he tore at our society's very fabric. We are here to ensure your pride doesn't cause further harm."

Government inspections. Official records keepers. Liaising with the Hudson's Bay Company. A list of all active archivists. A list of any other "secrets" the Archives might be keeping.

Bloody idiots didn't have a clue what they were asking. As though any guild in New London would be willing to part with their deeply guarded skeletons, laying themselves out for others to pick apart. Pulling up his collar and securing his topper low on his head, he turned sharply and marched toward the iron walkway that would take him to the Archives.

Guild Master June had put him in charge of government relations while the rest of the Elders were busy with reconstructing their refuge. The physical structure of the building itself would take time to repair, the memory vaults having suffered the greatest amount of damage after the Archives' central machine had gone into shutdown. Emmet along with every available archivist had been enlisted to help with inventory. Rows upon rows of shelves, each one containing dozens of memories, taken from New London's deceased. So many memories lost, lives once stored for future generations snuffed out of existence.

Maybe they were better off now. Finally gone on to the afterlife.

No. The memories of the dead were a commodity so precious they couldn't afford to lose a single one. Every effort was being focused on the rebuilding.

But it was the damage to the reputation of the archivists themselves that would be the hardest to fix.

They'd unwittingly created the most devastating killer New London had ever known. The zombies, as the public loved to refer to them, were a menace to both the living and the dead. They needed to be controlled, watched; otherwise, how could the people of New London be assured that they would remain safe? How could they know if another Jack the Ripper was hiding in the basement of the Archives? It was a refrain he was tired of hearing. How could the Guild Masters expect Emmet to right the mountain of wrongs that now lay atop the soul of the city without giving in to the demands of the king and his representatives?

He was third son of the Duke of Bedford, not a fucking god.

Darkness had crept upon the city while he'd been stuck inside arguing with fools. The glow from the sulfur lamps left pools of shadows and light across the frost-covered cobblestones. Emmet walked to the side of them, not wanting to face the continuing assault on his sensitive vision. He'd foolishly left his radiation goggles at the Archives. More and more, Emmet was finding himself distracted, an unfortunate habit that in the end would cause him physical harm if he continued.

The dark halls and cavernous rooms of the Archives provided him with respite from the growing radiation in the New London air, a reminder of their war with the French. Things would only get worse for him once he underwent his first extraction. His mind would slowly be filled with holes, picking away at his memories until he was left as a pale shadow of his former self.

Emmet adjusted his collar, pulling it tighter against his neck. He'd managed so far to put off his inevitable step to become a true archivist. While one by one his friends were assigned a mentor and an extractor, Emmet found other tasks, important responsibilities that required his presence anywhere but out on the streets of New London extracting memories from the deceased. It was only a matter of time. Soon the Archives would be repaired, the government would be appeased, and his name would once again appear at the top of the assignment roster.

His father would laugh if he knew how hard Emmet had worked to stay as far away as he could from the thing he'd begged to be allowed to do.

Bloody little fool. Go then, be nothing more than a harbinger of death. But don't expect to come crawling back. I'll harbor no zombies in this residence.

The gate that led to the iron walkways came into sight. The moving walkways that crisscrossed New London weren't policed by the King's Sentry or the Bow Street runners. Emmet could certainly afford to take a hackney, or could even have requested one of the Guild's carriages to take him back to the Archives, keeping him out of harm's way.

But where would the fun be in that?

The collector swallowed his copper as he pressed it into the slot. One of these days he'd love to find out where all the coins went.

As the gate closed behind him and Emmet gained his balance on the moving walkway, he took stock of his surroundings, cataloguing everything with a single glance and storing it in his eidetic memory. A group of three was in front of him, slumped forward in exhaustion as they stood silently. The iron walkway track joined in with a second, adding more bodies to the mix. Emmet slipped his hands into his overcoat, to curl his fingers around his pistol. Not that many were foolish enough to attack an archivist, but a person couldn't be too careful. He looked around once more, catching the eye of a burly man, who sneered at him. Emmet silently dared him to make a move by refusing to look away. The contact lasted only a moment before the man turned his face away from Emmet's.

It was a good thing the man hadn't pushed him tonight, given his foul mood. He'd been itching for a fight for weeks now, needing to find a way to burn off his excessive energy. Even a covert visit to the boxing club the previous week had done little to quell his need to hit, punish, vent his frustrations at the direction his life had taken. He couldn't risk losing that sort of control, not after he'd seen the result of what had happed to Jack.

No. Emmet knew he was under scrutiny by too many people to let his control slip now. Not simply because he'd gone against the Guild Masters' orders and helped his friends Piper and Samuel, but because he'd never truly been one of them. His brief dissention had simply reinforced what many already believed to be true—Emmet was only a part of the guild for his own benefit.

A man stepped up beside him, his long black coat, high collar, and bowler doing little to hide his surreal visage. Emmet hadn't been aware of his presence or his approach, which set the hair on the back of his neck on end.

Clearing this throat, Emmet kept his eyes forward. "Good evening, Administrator."

The Administrators were the secret enforcement officers of the Archives. While the populace of New London was often scared of the archivists, the archivists were equally scared of what the Administrators would do to them. They were an all too real boogeyman who coexisted with them, watching their every move.

Even Emmet wasn't above their watchful gaze or their rules.

"Good evening, Mr. Dennison. How was your meeting?" The man's voice was as flat as the dark night.

"As I'd anticipated. Tedious and a waste of the guild's time. I was able to deflect the majority of their requests, while ensuring the ones that required action would flow to the correct individuals so as to not inconvenience the Guild Masters."

"Well done, Mr. Dennison." His tone undercut the compliment.

There'd been rumors for the past several years that Emmet was being groomed to become an Administrator himself. They existed in the world of shadows, in the darkness where no one else would dare tread. Emmet had always been drawn to the darkness, the excitement of the unknown. It was what had drawn him to this job in the first place. As the son of a duke, Emmet could have been granted the position of liaison instead of archivist. But taking a lesser role was the only way he'd escape the far-reaching shadow of the Duke of Bedford.

Becoming an Administrator would give him unprecedented access to the inner workings of the city, the king, and each of the guilds. It was a position even his father wouldn't have been able to procure on his behalf and an opportunity Emmet wouldn't refuse if it was ever presented to him. Accepting that title would wipe the smug look off his father's face when he finally returned home.

If they ever made the offer.

The Administrator turned to face him. His pale skin and white eyes gave the man a ghostly presence, one that made it difficult for Emmet not to look away despite the unsettled sensation gathering in his stomach. Still, he straightened and maintained eye contact. If he were to become one of them, he better have the fortitude to confront what he may himself evolve into.

If the man was impressed with Emmet's ability to remain nonplussed, then he didn't show it. Instead, he stepped closer and lowered his voice. The sweet smell of tobacco had Emmet's mouth watering as the scent washed over him.

"A matter has come to the attention of the Administrators. One that could have serious ramifications for the guild if not handled in the proper manner."

Emmet could only imagine what that could be. Until recently, he'd had only marginally more information than some of the other archivists. While the Guild Masters took advantage of his status to gather information they'd otherwise not have access to, they didn't completely trust him. "I take it this has a degree of sensitivity?"

"Indeed, Mr. Dennison, one that the Administrators would like to handle as quietly as possible."

Casting a glance around where they stood, he noted that the forward group of three had taken an exit gate. Several people in front of them had drawn farther away and were casting uneasy looks there way, giving them a surprising amount of privacy considering their location.

"Mr. Dennison, the Administrators are giving you an assignment, one that the Guild Masters are not fully aware of. We expect it to remain privileged."

"Of course." Rarely did anything good come from secretive missions. His older brother Tobias, a captain in the King's Army and an intelligence officer, had often spoken of the negative fallout of such cases. Still, it was rather exciting to be on the action end of such a scenario, rather than simply listening to the story.

The Administrator's gaze never left Emmet, rarely blinking as though the added scrutiny would reveal something previously unseen. "As you are already aware, the Hudson's Bay Company insisted on sending an engineer to assist us with the rebuilding of the Archives' central machine and to check the structural integrity of the memory vials. Their claims of being the original architects and therefore having a greater fundamental understanding of how the central machine functions were persuasive. The king's insistence sealed our fate. We are to play host to a clockwerker."

There had been a serious breach of containment when Piper and her now husband and former archivist Samuel had been on the trail of Jack the Ripper. The Guild Masters had managed to keep the general public in the dark regarding Jack's true identity. Master Ryerson, who'd been responsible for the whole debacle, had been *handled* by the Administrators and hadn't been seen since that fateful night. As for Jack…his body might still be alive, but his brain was dead and personality gone.

What they weren't certain of was if the archived memories of the deceased men, women, and children of New London were still preserved. And if so, if the central machine, and, by extension, the Archives themselves, was capable of continuing on. Without it, then their entire guild would cease to be of any use.

"I am. I assume this clockwerker is causing some problems for the guild?"

"In a manner of speaking." The Administrator licked his lips. A nervous tic, or simply a tell that whatever he was about to say wouldn't be pleasant. "We have received information that has led us to believe there is a possibility that Master Ryerson didn't act alone. The information we have indicates there is a member of the Illuminating Company in New London and that Ryerson might have been providing this individual with information."

"What is that?" God, there was a time when he knew every major organization in the New London, now he couldn't keep track of them all.

"They are the main competition to the Hudson's Bay Company. With Ryerson now gone, our informant believes that the HBC engineer will be a target. That they will try to take the clockwerker and force them to reveal their knowledge of the Archives."

No. "You want me to play *nursemaid* to this man?"

The other man smiled, his lips twisting up to reveal too-large white teeth and reddened interior flesh. "I think you'll find Tesla to be an intriguing subject."

"With all due respect, sir, I haven't worked my way through the ranks of the guild, spent my spare time acting as liaison between His Majesty and the Guild Masters, and providing the

Administrators with information from the ton that they would otherwise not have access to, to play nursemaid to someone that one of our apprentices is perfectly qualified to watch."

The iron walkway jerked and jumped on the track, causing Emmet to lose his balance. But as he reached back to grab hold of the rail, the Administrator moved forward. Emmet froze as icy cold fingers gripped his wrist, preventing him from moving.

"Mr. Dennison, I don't believe you understand. This is not a request, a suggestion, or an assignment you can pass off to one of your lackeys. You are to stay with Tesla. You will ensure that nothing happens while work is being conducted on the Archives. And you will see to it that no one from the Illuminating Company comes close to Tesla while *she* is under our protection."

Emmet swallowed hard, ignoring the rising pain. "She?"

"I believe this is our stop." The Administrator pulled away and stepped past Emmet before he could react. Forced to chase after the man, Emmet covertly rubbed his abused skin.

"Nicola Tesla is one of the greatest engineering minds of our generation. She has a way with machinery that would make the Clockwerker Guild envious. She's refused the normal protection of the HBC, and it is our responsibility to keep her safe while she fixes the Archives. The consequences of failure are too steep otherwise."

The Administrator stopped in the middle of the road, forcing Emmet to come beside him. "Why me?" It was a reasonable question, even if it was the last thing he should be asking. One didn't push the Administrators, lest they find themselves "handled."

"You haven't undergone an extraction. Most of your peers have performed at least one, but you've found every opportunity to avoid your initiation. It hasn't gone unnoticed that you pushed your way through the front door, only to drag your feet."

He turned his head only enough for Emmet to catch a glimpse of the disdain in his eyes. "Quite frankly, Dennison, at this point you're expendable. If someone is to die while protecting Tesla, we'd prefer it be you."

Emmet had been called many things over the years—boorish, prideful, secretive—though never once had he been considered nonessential. "I see."

"Keep her safe. See to it that she accomplishes her goal and gets back on the airship for Canada. Prove yourself."

Emmet stood rooted as the Administrator walked in the opposite direction of the Archives and disappeared into the darkness.

Expendable.

"Fucking little fool! You have no idea what the world is like beyond my protection."

"Then let me find out for myself. I need this, father."

No, that simply wasn't acceptable. He wasn't some by-blow to be used, cast aside, and then ignored. If they wanted him to play nursemaid to some slip of a woman while she puttered about her contraptions, then by God that's what he'd do. And once she was safely on her way to Canada, Emmet would have a rather pointed conversation with the Guild Masters. If the Administrators believed he was of no use to the guild, then it was more than likely others thought so as well. He'd prove himself, even if that meant taking an extraction assignment and tearing his mind to shreds.

Pulling back his shoulders and lowering his chin, Emmet continued home.

The large building that contained the Archives was one of the most foreboding structures of New London. The large gray stones rose high into the sky, leading to copper turrets topped by steeples. One of the earlier architects had the foresight to attach metal rods to the peaks, running cables down into the depths of the building. Piper and Samuel had once tried to discover where those cables had gone, to see if they could harness their power. They'd begged Emmet to come along, but he'd still been more than a little prideful and standoffish at that point. It had turned into one of Sam and Pip's many childhood adventures, a plan that never quite came to fruition, but that they'd enjoyed nonetheless. Emmet stood on the outside and watched.

He'd never admit it aloud, but he missed having Piper around. Once she'd healed from Jack's attack, she'd declined to be reinstated as an archivist and had accepted a position with Samuel at the King's Sentry. Now they worked side by side and had recently been married.

His friend Jones performed his first extraction sooner than originally scheduled. He had been called to withdraw the memories of the king's second cousin. The experience had left him shaken so badly Emmet knew he'd been correct to put off his own initial extraction as long as possible. When Emmet tried to engage Jones after he'd been released by the doctors, his friend simply shook his head, leaving Emmet standing alone in the corridor.

The winds whipped around him as he made the lonely approach up the steep staircase to the main Archives entrance. He had no reason to feel anything but determination in regard to his current predicament. He'd chosen this life over countless other options, roles that would have provided him with wealth and status, even as he blended in with the rest of the younger sons in society. So why the hell did Emmet feel as though his life was slipping away from him?

The foyer of the Archives was unsurprisingly empty. Opening his coat and removing his topper, he strode to the lift that would take him to the residential level. His rooms had always been bigger than what the other archivists had been allotted. There had to be some advantages to his standing, and Emmet had always felt a great deal of comfort there. Tonight he'd seek out his solitude, consider the Administrator's assignment, and decided how best to proceed. A plan would be necessary to ensure all would go the way he wished.

"Mr. Dennison, sir!"

Emmet turned to see one of the apprentices—Reggie, Regan, Ryan...something—running full speed toward him.

"Slow down!" The boy skidded to a stop several feet away, his eyes growing wide. "The Archives is no place for a foot race."

"No, sir. Sorry, sir. But Master Tolan sent me to get you as quickly as possible."

Tolan was one of the elder Guild Masters, the person in charge of the Archives vault and by extension the central machine. Emmet had always considered him more than a little mad, though that was to be expected seeing as the man rarely saw the light of day. If Tolan was after him, then it was likely there was a true issue.

"What's the problem then? Spit it out, boy."

The lad blinked at him, shuffling from foot to foot. "Umm, I wasn't quite sure what Master Tolan said, but it had to do with that *woman*."

The emphasis was no doubt Tolan's and not the boy's. "Someone meddling with his gears?"

"She took off a panel and disappeared into the works." It was said with a certain degree of awe. "Master Tolan said you were supposed to keep her in line and that I was to fetch you as soon as I could."

No doubt the Guild Master threatened the lad with vault cleaning duty if he didn't perform the task as quickly as possible.

Having been on the receiving end of that particular punishment several times over the course of his apprenticeship, Emmet could appreciate the boy's haste.

Still…

"Master Tolan said I was responsible for her?"

The boy nodded twice so hard, Emmet feared for his head. "Yes, sir. He said that's what the…what they…"

"Who?"

"The Administrators told him." The words came out in a rushed whisper. The boy looked around as though simply saying their names would cause them to appear. Perhaps he was a smarter lad than Emmet first thought. So, it was to be known that he was watching the girl, but not of the need to protect her. Fine. A game he could well play.

"Thank you, Ryan."

"It's Roland, sir. I'll run ahead and let him know you're on the way." Without another word, he spun and bolted down the hallway.

So much for coming up with a plan.

Shoving his gloves into his pocket and tucking his topper beneath his arm, Emmet stepped into the lift and pressed the down button rather than the up. Roland would no doubt take the not-so-secret passageways that led to the basement. Most apprentices enjoyed traveling that way, testing their knowledge of the building from the maps they'd read. Even Emmet couldn't resist them when he'd been younger. Yet as time marched on he'd joined the ranks of the adults and now chose the more traditional routes.

The journey to the bowels of the Archives didn't take long. Certainly not long enough for him to work out what the hell was going on. It felt like he'd been in a state of flux since Piper and

Samuel had left him behind. Jones had been no help, too busy dealing with his own concerns.

The vault was closed, but the sounds of chaos slipped out into the hall. This wasn't what Emmet needed tonight. No, a nice drink of scotch and a cigar would have gone a long way to setting things right. Pushing the doors open revealed Master Tolan standing at the far end of the cavernous room, basted in the glow of the red light from the memory vaults, shouting into a giant hole in the wall. As Emmet got closer, he was able to see that several panels in the wall had been removed and placed on the floor.

"I demand you come out here at once!" Master Tolan stood in front of the opening, arms crossed. "Do you hear me, young woman?"

"I heard you have a pest problem, Elder." Emmet leaned against the side of the wall, ignoring the older man for the time being. "And I've been informed it's my duty to assist, whether I wish it to be or not."

"That woman has been nothing but a thorn in my side since her arrival." Emmet looked back at the Guild Master and tried not to laugh at the expression of absolute disgust on his face. "She's poked at and criticized every inch of my vaults since her arrival this morning, as though she knows more about this place than I do. I've devoted my life to ensuring everything works perfectly."

"I'm sure she meant no disrespect. You know what these Company people are like. Arrogant."

"That's saying something, coming from you."

Emmet cocked an eyebrow at Tolan. "I could always leave you to the task, Master."

Master Tolan waved in the direction of the hole. "Go fetch her, Dennison. I want her out of my house."

The dark passage was lined with pipes, conduits, and copper wires. They disappeared into the shadows, making it nearly impossible for Emmet to see where he was going, or what Miss Tesla was up to.

"Wouldn't it be better to send your apprentice in for the task?"

"Roland is a stupid boy, terrified of his own shadow." Master Tolan straightened and narrowed his pale gaze at him. "This is your assignment. Your responsibility. I will not allow you to fob it off on some idiot of a boy."

Shocked by the venom in the Guild Master's voice, Emmet nodded. He wasn't certain what had changed to damage Roland's reputation within the guild, but he needed to find out. As soon as he dealt with their interloper. "Of course, sir. I'll handle Miss Tesla and ensure she causes as few problems as possible with the Archives, least of all to your machine."

"Good." Without saying another word, Master Tolan turned and marched away, leaving him standing alone in front of a hole in the wall.

"Fine mess you've made for yourself, Emmet," he muttered.

Grabbing one of the headlamps the apprentices used while they were assigned to the deeper sections of the vaults, he slipped it in place and flicked the switch. A weak beam shone into the dark passage. Removing his overcoat and waistcoat, Emmet rolled up the sleeves of his shirt, hoping to protect as much of the fine fabric as possible.

He dropped to his hands and knees and began the journey into the guts of the Archives. "Ready or not, Miss Tesla, here I come."

* * *

Keegan picked up the copper casing and held it in his hands. The metal was tarnished and pitted, and deep scratches lined the top.

It was easy to see why a clockwerker would have discarded this particular piece. The work required to make it usable would have taken much too long.

Not that it mattered to him. He had all the time in the world.

This was the key to Mr. Edison's entire plan. The heart that needed to beat in just the right way to ensure the successful completion of their mission. Although it was empty now, Keegan could envision how the gears would fit, how they'd slip into place so they could dance together. The ticking would be like beautiful music, and he'd be the conductor.

He prayed Mr. Edison liked it. His boss scared him in a way that Glyn never did. While the older boy would yell and hit any Underling who didn't do as they were told, Keegan knew he wasn't in any real danger. Mr. Edison though…there was something evil about his new boss. Not that it wasn't anything he couldn't handle. Keegan would find a way to escape if need be.

Tucking the casing into his pocket, he climbed out of the junk pile behind the clockwerker's factory and checked to make sure the guards weren't about to come by.

"Psst!"

Keegan snapped his head around, locking in on the source of the sound. A dirt-smeared face poked around from the side of an abandoned boiler across the way. It was Gerry, one of the Underlings boys.

"Keegs, where've you been, eh? We was worried the zombies gotcha. Glyn's been askin' fer ya."

He couldn't tell Gerry about the warehouse, Mr. Edison, or their plan. Keegan didn't want to share his treats with the other boys. Nor did he want to risk anyone finding out what they were up to. If Glyn knew, he could ruin everything. It needed to be kept secret until they'd finished, at least. Then everyone would know. And it would be beautiful.

"Keegs? Ya comin'?"

Pulling his radiation goggles down across his eyes, Keegan turned his back on his friend and ran.

Chapter 2

Emmet was starting to believe Miss Tesla was part mole. He'd spent the better part of the past fifteen minutes picking his way through conduits and cables, his hands and knees pressed against the hard riveted floor, abusing his skin as he went. It shouldn't have been so difficult to locate one woman in here. He'd spent a large portion of his life finding his way through the nooks and crannies of the Archives. She'd been here, what, a few hours?

The temperature rose exponentially the farther he got into the works. The girth of the pipes grew, making the metal a dangerous companion in his search. Careful not to come too close to the exposed heated parts, Emmet turned sharp corners that lead down what appeared to be a service passage. With few other viable options available to him, he pressed on.

"Miss Tesla?" Calling for her had proved to be damn near futile. She was either unable to hear him, or incapable of speech.

Or perhaps she too had no respect for Emmet.

Stopping God only knew how far deep into the Archives, Emmet closed his eyes and listened. She had to be here. He pushed past the whooshing sounds of steam being forced through the pipes above him. Ignoring the clicking and grinding noise of gears meandering about their business, he tried to hear anything that sounded out of place, off, a thorn in the side of the mighty Archives machine. Because it was becoming painfully clear to him that Miss Tesla was exactly that—a thorn intent on causing him grief.

Tap, tap, tap, tap.

There she was.

Before Emmet got three feet deeper into the machine the tapping stopped. Of course she'd take this moment to rest.

"AHHHHHH!"

Her scream echoed through the metal and filled the small space, setting his heart racing. *Shit, she's hurt.* Without opening his eyes, he shifted his body position so he now faced the direction of the scream. Mentally, he recalled the basic map of the Archives that all acolytes were expected to memorize upon their arrival and added to it his own expanded knowledge of the building. Starting off again at a faster pace, he prayed he wouldn't be too late to save Tesla from whatever evil had befallen her.

"Miss Tesla!" *Blasted woman.* "I'm coming."

"Miss Tesla? Shit." He sucked in a breath and lifted his knee from where he'd placed it carelessly on a metal seam that sliced into his trousers and flesh. "Goddammit."

"Swearing announces a small mind that lacks the imagination to use words creatively."

Emmet looked up to see a slip of a woman leaning back against an outtake pipe. Her chin-length brown hair was tucked behind her pixie-like ears, and her lips were turned up in a soft smirk. She looked as though she held a dozen flippant remarks back with the greatest of restraint.

"You're not hurt?"

"Hurt?" Her full lips pulled into a frown. "Why ever would you think I was hurt?"

"You screamed."

"Ah." She shrugged. "A cry of frustration. You're one of the apprentices? Bit old aren't you?"

The throbbing in his knee increased. "I'm *not* an apprentice. I was asked by Master Tolan to fetch you."

Emmet sat back on his bottom, hoping to examine the damage to his leg. For his trouble, he smashed the back of his head against a pipe behind him hard enough to set his teeth rattling.

"Bloody hell."

"At least your vernacular is consistent." Her voice was heavily accented, sounding more gypsy than the Canadian he'd assumed she'd been. "And far more interesting than that Guild Master."

"Master Tolan is not one of our more practiced conversationalists. I'm Mr. Dennison."

"Yes." Though what she was agreeing to, he wasn't certain. She let her gaze slip to his abused knee. "You are bleeding, Mr. Dennison. I would offer to assist you in your time of need, but I fear I am less adept at dealing with the human body than I am with machines." Reaching into her pocket, she pulled out a handkerchief and tossed it his way before turning around and continuing to work on the open panel.

He checked to ensure that the handkerchief was clean, noticing a small *NT* monogram in the corner, before he pressed it to the freely bleeding wound. He'd need to stop by the medical bay, one of his least favorite places, if the blood didn't stem soon. "May I ask what you are doing in here, miss? I was under the impression you were to help with repairs to the ventilation fans. The last time I checked, the fans were embedded in the ceiling."

"Yes, they are. And that's what I'm doing. The root cause of the problem is often hidden from plain sight. Fixing it requires persistence and imagination." She poked her head back around the corner to wink at him, her gaze shifting to his knee again before she turned back to her work. "I had to go digging."

"I would think a woman such as yourself wouldn't be subjected to working in these cramped and filthy conditions." Truth be told, Emmet was ready to grab her by the shoulders and pull her out to the wide open space of the vault. It was growing increasingly difficult for him to breathe as the pounding in the back of his skull started to increase.

"I find your comment quite amusing as you've only just met me and don't know what type of woman I am in the least." She threw him a look over her shoulder. "Curious, but an unsurprising reaction given the type of man you are."

"What, an archivist?"

"No, upper-class. Your type thrives on categories. You enjoy shoving the rest of us into neatly secured boxes that reflect who we should be and what we should do."

It was true that the duke would have evaluated and dismissed Miss Tesla the moment he heard her speak. While clearly intelligent, she wasn't at all the proper young woman that would integrate neatly into his father's world. Emmet liked to think he was far more enlightened than the rest of his family, but perhaps the apple truly didn't fall far from the tree. Yet another trait he'd need to improve upon.

"I've renounced most of my blue-blood ways. I can assure you if I hadn't, I wouldn't be in my current position."

"Trapped in a hellishly small conduit with precious little light and next to no fresh air?"

"No. Alone with a woman."

She snorted. "Oh. That. One quickly forgets about propriety

when dealing with minus thirty degree centigrade temperatures and forced to huddle together with the closest body for warmth."

"Centigrade?"

"Sorry, we started using the metric system at the HBC. More accurate and one of the few good things the French have given us. That's negative twenty-two." Reaching up behind a pipe, Tesla scrunched her face up in concentration while she fiddled with something. "Now that dial shouldn't be set to that. I'm surprised you haven't been blown up."

"Are you supposed to be touching that?"

Her lips curled up into a grin. "There we go. Now I just need to recalibrate the flux capacitor...and I really should update your regulatory system. I have a new electrical current system that would really do wonders for this place."

Nicola pulled back and began to hammer on one of the smaller pipes. Either because of the blow to his head or the dim lighting of the place, Emmet couldn't help but think she was really quite lovely to look at. If only her personality wasn't so manic he'd consider forming an arrangement with her while she was visiting the Archives. Not that a sexual relationship would be condoned officially, but he got the impression that Miss Tesla didn't abide by convention.

"Miss Tesla, are you nearly finished? I would suggest we return to the main—"

"Ah ha! I knew there was a malfunction in the pathway."

"Miss Tesla, I really much insist that you—"

"All I need to do is this and we should be all—" A loud echo shook the pipes around them, which was quickly followed by an ear-splitting hiss of steam.

"Duck!" She wiggled herself away from the pipe and threw her body across Emmet's, sending them both crashing to the floor.

The air was knocked from his lungs and the weight of her body made it difficult to breathe once more. His headlamp fell from his head, landing a short distance away to cast a light diagonally above him.

Before he could protest his further abuse, an explosion of steam shot above their bodies. Tesla pressed her face to his neck and stretched her arms and legs as wide and as flat as she could go. The result was having the entirety of her lithe frame pressed across his torso. Emmet held his breath, trying not to notice how perfectly her body fit against his, how her scent was a mixture of something floral with grease. It made for a strange combination. It took him every effort not to reach up and wrap his arms around her.

When the air finally cleared of steam and Telsa lifted her face, he got a good look at her features. Her short hair was dark brown, presenting an interesting contrast to her crystal blue eyes. Her complexion wasn't as fair as his friend Piper's, nor was her face as rounded. Miss Tesla's chin came down to a point that highlighted her square jaw. She wasn't pretty by the societal conventions of the day. Then again, Emmet rarely paid society much mind.

If he were forced to put her into a box, as she'd accused him of doing, he'd call her striking.

She grinned down at him, got up onto her hands and knees, and held out her hand. "I believe full body contact now qualifies us to be on a first name basis. At least while we are still in danger of being steamed alive. Nicola."

He had to give her credit, she possessed a sense of humor, albeit a slightly twisted one. Taking her hand, he gave it a gentle squeeze. "Emmet."

"Well, Emmet. I've managed to unblock the heat exchange

pipe that was preventing the steam from flowing fully to the drive. Now I will be able to begin the reconstruction of the fans and get your vaults up and running once more."

It had been years since he'd been with a woman in any meaningful way. Members of the Archivist Guild were forbidden to have relationships before they were cleared for active duty. After that, opportunities were limited. Who wanted to engage in a sexual relationship with a zombie? This left only the occasional tryst with another archivist, and that rarely went well. Their lives weren't conducive to relationships, Piper and Samuel being a notable exception.

So, finding himself on his back, an attractive woman straddling his body in such a way that he was able to see the swell of her breasts from the plunging neckline of her vest, made his body turn traitor. Widening his legs to press his thighs to the inside of hers drew a smirk from her. *Dammit.* Shifting once more to decrease the contact, Emmet pushed the amorous thoughts from his mind.

"Miss Tesla—"

"Nicola."

God preserve him. "Nicola. Might we now return to the vaults? I'm afraid my body is unable to suffer from any further abuse." Nor would he be able to maintain the illusion of being a gentleman much longer.

"Of course. I wouldn't expect an archivist to be able to deal with these conditions for long." With a smirk, she swung her leg over his body and deftly climbed past him toward the exit.

He couldn't move. Not because he was physically unable, but he wasn't certain he could withstand another assault from the force that was Nicola Tesla. Perhaps if he hid here long enough someone else would take this task from him? No, the Administrators had made it clear this was his duty. Plus, it wouldn't do to stay lying on the floor in the dust and muck. The walls would begin to close in around him before long, robbing him of breath.

And Lord only knew the trouble this woman would get up to without his presence.

The return journey back to the vaults was slower, if more direct. Emerging from the darkness and out into the cavernous space lifted the growing weight from Emmet's chest. He'd never been fond of enclosed spaces, but he refused to let them get the better of him. As he maneuvered his body from the opening, finally able to rise to his full height, Emmet knew he'd taken too long.

Nicola and Master Tolan were standing face to face next to the small antechamber off the vault area. The Master was ramrod straight, his finger in her face. Emmet didn't need to hear the words to know the Elder was unleashing a verbal lashing that had the ability to make grown men weep. Nicola simply nodded, her hands laced behind her back and that little smirk of hers fixed on her face. Her clear disregard for the Guild Master would only serve to further infuriate the Elder, making the situation far worse than it needed to be.

Emmet wasn't certain which one of them he'd be rescuing, but it was clear he needed to intervene. Ignoring the throbbing in his head that had grown into a pounding, he limped over. A fresh trickle of blood rolled down his leg as he went.

"And if I catch you down here tinkering with my equipment alone, I will have your head wiped and your body tossed onto the next ship back to wherever the hell you came from." Tolan pulled in a deep breath, preparing himself for another round of yelling.

Stepping beside Nicola, ignoring how she was nearly as tall as himself, Emmet held up his hand and prayed the Guild Master would not make this any more difficult than it already was.

"Master Tolan, if I may. I believe Miss Tesla has managed to fix a significant concern. Am I correct in that assessment?"

"You are, Mr. Dennison. I was about to inform your colleague that I have accomplished all I am able this day."

"He is not my colleague." Master Tolan narrowed his gaze. "He's barely more than a child."

Now free from their confined location, Emmet was able to fully appreciate the way her chin-length brown hair caressed her cheeks. There was no hiding that mischievous glint in her eyes either, which Emmet knew would only further infuriate Tolan.

"Have you been shown to your quarters? I would be more than happy to escort you." Keeping her safe would prove more of a challenge than he'd first anticipated. If there was an opportunity to lock her up somewhere, a cell perhaps, Emmet would take it.

Nicola turned to face Emmet, clearly dismissing Master Tolan and his rant. "While I appreciate the sentiment, the Hudson's Bay Company has secured rooms for me at the George Inn. I shall find transportation there and will return to work first thing in the morning."

Wonderful. How was he going to keep her in his protection until such a time as the Administrators were convinced there was no threat to her? "But Miss Tesla, I assume this is your first time in New London. Surely your employers will grant you a brief respite from your daily duties and allow you to enjoy some of the joys our city has to offer. Dinner, perhaps? I would be pleased to show you around before escorting you to the inn."

As far as distractions went, this one was obvious. Still, Emmet was relieved when she cocked her head and eventually nodded. "I must admit, I've been curious about the city. Since I left my parents and moved from the Austrian Empire to Canada, I've missed certain fundamentals that society can offer." She threw

Emmet a wink that even Master Tolan would have seen. "Perhaps an evening meal with tolerable company is the perfect start to my adventure here."

Without waiting for Emmet, Nicola marched over to the table in the annex room and reemerged with a long leather greatcoat. The myriad of pockets would have been sufficient to conceal any number of weapons, tools, and devices. Slipping it on, and pulling a leather newsboy's cap from the side pocket, Nicola grinned at him once more. "Shall we?"

"I would wish you the best, Dennison," Master Tolan muttered. "But I expect you to do your duty properly."

"Of course, Elder. I would never do anything to bring shame to the Archives." *Bastard.* Emmet retrieved his own greatcoat and topper and strode after the infuriating woman.

Nicola stood at the door to the lift, hands secured behind her back and leaning in to inspect the control panel. "This should be upgraded. We haven't used glass tubes to indicate pressure levels in at least a decade. I have a few extra diodes I can install to improve the efficiency. It would greatly increase the speed of the lifts as well. As soon as I'm done repairing the central machine, I'll tinker around a bit."

"I would suggest mentioning it to the Guild Masters council first, but I fear they'd do you bodily harm at this point."

Her snort was unladylike and slightly reminiscent of Piper. "Then they are old-minded fools. No wonder this place is falling down around them. They are unwilling to bring the Archives into the nineteenth century."

The lift door slid open and Emmet waved Nicola in before him. With the bulk of her leather coat draped around her, he wasn't able to catch a glimpse of her body. A shame, given how striking she was.

"If you don't mind, I would prefer to change my trousers before I take you about the city." With a pointed look down, Emmet knew there was little chance of saving them. "The establishment I hoped to take you to frowns upon exposed flesh wounds."

"Of course. I'll wait for you in the foyer—"

"No."

Nicola blinked, the first indication that he'd actually been able to catch her off guard. "Pardon?"

"It seems in your short tenure here you've already managed to annoy not only the Guild Masters, but also the Administrators. While I know you can't appreciate the full meaning of that, trust me, it's not a positive thing. You are to stick by my side while you are in the Archives, which means coming with me to my quarters."

Emmet was certain not even the Administrators would have forced him to bring Nicola with him in this instance, but he'd enjoyed watching the blush cross her fair cheeks. It made her already startling blue eyes all the more stunning. Yes, this was a woman he'd enjoy teasing. It would at least make his assignment more enjoyable.

"I see." As quickly as her discomfort arose, it was gone. "I believe it's only fair to warn you that I have no interest in men. It see your lot as a distraction from my inventions, my science. If you're trying to seduce me, then it will all be for nothing."

They switched lifts and Emmet pressed the button for the residential level. "I appreciate the warning." Did she not understand that such a statement was practically begging for a man to take her up on the challenge? It poked at a primal part of his brain that he did his best to deny. *Take. Own. Mine.* He knew others who wouldn't be able to resist such temptation.

The lift jerked to a halt, causing Nicola to lean in again, muttering something about bearings and balance, before she finally followed him into the hall. She stopped only long enough to take in her surroundings before falling into step beside him. "Well, this is pleasant."

Emmet looked up at the large stone walls, lined with steam pipes and dotted with the flickering lamps that provided minimal light to the interior of the building. "It's better than some guilds."

"In Canada the Company started its organization in a fort. They've since gone on to build several estates in which they conduct their business, our research... and other things. I have a fireplace in my room. It's quite cheery."

"And cold." He'd heard about some of the conditions in the new lands. He shivered. "I've heard reports that the snow can reach up to a man's waist during a storm."

"You get used to it."

Emmet led her to the end of the hall and stopped in front of the door to his quarters. "Can I trust you to wait here?"

Nicola grinned, rising onto the tips of her toes as she gawked at the various steam lamps and their housings that lined the hallway. "Of course."

Dear God. "Never mind." He grabbed her by the arm and pulled her behind him into his rooms. "Stand here."

"Would you like me to face the wall? I can at least do that much, to protect your modesty."

Emmet growled. "You're the one who claims to have no interest in men. With such a liberal state of mind, you should have no problem with my state of undress." Tossing his greatcoat to the bed, he loosened his belt and let his torn trousers fall to the floor. "I will only be a moment."

Ignoring her as best he could, Emmet retrieved a fresh pair

from his modest chest of drawers. His father would have a fit if
he saw the conditions that Emmet lived in. Though they were
far more comfortable than those of his fellow archivists—he'd
received special permission to bring along several pieces of
furniture—Emmet lived in relative squalor compared to the rest
of his family. He'd learned tricks to folding his own clothing to
ensure wrinkles didn't exist. If they got too bad, he could always
hang them in front of a steam vent until they fell straight.

That particular trick wasn't necessary today as the trousers fell
as they should before he pulled them on. Unrolling his sleeves,
he took quick stock of the condition of his shirt. Soiled, but sal-
vageable. He pulled it off and placed it in the clothing bin, before
fetching another.

"How long do you plan to stay in New London, Miss Tesla?"

"It's Nicola." There was a waver to her voice. "The Company
had intended on me being here at least a month. I suspect it will
take me longer than that to effect the repairs."

Emmet turned back to face her. "More than a month?" God,
would he need to nursemaid her the entire time? "Can you
request assistance to speed up the process?"

It took him a moment to realize she was no longer looking
directly at him. And the blush on her cheeks had darkened. She'd
picked up a tiny bird automaton that Piper had sent him several
weeks ago and was studiously examining the underbelly. Well,
well. It seemed Miss Tesla wasn't as unaffected as she wanted him
to believe.

"The Company didn't have anyone else with my particular
skill set that they could spare for the journey. However, there is a
local man I may need to enlist if things prove to be too challenging for me to complete alone."

Leaving the bulk of his opal-faced buttons undone, Emmet

closed the distance between them. "You realize anyone you wish to bring in who isn't an employee of the Company would need to be approved by the Guild Masters first?"

He could feel her body heat rolling off her and detected the faintest scent of lilac beneath the oil and metal that clung to her. Emmet was a fool to believe he wouldn't be interested in bedding this woman. Taking longer than he normally would to fasten his cufflinks, he kept his gaze locked on her.

Nicola cleared her throat, pulled her shoulders back, and met his gaze evenly. "The man I have in mind is a Company man and will be more than acceptable to your Guild Masters. He's currently...on leave, but still one of us. Once I've completed my assessment of the necessary work, I will contact him."

There was nothing Emmet admired more than strength of character in a woman. Except perhaps a perfect set of breasts. One day he'd need to determine if Miss Tesla's fit into that particular category.

"I believe I'm ready now. Would you like to stop by your rooms first so you can change as well?"

She ran her fingers through the short strands of her hair and checked her face in his mirror. "Yes, the opportunity to freshen up would be appreciated. I would terrify onlookers."

There was a smudge of grease on the side of her jaw. Emmet walked over to the basin in his room and dampened a cloth with warm water before bringing it to her. It would have been easy enough to hand the cloth over, or give her a few moments of privacy to clean up before they left. Instead, he ran the damp fabric over the dust and dirt, cleaning away the evidence of her day's work.

"There you go." His words sounded rough as he spoke. "That should do for now."

Nicola's eyes had grown wide and her throat bobbed as she swallowed hard. "Thank you."

He cleared his throat and stepped back. "I'll order a carriage for us. I wouldn't recommend traveling by the iron walks this time of evening."

She nodded and flipped her newsboy's hat back onto her head. Whatever had passed between them flitted away as quickly as it had arrived. "Lead the way, Emmet. I'm hungry."

What he really wanted was to pull that blasted leather coat from her body and press her back to his bed. "Of course. Follow me."

* * *

Keegan tipped the bag, now empty of sweets, into his mouth, hoping to catch a few more crumbs. He'd never had sweets like this, anything for that matter that tasted so good. Mr. Edison had been gone from the warehouse when he'd returned with his latest finds from the scrap yard, so Keegan simply set to work. He knew what needed to be done, even if his boss wasn't here to tell him. If he did a good enough job, maybe he'd get another bag or an extra roll with his supper.

His fingers were now black and his nails had chipped from the effort of polishing the metal. The muscles in the back of his neck and shoulders hurt from slumping forward over his tiny workbench. Even his mouth was sore from being dry. None of that mattered to him; only the condition of the metal and how much he wanted to impress Mr. Edison mattered.

Everything would be fine then.

Giving the casing one final wipe down, Keegan held it up to the light. The reflection bounced off and cast beautiful images across the filthy walls. It was the most amazing thing he'd ever seen.

"Well, well. I see someone has been busy."

Keegan looked up to see Mr. Edison standing in the doorway, two men he'd never seen before behind him. One looked as though he'd been through a fight. His nose was bloodied and twisted, clearly broken. The other man's face was so pale he could have passed as a ghost. Their gazes darted from the floor to Mr. Edison and back again. Keegan dismissed them and turned his attention to his boss.

"I found this for the casing. It needed some love."

Mr. Edison held out his hand, revealing bruised knuckles. "Let me see."

He shouldn't be hesitant, but he couldn't help but look at Mr. Edison's hand.

"They didn't do what I told them to, so they paid the price." He smiled down at Keegan. "You can appreciate that, can't you?"

Whatever it was they were building wouldn't belong to him. Keegan was only the lackey, the mite that crawled through the muck and mud to find the bits and bobs that his boss needed. Still, he knew this casing was special just as sure as he knew the metal could be restored. It would be his way to leave a mark on the machine, to lock in his rhythm, which would pattern the melody. Keegan knew this as surely as he knew his own name.

Mr. Edison said nothing else, but Keegan could tell by his frown that he needed to act now or he might be subject to a similar fate as the others. It hurt to stand up. His legs ached from lack of use and his lower back felt as though one of the older Underlings had kicked him hard. Still, he forced himself forward and gently placed the casing in his boss's hand.

"Yes, sir. It was all banged up and dirty. Most people would have ignored it. But I could feel the music in the metal. It still had a song it wanted to sing."

"Very impressive." Mr. Edison turned the casing over and over, even pulled out an eye magnifier to inspect it up close. "You've worked wonders, lad."

"Thank ya, sir, Mr. Edison."

Handing the casing back to Keegan, the older man smiled down at him. "This makes me even more pleased to be presenting you with your first official pay."

The silver was cool as it was pressed into his palm. All he could do was stare at the coin in his hand. Keegan had never had so much coin in his entire life. Well, at least not this much that he didn't need to hand over to Glyn. "Wow."

"I also procured you a jacket and a pair of trousers that should fit. I can't have my employees freezing on the job." Mr. Edison handed them over, and Keegan couldn't stop himself from running his fingers over the fabric.

The heavy wool was a luxury Keegan had never experienced before. More valuable than the silver, this was something that could save his life for years to come. Something the others would be jealous of if they ever knew. "Thank you."

"You might also want to check your pocket." Mr. Edison smiled, though it didn't quite make his eyes sparkle the way it did with some folk. It was strange how he'd never noticed that before.

All of which Keegan quickly forgot as he wrapped his fingers around the now familiar paper bag of sweets. "Thank ya so much, Mr. Edison." His mouth already watered with anticipation, the memory of the pleasant rush that rolled through him once the sugar melted into his stomach.

"I think that's enough for today. Why don't you go back to

your room? I've had the boys put a bed in there for you. There are blankets as well. No sense having you be uncomfortable, especially since you've been working so hard."

A bed, money, clothing, and sweets? Keegan might very well have died. This was better than any heaven he'd ever heard of. As long as he did what Mr. Edison wanted, everything would be wonderful. Without protest or escort, he made his way back to the place he'd once considered a cell. Had it only been a few days? *Who cares. This is where I belong now.*

Keegan was so wrapped in happiness, he didn't even mind when one of the men with Mr. Edison closed the door to his room and locked him in. He had no intention of leaving.

Ever.

Chapter 3

Nicola was grateful when they arrived at the George Inn and she was able to make a mad dash to her rooms. While she'd done her best to downplay the state of her appearance, she normally made a point of dressing in a far less grubby manner when working, not to mention entertaining. If anything, Nicola was more particular about her appearance than many of the upper-class ladies she'd met over the years. While she never wore gowns or attended balls, she had her own sense of style. It wasn't a matter of arrogance or status, but of necessity. Her mind was easily distracted if she felt there was something out of place. By dressing in neat, functional clothing, she could ensure her mind was where it should be, not bothered by how much flesh she'd exposed for her male colleagues to see.

One look in her mirror and she wanted to scream. While there was no dirt on her face, her hair was tousled and now stuck out in a multitude of directions once she removed her cap. Emmet was currently sitting downstairs, projecting the perfect image of tonnish elegance, and she clearly looked the part of an insane clockwerker. He was unlike every other archivist she'd met, giving off more airs than the others. His attitude was different, more refined than the Masters she'd met, and she couldn't help but wonder if he was as much an outsider as she was.

She touched the spot that Emmet had cleaned earlier, wondering if it were possible for him to have left a mark upon her skin. It certainly felt as though he'd branded her with that gentle caress. *Foolishness.* She'd never had any sort of interest in men before now, so it was madness to let her base attraction get the better of her now. Quickly removing her corset and shirt, she changed both into something far more suitable for their meal. A pale blue shirt and chocolate brown corset that bore the mark of the Company were perfectly offset by her doeskin breeches. She gave herself a quick once-over to right the remains of her appearance and made her way back to the dining room.

The innkeeper had given Nicola a wide berth for the most part since her arrival. The man stared at her now as she descended the stairs and nodded to a table in the far corner of the room.

"He's in there."

"Thank you." She gave him a little bow and pretended to not see his sneer.

Continuing to ignore the curious glances from the other patrons that she suspected had more to do with her uniform than anything else, she made her way to where Emmet sat.

"Sorry for the delay." Ignoring the waiter, she pulled her chair out and sat with a less than ladylike thud. "I can't believe you wanted to be seen with me in public. I looked dreadful."

"Miss Tesla, I doubt anyone living or dead would lay that complaint at your feet."

"Damn." She stared at him, growing annoyed at the faux-innocent look he could do with ease. "I hate when you do that."

"Do what?" He laid a napkin across his lap and focused his

attention on righting it. "I don't believe I've done anything impolite."

"Your use of compliments is rather distracting." She narrowed her gaze when she saw his lips twitch into a small smirk. "Stop them."

"You don't want me to pay you compliments? I have to say you're the first woman I've ever met who is of that particular opinion."

Even Simon—her supervisor and sometime friend—and his incessant need to tease her didn't lay it on quite so thick. "A genuine one is all well and good, but you're trying to soften me up for some nefarious purpose. I won't be won over quite so easily."

"I would never assume you would be, Miss Tesla."

The waiter hovered a few feet away from their table. She couldn't tell if he was trying to be inconspicuous, or if he was terrified of approaching them. It had been fascinating to her to see the reactions of the regular New London residents to members of the various guilds. Emmet wore a pin, clearly visible on his coat, indicating he was an archivist. The waiter stared at it as he crept closer, then into Emmet's eyes, before dropping his gaze. He cleared his throat in a slightly nervous manner. "May I get you something from the kitchen?"

"Chicken pie and a pint." She leaned in and met Emmet's gaze. "How much do you know about the Company?"

The waiter made a high-pitched noise. "Sir?"

"The beef and a glass of your best Cabernet." He waved the man away, and he scurried to the kitchen without another word. "No more than the rest of New London. I know that you're more secretive than the Guild Masters and richer than the king."

"Yes, the owners do tend to have their fingers in more pies that should be allowed." Simon wouldn't want her discussing business with someone outside of their influence, but Nicola had always been curious about what others thought of them. "With the number of guilds here in New London, I'm surprised we have any reputation at all."

Emmet waited for the innkeeper to set down their drinks and leave before he answered. "You're reputation is rather more potent than you realize." He opened his mouth to say something more, but snapped it closed and chased the silence with a sip of his wine.

The hanging implication got beneath her skin like a raid of ants upon a dollop of jam. He wasn't speaking about the Company at all, but her directly. "Who is interested in my reputation?"

"So how did a woman such as yourself find employment with the Hudson's Bay Company?"

"That's diversion if I ever heard it."

He chuckled. "You have your secrets…"

Nicola swallowed down a generous portion of her beer, relishing the warm liquid as it journeyed to her stomach. It was the only way to stop herself from laughing at his teasing tone. She was *not* going to succumb to his flirting, if that's indeed what he was doing. Were archivists even allowed to flirt? "I was approached after I had a bit of a falling out with my last employer. Leaving the continent seemed prudent at the time, so I moved to Canada and have been there ever since."

Emmet ran his finger along the top of his wine glass, the smile falling from his lips. "Seems like a long way to run to get away from a bad relationship."

The last thing she wanted to do was get into her relationship with Thomas. While she didn't know Emmet well, she couldn't imagine he'd look too favorably upon her actions. "As I said, it was prudent."

He took another sip and leaned back in his chair. She wished he would meet her gaze again, rather than stare into his glass. He really did have lovely eyes. "You don't seem to be the same as the other archivists. I sense you have a story of your own that you keep hidden."

"Touché." He didn't break eye contact with her the entire time, and the intensity in his gaze sent shivers through her body. "Let's just say I didn't run quite as far away as Canada to escape my demons."

"Employer?"

"Father." He pinched the bridge of his nose, the action causing his social mask to slip. She didn't know about poor relations with one's family, but she recognized the heartache he projected, even if it was for a moment.

Here there be dragons.

"Well, if you had to run anywhere, the Archives seem to be a rather interesting place to go."

Leaning back in his seat, Emmet flattened his hand on the table top. He had long fingers that would have been just as adept at holding a book as a gun. Nicola wasn't certain why his hands were such a fascination for her, why she could imagine them reaching out to touch her arm, cup her face. She also knew that those were the same hands that would one day touch a dead body so he could extract its memories.

Emmet chuckled and the dark shadow that crossed his face vanished. "Rather than dig into our respective pasts and go places that will cause us both discomfort, why don't you tell me about some of the projects you work on in the freezing cold of Canada."

As quickly as her unwanted attraction to Emmet threatened to rear its head once more, it vanished. She didn't need a man, need a relationship, romantic or otherwise, in her life to make her complete. The only thing she loved more than conducting her experiments was being given an opportunity to talk about them. "How much do you know about alternating current transmission systems?"

For the next hour, in between rounds of food and alcohol, she went through her ideas on electricity, talked about how it would be possible to provide it to every home for free, and discussed how it would be possible to convert society from steam power to electrical.

"Simon thinks I'm mad. He won't even let me discuss the possibility of a limited experiment with one of our local towns with our bosses. Something about being terrified for my life." She drained the rest of her draft and started looking for the waiter. "I think we scared the poor boy off."

"I can't imagine why."

Emmet had spent most of their time listening to her rambling on. For a while she thought he was simply humoring her, but then he'd pipe in with a question about some tiny detail of what she'd been pontificating about, proving that not only was he was paying attention, but he actually understood what she was saying.

"You could have stopped me at any time. As an engineer I do tend to ramble about my projects."

"If I hadn't wanted to listen to you speak, I would have found a way to leave long before now. It was a skill I learned early on."

"Oh?" It was strange how quickly she'd started to recognize his tells. Emmet would flatten his hand on the table where there was a topic that he didn't wish to discuss. He would cross his arms when he was trying to appear bored, but the quirk of his lips into a smirk gave his interest away. Currently, he was leaning both forearms on the table, giving the appearance of someone about to share a deep, dark secret with her. "And where would you learn such a thing?"

"As the third son of the Duke of Bedford, my father wanted me to be able to extract myself from conversations that were beneath my station. He told me it was an important skill." He flattened his hands once more and sat back in his chair. "It's getting late. I think your innkeeper would like to shut the room down."

Nicola was shocked when she looked around and realized they were the only two still in the place. Even their nervous waiter was nowhere in sight. "That explains why my mug hasn't been refilled."

"Let me see you to your rooms." He stood, and she was startled at his height. How could she have forgotten how tall he was?

"That's not necessary." She got to her feet as well, preferring to be on equal footing with him. He unnerved her in a way she didn't think possible. "I'm sure you wish to return home." He didn't respond right away. "Emmet?"

"Yes, you're right. I shall fetch you tomorrow morning, then. Say eleven?"

She snorted. "I intend to arrive long before then. I'm afraid to say I don't sleep much."

"Eight in the morning it is." He slapped his thigh, looking anywhere but at her. "Bright and early."

Oh. He was making this far too easy. "I can let you sleep in. I would hate to be the reason for bags to appear under your eyes. Send the carriage for me and I'll get there on my own."

"I don't think so."

Nicola waved him away and strode past the sneering innkeeper to the stairs. She'd gotten halfway up when Emmet's long fingers caught her by the forearm. Looking down at where they were connected, she was surprised to see the riot of goosebumps rising across her skin.

"Miss Tesla." His voice was low, rough, and it penetrated her. Damn, her name shouldn't sound that good. "I will fetch you in the morning."

There was a sense of urgency to his words. Yet another secret he held from her, or was this another matter altogether? Lifting her gaze to his, she ignored her foolish attraction to him and focused once more on what was important—her work. "I will be ready to leave by eight. If you are here, then you may accompany me to the Archives. If not, I shall see you in the central machine room."

He released his hold on her arm, allowing her to continue on her way. Nicola felt the weight of his stare long after she'd closed the door to her rooms.

* * *

"Please, Mr. Edison! I promise I won't mess up again."

Keegan listened to the man sobbing in the other room as he continued to file down the gear that had been causing him problems. He hadn't moved from the workbench his boss had set up for him all day. At first the muscles in his back screamed from staying in the same position for so long, but he soon got used to it.

"You're more useless than a piece of shit, Clayborn. You were to find one woman, that was all."

"She hasn't been seen, sir. I checked with my contacts."

"I have no patience for excuses."

"No, sir. Please!" His voice was cut off, the muffled noises of a beating taking its place.

Keegan reached over to his paper bag and pulled out another sweet. He shouldn't eat so many at once, but the pleasure they gave made everything better. His hands would stop shaking and his mind became lighter. His body became happily numb while his thoughts stretched out wide.

A scream echoed through the hall, followed quickly by the ear-splitting crack of a pistol. The noise filled Keegan's head in a pleasant way he knew it shouldn't. That was the sound of death, or failure. He should be terrified, but he wasn't.

The soft hiss of boots against the stone floor pulled his attention away from the gear. He looked up as Jonas dragged Clayborn's body out into the hall and away. A trail of blood marked their passing, and he couldn't help but wonder if the smell would turn his stomach as it got older.

Mr. Edison stepped out, looking at the retreating corpse. Keegan quickly dropped his gaze once more, focusing extra hard on getting those gears exactly right. He didn't react when he heard Mr. Edison enter the room and come stand beside him.

"What's your status?"

Keegan held the gear up to the lamp, inspecting his handiwork. "I've finished constructing and repairing all the works I need. I'll be able to start on the motor tomorrow, Mr. Edison."

Long fingers ruffled Keegan's hair, as Mr. Edison smiled down at him. "Excellent work. It's good to know that I have at least one employee I can count on. Even if you are a...what do you call yourselves again?"

"Underlings." Though Keegan was fairly certain he wouldn't be one of them ever again. "Ta, sir."

Mr. Edison chuckled. "You prove that a man can rise above his situation. That with brains and perseverance, there is nothing we can't control."

Keegan had stopped worrying about going back to his old life. He'd been miserable and pathetic; why would he want to run back to that when Mr. Edison gave him everything he could possibly want? "When yer done wit' yer project, are you going back to America? Do you have someone waitin'?"

He didn't mind that Mr. Edison didn't answer right away, and went back to working on the gears. But when Mr. Edison moved away, Keegan pulled his attention away from the metal and focused on the man. "Sir?"

"I have a family that I will need to return to."

Of course a man like Mr. Edison had a family. A wife and kids. "I bet they miss ya."

"I'm sure they do." He walked over to his workbench, leaving Keegan to his own devices. "We're behind schedule. I expect you to finish that motor by the end of the day tomorrow if we are to stay on track. You know the consequences if you don't."

Keegan's ears still rang from the sound of the gunshot. "I'll never let you down, Mr. Edison."

"I know you won't. And I want you to fetch a bucket and water and scrub up that mess." He waved his hand toward the hallway. "I don't want my place of business to be contaminated by such filth."

"The blood?"

"A fool's blood. Nothing worse."

"Yes, Mr. Edison." Keegan was no fool. He was smart and would find a way to make sure his life got better.

He had plans to stay away from Glyn and the Underlings. He needed them to come true. Failure wouldn't be an option.

Keegan wanted to go back to America with Mr. Edison. He wouldn't ask the question now; it was far too soon for that. But when the time came for Mr. Edison to leave, he would ask if he could go with him, present his case as a business deal. His boss would appreciate that, would see the value in taking Keegan with him.

Maybe he'd let him work for him in his factory. Not as a clock-werker, maybe as an overseer. Keegan would know if the workers were doing a right proper job of it or not. He could be important. He could be as tough as Mr. Edison, and just as smart. He'd learn what he'd need to and then he'd leave. Maybe he'd start his own company and someday have a family of his own.

Yes, that's what he wanted more than anything.

But he wouldn't ask the question...not yet.

Chapter 4

Nicola was a creature of habit. She'd established her routine as a child and had continued on that same course into adulthood. Her father had often tried to break her of her regimented ways, but would repeatedly resign himself to the fact she wouldn't change. Her brothers would tease her, do whatever they could to throw off her carefully constructed schedule, but Nicola would always continue on. Even her mother would admonish her for her lack of flexibility, but none of them had been able to disrupt the pattern of her life.

Moving to Canada and joining the ranks of the Hudson's Bay Company hadn't changed her. If anything, it had served to reinforce her behaviors. With few resources, cramped quarters, and a vast wilderness, she learned that routine and fastidiousness could save her life and the lives of those around her.

So why she'd woken up a full hour earlier than normal and had been unable to eat her normal breakfast of one hardboiled egg with toast and butter was a complete mystery.

Lies you tell yourself.

Nicola had dressed and made notes in her journal about

the scope of the repairs, and was now sitting on the small settee in the hotel room. She'd had a restless night's sleep after her encounter with Emmet on the stairs. Her body had betrayed her by aching in places she normally ignored—her breasts, between her legs—and she nearly succumbed to the temptation of relieving the unwanted pressure. She hadn't, which only served to put her in a foul mood. Coupled with her need to wait for Emmet, it had made Nicola nearly stir-crazy.

She'd considered making an early start of it simply to relieve the lingering tension. That was until she'd received a tube communication from Simon. She'd torn into the message tube without a thought, only to stop short when she read the words.

Hello, Nikki.

I hope you have found your accommodations satisfactory. I did try to procure you the best rooms possible, though I realize you won't fully appreciate them. If nothing else, consider this the best option available to you to allow for a restful night.

Something has come to our attention and I wanted you to be aware. Please promise me you won't react to this the way I suspect you will. A futile request I know, but I feel obligated to write it nonetheless.

There have been reports that Thomas is in New London.

Take a deep breath, Nikki. And now another one.

I'm only giving you this information to keep you informed and safe. I'm not certain he is even aware of your presence, and if luck is on our side it will remain that way. I beg you to not go looking for trouble. That man is dangerous, especially to you. If he learns of your arrival in New London I have no doubt you'll become a target for him. For the time being, I want you to stay close to whichever bloody archivist they've paired with you. It will grate on your sense of independence, but your safety is paramount. I have far too many assignments that require your particular insight to lose you now.

I've also sent a communiqué to David informing him of the situation. Not that he'll have any love for receiving the message, but I know him well enough to know that you'll have support if necessary. I've enclosed his details at the end of this note. His brother is also an officer with the King's Sentry if you feel it necessary to include the authorities. Make sure you go through Rory if that is the case.

Get the vaults stabilized, make those Archives fools happy, and get back home. I know we've said a month, but I can get another airship to you far sooner than that if need be.

By the way, we've nearly completed the blueprints for the new motorized sled and could use your assistance on the motor. It still stalls in the freezing cold.

Best always,
Simon

She folded the note three times and set the paper in her lap. She did as instructed and took a deep breath. Then another. Neither did her any good.

Thomas bloody Edison was in New London.

Nicola had been little more than a girl when she'd gone to work for Edison at the European branch of the Illuminating Company. It was just after the French had finally agreed to a tentative peace with England and reopened their doors to business. The Americans, one of the few allies the French had, flooded in, wanting to take advantage of the new business opportunities. She'd seen it as her chance to prove to her family that she was ready to follow her dreams of creating the most amazing inventions the world had ever seen.

What she hadn't anticipated was that her employer was a thief.

She'd worked side by side with Thomas. On more than one occasion she'd marveled at how he understood her ideas and could follow her train of thought. He always seemed genuinely impressed and felt comfortable making suggestions that would enhance her work. The idea of partnering with such a man, someone with forethought and business savvy, was thrilling to her. Had she realized that Thomas had taken every single thought, laid claim to them as his own, and pocketed all the coin, minus her modest salary, she would never have boarded the airship to Paris in the first place.

Of course she'd confronted him, demanded an explanation for his actions. Instead of righteous indignation or blustering denial, Thomas simply wrapped an arm around her and gave her a gentle hug.

"You're my employee, Nicola. Everything you do, everything you are, belongs to me. I was simply taking my due."

She'd fled shortly after that, leaving a wake of destruction behind her that made the papers around the civilized world. No, Thomas would not let things go if he learned she was here. She'd set him back months, if not years, by burning his notes and damaging the prototypes that had belonged to her. Given what she knew of her mentor and former friend, Thomas would track her down and make her pay for what she'd done to him. Not to mention, he'd want to keep her from damaging whatever it was that currently held his interest.

Because if he was here in New London, then there was something illicit in the works.

The hard knock on the door startled Nicola. She took a breath and forced her body and mind to relax. "One moment please. I need to dress."

She scurried to finish her normal morning routine. Her crisp white shirt disappeared beneath the leather corset fitted below her breasts. The metal boning provided her with additional support for those days when she spent far too much time slumped over her workstation. The doeskin trousers hugged her legs comfortably. Their acquisition had been her biggest change since her arrival to Canada. The natives used the fabric to trade for supplies, despite their disdain of the technological marvels the HBC could provide them. The moment she'd slipped her first pair on, she knew she'd never wear linen again.

Another knock, louder and more insistent. Righting her utility belt and tucking her hair behind her ears, she marched over to the door. "Yes?"

If she'd thought Emmet Dennison looked dashing the previous evening, this morning he was downright devastating. Black trousers that fit well enough to accentuate all of his assets, a tailored white shirt and black waistcoat, and a modest top hat that betrayed his family's fortunes. Of all the archivists she'd met since her arrival, Emmet was by far the most handsome, the most elegant. She had no doubt that made him one of the most dangerous.

"I trust you had an agreeable evening after my departure, Miss Tesla?" His gaze slipped from hers and surveyed the room behind her. She wasn't certain if it was simple curiosity, or if he was looking for something in particular. Interesting.

"I did. I hope yours was as pleasant, Emmet." Oh, how

she loved to watch him twitch every time she used his given name. It had been years since she'd bothered to stand on ceremony. Like everything else, there wasn't room for titles at the Company. Having the chance to toy with someone who clearly thought a great deal about standing and propriety was far too much fun for her to pass up. It had become a game of sorts, to see if she could make the muscle in his jaw jump as he clenched his teeth.

And there it went.

Emmet simply sucked in a short breath, giving his head a nearly perceptible shake. "I thought you might appreciate taking the irons this morning rather than the carriage. It would give you an opportunity to inspect your employer's work firsthand. They are one of our city's greatest inventions."

In truth, she'd been fascinated by the mechanical horse pulling the carriage the previous evening. She'd seen many automatons over the years, but not one so elegant as that. The steam-powered creatures possessed an inner light that gave them lifelike qualities. The pistons and gears flowed together, sliding one inside the other without the aid of grease or oil, metal ligaments and tendons. The illusion made them appear all the more real. She could appreciate why the residents of New London were unnerved by the beasts and did what they could to avoid being in their presence, but the opportunity to experience firsthand one of the inventions she'd previously only heard about was one she couldn't resist.

"Thank you. I have to say it's something I've been looking forward to." An understatement, but there was no need to be crass, either.

Emmet was surprisingly tight-lipped as they descended the stairs of the George Inn. Even in this most progressive of establishments, an unattached woman and man coming from the direction of the rooms raised a few eyebrows. Thankfully she didn't have to worry the way some women did about their virtue and the need to land a husband. Nicola earned more money in a year than most of the ton saw in their lifetime, and her position as clockwerker and engineer gave her latitude many women didn't enjoy.

The morning air was crisp, still holding the chill from the night. It wasn't as cold as she'd grown accustomed to, living on Hudson Bay. She didn't bother to fasten her buttons, enjoying the breeze as it washed over her. The occasional fleck of snow would blow against her cheek, dampening her skin.

She was surprised to see Emmet withdraw a pair of radiation goggles and slip them over his eyes. The pollution in the air, while obvious, didn't seem that oppressive to her and certainly had had no ill effects on her in her short time in the city. Perhaps it was cumulative damage, or it affected those who were born here more than others? *Curious.* She'd have to ask Simon in her next communication.

"We won't get to the Archives if you don't stop inspecting my gear, Miss Tesla."

Oh. She hadn't realized she'd stepped closer for a look at the metal and the tinted lenses. Her lips were only a few inches away from his cheek, giving the impression she was about to steal a kiss. *Preposterous idea.*

Nicola couldn't afford to have these continued lapses in social propriety if she was going to last the full month in New London. "I apologize. I haven't had an opportunity to get a look at those goggles everyone around here seems to wear. I shall have to purchase a pair so I can examine them at my leisure."

"I can have the Archives provide you a set if your eyes are

growing sensitive." He took them off and held them out for her. Nicola shivered as his fingers brushed against hers. His skin was surprisingly rough and his hands far larger than she'd first realized. Not the elegance that many of the HBC clockwerkers and engineers possessed.

No, these were hands made for death and killing.

What was it about this man that drew her curiosity? She'd been in many a room with more than one man who would be considered attractive, even some who her mother would deem an ideal match for any eligible young lady. None of them had made her skin tingle from a casual caress. Nor did she blush when their gaze lingered longer than it should. So why then, had she felt a spark of…something when she'd turned to see him on all fours crawling through the conduit in search of her yesterday?

Pushing the unwanted thoughts away, she slipped his goggles over her hat and rested them across her eyes. The nosepieces were too wide for her face, causing them to slip down from their weight. Little good they did her, as she was still able to clearly see him from over top of the lenses.

The blasted things even smell of him.

"The glass has been coated with a protective layer. Each guild seems to have their own special formula for keeping the radiation from affecting our eyes. I've tried several types, but these ones are the best I've come across."

Using her forefinger, she pressed the goggles up by the bridge to get the full effect. The world distorted as the glass slipped into place and she turned her head, looking at the early risers on their way to their employment. The lines of their skin were more pronounced, their hair darker. And yet, they seemed to have an aura cast around them, a glow that could be anything or nothing whatsoever.

"I haven't noticed any issues with my eyes since my arrival." She pulled them up and let them rest on the bridge of her hat. "Did the guild provide these to you? They are exceptional."

"My father. He had them made especially for our family. Even his wayward son received a pair." Nicola heard the note of bitterness in Emmet's voice. Or maybe that was disappointment? She often confused the two emotions in others.

"Thank you for showing me." But as she reached for them, he stopped her.

"You keep them. At least until we get you a pair of your own." Again, she shivered as he slid his fingers across the back of her hand. "I would hate for you to do any damage to those beautiful eyes of yours."

Whatever witty retort would normally sit on the end of her tongue, ready to leap upon a man who dared attempt a flirtation, evaporated as sure as the water does on a hot day. He thought her eyes beautiful? No one, not even her parents, had ever called her such. Simon had once told her the strength of her personality consumed others to the point where they stopped seeing her as a woman, instead viewing her as one would a force of nature.

Still, she couldn't take something that held value to him. "I'll be fine. You keep them, as they are obviously special to you."

"Please." Emmet's voice had taken on a rough quality, giving him an air of sudden vulnerability. "I insist."

She didn't like this change in him. It was stepping away from their banter of the previous evening and moving them into a different realm. Better to counter and get them back to familiar ground. "Dare I take something the Duke of Bedford intended for his son? I couldn't possibly—"

"I'm no son to that man. Take the bloody goggles."

Her chest seemed to constrict on her, making it difficult to breathe. Is that why he'd left and joined the Archives? She couldn't imagine the pain of being pushed away by one's family. Rather than add to his burden, Nicola cleared her throat and offered him an awkward smile. "Thank you. They will be most helpful."

Emmet finally looked away, turning his gaze in the direction of the Tower. "The iron walks are this way. We can get onto an interchange up ahead."

Nicola watched for a moment as he walked away from her. She didn't understand this man or his actions. One moment he seemed to be undressing her with his eyes, and in the next moment he threw up an emotional barrier so obvious even she had no difficulty seeing it. Oh well, she had a month in which to figure him out. It would prove to be an interesting experiment if nothing else.

The gates to the iron walk interchange were imposing, if slightly run-down. The Company's logo of two stags crowned the entrance, a stark reminder of the entity to which the city owed this modern convenience. Typical and certainly the sort of thing she'd expect from her employers. The sight of a beat-up copper box caught her attention upon their approach. "There is a fee? A reasonable one I hope."

"For most people the irons are a necessary evil. The jobs pay little and housing is expensive. The distances between the two are occasionally great to accommodate the discrepancy." Emmet didn't hesitate as he pulled two coppers and slipped them into the collector. With a soft groan of metal on metal, the gates slid open, allowing them access. "Yes, there's a fee, but it does allow residents to find better employment with some measure of convenience."

"Marvelous." She stepped onto the moving metal grate, stumbling only slightly as she regained her balance. "I would love to see several of these in the larger Canadian cities. I fear it will take a great many years to get there due to the harsh conditions and the pace at which the blasted government works. There's something to be said for having monarchy breathing down one's elected officials' necks."

"If anyone could make it happen, I'm sure it would be you."

The compliment had her spinning around to face him. Not that he wore any indication that he'd uttered the words. "Me?"

"The Company."

Infuriating man.

"Do I annoy you, Emmet?" She made sure to stress his name, knowing how best to needle him. "I must admit while I do normally elicit frustration from the men in my company, you're the first who confuses me."

One moment he was standing quietly at her side staring forward, and the next Nicola found herself pressed back against the handrail and a very annoyed-looking archivist glaring down at her face. His nostrils flared as he breathed in, his gaze narrowed on her. It was more than simply having attracted the attention of a handsome man, and blast it to hell he was stunning, it was the first time she'd been in close proximity to such a powerful man. More than physical domination, Emmet had a power to his spirit, his personality, that called to her in a way no other had.

Emmet had an edge to him, a darkness that he tried to hide from the rest of the world. She wasn't certain how she knew that, but it was there, peeking out occasionally from beneath his façade of bored society man who was playing at being an archivist. Perhaps she saw it because she had a similar darkness herself.

"Miss Tesla, I feel it's important for me to clarify my position." The muscles in his jaw jumped as his gaze roamed across her face. "I am here to ensure your safety while you visit New London and fix our central machine. Once that is done, I will escort you to the first airship heading to Canada so I can get on with my life. While I enjoy our banter, I would prefer to keep our relationship…professional."

She had no doubt that many others would have been put off by Emmet's curt speech and demeanor. Nicola might have been if she didn't have to work side by side with some of the most socially inept men and women on the planet. But she'd seen this type of reaction before. The attack that was meant to stem any potential fronts before they could be brought against the individual in question. Emmet was building a wall, though for the life of her, Nicola didn't know why.

What she wasn't prepared for, and in the end what nearly did her in, was how their bodies seemed to slide perfectly together, like gear teeth that only had one possible partner to make the works move smoothly. Being only an inch or two shorter than him, Nicola knew it would be easy enough to press her face into the crook of his neck, resting her cheek on his shoulder so she could wrap her arms around him. This was more than the brief connection they'd shared in the conduit tunnel the previous day. There'd been an immediate threat of injury, forcing her reaction and dulling any sexual awareness she might have had.

No, this was something else. *Heavens, what's the matter with me?*

"I…" Clearing her throat seemed to break the spell that had descended upon them. He pulled back, giving her room to once again stand tall. "I am always professional. I have every intention of ensuring the central machine is back to fully functioning capacity as quickly as possible. While this visit has proven amusing, I do have duties waiting for my return."

He stared into her eyes for several heartbeats longer before he finally stepped away. "Of course. Then it's settled."

They spoke very little after that. Memories of Emmet's teasing nature and soft smiles from the evening before were now gone. She was sorry to see that fade away. It had been a wonderful change from the clinical manner with which most of her male colleagues normally treated her. In the workshops Nicola wasn't a woman, but simply another brilliant mind that the Company had pulled together to work on their inventions. Until this moment, she hadn't realized that there was a small part of her that had wished someone would see her for all aspects of her being—woman and engineer.

Yes, it had been nice to be seen as something more than a brain that had the ability to solve the most complex of issues, even if it had been fleeting.

Oh well. Nothing could have come of the light flirtation at any rate. She had no time for a man, and she doubted he'd be willing to step away from his life as an archivist to move to the chilly banks of Hudson Bay. Pushing those thoughts away, she focused on the real problem at hand—Thomas Edison.

Somehow, she'd need to find a way to slip Emmet's watchful eye so she'd be able to discover exactly what Thomas was doing in New London. Whatever it was, she knew it would be no good, and it would be best for everyone if she learned the details and reported them back to Simon. He'd be furious that she'd ignored his warning to stay as far from Edison as she could, but he'd understand in the end.

Yes, she'd fix what needed to be fixed and then she'd do a little covert sightseeing.

Their return to the Archives was met with far less chaos than it had been when she'd arrived the previous morning. Nicola couldn't help but be fascinated by all the bits of arcane technology that comprised the place. Gear works powered by steam, boilers that were fed coal, pipes that would eventually break through the force of the superheated water.

A place such as the Archives would be the perfect place to test out her theories of sustainable electric current. Not that Simon would give her permission to do such a thing, not before the Company had an opportunity to determine if there were other uses…commercial applications that they could capitalize on. Well, that and the safety testing they insisted upon. But the temptation to slip in a few circuit boards and test her ideas on a limited scale was strong. It would be a wonderful way to get a leg up on the others, once again looking brilliant when she got back to the Company laboratories.

As she walked into the vault and her gaze was drawn to the rows upon rows of memory vials, Nicola knew there was too much at stake here, too much knowledge to simply risk damaging what the Archives had collected over the years. They could stand to have something a bit more secure, something with a backup or a fail-safe redundancy. It should be easy enough for her to implement, and she could sneak in a few of her theories about the current…

"Are you going to gawk all day? If so, I'd be more than happy to fetch a book from my quarters."

Nicola spun around to face Emmet. Unlike the sharpness of his words, there was a soft smirk on his face, one that reached his eyes.

Damnable confusing man.

"I was simply coming up with my strategy for the day."

Removing her leather overcoat, her hat, and his radiation goggles, Nicola marched over to him and pressed the bunch into his arms. "I shall start with the fans."

Emmet looked up. "And how do you propose to do that?"

She'd brought her kit bag when she'd arrived yesterday. Ignoring the way Emmet's gaze followed her she made her way over to the large metal box and withdrew one of her favorite toys.

"Dear God, what's that?"

"I thought the archivists were all atheists."

"Miss Tesla…"

"It's a grappling device. I've only had one other occasion on which to use it."

The harness had been an addition after her misadventure with the scaffolding in Paris—a mistake she'd not make a second time. Setting the harpoon-type gun on the floor, she stretched the harness on the floor, stepped into it and pulled it up. The metal hooks slid into the loops on the top of her corset, giving her an added measure of protection. Nicola then picked up the gun, aimed at the side of the fan unit in the ceiling, and fired.

The echo of the hook piercing the metal reverberated through the entire vault. Master Tolan briefly emerged from the small antechamber room, looked up, shook his head, and left once more, his mutters unintelligible given the ambient noise.

She patted down her utility belt, ensuring she'd have everything she needed for the time being. Looking over at Emmet, who still held her clothing, she smiled. "You might want to fetch that book now."

With a wink, she hit the retract button and let the grapple do its job, pulling her weight up. In the few moments it took to winch her way up, Nicola felt all her troubles fall away. She was free, flying where no one would catch her. There was no infuriating Thomas Edison, confusing Emmet Dennison, frustrating Master Tolan, or protective Simon. It was only her and her inventions.

It was the best feeling in the world.

* * *

Keegan sat on a mat on the floor, his back against the wall as he worked. The copper casing was warm in his hands from his near continuous touch. He'd been trying to find the best approach, where to make the seams, the holes, how best to work the necessary cogs together. It had been harder to focus this morning. His mind flicked from one thought to another and his hands shook so much he'd dropped the casing once. Mr. Edison had told him he wouldn't receive another bag of sweets until he finished the job he'd been given.

"I don't pay before the work is completed. What would be the incentive for you to do your best then? Now do what you've been told."

"Yes, Mr. Edison." So Keegan found a spot close to his boss and set right to work. This way he'd know exactly how hard Keegan worked, the effort he'd put in. And if Keegan was very good, Mr. Edison might give him his treats early.

It was strange how quickly he'd grown accustomed to the taste, how he practically craved it after such a short time. Thankfully, the supply appeared to be unlimited as long as Keegan did what he was asked.

Mr. Edison had been sitting at a desk that the men had managed to find somewhere in the building, reading some sort of documents. He wished he could read so he could find out what was making his boss chuckle and frown. Maybe if things went well and he did everything Mr. Edison wanted, he'd be able to convince him to teach him a few words.

That would be amazing.

The echo of feet clopping in the hallway had Keegan looking up. The men had been in and out all morning, muttering the occasional few words into their boss's ear. But Keegan could tell that something else had happened, something important to cause them to run that way. He might not be able to read printed words, but Keegan was fluent in the language of the body.

"Boss." The big one came into the room first. He wore a dusty old bowler and a worn leather jacket. He looked no different than them men who ran the press gangs, pulling Underlings off the street and shoving them onto airships headed for Lord knew where. "We found her."

Mr. Edison got to his feet, his papers abandoned in a pile on the filthy desk. "Where?"

"The George Inn. She came out this morning with some bloke. A lover?"

"Tesla is a cold fish. She wouldn't know what to do with a man if he forced himself upon her." Mr. Edison tapped his finger to his lips. "No, it's probably one of the archivists. That bitch has been holed up in that building of theirs."

The smaller man stepped into the room. Keegan was drawn to the large ring that spread his earlobe wide, like a grommet for a sail. "That might make things easier."

"Two birds, one stone." The larger man grinned. "Do ya want us to grab them?"

"Enough." Mr. Edison turned to Keegan. "Keegan, I need to

discuss a business matter with my associates. Take your things and continue your work in your room."

Disappointment swelled through him. This had been the first time in days that Keegan had felt like a part of the group. There was something huge going on, and he knew if Mr. Edison gave him a chance, Keegan would be able to prove he was more than a tinkerer. Still, if he wanted to keep his boss happy, then he needed to do as he was told. Getting to his feet, he slipped the casing into his pocket. "But, Mr. Edison—"

"Now!"

Keegan's heart pounded and his hands shook, but he nodded and started to shuffle toward the hallway. "Yes, sir."

"Boy." Keegan turned and, to his surprise, Mr. Edison pulled out another bag of sweets. "Not all of my employees are as wise as you are. You know where your loyalties lie, don't you."

"Yes, Mr. Edison sir." His mouth began to water at the sight of the rumpled paper.

"Things are about to change. I need to make sure my best employees are ready."

Keegan nodded, ignoring the way his head spun. "I'm ready. I'll do whatever you need me to, sir."

Mr. Edison smirked. "Of course you are." He tossed Keegan the bag. "Now go."

"Thank you, sir!"

Keegan's head spun as he staggered past the men. His feet didn't want to cooperate with him. Maybe he'd been sitting too long. Using his hand as a brace against the wall, he made his way back toward his room.

"Won't those things kill him?" The voice of the smaller man drifted from behind him.

"Hard to say." Mr. Edison's voice didn't sound right. Maybe

Keegan should rest before he worked again. He had been pushing himself harder than he normally did, even when Glyn was after him. "Now, tell me about Tesla."

Yes, a rest would be good. He'd close his eyes for a bit and dream about the cogs. He'd be able to see them dance in his dreams, and then he'd make them real.

Chapter 5

If Emmet thought his first meeting with Nicola had been challenging, he couldn't have anticipated what was to follow over the next week. They'd fallen into an odd sort of schedule over the preceding days. He'd meet her at the inn, more often than not needing to go up to her rooms to fetch her and finding her tinkering with some gadget or other. They'd pass a brief, if not pleasant, conversation that was not in any way tinted with any sort of underlying sexual undertones whatsoever, until they reached the Archives.

Then he'd be forced to watch her work.

It was bordering on torture to have nothing to do but stare at her lithe body as she climbed up walls, through walls, around steam pipes, grease and dirt clinging to the exposed parts of her skin. His gaze would drift to the swell of her ass as she'd bend over. If he'd had something to do, it would have been easier to distract himself, but he had to sit here, without purpose while others worked.

Emmet had thought he'd always had a purpose at the Archives. He was the one who could get things done. But the more he watched Nicola work, the way she'd be able to solve a complex problem that had confounded the archivists who'd been responsible for managing the workings of the building, seemingly out of thin air, amazing him.

It was a talent she shared with his friend Samuel. The sergeant had always had an odd affinity with machines. Emmet had watched him tame one of the mechanical horses, putting it to sleep, if such a thing was possible. And Piper had one of the most amazing minds and capacity to care that he'd ever seen. His father would have a heart attack if he'd known Emmet had wished to have been romantically involved with a Welsh orphan. No, it was for the best that his friends had reconnected and that their lives were back on the course to happiness.

While he was forced to nanny an insane woman.

With nothing but time and inactivity consuming his days, he'd taken to pondering his current situation. Emmet needed a role, a place to fit, something that was his. Something with meaning. Unfortunately, he didn't have a bloody clue what that *thing* might be.

"So this is where they've hidden you?"

Emmet looked over his shoulder to see his friend Alastair Jones standing there. He couldn't help but look immediately into Jones' eyes, to the now visible white ring circling his pupil. It had changed his friend's appearance in a way that Emmet wouldn't have thought possible. Drawn and pale, Jones looked as though he were close to death, not a young man of one and twenty. *A zombie indeed.*

"I've been banished to purgatory." Emmet turned around and lifted his book once more, knowing Jones wouldn't appreciate his scrutiny. "Forced to sit and stare at the walls. I'm surprised to see you wandering down here. To be honest, I'm surprised to see you looking as good as you are, given how short a time ago your extraction was."

"Apparently I am gifted." Jones moved to the side and plucked the book from Emmet's hands. "I've recovered far faster than most. Piper is the only other one to have responded this well in recent years. Hooray for me."

Emmet resisted the urge to cringe. The ability to recover quickly from having one's memory wiped after an extraction was rare. It would mean Jones would be slated for more cases faster than the others, each one stretching the hole in his eidetic memory until it would eventually ruin him.

The average archivists who survived their service typically went on to serve as Guild Masters, mentors to the apprentices. They would be assigned their students, shuffling the ones suited for memory extraction duties from those who would serve the guild in other roles. But men like Jones didn't live long enough to claim such a post.

"Are you well?" Emmet stood, knowing he wouldn't get a truthful answer from his friend if they weren't eye to eye. "I must admit, I've been worried."

Jones smiled. "Not really. Piper tried to explain it to me once, what it felt like after the memory wipe. She said it was as though her brain were itchy, as though she knew there was a wound and she wanted to pick at the spot but lacked the capacity to reach it." He licked his lips and looked over Emmet's shoulder. "But that's not exactly right."

Emmet didn't want to be fascinated by what Jones had to say. Still, he couldn't deny his morbid curiosity about what the experience was like. Someday soon he'd know firsthand, but until then...

"Do you remember when we were children and I'd burned my

arm?" Jones reached out and touched his cloth-covered forearm. "Remember how the skin gave off heat and I said I could feel my heartbeat pulsing around the wound?"

"Yes." Emmet cleared his throat, hating how tight he sounded, that he couldn't ease his friend's burden. "You couldn't bear to have anything near it, even the bandages the doctors made you wear."

"This is worse."

"Shit." And Jones would be subjected to this over and over until he was left a shell of a man.

So would he.

It wasn't fair.

Before Emmet could say anything else a large metal casing fell to the floor several feet away from where they stood. The clang was so loud and unexpected that he jumped and Jones let out a less than manly scream.

"What the bloody hell was that!" Jones scurried back several steps, his gaze locked on something above them. For a brief flash, he was his old self again.

"That was the reason I've been stuck in this hole." Emmet watched Nicola as she slid down the length of rope she'd used to go up and down to repair the fans over the past week.

"I'd heard about her." Jones relaxed and moved closer again. "Is she like they say?"

"Frustratingly pigheaded? Yes."

"No, I meant attractive." Jones cleared his throat and shot Emmet a shy smile. "I overheard some of the apprentices talking. They claim she's quite lovely, though you know how boys can be. Though I see in this instance they are more than correct."

Nicola landed with a thud, unhooked the rope from the rigging she wore, and slipped from the harness. Her corset and form-fitting pants left nothing to the imagination, clinging to her firm thighs and thin waist. Emmet had done his best to ignore her more enticing feminine qualities, but with each passing day that had proven more difficult. Snapping his book shut, Emmet got to his feet and tossed it on the chair.

"*Lovely* isn't the term I'd use for her." What else could he say about the woman who'd done little more than infuriate him for the past week? Any comment he'd make would put him on a path that would lead to problems. Best if he shoved away his baser attractions toward her until she was gone. Then he'd let those thoughts get him through his lonely nights.

Emmet turned away from watching Nicola, and caught sight of Jones' smirk. "What?"

"Not a thing." It was the first time Emmet had seen the sparkle return to his friend in ages.

"That's not the look of a man with nothing to say." He crossed his arms and faced his friend. "Out with it, man."

Jones was full-out grinning now. "Funny, I was going to say the same thing about you?"

"Pardon?"

"You look like a man with plenty to say. But for once in your life you seem to be keeping the comments to yourself." Jones nodded toward Nicola as she made her approach, their gazes already having found each other. "Mind presenting me to our guest, Dennison?"

Most women would abide by social convention and wait for Emmet to conduct the social niceties by providing an introduction. He should have known that Nicola wasn't one of those women. Nudging Emmet aside, she held out her hand for Jones. "Hello there. Nicola Tesla, at your service."

"Alastair Jones, ma'am." Bending over her hand, Jones kissed the back of it before smiling up at her. "A pleasure."

"My, my. I find it hard to believe that a gentleman such as yourself is friends with this cad." Nicola patted Jones' hand before he released her. "Though I suppose given your environment, you have few choices of friends."

"It's a burden I've endured for years now."

Emmet wanted to be angry at Nicola for presuming to know the constructs of his friendships. If this exchange had taken place a year ago, Emmet would have flown off and put her in her place. But before his mouth caught up to the arrogant side of his brain, he noticed something. Nicola wasn't treating Jones any different.

She was treating him as a normal man. He knew she was aware of what the rings meant. She'd been here long enough, and had asked him more than a few pointed questions about the effects of the extractions, to appreciate their significance. But she didn't seem to mind, allowing herself to flirt and chat with Jones the way she had with him. She was doing what Emmet should be naturally. Something he'd forgotten to do himself.

Clearing his throat, he waited until Nicola turned to face him. "If you're done attacking my character—"

"For the time being."

Emmet growled. "How are your repairs going? Done? Ready to fly home? Tonight, you say? I shall fetch you an airship promptly."

Jones didn't bother to hide his ever increasing grin. "Oh, he only gets like this when he's really annoyed. Well done, Miss Tesla. I've only known a few others who've accomplished that task with the same degree of ease you've shown."

"Please, call me Nicola."

"Well, I'm Jones to all my friends around here. I'd be pleased to count you amongst them."

Nicola winked at Jones. "The honor is mine."

"Shall I leave you two alone?" Their playful flirting shouldn't bother him the way that it was. He had no designs on her time, or reason to be seeking her affections. Jones was a good friend and the banter was harmless. Still, there was something that had gotten beneath his skin watching their back-and-forth, something Emmet wanted to dig out before it took root.

When Jones shook his head and clapped him on the shoulder, Emmet's relief was palpable. "No need, Dennison. I was only stretching my legs. I'd best return to my quarters for a rest. Nicola, it's been a pleasure." One quick kiss to her hand and he was gone.

Emmet watched as Nicola's gaze followed Jones' departure. There wasn't any desire or longing, a look he'd grown accustomed to seeing on his friend Piper as she'd watch Samuel. No, this was curiosity.

"How long ago did he do the extraction?" He'd half expected her to have a clinical tone, that detached curiosity she'd mastered. It was a surprise to hear instead concern.

"Nearly three weeks ago. He's a natural."

She cringed. "Do you know when they'll send him out again?"

"No, but I imagine it won't take them long to find another. People are always dying in this city."

She turned and took one of his hands in hers. Her fingers were grease-smudged and her nails discolored from dirt. But her skin was still soft and fit perfectly to his as she held on. Nicola looked into his eyes, causing his heart to stutter.

"I know he's your friend and I'm certain you've already noticed this, but your Jones is hurting quite desperately. And I need to assure you that I'm one of the least socially adept people of your acquaintance. If I've noticed—"

"I know." He swallowed past the sudden lump in his throat.

"I've been concerned. I did try to talk to him before, to let him know that I'm here for him, but he's kept me at arm's length. This was the first time I've seen him since your arrival."

"He'll need you. Friends are better than family in that regard."

"How?"

"Family cares because they must. Friends do because they choose so. That's why the pain of losing a friend hurts as much as losing a family member."

Nicola stepped back, turning to grab her gear. It was obvious that someone had hurt her terribly in her life, and even more so that she had no desire to discuss it. They'd both spent too much time in the dark in recent days, and clearly it was taking a toll on their mood.

"Let's get out of here."

She looked up at him, her harness draped over her shoulder as she adjusted her belt. "Where?"

"You said you wanted to see New London, let me show you."

"I'm still in the middle of—"

"Are you honestly going to stand there and tell me you can't finish whatever it is you're doing well within the time frame they've given you?"

She snorted.

"I thought not. Let's go and get some air. You claim our New London weather isn't as cold as what you experience in Canada, so you can't use that as an excuse. Unless you find my company so very distasteful?"

"Not at all."

"Well then?"

It was fun to watch her turn the idea over in her mind. Even better when he saw her enthusiasm spread across her face in the form of a grin and a sparkle to her eyes. "Why not. Even the Company doesn't expect its employees to work every day."

"Excellent."

"I'll get cleaned up and grab my coat. Then we can be off."

Emmet watched as she tidied her equipment and washed her hands in the steam basin that Master Tolan had brought for her after the second day of her complaining. He shouldn't be as fascinated as he was watching her scrub the muck and grime from her skin. Shouldn't enjoy seeing her run her fingers through her hair to smooth down the strands before tucking them behind her ears and coving them with her hat. These weren't feelings that a man should have for a woman who was in his care.

Not at all.

"I'm ready." Her grin was blinding. "So, what do you plan to show me, Emmet?"

He hadn't given it much thought, the suggestion being one of impulse. Nicola wasn't like the other women of his acquaintance, and none of his normal ideas seemed right. A walk in Hyde Park? No. A shopping excursion down Oxford Street? Hardly. It wasn't until he thought back to that first evening when they'd shared dinner and the conversation that had kept him amused for hours that he knew where to take her.

"How would you like to visit Big Ben?"

* * *

Nicola's hands had been shaking for the better part of an hour, though she'd done her best to conceal that fact. No one who knew her well would understand her fascination with something considered to be so simplistic in nature. It was a bell in the middle of a giant clock. But Nicola had desperately wanted to go inside, see the mechanism room, and watch the dance of the gears ever since she'd heard of its construction.

She wanted nothing more than to lean her head out the window and gauge the amount of traffic that blocked their way, to calculate the time it would take them to reach their destination. It would occupy her mind for a few moments if nothing else, help her to fight off her excitement and maintain at least the illusion that she was a mature individual.

"How did you say you could get us in? It was my understanding that visits were off-limits."

Dennison was seated in the carriage facing her. He'd been kind enough to take the rear-facing seat after she'd discovered that her stomach didn't agree with the rocking motion in such a position. "My uncle is one of the clockwerkers who designed the tower and the works."

"An archivist and a clockwerker in one family. A talented lot you are."

"Not according to my father."

She let the comment pass, having learned quickly that Emmet didn't speak about his father with any great kindness. It was yet another thing she wanted to learn about the man, another strange inconsistency in his life's story that called to her. Sooner or later, she'd unravel the mystery that was Emmet Dennison.

The afternoon had taken on a warmth Nicola hadn't anticipated given the time of year. Her skin had grown clammy beneath her leathers, making her discomfort grow alongside her anticipation. Soon, she'd be back out on her feet and making the climb up the 334 limestone stairs to the top. She'd need to consider leaving some of her gadgets secreted away in her coat behind in the carriage if she were to undertake such a trek. Though the mere thought made her uneasy.

The carriage jerked to a halt, nearly sending her forward into Emmet's lap. He grabbed for her arms, preventing her from falling all the way, but not enough to stop her from making contact with his body. For a heartbeat, time slowed around them and all Nicola could focus on were his intense and surprised eyes. Once more she fought the urge to push forward and kiss him. The carriage shifted, reminding them of their current situation. He helped her back to her seat, though with what appeared to be regret.

"We stopped." She tried to ignore the way his hands lingered on her, or how a nervous tremor flowed through her body. "Not normal, I take it?"

"No. The horses don't normally halt unless we've reached our destination. Or if there's trouble." Emmet withdrew his pistol from the inside pocket of his greatcoat. "I would ask you to stay in the carriage—"

She didn't even bother with a reply. Taking her own pistol from its hiding place in her inner pocket, she checked to ensure she had a full complement of bullets loaded. "I'm ready."

Surprisingly, Emmet didn't protest her following him. He pushed open the door, pistol at the ready, and jumped to the cobblestones. Nicola wasn't familiar with the layout of New London, but she was fairly certain that Big Ben's Clock Tower didn't reside in the rougher quarters of the city.

"Took a wrong turn, did we?" She flanked Emmet, scanning the empty road for signs of trouble.

"I've never seen the horses go wrong before. Not unless Samuel was at them. And as much as my friend has good reason to make my life difficult, he wouldn't do anything to put your life in peril."

"I guess that means I best take a look." If there was a mechanical glitch, then she was the best candidate to conduct the repairs. Tucking her pistol back into its holster, she made her way to the side of the metal automaton and removed the panel along its flank with a *pop*. The horse protested with a burst of steam through its nose, and stamped down twice.

"Oh, settle down. I'm just peeking." The beast turned its head, as though it were listening to her words. "I promise I won't mess up your works. You're far too beautiful a creature for that. Plus, I'm far too talented."

Another release of steam and then the horse settled. *Fascinating.*

After a few moments of checking the tiny gears and intricate pumping mechanisms, Nicola knew that everything she'd ever thought about the horses paled in comparison to their reality. These weren't simple automatons; they were practically engineering works of art. There was more to these creatures than steampowered cores. They wouldn't be easily influenced or altered by someone who didn't have intimate knowledge of these types of mechanisms. In fact, Nicola only knew of a few men who would have been able to pull these creatures off course.

Reaching deep inside to run her fingers along one of the inner sets of gear teeth, she was nearly immobile when Emmet tensed. "What's wrong?"

"Miss Tesla, we need to move. Now."

"I thought you said we were safe—"

"Someone is approaching."

Nicola was able to crane her head around to see a group of three men racing toward them.

"Can you fix them?"

Nicola looked back at where Emmet stood. "This one isn't broken."

"Shit." Emmet cocked his pistol and sunk further into his stance. "We're out of time. Run."

Squashing her regret at being unable to explore the inner workings of such fabulous craftsmanship, Nicola pulled her arm back only to have her sleeve catch between the gears. She pulled again, harder this time, but the fabric of her sleeve was jammed.

"Miss Tesla!"

"I'm stuck." She jerked repeatedly in a vain attempt to free herself. "I can't—"

The men were upon them. Emmet fired his pistol, hitting the largest of the trio in the shoulder, sending the brute staggering back. It was the only shot he managed before his pistol was knocked away. The uninjured attackers jumped on him, their fists landing in Emmet's stomach and chest. Nicola's body shook as she was forced to helplessly watch the assault. "Emmet, behind you!"

The wounded man had regained his composure and picked up a brick. Emmet ducked beneath the swing of the next punch coming his way, landing one of his own. The wounded man tried to get behind Emmet and swung the brick at his head. Emmet somehow twisted out of the way to avoid a fatal blow, but the brick connected with his shoulder. His scream of pain fired Nicola's determination.

"You bloody metal beast, let me go!" She yanked harder on her sleeve until the beautiful sound of fabric ripping reached her ears. "That's it."

Emmet was thankfully holding his own against his attackers. When one man grabbed his arms from behind, Emmet lifted his feet and kicked an approaching assailant in the chest and face. The brute fell to the ground and didn't get back up. His compatriots retaliated with brutal force. Nicola's breath caught as the man with the gunshot wound had somehow found the strength to land several short, sharp blows to Emmet's gut.

He wouldn't be able to hold out much longer.

Nicola braced her foot against the side of the horse and pulled back. "Let me go!"

The beast lifted its head and steam exploded from its nostrils. With a thunderous step forward, the gears moved enough to free Nicola. "Yes!"

Her yell and the horse's movement was enough of a distraction to draw the attention of the attackers. They threw Emmet to the ground where he stayed unmoving.

Shit. "Hello, boys. Wonderful city you have here."

The uninjured man pointed a grubby finger toward her. "Our boss wants te see you."

"Does he?" She nodded and took a step back. "Well I'm afraid my schedule is completely full at the moment. Your boss will need to make an appointment. Say, a week from Tuesday?"

"Grab the bitch and let's go."

Nicola's back hit the side of the horse, blocking her escape. It snorted, sending another burst of steam before it turned to face her attackers. Both men stopped dead, their eyes locked onto the automaton. Sensing an opportunity, Nicola reached over and patted the horse on the neck. "As I mentioned, I'm really quite busy. Now, I'm going to get my friend and we will be on our way."

Nicola was nearly as surprised as the men when the horse stomped its hoof upon the cobblestones. The vibrations seeped into the souls of her feet and up her legs as the creature began to move toward the men. With a noise that sounded as though hell itself was upon them, the automaton charged their attackers. Emmet somehow rolled away out of the path of the retreating men and stumbled to his feet. She raced toward him and grabbed his hand, not bothering to check his injuries. There'd be time for that when they were safe. "I believe you said *run*." Without further conversation, they raced into the small alley that jutted off from the far side of their current position. She moved with him as though they'd been doing so for years, in perfect unison that might have appeared choreographed to an onlooker. The space was narrow, as though the buildings had emerged out of the ground too close together and formed a symbiotic relationship. Emmet's wide shoulders scraped as they struggled through, slowing their advancement.

Nicola kept a constant watch behind them, expecting a pursuer to emerge from where they'd come to give chase.

They emerged from the tight walkway, tumbling out into the blessedly wide alley. The confined space had no ill effect on her, but a quick glance at the pallor of Emmet's face revealed he'd reached a breaking point. He stumbled a few steps before leaning forward to rest his hands on his knees. "Sorry. Need to catch my breath."

One moment he was leaning over catching his breath, and the next he'd collapsed to the ground. "Emmet!"

Abandoning her gun on the ground beside him, she quickly went to work pulling open his cravat and the buttons around his throat. Dammit, he didn't look *that* undone by his injuries, certainly shaken but nowhere near close to losing consciousness. It was then that her fingers brushed against something hard and long protruding from the side of his neck. She tugged it free with ease and brought it to eye level for inspection.

A dart.

Thomas.

There was chuckling, and another brute materialized, as big and ugly as the previous three.

"Well, good afternoon." Tightening her hold on Emmet's shoulder, she hoped to rouse him from his drugged stupor with a few shakes. She didn't want to abandon him in the middle of the alley, but if one of them didn't escape then no one would have a clue where they might be or who was responsible. When Emmet didn't move, Nicola shifted slowly, preparing to bolt. "It seems you've rendered my companion unconscious. That's extremely uncharitable of you."

Either the man was dim and didn't understand a word of what she'd said or he was doing his best to intimidate her. Instead of rising to her verbal challenge, his gaze shifted behind her. Two of her pursuers emerged from the alley behind her, blocking all obvious signs of escape.

"Think yer going somewhere, miss?" The man with the dart gun grinned at her.

The tiny dart bit into her skin, sending a flash of pain through her body. She hadn't seen the other man move, but she caught sight of a long tube in his hands before the darkness consumed her. Her last waking thought was of Emmet and how wonderfully warm he was beneath her body.

Chapter 6

Keegan sat on his cot, back pressed against the wall, and stared at the couple in the cell across from him. Mr. Edison hadn't said a word about bringing others to work for him, though it really shouldn't have come as a surprise. The project was large and would take far less time if Keegan wasn't the only one with his hands dirty. Still, he couldn't help but be annoyed.

The man was an archivist, Keegan could tell from his clothing. What Mr. Edison wanted with a zombie was beyond him. They were horrible people, worse than the clockwerker guild, if half the stories he'd heard were to be believed. Then there'd been that Jack the Ripper a few months back. Even Glyn had been scared, not that he said as much, but Keegan could tell. Word was that the killer had been one of them zombies gone mad. He wasn't sure that was the truth, but in his experience the rumors that the Underlings unearthed were more often true than not.

It was the woman that had Keegan more than a little curious. He'd caught sight of something on her jacket before the men had thrown her on the floor, something he thought looked like the stag's head that rest above all the iron walks. If it was, that meant she was with the Company. Keegan had never actually met anyone from there, though like every citizen of New London, he reaped the benefits of their technology. He didn't have an opportunity to look at the symbol again before they stripped her of the greatcoat.

Why would Mr. Edison want someone from the Company? It didn't make sense if he was trying to keep his invention a secret.

"Keegan, my boy. Come out please."

His stomach growled and his fingers shook as he slowly pushed his way off the cot. Sleep had been getting harder and harder to come by, though he still took the rest breaks Mr. Edison insisted upon. There was no point in arguing with his employer, something Keegan had learned early on. In the past two weeks of his new life, he discovered that being in proper employment with a proper boss wasn't that much different than being an Underling, forced to do what Glyn wanted, when he wanted it. At least the food was better.

The light was bright as he shuffled out into the hallway, forcing him to shade his eyes. "Yes, Mr. Edison?"

His boss stood in the entrance of the work area. With a crook of his finger, he beckoned him in. "There's something I want to show you."

Keegan's heartbeat picked up. Oh, he loved it when Mr. Edison had things to show him. They were normally interesting gadgets, things that he'd get to tinker with until Mr. Edison was pleased with the progress and spirited them away. Still, those few hours when he'd be permitted to caress the metal gears, adjust the springs and cogs with a mental push, were some of the best time he'd ever spent.

Creeping forward, Keegan followed where Mr. Edison had disappeared. What he wasn't expecting to see as he entered the room was that the floor had been covered with various bits and bobs, metal casings, springs and cogs. Some of the items he recognized from previous sessions, things he'd already put his mark upon. Others were new, still rusty and damaged, with their potential still hidden beneath the surface.

"Wow." His whisper filled the quiet of the workroom. "What's all this, Mr. Edison?"

"This, my boy, is going to be your project. The most important of tasks that I require you to undertake. I had intended to do the work myself, but you've more than proven your abilities." There was something odd in his voice, something Keegan couldn't put a name to. "For the next couple weeks, building this machine will be your one and only priority."

If this had been Glyn telling Keegan what to do, restricting his movements to the Underlings' home, he would have rebelled. Sure, he didn't mind following orders, but he hated being held back, trapped in one place with nowhere to go. Funny, he hadn't felt that way even once since he'd been brought to the warehouse.

Instead of protesting, Keegan stepped past Mr. Edison, and began to inspect the objects. "What do ye want me to make, sir? I can see lots of things I could do with this stuff."

Normally his boss would make a smart comment, something that would make Keegan smile or think. When nothing came, Keegan tore his attention from the casing and looked up at the older man. "Sir?"

It was odd, but Keegan hadn't noticed how old Mr. Edison was. Not ancient like some of them highbrow gents walking around with their white hair and beards, looking near dead in their black suits, but older than Keegan had first assumed. More than that, he was sad.

That was an odd thing.

"This is a special project." Mr. Edison narrowed his gaze and cleared his throat. "A special project for a special boy. I need you to make me an automaton."

"Oh." Yes, he could see that now. There were enough bits and pieces here to build something beautiful, sleek, and powerful. "You want me to make a person?"

"I do. A woman, to be more precise."

Keegan had heard rumblings about men who'd go to the darker parts of New London seeking out the comforts of local whores. With all that nasty Ripper business, them women had been complaining about lack of business. He didn't figure Mr. Edison for the type of man who'd want to be with a whore, but being with an automaton was... strange.

"You want a metal girl?" Keegan picked up a spindle, mentally calculating how long it would take to rewind the metal spring. "I can find ya a nice girl if that's what yer lookin' for, sir. Glyn has a bunch that he lets some of the older Underlings use when they have an itch they need scratched."

Keegan didn't register Mr. Edison moving, until his hands were around his neck, squeezing tightly. His head swam as he struggled to draw breath. The words his boss spoke grew more difficult to understand the tighter he squeezed.

"Don't you dare talk about it that way. I'm not going to fuck it, nor some whore. I can have any woman I want in my bed. You are to build her and she's going to be perfect. Do you understand me? Perfect!"

"Yes... sir." Keegan lost the ability to speak for a moment before he was sent crashing to the floor. His head began to pound even as he sucked in a lungful of air, and the tremors he'd been able to suppress racked his body.

Mr. Edison stood over him, his hands balled at his side, his gaze unwavering. "I have no doubt you'll do what I ask. You're a smart boy and a hard worker."

Keegan didn't normally get scared, even when situations looked bad for him. He'd always been able to find a way through using his wits. But as Keegan looked up into Mr. Edison's eyes, his stomach turned and, for the first time since the first few hours when he'd been brought here, fear gripped at him. He'd seen that look before, on the faces of men out on the streets. Those weren't the sorts Keegan associated with, the type as likely to stab you in the back as they were to pay you for your troubles. He needed to be careful.

"I'll make her perfect, sir." Keegan slowly pulled his legs under him so he could crawl toward the nearest casing. "I can picture her in my head. This piece here, it's wide and smooth. I can make this into her back."

He scrambled over to another piece. "Here. This one doesn't look like much, but I can use this for her hand. Her fingers will be nice and long. Pretty."

When something glinted in the corner of his eye, Keegan recognized it and scrambled for it. "Now I know why this one spoke to me as it did. This is going to be her heart."

"Yes." Mr. Edison's hands relaxed. "I knew it the moment you showed it to me."

"It's special, sir. I could see how everything connected the moment I laid eyes on it." He grinned as the tension eased from the room. "I can do this for you, Mr. Edison. She'll be perfect for you."

The darkness that had held Mr. Edison in its grip eased. He smiled and in a flash was back to the kindly man Keegan had grown to like. "Of course she will. You're a bright lad, which is why I hired you in the first place. You've the best apprentice I've ever had."

An apprentice? He'd never been one of those before. "Thank you, sir, Mr. Edison."

"I forgot to ask if you'd rested. I want to make sure your mind is fresh before you begin working in earnest."

He hadn't. But with his body and mind buzzing from the tension, there was little chance of him sleeping at this point. "I'm good. Maybe a bit hungry."

"I'll have one of the lads put some food on a tray for you. They have their hands full at the moment, so it will take time."

"S'okay." He widened his eyes just so, knowing the impact it would have. "I'd take some more sweets if ya had 'em, Mr. Edison, sir."

That elicited a chuckle from his employer. "I'm fresh out, but I'll make sure to get more soon. In the meantime, see what you can manage for now."

Keegan knew he shouldn't ask, that it was a part of Mr. Edison's business that the less he knew of the better it would be for him in the long run. But if Keegan had one fault, it was his curiosity and his inability to put a cork on it. "Who are dem people in the cell? If you don't mind me asking."

"I do mind." He turned his back to Keegan and continued toward the door. "For now, consider them nothing more than pests to be dealt with."

"Yes, Mr. Edison."

Glyn used to say the same thing about boys who caused the Underlings trouble. Their bodies would turn up days later, barely recognizable. If Mr. Edison was even half as vindictive as Glyn, Keegan would find himself alone again soon enough.

* * *

Emmet was conscious long before he was able to open his eyes. While he knew something was wrong, that something bad had certainly befallen him, his brain wouldn't share the information. So rather than twist and turn, he lay still and tried to remember. It was then that he heard the voices, shouting in the distance chased by the clanging of metal. That wasn't a typical sound from the Archives, not in the least. Which would make sense given he'd left there earlier, went on a trip with—

"Miss Tesla?" His voice was rough, the words hurting as they were formed in his throat. Emmet licked his lips, trying to force some moisture back into his mouth. He'd been with her when something had happened. The memories were as hazy as a summer morning in New London.

He should move, see what predicament he'd landed himself into and if he had any hope of getting out of it unscathed. With effort he opened his eyes and found himself facing a stone wall. So he was inside…someplace. His next attempt was to move his hands, which were surprisingly free from restraints. Whoever had placed him here either was not worried about his escape or had other contingencies in place for such an eventuality. Emmet would need to be cautious.

Wiggling his fingers brought the circulation racing back, and before long, his arms were inflicted with the sensation of pins and needles. God, he hated that. It was the incentive he needed to struggle into a sitting position, giving him the vantage point he needed to see where he'd landed.

A cell. The bars on the door appeared to be old and not a part of the original design of the place. The welded hinges were sloppily done, as though the craftsman was either in a hurry or under duress. If luck was on his side, that would mean there was a weakness to the hinge, something he'd be able to manipulate to his favor. Emmet filed that point away as something to explore at a later time. Not until he knew where he was and who'd put him here.

A soft moan from the cot beside him jarred his sluggish brain. Emmet forced his body to move, crawling the short distance across the cold stone floor to the edge of the wooden frame.

"Miss Tesla?" His fingers brushed warm linen and flesh as he reached up. Thank God she was still alive.

Pulling himself up onto his knees, Emmet carefully rolled her onto her back. Her short hair slipped off her face to land on the thin blanket beneath her. This was the first time in their acquaintance that he'd seen her this still, this passive. Her lush lips had parted, revealing the barest hint of white teeth and pink tongue. Her long lashes lay at rest against her lids, hiding her bright blue eyes from his sight.

This wasn't right, seeing her this way. Nicola was the living embodiment of an energy ball. The air practically sparked around her as she moved, laughing and working with an enthusiasm he'd rarely seen in another. Even when she was in repose, she was rarely still. He'd watched her sitting at a desk, pouring over notes or reading, while her hands or feet were moving, tapping.

Emmet hesitated for a moment before brushing a stray hair from her face. She was so warm; the scent of woman, oil, and lilac he was still surprised she smelled of was still fresh on her person. For the first time in years, since long before Piper had given her heart to Samuel and left the Archives, Emmet wanted. He wanted this woman, wanted to feel her lips beneath him, her naked flesh as he slid between her legs, hear her moans in his ear as he brought them both to that blissful state of pleasure. It would be so easy to lean down and kiss her until she woke, to take some of that energy and lust for life Nicola possessed for himself.

He wanted, but knew he could never have. Not in any permanent way, which made it less than appealing.

Pulling back, he gave her a gentle shake. "Miss Tesla?"

She licked her lips and a soft moan escaped her. Whatever had been done to him clearly had struck her as well. She was no doubt going through the same painful stages of awakening as he had. Leaning in, he ignored his body's reaction to being so close to her, and whispered into her ear.

"Miss Tesla, we are safe for the moment. We appear to be in a cell, but unharmed. I know you can hear me, even if you can't speak yet. Relax and let your body do what it must. I'll see if I can determine where we are and if we can escape."

She moaned again, her lips moving as she tried to speak. Emmet placed his ear above her mouth, trying to catch the words. But the only thing he managed to make out was a single name.

Thomas.

Emmet pushed away from the cot, ignoring the way his head spun from the sudden movement. Of course, he knew very little about her, or her life back in Canada. Why he hadn't considered the thought that she had a lover, a man who was important in her life, he wasn't certain. Still, hearing another man's name on her lips was the splash of cold water he needed to break him out of his youthful obsession.

"We shall get you back to your Thomas soon enough, Miss Tesla. But first I must conquer this door."

Emmet's feet were numb, causing him to stumble as he moved. From his new vantage point, he was able to see partway down the hallway. There appeared to be a room from which the noises were coming. He could make out two distinct voices, one of whom sounded like that of a child. It was quite likely they'd been taken by one of New London's many street gangs, perhaps with the hopes of offering them up for ransom. The archivists weren't likely to pay for Emmet's release, but there was a chance that the Company would. He couldn't rely on that happening, though, and turned his thoughts to escape.

"Emmet?" He turned to see Nicola struggling to sit up. "Where are we?"

"A cell, in what looks to be a warehouse of some sort. I'm not certain."

"Are there guards?"

"Not that I can see, but we're not alone."

A loud clang followed by a chuckle was quickly chased by the sound of approaching footsteps. Emmet shifted so he was standing fully in the doorway, blocking Nicola from outside eyes. She wouldn't be strong enough to help him at any rate; best to keep her as safe as possible. The brute who stopped in front of him looked to be an escapee from the bowels of the Tower. A tattooed dagger was prominent on the side of his neck, adding a further degree of menace. No doubt if Emmet were to ask Samuel, the sergeant would have been able to identify the man and which crime organization he belonged to.

Keeping his gaze even, Emmet smirked. "Fine day, it is."

The brute grunted. "Yer awake."

"Stating the obvious. An indication of your level of intelligence and your status in this kidnapping. Let me speak to your boss."

"Fuck off."

"I'd be more than happy to do just that, but I appear to be locked away." Emmet kicked the bottom of the bars. "Unless you'd like to open up for me. Then we could have a proper chat."

"Our guests are awake?" A new voice, American from the sound of the accent, reached him.

Emmet waited until the approaching footsteps revealed a middle-aged man, well dressed and of good health. He looked Emmet up and down before waving the brute away. "You're an archivist."

"I am." Emmet waited, knowing this man wouldn't be easily goaded into revealing information.

The man's gaze returned to his eyes and Emmet had no doubt what he was looking for. "An unproven one. I guess that explains why they had you minding your guest rather than out on the streets doing real work."

The barb was intended to wound, but Emmet's skin was far thicker than that. "We all have our ways of serving the guild."

"I'm sure you do." He stepped closer to the bars. "Do you know who I am?"

"Not specifically. But you work for the Illuminating Company."

"Work for?" The man smirked. "A shame that my reputation doesn't have as far a reach as I'd assumed. It's a blow to the ego, don't you think, Nicola?"

Her hand touched Emmet's arm, encouraging him to move to the side. "I'm certain your ego can withstand it."

"Care to give the introductions, my dear?" There was something in the man's voice, not quite hate, but certainly close enough that Emmet immediately went on the defensive.

If Nicola was scared, she certainly gave no indication. "Emmet Dennison, archivist, please meet Thomas Edison, founder of the Illuminating Company and idea thief."

"Now, now, my dear. We've been over that before. You were in my employ and therefore those inventions rightfully belonged to me."

"You're a lying bastard who's forced to steal what others create because you are too damned stupid to invent the things yourself." Her body shook as she spoke, her hands balled at her side. "I shall never forgive you for that."

"I don't need your forgiveness." His smile didn't quite reach his eyes. "But I do need your brain."

Nicola snorted. "As though I'd ever help you again."

"You don't have a choice." Edison turned his back on them. "Bring them water and food. Only enough for one though. I wouldn't want to waste all our resources."

Emmet refused to move until he knew for certain that they were gone. Once the footsteps disappeared, he rounded on Nicola and took her by the shoulders.

"What the hell does he want?"

"How am I supposed to know?" Yet, she couldn't quite look him in the eye.

"Because I've come to realize that you know a hell of a lot more than what you let on. So I'll ask you again, what does the bastard want?"

Nicola walked unsteadily over to the cot to sit none too gracefully on it. "I believe he wants me."

"I gathered as much. It was the reason I was assigned to stay with you." Her head snapped up in surprise, but he ignored her. "Why does he want you specifically? What is it that you have that he needs? If we know that, then there is an opportunity we can use it as leverage to get us out of this place."

Nicola didn't respond, and instead picked at the material of her trousers. He couldn't be certain what she was thinking, and he was almost to the point of not caring. Clearly, she was holding back information that he needed if they were to have any opportunity of getting out of this in one piece.

"Miss Tesla?"

"Nicola. My name is Nicola." She patted her thighs softly before looking up. "Thomas wants me because of what I did to him. See, I was in his employ for a time. I was young and the opportunity was quite exciting. What I didn't understand was that he took my ideas for his own. Got rich off them."

"This is about money?" Having never wanted for anything in

his life, Emmet often found it difficult to relate to such matters. "Surely the Company can pay for any damages done."

"If only it were that simple." For the first time since their acquaintance, Nicola lost her cockiness. "I didn't exactly leave the Illuminating Company on the best of terms."

"Oh?"

"I might have, perhaps, blown up his warehouse on my way out the door." Nicola finally met his gaze and smiled. "He's had a price on my head ever since."

Chapter 7

The cold from the stone wall had long seeped into her back, causing the skin to go numb. Emmet hadn't said much to her after her confession about her relationship with Thomas. Not that she expected him to fully appreciate her point of view in matters, but a bit of sympathy wouldn't have gone amiss.

Once their meager meal had been delivered, Thomas had left them surprisingly alone. Nicola had no doubt he was plotting out the best way to turn this situation around to his advantage, perhaps spending time to build an adequate torture machine to shove her into. Being faced with that would have been far more comforting than being forced to sit in this cell left to ponder her fate. She hated inactivity, hated not being able to get her hands dirty and keep her mind in motion, but there was nothing for her to do here.

Thomas clearly knew how best to drive her mad.

Emmet was still inspecting the hinges that held their cell door in place. He was convinced they were the means to their escape. She could offer to help him, put her nervous energy to good use, but she got the impression her presence wouldn't be welcomed.

To hell with it. "Unless you have something hiding in your pockets that can cut through iron, I don't see how you plan to work those hinges free."

"I'm simply learning everything I can about our environment."

"Well, if you ask me—"

"I didn't." His voice was muted somewhat by the wall, though his annoyance came through clearly.

"Why are you so annoyed with me? I didn't deliberately put you in danger. I only learned of Thomas' presence in New London a short time ago." A part of her wasn't sorry in the least that they'd been captured by her former employer. It saved Nicola having to wander the streets of a strange city trying to locate him. "It's not my fault he's out to get me."

"Except that it is." Emmet pressed his head against the door for a moment before throwing a glace her way. "You blew up his bloody life's work."

"*After* he stole mine." She crossed her arms and narrowed her gaze. "It was only fair."

"I'm sure he doesn't see it that way."

No, Nicola knew Thomas wouldn't feel anything but anger and betrayal regarding her actions. His work was everything to him, meaning nearly as much as his precious reputation. She'd watched him push aside his family, his wife and children, to capture as much money, power, and glory as he could muster. Nicola had always felt bad for his wife, Mary. They'd worked side by side for a time in Thomas' shop, until Mary had caught Thomas' eye. They'd married quickly, and Mary, once Nicola's compatriot, became the mistress of the Illuminating Company.

But Mary had lost the spark of personality after the marriage. Every time Nicola would see her at the warehouse, she noticed that she'd grown quiet, withdrawn. The last time she'd seen her before Mary flew to America, Nicola had begged her to seek a doctor's aid for her headaches. She'd often wondered what had become of her friend. Though the idea of asking Thomas how she fared was less than wise.

With her departure, Thomas grew more driven, and the bulk of his attentions had fallen onto Nicola.

"Let me see that bloody door." She crossed the distance, shoving Emmet aside. "You're an archivist, not an engineer."

"I'm also not an idiot." But he gave her the space she needed.

The hinges were steadfast, though she could see there were a few stressed locations that, given the right equipment, would give way under duress. The problem being, she didn't have access to anything that would inflict the proper damage.

As she began to inspect the iron beam that held the hinges, she heard a small cough and the stumbling step of someone approaching. Emmet put his hand on her shoulder, pulling her away from the door, but not so far that she wouldn't be able to see the approaching person.

What she didn't expect was the thin waif of a boy to poke his head around the corner. There was an odd distant look in his eyes, as though he wasn't able to focus on them. The boy gave his head a shake, before offering them a small smile.

"Hullo."

"Hi there." Nicola waved. "What's your name?"

He cocked his head and frowned. "It's Keegan."

"Keegan. That's a good name. Solid name." Nicola stepped closer to the bars, ignoring Emmet's soft hiss. "I'm Nicola and this is Emmet. He's a bit of a grump though, so I mostly ignore him."

Keegan smiled and inched closer to the cell. "Why are you two in there? Did Mr. Edison offer you a job, too?"

Interesting. "I used to work for Mr. Edison, years ago in the Paris location. Are you one of his clever lads? He always seemed to find the smartest people to work for him. And I can say that because I was one of them."

"I help make the metal dance." Without any further comment, he turned and went into a cell of his own.

The door was open, and it was apparent that no one was forcing the boy to stay here to work. Still, there was something odd in his behavior, something that didn't sit right with her. "What do you mean you make the metal dance, Keegan? Is that something you can show me?"

"I'm tired, miss. Maybe later. After I've eaten my sweets."

If Keegan had any food, he made no move to eat it. Instead he curled up on his cot and closed his eyes. It had been years since she'd seen that level of exhaustion in another person. She'd only experienced it herself a few times, and never since she'd begun her tenure at the Company.

"Poor mite is worn out."

Nicola barely managed to suppress a gasp at Emmet's unexpected words against her ear. He'd moved up behind her while her attention had been focused on Keegan, and now his body was so close she could have swayed little more than an inch and they would be in complete contact. Her traitorous body reacted to his proximity in a way she wouldn't have assumed herself capable of before now. Her nipples were hard, and a warmth she'd never felt as the result of being with another person consumed the sensitive spot between her legs.

This was a rather inconvenient time to develop a physical attraction to a man.

Doing her best to keep her body as still as possible, Nicola nodded. "I've only seen that state a few times before. I suspect he'll have a difficult time sleeping, even if that's the one thing he wants most in the world."

"What do you think Edison wants him for? Surely, a boy of that age would have little to offer to an engineer."

"Sometimes age doesn't inform ability." Did he know what he was doing to her by standing this close? She wanted nothing more than to turn around and slap him for eliciting this reaction from her. "Would you mind stepping back?"

His hot breath tickled the side of her neck as he chuckled. "It's easier for me to speak quietly if we are close. What are you afraid of, Miss Tesla?"

Without touching him, she turned so they were now face to face. "I'm afraid of nothing."

It was odd looking into Emmet's eyes. He bore the same level of callous indifference that most of the archivists wore, though he didn't bear the physical scar of having performed an extraction. But every so often, she'd catch a glimpse of something else, lurking. Was this behavior simply a shield for him, a means to keep himself on an even footing with the others of his guild? Or was he hiding the true man beneath the surface, waiting to explode out into the daylight?

"Miss Tesla—"

"Nicola."

He closed his eyes for a beat. "We need to get out of here. I believe our best way of doing that is to discover exactly what it is Edison is planning and put a stop to it."

She'd never wanted to kiss a man before. Not with any real feeling behind it. Not with any intention of taking things further. So why she was tempted to close the small distance between them, press her lips against his and quell her curiosity of what he would taste like, was as much of a mystery as what the hell Thomas was doing in New London.

"The Administrators suspected the French are looking to gain a foothold in New London. I was told that the person who was out to capture you was working with them."

The mention of politics was a surefire way to kill any amorous feelings she was beginning to have. Stepping away to grant herself a chance to clear her head, she sat down on the cot. "I wouldn't be surprised if Thomas was working with them, but that wouldn't be his only goal. More of a means to an end. He doesn't have political aspirations beyond gaining influence to assist his own interests."

"A rather dangerous means from my perspective."

"If Thomas came all this way, he has a reason. One that will be far more dangerous than an alliance with the French. Or at the very least more specific."

Emmet chose that moment to pull his cravat off, leaving him in only his waistcoat and shirtsleeves. It was a look she'd seen on countless men over her years of working with the Company, and yet somehow on Emmet it gave him the appearance of something dangerous. And appealing in a sexual manner.

"I'm surprised they left us in here together." He patted down his pockets. "Though they seem to have relieved us of anything useful."

"This place doesn't look as though it's in the best condition. They probably don't have another cell available."

"Let's hope it stays that way. With the two of us being here, we'll at least have a chance to plan an escape."

Nicola looked past Emmet across the hall. "What about…?"

"We'll take him if we can. If for no other reason than he's been here longer and might have a clearer picture of what's going on."

"Fair enough."

With nothing left to do or say, the nervous impatience threatened to rise up inside her once more. "I hate waiting."

"Try to rest. We don't know when we'll need to move. I'll wake you if anything happens."

Rolling onto her side, facing the wall, she sighed. There was nothing for it but to try to rest. Even if her sleep would be filled with images of her feeble attempts to seduce Emmet.

* * *

He'd lost track of how much time had passed since he'd gained consciousness. Instead of taking his own rest, Emmet kept watch, cataloguing every sound that reached him. He'd detected at least four different voices, all except for Edison bearing local accents. That would make it easier to track the ruffians down upon his escape.

The distance from where the men were was significant enough that Emmet was unable to make out their conversation, no matter how much he concentrated. Add to that the loud, uneven breathing from the boy across the hallway, and Emmet knew his vigil was a pointless endeavor.

When he finally heard someone approaching, his agitation had grown to a state where he was fit to punch through stone. The sight of the three brutes they'd encountered in the alley now standing outside their cell did little to reassure him that the next few hours would be pleasant.

"Shall I don my coat? I would hate to appear less than presentable if I'm meeting guests."

"Don't be a smartarse," the middle one snapped. "Get them both out here."

"Miss Tesla, I believe we are about to find out why our presence has been requested." He didn't need to look to know she'd also heard their approach and had gotten up from the cot.

It was odd how quickly he'd become attuned to her ways. Emmet had a similar relationship with Jones, Piper, and Samuel, but that stood to reason, given the closeness of their relationships, and he had never had that kind of closeness with someone from outside of the guild. Not even his family, though that was hardly a surprise.

Unwilling to let Nicola go first, Emmet stepped out and was immediately punched in the stomach. The contents of his gut threatened to spill as additional blows rained down on him. Nicola's cries were swallowed up by his grunting and the ringing in his ears. He tried to fight back, but the attack was so sudden and consuming, it was pointless. Giving up, he allowed himself to be dragged down the corridor to a much larger space. In a way it reminded him of one of the chambers in the Archives—too large to be of much use to anyone, yet given the right circumstances it would prove invaluable.

Emmet allowed himself to be shoved back first against a metal post and his hands bound behind him. While escape wouldn't be possible, from this vantage point he'd be able to take in as much detail as possible, all of which could prove useful at a later time.

The warehouse had been cordoned off, the focus of their occupation being little more than a third of the area available to them. Clearly, Edison was building some contraption or other, one that required a significant amount of space. Steam pipes lined the walls and up across the ceiling. They were suspiciously quiet, an indicator that the building was far from being in the best of condition. Without steam, the chances that the equipment left behind would work were slim at best. Add in the grime-coated windows and rust-covered iron and Emmet couldn't imagine the clockwerker being able to accomplish much of anything in this location.

The air here was far colder than in the cell, though Edison

had taken pains to bring to life some of the heating. If this was where the boy had been working, it was a wonder he hadn't frozen before now.

Edison stood with his back to them, examining something or other on a workbench. To Emmet's eyes, he looked to be in good health and in full control of his faculties. No madness driving his actions, as there had been with Jack. What he wasn't certain was if that made the inventor more or less dangerous.

"Really, Thomas, if you were planning on taking over New London, couldn't you afford a better workspace than this? It's sad to see you fall to such lows." Nicola's tone was light, dismissive, as though she wasn't bothered in the least by what was transpiring around her.

Maybe that's what she wanted Edison to think, but Emmet wasn't convinced.

"It suits my needs. Please have a seat."

Nicola was forced onto a chair in the middle of the room, too far away for him to be able to do anything to assist should she run into trouble. Not that he was much good to her with his hands bound, but Emmet was resourceful if nothing else. The moment the brutes left him alone and turned their attention to Nicola, he began to test the restraints to see if there was any weakness to them.

Nicola crossed her legs and placed her hands in her lap. She looked to be a woman humoring a suitor she already knew she wouldn't accept. "What do you want, Thomas? If you're planning on killing me, I would appreciate it if you'd simply get it over with."

"In due course, my dear. In due course. Before I have the boys here slit your throat, I thought you might be interested in seeing this."

He turned to face them, and in his hands he held a large glass orb. Emmet would have dismissed it quickly as irrelevant, until he caught sight of something odd in its center. A soft green light that appeared to have no apparent light source. His hands momentarily forgotten, Emmet tried to lean forward as much as possible to try to catch a better look at the object.

Nicola stood, ignoring the way the brutes closed in on her, and took the orb in her hands. "Well, well. This is fascinating."

"I thought you might approve." Edison leaned back against the workbench. "It's far sturdier than it appears. I assure you, if you were to drop it no harm would come—"

Nicola let the orb go, and it landed on the stones with a mighty *gong*. The light flickered for little more than a second before returning to its full strength. "What's the shell constructed from? Surely not glass. It's far too light for that."

Emmet's heart had stopped when the orb connected with the stone. His attention had been fixed on Edison, who was staring at Nicola. In an instant, it appeared as though Edison would make good on his earlier promise to slit Nicola's throat. She was clearly too taken with the new material to fully appreciate the danger she currently resided in.

"What the hell is it and why do you need us?" His throat was sore from where he'd been punched, but thankfully his voice still held its edge.

"Ah, yes, the archivist." Edison plucked the orb from Nicola's hands and sauntered over to Emmet. "I couldn't believe my luck when the boys told me they captured both of you. While Nicola was my prize, having you here will certainly make the next phase of my project far simpler."

As he brought the orb closer, Emmet realized what exactly it was he was seeing, certain obvious truths that anyone beyond the walls of the Archives would not have access to. Something must have shown on his face, for as Edison stopped before him and held the orb up, he chuckled.

"Your archivist is a bright one, Nicola. Though from the look of him he's still untested."

"I wouldn't worry about him," she said as she shook off the guards and came closer herself. "I've learned he's annoyingly perceptive and far handier than I originally gave him credit for."

"High praise coming from you." Edison held the orb directly in front of Emmet's eyes. He could see it all, the filaments and tiny casings, the pathways that would be formed once it was filled. "You know what this is?"

"Yes." Far larger than the refined tubes the guild used, it would still serve its purpose. "It's a memory vial."

"A what?" Nicola stepped close, her gaze shifting between Emmet and the orb. "Not possible."

"Oh, but it is." With a flourish, Edison pulled the orb away and the guards moved in to put Nicola back into her chair. "I've found a way to construct a memory vial. But more than that, I know how to access the memories."

"Not possible. That isn't even common knowledge within the Archives."

"No, but certain Guild Masters who have dealings with the French are quite happy to sell your secrets for a tidy profit."

Ryerson. The bastard.

Emmet should have known that there would be additional issues resulting from Ryerson's fall from grace. If he could kill the Guild Master all over again, he would. "I'm certain he sold that tidbit of information because he knew there was no way the French would be able to make use of it. The extractors are all accounted for and are under the strict gaze of the guild."

"You're quite right. The Frenchies didn't have a clue about how best to use their prize. Nor did they have the refined equipment to produce the glass needed. It seems they too are still suffering the effects from your little war." The orb was placed back on its small pedestal, casting its surreal glow across the surface of the workbench. "I, however, know a thing or two about materials. And more than enough about getting what I want. That's where the two of you come into play."

"You don't honestly think we're going to help you?" Emmet tried to loosen his bonds as he spoke, the urgency of the situation increasing with each realization.

"Of course you will." It was strange how calm and confident Edison was. Surely his outcome wasn't so certain that he could afford to take the risk of informing them of the details, or relax his guard even a little. "You see, Mr. Dennison, you will do what I ask or else I'll kill Nicola here. I've been told that your Administrators don't take too kindly to their operatives failing."

"And why would I help you?" Nicola shifted in her chair so Emmet was able to catch a glimpse of her nose and plump lips in profile. "For that matter, why would you want me to assist? Given what I did the last time we were together, I would assume you'd want me as far away from your projects as possible, lest I find a way to blow them up."

Emmet strained against his bonds when Edison moved around behind Nicola's chair, grabbed her by the chin, and wrenched her head back. "You'll help because you can't stand leaving an engineering mystery left untouched. And if you don't I'll have the boy who is currently asleep across from your cell tortured for every second you refuse. If you think I'll hesitate to kill the street rat, you're a bigger fool than I thought."

"You bastard. You wouldn't dare…" But even Emmet could

tell from the tone of her voice that she wasn't at all convinced of that.

"Wouldn't I? A lot has happened since you and I last spoke. I've seen things, done things that have changed me. I will kill to get what I want." Edison finally let her go, but didn't move away. "I'm not the same man you once knew. Don't make me prove it."

Fuck. Emmet jerked against the pole. "How can you access the memories?"

Edison didn't grace him with even a causal glance. "All in due time. For now the two of you have a task to do."

"What?" Nicola rubbed at her throat. "What do you want from us?"

Edison grinned, and for the first time since he'd been in the presence of Jack, Emmet felt fear.

"You're going to build me a memory extractor."

Chapter 8

Nicola couldn't stop the periodic shaking that rolled through her body. They'd been escorted back to their cell and left alone to ponder the implications of Thomas' words. He wanted her to build a memory extractor, implying that he was planning to kill someone to steal their memories and then put them to use.

Before I have the boys here slit your throat...

Was he going to pillage her head, steal the thoughts and ideas she'd stripped from him all those years ago? She wouldn't put it past the bastard to attempt such a thing. This would be theft of a barbaric nature, the ultimate crime that would provide Thomas with every thought, every leap of logic she'd ever had. If he'd found a way to make use of those memories afterward, there would be no way for anyone to prove the inventions weren't his own.

The plan was beautiful in a diabolical way. The crime was far worse than her murder alone.

"I don't understand what the orb was made from." Emmet paced around their cell, full of tension and fury. "Glass would have shattered when you dropped it, even if it was thick. I've seen other attempts to replicate memory vials. None were that complete."

"It's Parkesine."

He stopped in his tracks, turning to frown at her. "What? I've never heard of that bloody stuff."

"Created by Alex Parkes, a company man who was a bit on our fringes a few years back. He showed it off in 1862 at the Great International Exhibition. It's an organic material, something that can be heated and molded. Odd stuff, but very effective when one needs lightweight material."

They'd begun to use Parkesine at the head base in Canada. It held up better in the cold than glass and turned out to be far more durable given the extreme temperature changes. Of course, Alex's original formula had been tweaked since its arrival, but that was standard for anything that found its way into the hands of the HBC. No man, woman, or thought was left free from the stag's mark.

Emmet waved the idea away. "Fine. Not that it will matter. Even if we could build an extractor, I have no intention of doing so."

Nicola let her gaze linger on his stubble-covered face, unable to help but wonder what it would feel like against her fingers, her face, her lips. "We have no choice."

"There is more at stake than one life if the wrong person has access to a machine such as the extractor." Emmet straightened so much he appeared to swallow a significant portion of the room. "We just got one madman off the streets of New London. I won't allow another to roam so quickly."

She knew better than to ask further details about the infamous Jack the Ripper. Instead, she got to her feet and cautiously approached. "What was it that was so offensive about what Jack did?"

"You need ask? He brutally took the lives of defenseless

women." His scowl deepened and something flashed in his eyes. "That should provide more than enough offense."

"So that is unacceptable to you, but the murder of a child, one who is either being drugged or is mentally incapacitated, is fine?" She waited for her words to penetrate, watched as his face twisted into a portrait of disgust. "I thought not. You and I will do what Thomas has asked. We will build his extractor and the damn thing will work. I will not have the life of that boy on my head."

"Miss Tesla—"

"But we will do so in the slowest manner possible." She knew she was putting her life in peril, but she would never be able to live with herself knowing an innocent's life had been taken as a result of her inaction. "We will buy ourselves enough time not only to discern Thomas' intents, but to find a way out of this mess. If we are very lucky, then we either will be rescued or will have found a way to escape long before then."

Emmet nodded. "You believe he'll kill the boy? That it's not some ruse to get your cooperation?"

There was a time when the idea would have struck her as preposterous. But there'd been something about the look in Thomas' eyes that chilled her through and through. "Without a doubt."

His gaze held hers steady. While she knew Emmet was a hard man, someone who didn't back away from trouble, those fleeting glimpses of caring would poke through the prickles of his shell. It was in moments such as these, where the concern for a child's well-being overrode what logic dictated, that Nicola began to understand her attraction to him.

Her breathing became labored and stuttered as she let it out. Every inch of her body had grown aware of his presence in a very real way. She could feel the space between them, knew it would take very little movement before they'd connect. He'd be warm. The scent of him would roll over her, making her drunk with want of more.

She should look away, should put some distance between them. Even back at the Company, men and women were rarely left alone together for this length of time. Sexual relations weren't prohibited, but they more often than not got in the way of productivity. Yes, nothing good would come from this feeling of want building inside her. They couldn't exactly act upon their desires trapped in a cell where anyone could happen by. No doubt, Thomas would use any hint of a relationship between them to his advantage.

If Emmet shared her sentiment, he didn't show it. Without having seemingly moved, Nicola found her chest pressed against his. Their arms still remained at their sides, though Emmet had lowered his face so their lips were inches apart.

"Miss Tesla?" The heat from his breath caressed her skin.

She let her eyelids slip down, blinked so slowly she could have been intoxicated. "Nicola. If you're about to kiss me I would ask that you at least call me by my first name."

"Nicola." There was something rough to his voice, his accent thick as it rolled across her name. "This is a terrible idea."

"I'm full of terrible ideas. It's sometimes hard to separate them from the good. Experimentation is the means to achieve success, to tell which is which."

His soft chuckle soaked into her body, heating her deep in her core. "We are hostages in a cell. If they know—"

"Thomas will already use you against me and vice versa. We might as well reap the benefits while we're able."

She didn't want to think about how she often did this, would find a way to distract herself from a situation she didn't want to face. The last thing she wanted was to continuously flip through the ways Thomas could kill her and take her thoughts. No, it was much better to face this reality, the enticement of an attractive man and the pleasure of a kiss.

Her inexperience was something of a bother to her. She'd often brushed aside the fumbling attempts of her colleagues, even while wishing she'd meet a man who would spark that inner flame, give her a reason to ignore her brain and focus on her body. As Emmet reached up and cupped her face in his hands, she knew he was the one.

"Have you kissed a man before?" His lips brushed hers, so close to giving her what she wanted.

"Yes. It was horrible."

"I hope to improve upon your experience."

"Please do."

"Even though this is a terrible—"

"Emmet. Kiss me."

One moment she was speaking and in the next his mouth was devouring hers. There was nothing soft about him, the way his thumbs caressed her cheeks as his tongue pushed its way past her lips, nor the muscles of his chest against her. Nicola lost herself in a sea of sensation, the scent of him, heat from his body, the soft touch of his tongue against hers. A moan escaped her as he slid his hands down the side of her throat to her shoulders, pulling her even harder against him.

That contact jolted Nicola into action. Never content to simply be a bystander, she began her own exploration of his person. Circling around to his back, she slipped her hands beneath the fabric of his waistcoat so they were trapped between the wool and his linen shirt. It was easy then to feel the muscles beneath her touch, enjoying the way they'd flex beneath her fingertips as she scratched across them. What she wouldn't give to see his body stripped free from the layers of material, to explore without fear of being caught. Emmet must have had a similar thought, as the next thing she was aware of was his hands teasing her back just above the line of her corset.

"I hate these damn things." He sucked on her bottom lip. "Too difficult to remove with any speed."

"More importantly, too difficult to redo with any speed." She smiled and nipped at his chin.

Nicola would have planned for an additional witty remark if it weren't for the light coughing from the cell across the hall. For a moment, she'd forgotten that they weren't alone in this, that there wasn't a child involved who appeared to be so far under Thomas' spell she wasn't certain how to extract him.

"Shit." Emmet muttered as he stepped back.

Indeed. She moved around Emmet, ignoring the way her body longed to fall back into his embrace, to stand before the cell bars. "Keegan?" The boy didn't move immediately, though she could see his eyes had opened. "Are you well, Keegan?"

With what appeared to be great effort, he pushed himself into a sitting position. "Aye."

"You were coughing. If you are coming down with something you must tell Thomas immediately." While she wasn't certain what the boy's role was in Thomas' plans, if he was here then it was significant. Thomas wouldn't risk anything happening to Keegan until his job was completed.

"I wouldn't want to bother Mr. Edison. Not when there's so much work to get done."

"What work?" Emmet shouldered his way beside her, far closer than he would have before their kiss. "What does Mr. Edison have you do?"

Keegan got to his feet and shuffled out into the hallway. Unlike the previous day, he looked a bit more rested, though Nicola didn't care for the pallor of his skin or the way his cheeks were sucked into his face. The boy needed food, proper rest, and a warm place to recover. If there was once a spark to his eyes, it had been extinguished.

"I help find the metal. The bits that will work with the cogs and gears. Mr. Edison . . . he hadn't told me for what." An obvious lie. "It's important though. I'm important. I know that." Keegan smiled, his lips cracking as he did. "If I do a really good job I get treats along with my coin. Don't tell Mr. Edison, but I would be happy just to have the treats."

"Oh, I'd never tell him." Nicola smiled as brightly as she could manage. "I would love to try some of the treats if I could. Maybe the next time you have a few."

"Maybe." He turned to look down toward the workroom. "I should go."

"What are you doing today? Finding more metal?"

"Oh no. Today I have an important task. Very important."

She could feel Emmet shifting, the tension taut in his body. Emmet asked, "What is it?"

A well-placed elbow into Emmet's side sent him away from the door. "Don't mind him, Keegan. He gets grumpy when he hasn't had his breakfast. Though I have to admit, I'm curious too about what it is Mr. Edison has you working on."

Keegan blinked slowly twice before he shrugged. "You work for him now, yeah? That's why yer here."

"Yes, he's asked me to build a special machine for him. Emmet here is going to be my assistant."

"I am not—"

"So that makes us colleagues." Nicola carefully pushed her

hand through the bars, offering it to him. "Hello, good man. I look forward to working with you."

Keegan's face split into a grin. He slipped his hand into hers and gave her a surprisingly hard shake. "Yeah, me too."

"And in the vein of being friendly co-workers, it only seems fair for me to tell you about my project. I'll be building an extractor." She retracted her hand through the bars and braced it on her hip. "Do you know what one of those are?"

"That's one of the things them zombies use."

"That's right. Mr. Edison wants one for his own, so that's what I'll be doing."

Keegan cast another quick glance toward the workshop before he leaned in and whispered. "I'm not supposed to tell, but Mr. Edison wants me to build an automaton."

"How exciting! And you look to be the perfect person for the job." Nicola ignored the way her stomach turned at the idea. "Well, I wouldn't want to keep you from your task. You move along and we'll speak later. Perhaps we can exchange status updates. That's what we do at the Company."

Keegan's grin widened. "I'd like that."

"Well then, I'll report in after."

With one final wave, Keegan turned and sauntered to the workshop. Nicola managed to wait until the boy was from sight before rounding on Emmet. "An automaton? What the hell does he want with one of those and a memory extractor?"

Emmet ran his hand along the back of his neck. "He claimed he knew how to use the memories once they'd been taken. It's possible he's found a way to integrate them into the robot."

"Automaton."

"Whatever. If he can store the memories in the orb, and use the robot to access them, then that will provide him with a means unprecedented in the history of the Archivist Guild." He closed his eyes. "We can't do this."

"Do we have a choice? Thomas is a smart man. If we don't build what he wants, he'll kill us and still find another way to accomplish his goals. It will take him longer, but he'll get there eventually. Better for us to cooperate and learn what we can, figure out how to stop him, than be dead."

And just like that, she was back to worrying about her fate.

"I don't like this. Any of it." But she could tell from the slump of his shoulders that he knew she was right.

"I wouldn't expect you to."

With nothing else to do, and nowhere else to go, they both sat down on the cot. With their legs close together, Nicola took some comfort in the idea that regardless of what would happen here, Emmet was with her. "I hate waiting."

"I can tell." He patted her thigh. "We'll find out what his plans are for us soon enough."

Before I have the boys here slit your throat . . .

"Yes, I guess we will."

* * *

Keegan had started humming at some point during his time in the workshop. He'd liked talking to the pretty woman—Nicola—before he'd come here. Other than Mr. Edison, the rest of the men who worked here paid little attention to him. It was nice to have a conversation, be treated like an equal rather than some gutter rat who would rob a person blind. He would, but that didn't mean he enjoyed being treated that way.

He picked up his hammer and began tapping away at the sheet of metal that he'd placed on the bench. He'd decided that this would be the chest, because of the way it was nice and rounded. He'd make his automaton as beautiful as Nicola if he could. Not that the automaton would have hair, or skin that look smooth as snow, but he could make its casing shine, giving it the glow that Nicola had.

It would be stunning. And strong. She was that way, he could tell simply by talking to her. There was energy inside her, the way the metal had energy, and it bled around her body, glowing. It was weird, he'd never been able to see that before, not with people. Maybe he should mention it to Mr. Edison. There could be something wrong with Nicola, and Mr. Edison would be able to help make her better. Maybe.

Oh, that was the perfect curve for the chest plate. If he could find an equal sheet of metal for the back, then there would be lots of room for the gears and conduits. He'd even be able to make a special cage to hold the heart.

Yes, his automaton would be beautiful. She'd have a soul.

Chapter 9

Once again Emmet found himself sitting in a chair, forced to watch Nicola work. It shouldn't have come as much of a surprise, given his skill set and what it was Edison wanted accomplished, and yet it annoyed him to no end to once again be perceived as useless.

"I'm not going to be able to do anything productive if I don't have proper tools, Thomas." Nicola had been talking to her former employer with complete disdain most of the day. "I mean, really, you think I can manage these wires with a cutter that won't slice through warm butter?"

"Do you think I'm fool enough to give you access to tools you can use as weapons?" Edison flipped the page from the morning paper over. His feet were propped on the edge of a desk he'd claimed as his own on the far end of the work area. "You forget that I know how vast your ingenuity is. I have no doubt you'll find a way."

Nicola simply rolled her eyes and used her teeth to remove the casing of the wire.

Emmet knew he couldn't sit there for long without saying

anything. It wouldn't go well for any of them if he opened his mouth and said the wrong thing. Nicola was probably correct in her assumption that Edison would happily kill them and find another way to put his plan into action if either of them caused too many problems. Yes, he should keep his mouth closed.

"So you're going to sit on your arse while she does all the work? I thought you were some bloody genius or something?"

Edison turned the corner of the paper down, casting a glance Emmet's way. "I guess it would be expecting too much for you to refrain from speaking."

"If the Guild Masters haven't found a way to silence me, I doubt you could."

Nicola snorted. "Don't bother, Thomas. He's surlier than you. Though far more pleasant on the eyes."

"Oh, please. You couldn't wait to get rid of me. I know for a fact you were planning to ditch me on our outing."

"Well, maybe if you weren't such an insufferable prig who thinks he knows what a woman should be rather than treat us like sentient beings, I wouldn't want to bash your head in."

They'd agreed it was for the best to cultivate the idea that they weren't the closest of companions while in Edison's hold. If anything, Edison might see them remaining in the same cell as additional torture for them both. It would do neither of them any good if one was used against the other. Though with Nicola, he wasn't entirely certain if she was faking the comments, or if that's how she really saw him.

"If you two can't behave I'll find a way to muzzle you both." Edison flipped the corner of his paper back up and continued reading.

Nicola glanced once more at Emmet and rolled her eyes. Despite her obvious fears of Edison, she seemed to be able to

handle them well enough. It was one of the things he was starting to realize about her, this innate ability she had to move
forward with a job, regardless of how she felt. Emmet admired
people who could do that, chose to spend time with them whenever possible. In a pinch, he knew he'd be able to count on them
to do the job, whatever that might turn out to be.

Rolling his head to stretch the muscles in his neck, Emmet
mentally reviewed all the information he had available to him
that could potentially help. The Administrators would know of
their kidnapping by now and would be out searching for them.
He wasn't certain of their location, but the search team would
use the carriage as their starting point to begin their search. If
the horses had been left in their original location.

Speaking of which…

"How did you stop the horses?" He sat straighter in his chair,
his mind racing now that he'd thought on the topic. "For that
matter, how did you draw them off course? I've never heard tell
of that happening before."

Edison sighed as he let his feet fall to the floor. "You won't let
me finish my morning paper, will you?"

Emmet shrugged. "If you've chosen to tie me up here, then
expect me to speak. Otherwise leave me back in the cell. I don't
care either way."

"I shall keep that in mind for tomorrow. Or maybe I'll simply
gag you." Edison walked behind Nicola, her body stiffening for
a moment as he passed. Emmet pretended not to notice, keeping his gaze locked on the other man. "It was a simple thing,
really. I'm surprised more citizens of this city haven't attempted
it before now."

Stopping by Emmet's side, Edison pulled a small black box
from his pocket. The casing was hinged, and with only the flick

of his thumb was he able to flip it open, revealing the guts of the machine. "I like to call it a dampener. It sends out small pulses that can disrupt the workings of an automaton. If I trigger a pulse at the right time, I can send the automaton off in a different direction than its original path."

"Bloody bastard." Both men turned to look at Nicola, but she continued to work on wiring her panel and said nothing else.

Interesting. He'd have to ask her about that later on. "The people of New London have no desire to hop into a zombie's carriage. They're not fools."

"Yes, they seem unusually scared of your lot. I find it rather amusing. You're simply pulling and mapping out the pathways of the mind. Moving a blueprint from an organic machine to a storage medium."

"Funny. Most people think we are extracting their souls." Emmet lowered his chin and smiled up at Edison. "I take it you're not a believer?"

"My relationship with God is none of your affair."

"Of course not. But you wanted to know why people don't try to stop the zombies. Not many are brave enough to walk into the pit with the vipers, risking their souls."

Edison stared down at him for a good long time. Emmet had borne such scrutiny many times before, from both family and strangers. He allowed the silence to stretch on, to pull at Edison until the man felt the weight of it upon him. Edison looked away, but didn't move. Much like Nicola, this man wasn't afraid to face a challenge head on. It made him more dangerous than most.

"Do you believe?" Edison's voice had dropped, had lost its condescending edge.

"In souls?" He'd been raised with the church as a child, much like his peers. He'd learned the readings, hymns, been able to recite the stories upon request. It was only after he'd moved to the Archives that he'd renounced all religions as foolishness practiced by the small minded. "Are you seriously asking an archivist that?"

"Answer my question."

Emmet fought hard to keep his gaze upon Edison. He bit the inside of his bottom lip, enjoying the small rush of pain. "I do."

"I see." Edison slipped the dampener back into his pocket. "Is that why you haven't performed an extraction?"

"It hasn't been my time."

"Liar. I'm very good at spotting liars."

Takes one to recognize one. "I am very adept at receiving other assignments when my name appears at the top of the extraction list."

Emmet hadn't allowed himself to think too long upon what it actually was they were taking from the dead. It was easier to believe what the Guild Masters told them as acolytes, that these were little more than pictures that still resided in the deceased brain. They were doing them, their families, the city of New London all a favor by preserving these experiences. It would benefit future generations to have these human stories recorded and stored.

It couldn't be a person's soul they were taking. If they were, then that would mean there was a God. Wouldn't he do everything in his power to cleave those to his bosom? Why would he allow them to be snatched from his grasp and forced to live for all eternity in a small vial?

No, best not to think too long upon that.

"I thought as much. Still, you won't be getting out of this duty, so best prepare yourself to join your friends and become a zombie yourself." There was something in Edison's eyes that hardened.

It was odd to see the steel beneath his surface rise up in such a manner. "You're the perfect conduit for the job I have in mind."

"Who? I don't see any corpses lying around here. Do you plan on killing someone?" Even though Nicola hadn't said as much, he knew she was terrified Edison planned on taking her life. If truth be told, he was more than a little concerned in that regard as well and would fight its happening tooth and nail.

"All in good time. For now, our little Serbian genius needs to build a working extractor. Then we'll talk more about souls and storage."

Edison waved the guards closer as he strode from the room. The large, brutish men quickly shifted away once Edison was out of sight. While Edison might not have any fears about being in the company of a zombie, his men certainly did. It took little more than a well-placed smile to send them scurrying away.

Nicola stood and stretched her back in an exaggerated manner, not too subtly looking his way and cocking an eyebrow. Of course she'd want to know what Edison had said to him. He gave his head a small shake and prayed she'd listen to him for once. Instead, she took the panel from her workbench, wires dragging on the floor behind her, and strode toward him.

"Whatcha' doin', miss?" The closest of the guards stepped in front of her to block her path.

"He's the only one here who has seen one of these extractors work." Holding it up, she looked around the hulk of a man to point at Emmet. "I need to have him double-check my connections to make sure I'm building this correctly."

"Yer not to go anywhere near—"

"I'd be more than happy to tell Thomas you wouldn't let me confirm my work. I'm sure he won't be upset at all if our little experiment doesn't work."

The man grunted and pushed Nicola toward Emmet. "You have five minutes."

"You're too kind." She grinned and strode forward. "Nothing like having our resident zombie available to check my work."

"Don't call me that."

Nicola flipped the board around, showing off the exposed wires and connections she'd soldered to the board. "I didn't know you were so sensitive, Mr. Dennison."

"I'm not." It only took the quickest glance to see that she'd made tremendous progress given her limited time and tools. "You're moving too quickly."

"I am?" She looked down and grinned once more. "I can't help it. I only have one speed when I'm working on a puzzle. Forward."

"Even if you might be the first and only test subject for the use of the extractor?"

"Unfortunately so. Shall we mark it up to a character flaw and move on? Now, what did Thomas say to you?"

"He asked me if I believed in the human soul. It was an interesting philosophical discussion."

"The bastard is toying with you." She closed her eyes and huffed softly before focusing her steely gaze back on him. "None of this makes any sense. It doesn't at all seem the sort of thing Thomas would do. I can't see the profit in it, and believe me when I say that profit is of paramount importance to him."

Emmet couldn't profess to know the man as well as Nicola did, but he knew she was wrong in this instance. "I'll continue to engage him in conversation, see if there is anything else I can learn from him in our talks."

"Good. I'll continue on this for now until we know what the hell is going on. I'm also working on a bit of a backup plan." She winked at him. "Just in case things take a turn for the worse."

"Don't do anything stupid. The Administrators will be out looking for us. It's only a matter of time before they—"

A clang echoed through the large warehouse space, grabbing everyone's attention. After several heartbeats, Keegan appeared from around the pile of scrap in the far corner. Shit, Emmet had forgotten about him, that he'd even been present in the room. The gangly waif of a boy was carrying a large curved sheet of metal. Ignoring the guards, he drifted toward them, staggering unsteadily as he weaved his way through the clutter of the room.

Nicola set the panel on Emmet's lap and turned. "Keegan? Are you well?"

The boy said nothing, stopping far closer to her than Emmet cared for. He cocked his head to the side, as though he was taking mental measurements, finally nodding after a time.

Nicola looked once more at Emmet. "Keegan?"

The boy stepped close and pressed the curved metal against Nicola's chest. She froze as the color drained from her face. *No, this isn't for her. It can't be.*

"Keegan," he said as softly as he could manage, "that's a very nice piece of metal."

"I knew I forgot something, but I didn't know what until I saw her."

Nicola sucked in a short little breath, as though she was terrified to move away. He wanted nothing more than to wrap his arms around her, calm her, take her as far away from here as he could so nothing would be able to hurt her. Jerking hard on the restraints eradicated any remaining thoughts of escape.

Best to try a different approach. "What did you forget? It looks perfect to me. The metal is smooth, polished. Hell, I can see my reflection. Looks like I'm in desperate need of a shave."

If Keegan heard him, the boy didn't acknowledge him. "You

see, it was right there, but I never really spend much time lookin' at ladies. The gents on the street don't like it when Underlings like me turn our eyes to their women. So it's best not to look. But I like lookin' at you, Miss Nicola."

"I...I like looking at you too, Keegan." Her voice shook as she spoke. "What did you forget?"

"The breasts." He looked up, wide-eyed. "Pardon, Miss Nicola. I know it's not polite to speak about the body to a lady, but we're workin' together, so I thought it was okay. I forgot to add a place for the breasts. No one will know she's a she otherwise. I need to fix that. I'll need more metal. This won't be big enough" In the same dreamlike state, he turned and shuffled away. "Breasts," and he giggled. "Bubbies. Boobs."

They watched him disappear once more to the back of the work area, off to add breasts to his creation. Nicola let out a stuttered breath. "I'd best get back to work."

"It might not be what you think it is." It was an almost lie, but one he didn't mind saying. "We don't have all the facts yet."

She looked at him quickly, before turning away. "I know you're not that much of a fool. He's building an automaton for my memories. Thomas plans to kill me."

* * *

Keegan was so excited about the completion of the chest plate. He still didn't know why he hadn't thought of adding breasts before today. Of course she needed to have them; he was right when he'd told Nicola that they were needed so the world knew she was a *she*. Mr. Edison would appreciate his attention to details, might even reward him.

His hands were shoved deep into his pockets, though they

continued to shake even there. It was why he'd been forced to stop working. His fingers couldn't hold the iron needed to solder the connectors to the chest plate. If they weren't exactly right, the cogs wouldn't do what he wanted, the metal wouldn't dance in exactly the right way, and she would be *wrong*.

There was no way he'd let that happen.

He continued to wander down the hallway that the guard had pointed him toward. Mr. Edison was somewhere down here, and that meant his treats would be here too. He always felt better once he'd had a few of his treats in his tummy. It was better than a hot bowl of stew and some beer to warm him up and settle his nerves.

A soft murmur reached his ears, and Keegan slowed down to try to detect where it was coming from. There were several doors along this way, all of them closed. Mr. Edison could be behind any one of them, conducting very important business. He wouldn't appreciate Keegan interrupting something simply so he could have more treats. No, it was best to wait here until he came out and then ask.

He continued to look around until the sound of Mr. Edison's voice grew louder. There it was, the door. Now all he had to do was stay small and be patient. He was good at that, had been forced to learn it quickly as an Underling, else Glyn would land a slap to his face. He'd only made that mistake once before he learned. Small and patient.

Time held little meaning for him since he'd come to the warehouse with Mr. Edison. He wouldn't have known if it had been minutes or hours that slipped by while he stood in the hall. Eventually, the door opened and one of the men was thrown out, his body landing against the wall with a wet sound. Mr. Edison emerged, his entire focus locked on the man as he strode to where he lay and kicked him hard.

"You've failed me for the last time." Mr. Edison kicked the unmoving man once more. "If she dies—"

Keegan must have made a sound, because one moment Mr. Edison was facing the wall and in the next he spun around to face Keegan so fast and smoothly that it made his tummy sour.

"What are you doing here, boy?" There was something in his voice, a note similar to how he was at the workshop—angry and mean. Like Glyn. "Speak!"

Keegan couldn't help but look at the unmoving man on the floor. There was a piece of him that knew he should be upset by what he saw. And still he wasn't. Keegan forced his gaze back to his employer's. "Mr. Edison, my hands won't stop shaking. I was working, but I didn't want to make a mistake. So I thought if I could have a few of those treats. Not a whole bag, I know I haven't earned those yet, but just a few, it would help. I can get so much more done when I've had my treats."

Mr. Edison opened his mouth to speak, but no words came out. He closed the distance between them and placed a hand on Keegan's shoulder. "Let me see your hands."

He pulled the left one from his pocket and held it up. It was the better of the two. He didn't want Mr. Edison to think he was too bad off. Then maybe he wouldn't want him anymore. That he'd find another boy who could make the metal dance in just the right way and he'd leave Keegan alone once more.

"It's just a little shake. Just a little bit. But I don't want te make a mistake. I'd do anything te be so good for you, sir."

Mr. Edison took his hand in his, giving it a little pat. "Yes, just a little shake. Nothing that a treat won't fix up."

The tight knot in his chest relaxed and Keegan knew he'd be able to keep working. Everything would be fine. "Thank you, Mr. Edison."

The arm across his shoulder, directing him away from the secret room, was a pleasant warm weight. Yes, Mr. Edison still liked him and that was the best feeling in the world. Almost as good as the sweets.

"You're a good worker, son. But I want you to stay away from here. Understand? Don't come back down this hallway unless I tell you specifically."

"Yes, Mr. Edison. Sir?" He looked up, surprised when he noticed the same strange aura around Mr. Edison. "I was busy building the automaton but then I finally realized I'd forgotten. I gave her breasts. Is that all right? She's a she and should look like one."

If he was shocked by the announcement, his employer gave no indication. "Breasts, you say? Yes, that seems to be the right thing to do. That is exactly right, exactly what I was hoping for. You've earned yourself another treat and an extra roll for your supper."

Well then. This was turning out to be a good day. A very good day indeed.

Chapter 10

It was full dark when they were escorted back to their cell. Nicola's back ached from the uncomfortable angle that she'd been hunched in for hours on end. It wasn't the sort of thing that normally bothered her, or that she'd even be aware of. Ever since Keegan had placed that metal casing against her chest and declared that it needed breasts, Nicola hadn't been able to relax.

Food had been left for both of them this time, a reward of sorts she suspected for the progress they'd made. Emmet took his plate and moved to the far side of their small cell, giving her a bit of space and time to think. She wasn't certain how he knew that's what she needed just then, but the gesture was appreciated.

She was building a machine that would be used to pull her memories from her head and embed them into an automaton.

The plate was a weight on her lap, and for the time being the temptations of food weren't winning. Setting it aside, she rested her head in her hands and did her best to not think about the consequences of what she was doing. If she didn't build his infernal machine, she was convinced they'd be killed and Thomas would find a way to construct it himself. She also couldn't bear the idea of leaving Keegan behind. The longer she spent in his company the more she believed that he was under the influence of some sort of narcotic. It wasn't at all the sort of thing Thomas had done in the past. She couldn't imagine what had happened to change him from cutthroat businessman to this unfeeling monster. It must have been something terrible to push him so far over the edge.

"You need to eat."

Nicola looked through her fingers at Emmet. Stubble now covered a generous portion of his face, giving him a rough and rugged look. He'd removed his cravat, exposing the entirety of his throat. Beautiful naked flesh that had never been a temptation to her before now. The memory of their kiss flared in her mind, shaking her body to life in a way she didn't know how best to handle.

"I'm not hungry." Lowering her gaze, she decided avoidance was the best option.

"That doesn't matter. You need the food to keep your strength up. Edison will push you to your limits, you know that."

"I'm not hungry." *Insufferable man.*

She didn't realized he had crossed the cell until he stood before her. Longer fingers pushed into her hair, encouraging her to look up. She didn't want to. She was far too tired to resist him and the comfort she suspected she'd find in his arms.

"Miss Tesla…" His voice drifted off, waiting for her usual correction. But what did her name matter if her very essence was to be sucked from her brain?

"He's going to kill me. He's going to use that device to pull all my experiences, thoughts through that box and into the automaton. I won't need to worry about eating then. I wonder if I'll be able to feel anything at all?"

Emmet dropped to a squat, reached for her wrists, and pulled her hands away from her face. With nowhere left to hide, she was forced to look into his concerned eyes.

"You're forgetting something critical." His lips were tugged into a frown, though whatever was causing him distress wasn't enough for him to look away. "Even if you successfully build that box, someone still needs to operate it."

The meaning behind his words didn't sink in immediately. It wasn't until she really looked at his hazel irises, the perfect undisturbed depths of color, that she realized.

"You'd be the one to do it."

"It's why he went to the trouble of bringing me here rather than simply killing me, or leaving me behind. He knows that a regular untrained mind wouldn't be able to survive the process of extracting the memories. He needed an archivist, and I seem to be the only one on hand."

God, that made things so much worse. While she would be dead, Emmet would have to live with his actions. Knowing he was the one responsible would haunt him. She didn't need him to say the words to know that.

Leaning in, she kissed him softly. "I'm so sorry."

"I won't do it. You need to know that regardless of what happens, I won't hook you up to that box."

"You might not have a choice. Either way, I'd be gone. If it's going to happen, I'd feel better knowing it was you looking after me."

Emmet gave his head a sharp shake. "The extraction process isn't what you think. I won't be simply transferring your thoughts into an automaton, and I'm still not convinced that is even possible. I pull your memories into my mind. I'll be able to hear your voice in my head, your fears, everything. I have a friend who was stuck with the memories of a prostitute for several days. It was as though she had another living person in her body."

The mere thought was horrifying to her. "But…how do you live that way?"

"We don't. The extracting archivists have the memories purged from their brains, leaving permanent holes in their minds. It's what leaves the ring in our eyes. If I were to do the extraction here, I would need to find a way back to the Archives before the process drove me mad."

Nicola pulled back, but didn't break contact completely. "I…I hadn't realized that's what they did to you. You mean your friend Jones—"

"Has a hole in his memory. So does my friend Piper, who was smart enough to walk away from the guild. Someday it will be my turn." Emmet refused to back down and leaned closer, removing the breathing room she'd procured for herself. "I have no intention of you being my first extraction. Do you understand me? We'll find some other way to handle this."

"Yes."

"Good." His gaze dipped to her lips once more. "I'm going to kiss you now."

"Is that wise?"

"Most definitely not."

Her eyes slipped closed as his nose brushed alongside hers. Gone was any hesitation she had from that first time. No, they were both rattled, scared of what might become of them, and Nicola knew if this was the location of her future death, she needed to take what solace she could in the arms of this strong, handsome man. To hell with what it did to her ability to concentrate. Little good her keen mind would be if Thomas got his way.

Unable to resist the temptation of his exposed throat any

longer, she reached up, brushing her fingers across the warm skin, loving the way the muscles shifted as he swallowed. She pushed on, cupping his neck with her hand until her fingers tangled in the fringes of his hair. The hair was soft against her skin, which only served to encourage her to touch him more.

A moan slipped from her as Emmet mirrored her actions. With one hand cupping her head and the other sliding around the small of her back, it was easy to let him tug her forward until her knees touched the inside of his thighs. She'd never been this physically close to a man, nothing beyond the occasional brush of shoulders, arms, or legs. She'd never wanted to move forward with a physical relationship before now, not really. As Emmet deepened the kiss, their bodies increasing in contact, she knew this was exactly what she wanted. What she needed.

Letting her hand slip down to his waistcoat, she pulled open the buttons. As soon as the heavy material fell open, she tugged his shirt free from his trousers.

"We can't." He muttered against her mouth. "Not completely."

"Want to touch you." When the linen was free from its constraints, it was easy enough to run her hand across his stomach. Muscles and hair, heat and strength, sensations she memorized as best she could. While she might be a virgin, she wasn't a complete innocent. Working day and night with men, even those who are reserved in sexual matters, one couldn't help but pick up a few smatterings of information. Nicola knew if she were to cup the front of his trousers just here...

Emmet sucked in a sharp breath, before nipping her bottom lip. "Minx."

"You like that?" It was obvious he did from the heavy weight of his erection in her hand, but the scientist in her craved the confirmation. "I don't want to hurt you."

"You can't." He lowered his face to the side of her neck, kissing the sensitive skin. "You're a virgin."

"Yes."

"You shouldn't know these things."

"And yet, I do."

"You should be offended by these actions."

"And yet, I'm not."

His chuckle rocked her body and sent a wonderful tremor through her. "You must terrify the clockwerkers in Canada."

"Daily."

In one easy motion, Emmet pushed her down so her back was flat against the small bed, leaving her legs to dangle off the edge. It not only gave her a perfect view of his face, but of the hallway and Keegan's room. They were alone, but it was unlikely they'd stay that way for long.

"Keep watch," he whispered as he opened the front of her trousers. "Just watch and let me make you feel good."

"But—"

"Don't argue, Miss Tesla."

"Nicola—Oh, God!"

In one easy motion, Emmet slid his hand into her trousers, pushing past the cotton undergarments and into the soft curls between her thighs. He shifted so he lay stretched out on the bed, his back to the cell door, protecting her from anyone who might happen to pass by. She was still able to see over his shoulder, though her attention had waned quickly given the wicked sensations he was pulling from her body with his fingers.

With his free hand, he opened the front of her shirt, undoing the buttons as far as her corset would allow. It was enough, allowing him access to her breasts and her hardened nipples.

"I'm smaller than most women." She might be perfectly

proportioned, but they were nothing that drew the attention of men. Before this moment, she'd always been thankful for that. Now, she hoped he wasn't put off.

"I know many men who believe that a woman who is well endowed, whose breasts are bountiful to the point of barely being contained by their clothing, is the most perfect sight a man can behold. I am *not* of that opinion."

His tongue brushed the peak at the same time his finger pushed further into the secret core between her legs that she'd touched a few times during the long, cold winter nights when her heart ached for human touch. The caress was soft, not enough to drive her mad, but certainly enough to nudge her in that direction. Despite the fear of discovery, Emmet appeared in no hurry to bring things to their pleasurable conclusion.

"I have always had an attraction to women whose breasts could fit perfectly into one hand. It gives me the opportunity to tease," he sucked the peak hard into his mouth, torturing the end with his tongue before pulling back with a wet pop. "I love to tease."

"You're a complete bastard." She squeezed her fingers into his hair, ensuring he wouldn't move away before she achieved her release. "More."

"I wish we were back at your rooms. I've heard the George Inn has wonderful facilities. Comfortable beds. I would keep you in it all day long so I might lick and taste every inch of your body."

She moaned, dropping her forehead to the top of his. "Please."

Emmet increased the pressure on her clitoris, rubbing it in soft circles. "I want to feel your legs around my body as I push my cock into you. I want to be the one who takes your maidenhead."

Any witty remarks she normally would retort with refused to form. She could feel and hear the wetness between her legs, knew her body was ready and willing to allow him to do exactly what he was describing. The thick cock she'd touched minutes ago would pierce her body in the most pleasurable way possible.

"Would you like that? Would you want to feel me inside you?"

"Yes." She shuddered, her body inching its way closer to release. "Yes."

"When we get out of here. The second we are both safe, I plan to do just that. Against a wall, in a bed, on the floor. I'm growing less particular by the second. Consider yourself warned."

Without further discussion, Emmet increased the pressure again, this time matching the flicks of his tongue against her nipple perfectly with the circles on her clit. Nicola's mind shut down, words and logic meant nothing in the face of such overwhelming physical sensations. The beats grew in strength as the tingles of pleasure rose. On and on he brought her closer to the edge, until her body couldn't stop shaking. Without thinking, she sucked in a gasp, needing the moan. He covered her mouth with his free hand, a silent reminder of how dangerous their interlude was.

Not that she cared, not while he was playing her body so perfectly. She'd never felt this intensity before, had never been able to give herself this amazing release she'd heard whispered about in the dark of night by those more experienced than herself. But now she understood, knew that it was possible, knew that Emmet had a level of experience she hadn't considered before. And while he might not know her, he knew enough to take control and give her this.

"I'm...I..." She whispered against his hand, her words muffled. It didn't matter, as he seemed to understand.

In the next moment, he increased the pressure one final time. It was too much for her to manage. Squeezing her eyes closed, Nicola bit down on the heel of his hand as waves of pleasure crashed through her body. He pressed her forward, on and on until the sensations crested then subsided.

"So beautiful." He pulled his hand away from her mouth and lifted his head to claim a kiss. "Unexpected."

She didn't know what he meant by that, and, quite frankly, she didn't care just then. Even as her body still shook from its release, she knew she needed to reciprocate. With a quick glance to the hallway to ensure they were still alone, she pushed him back against the bed, reversing their earlier positions.

"I'm not sure how best to do this."

"You don't need to."

She rolled her eyes and continued her earlier task of opening up the front of his trousers. "Don't be so noble. I believe you renounced such sentiments when you joined the guild."

Emmet sucked in a gasp as she wrapped her fingers around the bulge in his undergarments. The fabric had grown damp near the tip of his cock, allowing some of the flesh to be seen through the transparent cotton. He covered her hand with his own, stopping her and forcing her to look him in the eyes.

"Have you touched a man like this before?"

"I told you, I'm a virgin."

"That doesn't mean you haven't done this."

Oh. She hadn't considered that. "No. I've…never really had much interest in men before now."

"Have you seen a man's cock before?" There was something about the bluntness of his speech that sent another tremor of pleasure racing through her. Words failed her, forcing her to shake her head.

"Relax your grip and let me free myself." He waited for her to comply before adjusting his clothing and slowly releasing his shaft to the cold air.

Oh my. She swallowed hard, her mouth suddenly watering. "You are an impressive man, Mr. Dennison."

He cocked an eyebrow. "And what is your basis for comparison, Miss Tesla?"

"Woman's intuition." If any of the engineers back at the HBC were in possession of such a wonderfully proportioned member, Nicola would fall over dead from shock. Mind you, it would explain a thing or two about Anderson and the comment he'd made regarding Simon. "May I?"

He didn't move as she wrapped her fingers around the heated shaft, or even when she gave him a tentative stroke. It wasn't until she set an easy pace that he seemed to be unable to resist any longer. On the next down stroke, he bucked his hips to meet her hand. It forced the tip of his cock to grow ever redder in color and damper.

"You are a wicked woman." He threw his arm across his eyes and turned his face away from her. "God help the men of this world."

It was mesmerizing watching him. She couldn't help but categorize the reactions of his body as she touched him. The gentle hitch in his breathing was the most fascinating thing she'd witnessed when she twisted her hand just so. The flush that covered his throat and chest renewed her arousal, especially as she leaned in and placed a kiss on his bare skin. The idea of kissing his stomach, licking the tip of his cock, running her hands through the thick hair between his legs, shouldn't hold appeal, but it was growing increasingly difficult to ignore those thoughts.

The longer she spent in his company, the more she was growing attached to this infuriatingly stubborn man.

Nicola started when he reached down quickly and squeezed his hand over her own. He took over the pace, until the strokes flew over his cock at such a pace she was certain he'd come to harm. But when he bucked his hips one final time and come exploded from him, she could see that pain was the furthest thing away from what he was feeling.

His cock pulsed in her hand even once his essence had stopped coming. She stopped her strokes, but didn't release him, enjoying the sensations of his member softening in her grasp. They were still alone, still cocooned in their cell safe from Thomas, his plans, the archivists, and the Company. Right now, in this moment, they were Nicola and Emmet—a woman and a man, and nothing more.

Letting his arm fall from his face, he looked at her, heavy lidded. "As I said, unexpected."

She chuckled, because she had no idea how else to respond to such an unusual statement. "We need to clean you up."

"There is still some water in my glass. I can use some of the fabric from my shirt."

They spoke very little as they wiped away the evidence of their interlude. The silence made her once more aware of the dangerous nature of their situation. They could have been found out far too easily, giving Thomas an extra bit of information that he would use to torture them with. While she would never say anything to Emmet, she'd never forgive herself if anything bad happened to him as a result of her actions. Now with her clothing righted and her brain once more engaged, Nicola knew this couldn't happen again.

"I—"

Emmet silenced her with a kiss. "I know. It's too dangerous."

How was he able to do that? "I'm sorry."

"I don't regret it. Not for a single second." His thumbs brushed her cheeks one final time before he put some distance between them. "Just remember my promise."

"Pardon?"

"The moment we are free from here, I will be taking you to the closest bed and ravaging you."

There was nothing menacing in his words, though her body trembled at their intensity. "I look forward to it."

She just hoped she lived long enough to see that day come to pass.

* * *

Keegan stood a little way down the hall and listened. Nicola and the man had stopped talking. He'd been so tired after working for so long that for once he thought he'd be able to sleep. At first he wasn't certain what he saw as he stepped into view of their cell, but Nicola moaned and then he knew. He'd heard the whores out on the streets sometimes, knew they had a john with them, and he would turn tail and run. He didn't run this time though, his curiosity having gotten the better of him.

It was strange, seeing them grinding and kissing the way they were. He'd thought they didn't like each other from the way they spoke. Mind, he knew that people didn't always mean what they said to others. Maybe Mr. Edison would want to know this? If he could actually remember, he'd try to mention it to him tomorrow.

After a time of quiet, he shuffled back up the hallway, making some more noise than normal. When he got to his room, Nicola was sitting on the edge of her bed and the man, Dennison, was leaning against the opposite wall.

Neither of them spoke as he slipped into his room, though Nicola gave him a small wave. He still liked her. He'd have to try to get the automaton to wave the way she does. It would be nice to see when he finally got her up and running.

Yes, he'd do that in the morning.

Chapter 11

Nicola didn't think it was possible to lose track of time, but that's exactly what happened after a while. The guards would rouse them from their cell to work, leaving them in the workshop until she could barely keep her eyes open, before dragging them back. Emmet didn't seem as affected by the monotony of it all, didn't seem to mind the lack of sunlight or outside stimulation. Whether it was from all his time living in the Archives, or if he was simply better at hiding his emotions than she was, Nicola wasn't certain.

Thomas had appeared to abandon them as well. She wasn't certain which made her more nervous, having him watch or not knowing what he was doing. Keegan didn't seem to have any more insight than she did as to the whereabouts of their employer.

She looked over to where the boy was currently installing several cogs into an elaborate casing. Over the past few days she'd slowly made her way over to see exactly what it was he was doing. The work was flawless from what she could tell, even though the connections were so tiny she wasn't certain how he was able to do the work without the aid of a magnifying glass. It was strange to watch him work, the metal seemingly jumping into place with only the barest of touches.

Her own project was moving along far faster than she wanted. Now that the basic electronics of the control panel were set, it was simply a matter of connecting the leads and securing them to their posts. The extra Parkesine Thomas had provided to her made it simple to shape and install the indicator lights. From appearances, everything looked to be finished.

The guts of the machine would prove a more difficult challenge.

"Mr. Dennison?" She made sure to keep her voice as bland as possible. It was becoming increasingly difficult to keep her detached façade the more time she spent with him. "Might I have a word?"

"I'm locked to a post. I can't exactly walk away, Miss Tesla."

Oh, now he was simply being rude. Ignoring the barb, she hefted up the panel and carried it over to his chair. She couldn't imagine how frustrating it must be for him, tied up day after day with no opportunity to stretch mentally or physically. If she were in his position, she wasn't certain she'd be able to maintain the same level of restraint he'd show thus far.

"Now, now, Mr. Dennison, I'm simply in need of your opinion. There's no reason to take that tone of voice with me."

Setting the panel on his lap, the guts of the work exposed for his inspection, she crossed her arms and looked down at him. "I've managed the easy part. The connections have all fallen where they should. What I'm not certain of is how to proceed. As I mentioned to Thomas, I've never seen the inside of an extractor. I don't have the foggiest idea where to go from here."

A part of her prayed he didn't know anything beyond how to connect himself to the bloody box. The rest of her was far too pragmatic to believe that for even a moment. The members of the Archivist Guild prided themselves on gathering information. In the few short days she'd spent crawling around the inner workings of their central machine, she'd seen the lengths by which they impress upon their acolytes the importance of learning.

Emmet's jaw tightened as he stared at the wires. She knew he was making a decision, the same one she'd had to make herself. If he refused to share what he knew to help her make the extractor, she'd be forced to flail around until her failure was apparent. Thomas would have no use for them and they'd be disposed of. If he did help, then it was only a matter of time before she'd be killed and he'd be forced to take her memories.

Either way, an unpleasant outcome for both of them.

"I really can't stand leaving a project half finished." She cocked an eyebrow and gave him a look that was sure to annoy. "So do be a dear and tell me how to build this infernal thing. I'd rather not spend any more time in this blasted warehouse than necessary."

Emmet looked up, his frustration clear. "I'd be more than happy to assist, Miss Tesla. But I refuse to do so from this chair. If your former employer wants me to help, he will have to secure me to the bench so I can see what you are doing."

"All these demands." Thomas' voice filled the room. "I haven't had such bothersome employees since my lab was blown skyward."

There was a time when the mention of her crimes would have had Nicola squirming. There was a time when the sound of Thomas' voice sent fear knifing through her. No longer. With the exhaustion, hunger, and constant state of confusion regarding her feelings toward Emmet, she could no longer find the means to care.

"It's challenging to find good help when the working conditions are so poor," she shot back at him. She grabbed the board from Emmet's lap and strode back to her workbench. "Fine. If the two of you are going to continue to be difficult, I'll simply muddle through on my own. Neither of you are allowed to complain about the length of time it's taking me to finish."

"Now, my dear, I didn't say I wouldn't give in to Mr. Dennison's request." Thomas came up beside her, slapping her hand as she attempted to adjust a connection. "If you please."

He traced the paths of the wires, no doubt confirming that she was indeed doing her best work. If anyone would know what that was, it was Thomas. Although his ethics were questionable, his skill in engineering and knowledge of electronics was superb. She had no doubt that many of her inventions and ideas would have occurred to him in due time in the course of his tinkering. But Thomas was impatient and wanted his success to come as quickly as possible. No matter the cost.

"Very good. I'm pleased to see your skills haven't gone to waste over at the Company. It's a shame they haven't bothered to look for you since your untimely disappearance."

"You know them. A clockwerker is only as important as her last invention. They've had me doing cleanup duty for years now."

There'd been a time when Nicola had a romantic crush on Thomas. It was only after she'd learned of his relationship with Mary that those feelings evaporated into admiration. Even now, she couldn't deny that Thomas was a good-looking man, strong in purpose and spirit, but her amorous feelings were long gone. She didn't need a man at all, but if she were to have one he'd possess integrity, inner strength, and the ability to see her for who she truly was, and not simply a spirited woman with a spanner.

"I'd heard as much. The Company has sent you scurrying here and there, from airship to outpost and back."

What neither Thomas nor anyone else was aware of were the additional assignments Simon had ordered her to conduct while making said repairs. The only thing more dangerous than being a spy for the government was being a spy for one's employer.

"Jonas, release Mr. Dennison and bring him here."

Instead of the relief she wanted to feel, a knot formed in the pit of her stomach. "I don't actually require him to be here. I simply need him to answer some questions."

"I think it will do the two of you some good. It will give you an opportunity to work out this animosity you share." Jonas brought Emmet to the bench and secured one leg chain to the post nearest the table. "Get a shorter set as well to secure one hand to the workbench. It would be a shame if you decided to leave us prematurely."

"And miss out on all this excitement? I wouldn't dream of it." Emmet held still while his chains were reset. When Emmet was standing so close to Thomas, the differences between them were startling. Thomas was handsome, his dark hair was neatly brushed, and his blue eyes sparkled. He was charismatic and had the ability to draw a person's attention as he spoke. Even when he wasn't talking, she could tell his mind never stopped working, calculating his next move.

Emmet said little by comparison, but with a few careful movements, he could steal away the attention of those around him. He was physically larger than Thomas, stronger and by extension more dangerous. His hazel eyes were always moving, cataloguing his environment. She had no doubt he'd memorized everything he could of their surroundings. Trapped as he was, Emmet gave off the appearance of a man who would do whatever necessary to get free of their predicament.

Thomas stepped back, giving them room. "I expect you to live up to your end, Mr. Dennison. I would hate for anything to happen to Nicola here."

One moment she was standing; the next her legs buckled from beneath her as Thomas hit the backs of her knees, sending her crashing to the floor. The side of the workbench slammed against the side of her temple, sending the room spinning. It took several shakes of her head and many deep breaths before her world righted once again.

Emmet was shouting. She wasn't certain what he was saying, but he was most definitely shouting. He dropped as best he could into a squat and cupped her cheek.

"Miss Tesla?"

"Dammit! That hurt."

"You bastard." Emmet jerked against his chains. "That wasn't necessary."

"I simply wanted to assure you that I have no issues dealing with a woman. Now, we'll leave the two of you to work. I expect to see wonderful progress. Leaps and bounds from where you currently are."

The ringing in her head slowly subsided, though it was replaced with an ache. Emmet supported her weight as much as he was able, chained the way he was, and assisted her back to her feet.

"Are you well?" She could tell he was holding back, no doubt wanting to inspect the damage, but aware of the others watching them. "Do you need to rest?"

"I'm fine. Nothing more than a bump."

"Miss Tesla—"

"For the love of God. I think given everything we've been through you can call me by my name."

For the first time since she'd met him, something in Emmet's eyes softened. He dropped his hand and turned away from her. "You do like to push, don't you, Nikki."

Air refused to enter her lungs at the sound of her nickname on his lips. Even whispered, it was the most beautiful thing she'd ever heard.

"Of course I do. I'd die of boredom otherwise." She faced the workbench. "I take it you know exactly how to put one of these together?"

"I have no practical experience. As I said, the extractors are the same ones that we've used for years. However, I have seen the inside of one and I've had access to blueprints outlining the construct of the machine. It should be enough for you to successfully complete your task."

"I often thought having an eidetic memory would be a blessing."

"I can recall every single terrible thing that's ever happened to me. I can tell you in exacting detail what a torn open human body looks like. I can recall the smells as well, the stench that hung in the air when Piper extracted the memories of a dead prostitute. The exact way my father looked at me the last time we spoke."

His hand brushed hers as they reached for the same spanner. Nicola stopped, allowed the contact, needing the reassurance that it brought.

"I can describe," he whispered so softly, she could barely hear, "the flush of your skin when you're aroused. The soft way you sigh before you orgasm."

He ran his pinkie the length of hers, sending a shiver through her body.

"There are some benefits."

"I see." She pulled away as she felt the eyes of their guard land on her back. "We best get to work then."

* * *

Emmet never did have a head for engineering, or an affinity for automatons. His skills were always based in the practical, in people and his ability to manipulate them to do what he wanted. It was something he'd learned early on by his father's side, and he was far better at it than any of his brothers. Thankfully, his ability to recall the schematics he'd seen was enough for Nicola.

With little direction on his part, she'd easily picked up the thread of what he described and continued on from that point. The extractor contained gears, tubes, and energy sources, combined in such a way as to latch onto the memories of the dead. If Nicola understood the metaphysical aspects that manifested somewhere along the way, she didn't say. Instead, she would nod and proceed to insert the bits and bobs into place.

If it was possible for him to become even more disturbed by the power of the extractor, this would have caused him additional nightmares. How was it possible for something so mechanical, so pragmatic, to have the ability to pull the essence of a human being from their shell? But while the extractor was a feat of engineering, it was nothing without the human component, the battery that kick-started the process.

It was his mind that drew out the other. He was a magnet of sorts, with the unimaginable power to beckon to a soul. If that's what they were actually dealing with. No, that wasn't exactly right. He was more of a final component that closed the circuit and made the madness possible.

"I'm not certain I'll be able to attach the filament to the board properly. My fingers are unfortunately large." Nicola's voice was absorbed as she spoke into the box. "I might have to see if I can fashion some pliers to assist me. Not that Thomas will let me keep them for long."

"I'm sure you'll find a way to manage."

She looked up at him, frowning. "What's the matter with you? You've been a bear for ages now."

"Nothing." Everything. Things she couldn't understand. "I'm tired."

"Terrible liar. You need to work on that." She returned to her work without further prodding.

If she was correct and she was the intended recipient of the extractor, Emmet wasn't certain he'd be able to complete the task. He'd been with Piper when she'd had the prostitute's memories in her head for an extended period of time. She'd been convinced that the woman was actually still alive in her mind, still able to carry on a conversation, argue for her right to live. If Nicola was killed and her thoughts ended up in his mind, he wasn't sure he'd survive. To have grown to know someone that intimately, only to have the experience wiped away...

No, they needed to find a way out of this nightmare.

So he did the one thing he could, and hoped it was the right thing.

Speaking of which.

He checked to make sure Jonas wasn't within earshot before he slipped a stiff piece of wire from the spool that held it. "Can you cut this? Just a short piece."

She frowned, but did as he asked. "Why?"

Carefully, he doubled the wire over and slid it beneath the cuff around his wrist. "We need to start finding a way out of here. You're far too proficient in the creation of your inventions and we are running out of options."

"Of course I am. Only the best for the HBC." She stepped away to the opposite side to solder something, before returning with a rusted and bent file. "This might also be useful."

"Tuck it someplace here on the bench. I'll find a way to get it back to our cell."

And so they went, back and forth gathering bits and pieces over the next few days, like magpies in the hopes of finding things that would aid their escape. It was a slow and frustrating process, with the constant checks from their guards, Thomas' inspections, and Keegan's eerie appearances.

While Nicola had developed a soft spot for the boy, Emmet was still reserving judgment. He didn't trust that faraway stare, or the way he'd close his eyes and the metal in his hands would seemingly move on its own. His friend Samuel had that ability, so did Jack from what he'd gathered from the others. The affinity to make the metal move, to bring life to the lifeless, was nearly as disturbing as the archiving of souls.

"Damnation!" Nicola stepped quickly away from the bench, clutching one hand in the other.

"What happened?"

"The space was too tight to work. The pliers I made broke and I cut myself."

"We need a bandage!" But none of the guards made a move to help.

Keegan drifted to their sides, a small handkerchief held out. "Will this help?"

"Thank you, sweetie." Nicola took the cloth and pressed it to the wound. "I fear I might be done work for the time being. I can't feel my fingers for the throbbing."

Keegan stepped closer and took something from his pocket. "This might help."

The small white disk looked to be some sort of sweet. The edges had crumbled from being rubbed, giving it a waxy appearance. Keegan held it in such a way that he didn't want the guards to see, nor Emmet to be able to reach it. Odd indeed.

Nicola looked at it briefly, before leaning in to smell it. "What's this now?"

"A secret," his voice lowered to a harsh whisper. "Mr. Edison pays me with money, but also gives me sweets. I like the sweets. They make me feel so much better. I think they'll make you feel better too, Nicola. But please don't tell Mr. Edison that I gave you one. I don't want him to think I don't want them anymore. Because I do. All the time."

He held it up in front of her lips, giving her little choice but to accept the treat. Emmet watched as a range of emotions flitted across her face—uncertainty, surprise, and finally pleasure.

"Those are wonderful. I can see why you enjoy them as you do."

The boy's smile took up a surprisingly large part of his face. "I do. I can share some with you if you like?"

"We'll see. I don't want to take all your treats. You work so hard for them."

"I get bags of them when I do good. Maybe you will get some when you do good and finish your memory box. Then we can share."

Nicola shared a look with Emmet, one that belied her concern. "We'll see."

"I'm almost done with the heart. Mr. Edison will be pleased to hear that. I might even get an extra bag of sweets."

There was something wrong about all this. While offering treats to a child to buy his attention and affections was nothing new to Emmet, the fervor with which Keegan clutched these wasn't right. Once the boy shuffled back to whichever crevasse he'd been working in, Emmet pulled Nicola close.

"Did you swallow it?"

"Of course." She smiled as she tied the cloth around her cut hand. "They really were some of the most delicious treats I've ever had. Not that I get many back at the Company. Occasionally, we'll have something special made for us by some of the chefs, but most of the men aren't as particular regarding those things as I am. I really do love my sweets. Perhaps once we are out of here you can take me someplace for something special. That would be wonderful."

In a matter of moments, Nicola's eyes had glazed over and she'd stopped favoring her hand. It was as though she didn't have a care in the world.

"Opium. Or laudanum." Leaning in he smelled her breath, trying to see if he could catch a hint of the drug. "I think the sweets are most likely laced with opium."

"I wouldn't know. I've never had it before." She giggled and picked up a spool of wire. "I should get back to work. I'm good at working. Everyone always says so."

"Guards, we need to go back to our cell. Miss Tesla has injured her hand and needs rest."

Thankfully, she offered little resistance as they were led back to the cell, though she'd begun to sing a song in a language he wasn't familiar with. In between verses, she'd poke at the wound on her hand and say "Ouch." The added distraction of her erratic behavior made it easy for him to allow another bit of wire to fall to the floor and cover it with his foot before Jonas removed the cuffs from his wrist. The guard sneered at Emmet, slamming a shoulder against his before securing them.

Emmet held himself back until he was certain they'd been left alone. With a quick check down the hall, he turned and guided Nicola to the bed.

"Sit."

"There's no reason for you to boss me around. I have an employer and I happen to like Simon quite a bit. I've heard he's not interested in ladies though, which is a shame. That would explain Anderson's fascination though."

"Sit down."

"Fine." She plopped herself on the bed with a huff. "I'm growing tired of this place. We need to move soon. I want to go back to the inn. They have a lovely bed."

"I intend to do that once I know you are in a condition to be moved. Being drugged isn't the best of times."

"Pfff." She laid her injured hand in his. "I'm quite well. Never been better, in fact."

"That boy is addicted to opium. I'm fairly certain it was Edison who did the deed."

Emmet had heard of an archivist who'd taken to the poppy as a means to gain solace from the ever-growing hole in his mind. The man had reportedly jumped from one of the balconies while in a drug-induced haze. It was shortly after his arrival at the Archives, though at the time he'd believed it was simply a story that the Guild Masters told as a way of keeping the acolytes in line. He hadn't fully believed the tale until years later, when he'd witnessed another such suicide. The Administrators quickly hushed up the incident, but Emmet hadn't forgotten.

If Keegan was being drugged, then his life was already in great peril. If Edison decided to dispose of the boy once his task was complete, it would be difficult for a child with little means to earn enough money to support a drug addiction. He would need help or else be dead within the month.

Nicola had only ingested a single sweet, giving her temporary release from her pain, but hopefully not enough of a dose to acquire an addiction. She would need to stay away from the boy for the time being.

Using far more force than he normally would, Emmet held her hand down to examine the wound she'd previously hidden from him. "Let me see."

"So you're a physician now, too?"

"I know a thing or two about treating wounds."

She snorted. "Basic training for an archivist?"

"It is, actually." Any number of things could happen out in the field. "I managed to bring another wire back unseen. I'll attempt to fashion a lock pick once the others have settled down."

"Oh good. That means we can go elsewhere and get more sweets. Or kisses." She licked her lips and smiled up at him. "I do enjoy your kisses."

"Please shut up and sit still. You cut your finger quite deep and we need to make sure you heal properly."

There was little he could do given the distinct lack of supplies. A needle and thread would be necessary to close the gash and prevent infection. With her drugged, it would at the very least cut the pain. "I doubt they'll let me take care of this. I'll have to involve Edison."

"Don't." Her voice grew quiet, trembling on that single word. "Please don't."

"It needs to be stitched up, and I doubt he'll give me a sharp object to do the deed."

"Let it be then. I'll live."

"I can't. We need to fix this before things begin to fester. The last thing you need is to lose a hand."

Nicola grabbed his wrist and squeezed hard. "He'll kill me if I go with him."

"He won't. He still needs you to finish building the extractor."

She shook her head hard, her short hair flying around her face. "You don't understand. He hates me for destroying his lab, for ruining his work and running away. He wants to take everything that he lost from my head and put it in an automaton. I'll be trapped there forever."

Ignoring her wound, Emmet pulled her into his arms and held her tight. "I won't let that happen. I won't let him do anything to you, do you understand?" Dammit, he'd never had such strong feelings for a woman before. The simple thought of someone doing her harm fired a rage deep inside his chest. God help the person who laid a finger on her.

"You won't be able to stop him."

"Yes, I bloody well will." Without thinking, he pressed a kiss to her cheek, before trailing more down to her lips. She was soft and pliable, and if circumstances were different, he'd be more than willing to take advantage. "I can't do anything if your hand gets infected."

Sniffing and looking up at him with childlike eyes, she sighed. "Fine."

Emmet gave her one final hug before getting to his feet. Pausing only long enough to retrieve the wire and slip it into a hiding spot in the corner of the cell, he moved to the door.

"Edison!" The man was going to pay for every ill he'd caused to both Nicola and Keegan. "Edison, get in here!"

Time ticked on, but eventually the man sauntered down the hallway. "While I appreciate the stretch, I am a busy man, Mr. Dennison."

"She's hurt and needs stitches."

Edison didn't look beyond Emmet to see if what he said were true, and instead held his gaze. "Is that so?"

"She's no good to you if she loses her hand to infection." Even looking at the man made it difficult for Emmet to breathe. Rage squeezed at him, threatening to burst forth. "And despite my knowledge, I am no clockwerker."

"No," Edison said, lifting his chin, "you're not. Not much of an archivist from what I can gather, either."

"I'm more than enough for what you need, and you'll be hard pressed to find another."

If Edison had any concerns about Emmet, he didn't show them. "I'll send Jonas to get her. I'll make sure her hand works again. You see to it that this extractor functions. Deal?"

He stuck his hand through the bars, leaving Emmet to stare at it. It would be so tempting to simply grab him and smash his face against the bars of the cell. But while it would leave him feeling most satisfied, it would do little to aid them in their predicament. Emmet gripped Edison's hand firmly, not fully certain of what he was promising.

"Deal." One with the Devil, if Emmet believed such a creature existed.

* * *

Keegan couldn't get the tune out of his head. It was a soft little ditty he'd always seem to hum on occasion. *Da, de da, da de de dum.* Over and over the tune circled, until it began to spill from his lips.

Da, de da, da de de dum.

He'd taken to closing his eyes while he worked now. It was a strange thing, the darkness. Once it had frightened him, threatened to consume him whole, but now it had grown to be a comfort. It was in the darkness that he could hear the metal, could enjoy the colors that clung to people as they passed by. With his eyes closed, it was easier for him to see them and the patterns they created.

Nicola's was green; Mr. Dennison's was blue. Mr. Edison's would shift from red to yellow and back again. Keegan was starting to think that the colors were related not to their moods, but to something deeper that lived inside them.

The dark also made it easier to have the metal dance.

Da, de da, da de de dum.

The heart was nearly completed. A few more nudges of springs here and there and everything would come together. He'd taken to moving the pieces in time with the music, infusing some of the beauty from the notes into the casing. Oh, she was going to be beautiful! She'd dance for them all, and he'd be there to point and say, "There's my wonderful girl."

The final cog clicked into place and the ticking began. Opening his eyes, he ignored the way the light of the warehouse made his head ache and admired the elegance of his work. Before, he'd never have thought of the word *elegance*, let alone relate it to something he'd created. But Mr. Edison had said Nicola's work was elegant, and his connections were just as pretty, maybe better. She had to use her fingers and her teeth to get the components to do what they wanted. His way was elegant.

It was.

And perfect.

The casing of the heart was solid in his hands. He lifted it so it was at eye level, letting him peer into the small opening he'd left. The sound was a whisper to him, her yet to be discovered voice that encouraged him on.

Da, de da, da de de dum.

"You're beautiful." And he kissed the metal. "Time to put you in your new home."

While the others were moving around, sleeping, eating, he'd been busy creating. The metal body was nearly completed. The legs had been the second thing he'd finished to his satisfaction. It hadn't taken long to secure the metal feet to the legs, the legs to the hips. The torso came together quickly once he'd remembered to add the breasts. With the heart finished and ready to be placed into the chest cavity, the rest of his work would flow until finished.

"Well, well. What do we have here?"

Keegan knew he should turn around and look Mr. Edison in the eye, but he couldn't, not until he was finished. The metal cage he'd built for the heart was reinforced to ensure nothing would jar the delicate works. He slid the heart down the rails he installed to keep it steady and grabbed the soldering iron without looking.

"Keegan?"

Three spot welds were all that was needed to secure the heart in place. Backing away presented him with the completed project. Perfect.

The hand on his shoulder jolted him from his admiration. "Sir?"

Mr. Edison was frowning. Maybe he was mad that Keegan hadn't talked to him right away. Maybe he didn't like what he saw.

"It had to be exactly right for it to work." He licked his lips, but there was little moisture left in his mouth. "I wanted her te be elegant."

"She's that indeed."

Mr. Edison didn't move in to inspect Keegan's work the way

he normally would. Maybe he didn't really like what he'd done and was simply being polite. He knew adults would do that sometimes, so as to not hurt someone's feelings.

"I can make her better if you don't like her, sir."

"No, no, she's exactly what I'd hoped for." And he still didn't move in.

"Are ye sure? Cause I'll make her right—"

"You did fine, Keegan."

"Then why don't you want to look at her? You always look over my stuff to make sure I did it right. Are you worried that I did something wrong? I promise you, sir, I was careful. Made all them connections tight."

Mr. Edison squeezed his shoulder, pulling Keegan with him away from the automaton. Not that he wanted to go, but he'd learned early on not to go against what his employer wanted.

"I will be very proud to call her my own. She's very special to me. You've given her something I didn't think possible."

"What's that?"

"Beauty. You made her beautiful. She'd appreciate that very much."

It was strange, but Keegan knew he wasn't speaking about the automaton. "Who would?"

"Never you mind now." He reached into his jacket pocket and pulled out a flask. "Drink this. You sound parched."

"Don't I get my sweets?" The water was cool in his mouth and tasted wonderful.

"I think you need to eat something other than those. Too many will make you sick, and I can't have my best employee growing ill."

He didn't quite believe that, but there was no way for him to argue. "Yes, sir."

"Nicola has nearly completed the extractor. I believe that means we are almost ready to move on to the next stage of our project."

"What's that, Mr. Edison?"

"You'll see. It will be as beautiful as your automaton."

That was good. Keegan wanted the next stage to come. He knew it would be wonderful.

Chapter 12

Nicola's head felt stuffed with cotton. Thoughts would pass through her brain quickly, but her mouth couldn't move fast enough to express them, and they wouldn't linger long enough for her to make a second attempt. It was frustrating and almost as terrifying as the idea of Thomas stitching up the gash in her hand.

The chair that the guard had placed her in was far from comfortable. She squirmed to find a position that didn't grate on her nerves, or send additional strange sensations sliding through her. To make matters worse, she'd lost track of time, which only added to her aggravation. Thomas better hurry up and arrive to do this deed shortly, else she'd find a way to stitch herself up.

At some point while she waited her eyes slipped closed and a fitful sleep overtook her. It was only at the sound of the door creaking open that she sat bolt upright, her heart racing. Thomas stood looking at her, his hands laced behind his back. His smile appeared to be almost sentimental, and the sparkle in his eyes brought back memories of a pleasant time.

"I slipped." She smiled and held up her hand. "I'd be more than happy to stitch myself up, if you give me the tools."

"You forget I've seen your attempts at embroidery. For the sake of your hand and the completion of my project, I shall play physician."

They didn't speak while he gathered the tools necessary to mend her and sat down on the stool beside her. It was strange: The fear she'd experienced to this point dissipated as he took her hand in his and pressed his thumb near the wound.

"I'm afraid there is nothing to be done except to stitch this up." The needle bit into her skin, sending a burning pain through her hand and up her arm. "Do try to sit still."

"I'm trying." Thankfully, the numbness she felt made it easier for her to deal with the pain. "What is in the sweets you're giving the boy?"

Thomas cast her a quick look, but didn't stop his stitching. "Why?"

"He gave me one when I first cut myself. I've been feeling odd ever since."

"Opium. I wouldn't recommend eating another."

She'd thought as much now that the worst of the narcotic had worn off. "Why would you need to drug a child? Surely he wouldn't cause you that much trouble."

"It's necessary."

"It's barbaric, Thomas. What is he going to do once you are done with him?"

"I imagine he'll find his way back to his gang of hooligans, and either they'll deal with him or he'll die." He pulled the thread too tight, sending another burst of pain through her arm. "It's lovely to have this opportunity to chat once again. I've missed our intellectual sparring matches."

She would never admit as much, but there was a time when she enjoyed speaking with him, debating the possibilities of electricity and motors, the potential for inventions and automations. While she had some of that with the other clockwerkers of the Company, they didn't push her the way Thomas had.

"If you'd treated me with a measure of respect we might still be debating. I would have been content to work with you for years."

He hummed low before tying a knot in the thread. Leaning over, he used his teeth to break the thread. His breath washed over her wound, her wrist. She wanted to pull away, put some distance between them, but she wouldn't allow herself to show even that tiny bit of weakness.

"There we go. Right as rain."

She pulled her hand back and cradled it to her chest. "Thank you."

"I expect you'll be able to work again by morning. How is your progress with the extractor now that your archivist is involved? Is he slowing you down, or does the dullard actually have information you can use?"

The memory of Emmet stretched out beside her, his mouth on her breast and his hand teasing her body came to mind. No, *dullard* was the last word she'd use to describe him. "He's been helpful. He'd seen schematics of an extractor and is able to guide me through some of the more complex parts. What he lacks in understanding he makes up for in precise descriptions."

Thomas got to his feet, but didn't give her any space. His body was leaner than she remembered it being in France. "How much longer will you be?"

There was no sense in lying to him. She knew he would have done his own calculations and projections regarding a time frame. If she were to be longer, she'd have to prove to him beyond a shadow of a doubt the reasons why.

"Two days. Three at the most."

"Excellent. Keegan has nearly completed his end of the project. Then we should be ready for a trial by the end of the week."

"No!" She couldn't imagine what they would do to test the extractor. Emmet would need to hook himself up to the machine, and performing an actual extraction would leave the memories of the victim in his mind. To do two extractions at once might be enough to push him into madness.

"You don't expect me to risk everything I've worked this hard to accomplish on the possibility that the two of you are working to sabotage things?" His laughter lacked the warmth she'd once expected from him. "I think not."

She couldn't put Emmet at risk in this manner. Pushing herself up from the chair, she grabbed him by the wrist and prayed he'd listen. "Do you understand how the extractor works? Dennison's mind absorbs the memories of the dead and keeps them there. If you put him through a test, it will leave his mind infected with those thoughts, contaminate him, and potentially ruin him for your grand scheme."

Thomas shook her free. "You lost the right to inform my decisions when you blew up my laboratory."

"Listen to me—"

"Enough!"

Despite the force of his shout, she didn't back down. "What happened to you? The man I knew might have been an arrogant ass who took what he wanted for his own gain, but he wasn't cruel. You used to care about others."

The muscle in his jaw jumped as he sucked in a breath. "That man is long gone."

"Why?"

"When your entire world has been stripped away, when the

joy it held is snuffed out by the careless actions of a single individual, then caring for others means little."

Her words couldn't come. There was no retort she could make to defend her actions to him. She had been selfish when she'd destroyed the lab, knowing full well it wasn't only her inventions and ideas that would be lost in the fire. She'd wronged Thomas and couldn't expect to be granted his forgiveness.

Perhaps the old eye for an eye expression was accurate in this instance. Her life for the destruction of his life's work.

She said nothing as he led her back out into the hallway and past her cell, where Dennison still resided. She couldn't look at him, even when he moved to the door and called her name. Yes, it might be the opium still muddling her brain, making her compliant with her captor, but she knew it was more than that. Guilt was a hard burden to bear, especially after years of growth.

"I believe your hand will be fine for the work you need to do now." Thomas shoved her toward the bench and strode away.

The room was quiet except for the light tapping off in the far corner. Jonas stood by the main doorway, speaking with one of the other men. She should be looking for a way out, a weapon, something she could sneak back to the cell once she was eventually returned. But the light tapping had caught her attention and refused to give way.

Moving as though she walked through a dream, Nicola followed the sound. It wasn't until she saw Keegan that she realized she'd ventured into his territory. Odd, she hadn't come over here in the days they'd been working. Unlike Emmet, she hadn't been bound and was given mostly free rein of the room. Thomas had said the boy's part of the project was nearing completion, and yet she hadn't seen this female robot he was constructing.

Rounding the corner of the makeshift privacy screen, Nicola

stopped dead in her tracks at the sight before her. This wasn't a simple automaton. The body was perfectly proportioned—arms and legs stretched out where they should be, torso and chest expanding and contracting at exactly the right angles. The throat was long and elegant, and would have been the envy of any lady of the ton had any of them aspired to metallic perfection.

But it was the sheer size of the automaton that had struck her dumb. The creature was easily twice as tall as Emmet, if not taller, and at least as broad. It would be a force to be reckoned with, one that would prove difficult to stop if need be.

Keegan stood on a stool in front of his creation, thick goggles covering his eyes and a soldering iron in his hand as he secured the head in place. She could tell he'd taken time to place eye sockets with lids, lips that were swollen and almost natural looking, even given the downturned angle at which it currently rested.

She waited until Keegan noticed her presence before giving him a small wave. "Hullo."

There was something charming about the way he grinned at her, the large goggles filling a generous portion of his face. "Isn't she pretty?"

Beautiful and terrifying. "Yes, she is. You've been working hard to get her done this quickly."

Keegan shrugged. "I've gots nothing else te do. Working for Mr. Edison is a sight better than running with the Underlings."

"Who are they?"

"You don't know who the Underlings are?"

"I'm not from around here." She inched her way closer to the automaton, wanting to inspect the work without appearing to do so. "Though I have to say New London is lovely this time of year. You wouldn't believe how cold the Bay gets. Canadian winters can be a challenge."

"Oh. I forgot." He hopped down from the stool and walked around to the front of the automaton, fixing the hands so they rest neatly in its lap. "The Underlings are just a bunch of street rats. We beg and steal what we need to survive. Glyn would have my head if he knew what I had access to here in the warehouse and didn't bring any of it back."

"Yes, Thomas is quite generous." As she moved her head and body protested, growing weak. "Do you mind if I sit down for a moment? It's been a bit of a long day."

With surprising grace, he grabbed his stool and brought it to her. "You've been workin' just as hard as me. I'm sure if you ask Mr. Edison he'd give you a rest."

"I'm afraid Mr. Edison isn't too pleased with me at the moment."

"Oh. Whatcha' do?"

"I took something of his."

Rather than be offended by this revelation, Keegan seemed pleased. "You could be an Underling too."

"Maybe I could."

Keegan looked between her and his creation. He found a bucket, flipped it upside down, and used it as a seat. They looked at the automaton in silence, both lost in their thoughts.

"He's going to kill me." Keegan's soft voice shocked her into looking at him. "I'm not sure when I figured that out."

"Why do you stay here then? You're not locked into your room. You could slip out when no one was looking and get to safety." She turned to lean close. "You could go for help, bring the authorities here to rescue Emmet and myself."

"I can't." He sounded sad. "I can't leave her alone. Not when we're so close to being done."

She'd worked with others in the past who saw their creations as living beings. Metal cogs and gears infused with a living soul that only they could see. She hadn't expected to see such manic devotion in a person so young.

"She'll be fine if you leave. Thomas would never do anything to hurt her."

"He wouldn't be able to bring her to life the way I will. He wouldn't know how to make her sing and dance. *Da, de da, da de de dum.*" He got to his feet and began to sway to the melody of his odd little song.

Frustration cut through the dying haze of the opium, leaving her increasingly frustrated. "What if I promised to take care of her? I would make sure no one touched her until you got back with help."

"Da, de da, da de de dum."

"Keegan?"

Whatever spell he'd fallen under swept him away. Without another word to her, he slipped his goggles back over his eyes, moved the bucket to the side of his metal beloved, and resumed his work.

This was far worse than she'd thought. Whatever the opium had done to his brain, Keegan was no longer able to reason through the situation. She needed to get them all out of here as quickly as possible if they were to survive. If that meant she had to finish the extractor and use it to her advantage, then that's exactly what she would do.

"I'll be off then. I have work of my own to complete."

He kept humming, but offered her a quick wave in response.

No, Nicola couldn't afford to delay matters much longer, not if she wanted any hope of saving the boy. Her estimation of three days would need to be accurate. Which left her little time to devise a plan.

* * *

The song kept going round and round inside his brain. *Da, de da, da de de dum.* The tune was slowly changing over time, growing louder on each pass. At some point there was a soft harmony that added to its depth, sending a sense of peace through him.

He couldn't walk away from this. He knew Nicola didn't understand, but then again, how could she? She had no connection to the metal, to the beauty of the creature beside him. It would take time, but he would make sure they all knew soon enough.

"Now then," he ran his hand along the smooth metal of her shoulder, "not much longer. I promised you we'd be done soon and I don't break my word." He did, but never to her.

The harmony grew louder as he finished the final seam on the back of her neck. His fingers were raw from the heat, the skin red and angry, peeling in places it normally wouldn't. They should be painful, but he no longer seemed aware of pain, or hope, or fear, anything other than admiration and love.

He really did love her. And he knew she loved him in return, even if she wasn't able to tell him yet.

"Soon." He placed a kiss to her temple, not caring how the metal burned his skin. "I promise. Then we'll show the world how well you can dance."

Chapter 13

For the next two days, Emmet was forced to watch as Nicola worked like a woman possessed. With little input from him, she completed the lion's share of the work, bringing the extractor to its final stage. With each connection she formed, they inched closer to the inevitable conclusion, one that Emmet wanted to prevent with his entire being.

At night when they were returned to their cell, Nicola kept her distance. The physical separation was necessary, even if it wasn't wanted. The guards had begun to pass by more frequently, making it difficult for them to engage in any further intimacies. Instead of letting his frustrations grow, he channeled them into the creation of a key.

The wire he'd managed to smuggle back to the cell was thin and flexible. While alone it wasn't enough to aid their escape, when combined with the file he'd slipped into his boot, it was the beginnings of a tool that would spring the lock on the cell.

Emmet was squatting on the floor, his back pressed to the wall. He'd spent the better part of their rest time winding the wire around the file, securing it in such a fashion that it would not fall when forced into the lock.

"I need more of the bloody stuff."

Nicola was laying flat on the small cot, her eyes closed, but still awake. Her breathing was slow and steady, her body not quite relaxed against the small bed. "I'll be done with the extractor today."

Those were the words he didn't want to hear, even if he knew their truth. "Can you draw things out further?"

"Not without making Thomas suspicious."

Setting the key down, he crawled over to the bed. "Don't give up. We don't know what his plan is. He could be using this for anything."

"You're sweet, but we are well aware of his intentions. He's as much as said he will kill me. You'll perform the extraction, and my residual memories will drive you mad if you don't find help. If he simply doesn't kill you as well."

She'd been like this since her return from having her finger repaired. In the short time he'd known her this defeatist attitude was new. It was unbecoming in a woman with as much spirit as Nicola had.

Tipping her chin up, Emmet stole a kiss. Her lips had gone dry, but he moistened them with his tongue. She didn't respond, but he pushed, taking what they both needed—intimacy and kindness.

"Emmet," but the rest of what she intended was swallowed up as he deepened the kiss.

He needed her. The temptation to strip her down and take her as his own, consequences be damned, was strong. But she was exhausted and weak from lack of proper food and water. They were sore, tired, and in no condition to be engaging in the more pleasant aspects of courtship.

Courtship? He wasn't pursuing any sort of relationship with her, with anyone for that matter. He'd willingly given himself to the Archives, taken a vow to put the guild before himself. While the occasional round of sex tended to be overlooked, engaging in anything more substantial was forbidden.

It didn't matter that Piper and Samuel had found their way free and now lived a happy life together. His friends had always existed on the fringes of the order. They pushed the limits and beyond, not caring about the consequences. They came from nothing and had nothing to lose.

He risked his possible future as an Administrator. The only thing he had left.

He slowed the kiss, but didn't pull away fully. She reached up and began to scratch at the beard that now covered his face. It was pleasant, and a reminder of how far they'd fallen from their normal lives.

"I'd kill for a shave."

Her chuckle was soft, the first spark of life he'd seen from her in ages. "I like it."

"You'd be one of the few women to say so. If I were to step out in society looking this way, I'd leave a trail of swooning women in my wake. And not in a positive manner."

"Do you miss it? Society?"

Did he? It was an odd thing to think of. "Not in the way you might think. I'm the youngest son of a duke. I didn't enter society or attend balls except for family events. It grew tedious after a time, needing to attend the schools and functions as my father ordered. But sometimes I miss the freedom of travel, of going where and when I wanted. I'd follow my older brothers around like a dog would his master."

"That's all? You don't miss the balls, shooting parties, or whatever it is that young rich men participate in?"

"I miss the dirigible races." Oh, he'd had fun that summer. "My older brother Frederick snuck me onboard. I was too young to be there, according to my father, but I'd begged Fred and he worked his magic. I helped with the navigation. Good memory for maps and all that."

"Sounds exciting."

His father had been furious with them both when they'd returned. It wasn't until they showed off their trophy that his father allowed them to both continue. The summer before Fred joined the King's Army had been wonderful for all of them. For a time, Emmet had believed he'd be able to continue on in that fashion, that he'd be allowed to find his own way with the support of the duke.

How wrong he'd been.

"I'm nearly done with my key. If I can procure more wire, it should be enough to finish. One more night is all I need."

Nicola traced a pattern down the side of his neck, rising goosebumps in her wake. "I'll be finished with the extractor today."

"Put it off. Delay just one more day. If I can get the key made, we can slip out tonight while the guards shift. Jonas usually drifts off to sleep in the far room, giving us a window for escape. We can even take Keegan if you think he'll come."

Her fingers curled around his neck, massaging the tight muscles beneath. "You've been there with me. You have the bloody schematics in your head. It's obvious to any who looks that the machine is complete."

"Nikki—"

"Oh, now you use my name. When you're trying to get something from me. Typical male."

"Don't do this."

She turned to face him, bracing her weight on her elbow. "I'm doing nothing. I know it's a fault of character, this unfailing work ethic, but I can't change who I am. Once I saw the pattern, understood how the connections worked, it was only a matter of time. Today I'll finish the extractor, and tonight Thomas will kill me."

"Not if I kill him first." He no longer questioned this protective surge she elicited in him. He simply knew that if Thomas attempted to take her life, he'd do everything in his power to save her. Even if it meant sacrificing himself.

"You can't kill him. You'd never get close enough. After I'm dead I'll need you to find a way to prevent the extraction from happening. There are too many things rattling around in this head of mine that would be dangerous in the wrong hands. Or, barring that, if you have no choice but to do what he asks and I'm stuffed into Keegan's automaton, I need you to destroy it before you wipe me from your memories."

It was a difficult promise to make, and it would be an even harder one to keep. But if the consequences were as great as she suggested, he knew he had no choice. "I will do all I can to ensure nothing happens to you."

"Emmet—"

"If I fail, if he wins and I have no choice but to extract your memories, I will make sure the automaton is destroyed. I won't let your knowledge fall into the wrong hands."

If they weren't discussing her imminent demise, the smile on her face would have been sweet. "Thank you."

The stomping of heels on the stone floor pulled his attention. "Jonas is on his way with food and water."

"We must break our fast with enthusiasm. Today is the final day of our captivity."

The meal was meager at best as they ate in silence. Nicola's body had relaxed, her shoulders slumped forward and her head hanging lower than normal. He hadn't realized how dirty they'd grown in their captivity. Her once white shirt was covered in grease and oil streaks. Her hair rested limp against her face and her corset had long been removed, leaving her body open to him. Her appearance should strike him as horrendous, but all he wanted to do was pull her back into his grasp and rain kisses across her face and neck.

Lord, what has gotten into me?

When the time came for them to begin their work, Emmet stood close to her, wanting to offer silent support and encouragement. They would find a way to get through this, alive. He'd be damned if there was any other outcome.

Upon entering the workroom, he was stunned to see a giant metal woman standing by the bench. She easily towered over him, over all of them, her body appearing as anatomically accurate as he could imagine. Even down to her metal breasts.

"He finished her." Nicola's voice held a note of awe. "She really is quite beautiful. The Company would love to have someone as talented as Keegan on the payroll."

Where she saw beauty, Emmet saw the potential for disaster. This wasn't a simple vessel to house the memories of the dead. This was a creature that could be used for all the wrong reasons, that could be used for the complete destruction of New London.

"Our boy is a clever one."

Emmet hadn't noticed Thomas sitting in the chair. He appeared to be simply admiring Keegan's handiwork, though he too had the same look of awe that Nicola wore. Of course the damned clockwerkers would only see the beauty in the machine and nothing else.

"She's big." Ignoring Jonas, Emmet stepped closer to the automaton. The seams were nearly invisible along the torso, Keegan having taken the time to polish the brass and copper to a shine. And while the creature had no hair, he'd given her eyes, a mouth, and a nose, clearly feminine in appearance.

Reaching out to touch, Emmet jumped back when the creature's eyes flew open.

"And apparently she's been activated." Her eyes glowed, casting shadows across the floor that stretched to fill the void before them.

"Not yet. Not completely at any rate. The boy assured me that it's simply a response to our body heat. An automated on switch if you will. He really is an intelligent little waif. It's a shame I won't be able to take him with me back to America."

The eyes of the metal woman were staring blankly at the floor, but Emmet couldn't shake the feeling that she was somehow aware of them, of what was being said. Keegan had molded Parkesine into small orbs, each one giving the metal creature the appearance of life. There appeared to be no obvious light source, which was odd in itself. The brightness flared briefly as Thomas walked into her field of vision, before returning to its normal state. "You plan to kill the boy as well?"

"Murder is such a messy business. I fear he won't survive long as an opium addict on the streets of New London. Either he'll suffer the ill effects of the drug, or will be killed trying to find more. Either way, it's a loss to the clockwerkers of this city.

"Now, my darling Nicola, it's time for you to finish your task as well."

Without protest, she made her way to the bench to continue her work. Everything was near perfect, and Emmet realized it would take only a short time for her to complete her task. He knew this as well as the fact that the extractor wouldn't work.

He'd clung to that final piece of information as though it were a lifeline and he'd been cast to sea. As soon as they attempted to test the machine, he'd be forced to play his final hand. They'd either buy more time, he'd be able to finish his key, and they'd make their escape attempt tonight, or Nicola was dead.

No pressure, mate.

For the first time since all this began, he wasn't chained to the bench. It gave him freedom to walk around, see if there was anything he'd be able to use as a weapon, a means of escape. But when Jonas and the other guard arrived, Keegan in their grasp, he knew he wouldn't be able to make his move without putting others at risk. *Dammit to hell.*

Within the hour, Nicola set the wooden plank that contained her control panel on top of the makeshift box and stepped away from the bench. "It's done."

The muscles in his back tightened as Edison stepped up to inspect the work. The leads were checked, the tubes and filaments handled to ensure their proper connections. Edison had managed to find a set of goggles with blackened lenses. They dangled from wires connected to the bottom of the panel, swinging ominously back and forth. Overnight a number of suction cups had also appeared on the bench. Larger than the ones normally used in the extractor, they appeared to be sufficient to complete the task.

In other words, there was only one element missing.

Once he was satisfied, Edison turned to Emmet. "Time to see if it will work."

In a move smooth and fast, Edison pulled a revolver from beneath his arm inside his coat, spun, and shot Jonas in the throat. Nicola screamed and Emmet jumped as the body slumped to the floor with a hollow *thud*. Keegan simply looked down at the body cooling by his feet.

"Oh," he said softly, "I wasn't expecting that."

"Mr. Dennison, if you will, please drag the body to where you need it to be. I want to ensure everything is set up properly before we begin." Edison shifted so the revolver was now pointed at Nicola. "Promptly, please. I wish to finish our day on a positive note."

He wanted nothing more than to punch something—Edison ideally, but Emmet would settle for a wall. Ignoring the panicked look in Nicola's eyes, he made his way over to what remained of the guard and rolled the corpse.

"He needs to be flat. The connectors also need to be put in the right positions or else it won't work. The energy points need to be contacted to allow the memories to be pulled more freely from . . . from the body."

His hands shook and his stomach turned at the stench of blood. He'd seen his share of bodies over the years, but never like this, so recent. Blood pooled around the head on the floor, spreading across the stones, seeping into Jonas' clothing, covering Emmet's fingers.

He had to swallow the bile rising in his throat. "We need to move him. We need to clean him up."

"I'll help." Keegan dropped to his knees and slipped his hands beneath Jonas' feet. "Did you want to go now?"

The thought of this child being witness to such horror and responding with such disconnect made him as sick as the murder itself. "We don't need to take him far."

Emmet pushed the emotions aside, forced them deep down to a place where they wouldn't overcome him. Detached, clinical, an archivist. This is what he needed to do, to be. This is why the others didn't trust him. He hadn't borne witness to the final moments of another human being by performing an extraction, hadn't paid homage to the passing of a spirit to the beyond.

Polished black boots appeared in Emmet's peripheral vision. "Do you need to wait for the bleeding to subside?"

"No." More blood trickled down Jonas' neck. "Though it would be cleaner."

A white cloth fluttered down to land on Jonas' wound. "I have more if necessary."

Emmet let out a long, slow breath. "We need the box."

Time was slipping away from him. He began to undo the buttons on the body's shirt—the body, not Jonas, not his guard—exposing the chest. The skin was pale, red spots rising to the surface. In several hours the smell would grow oppressive, the body would stiffen and bloat, the features twist until they were unrecognizable. Not that Emmet would be there to see. Not that he'd be allowed to remember once the memories were taken from him if he was lucky enough to survive and make it back to the Archives.

Or he would also be dead.

The extractor was set beside him, Nicola's slight frame by his side. "Can I help?"

"No." He wanted her as far from here as possible. Didn't want her to get caught up in the inevitable aftermath. "I'll need space."

He'd done the placement of the connections many times in the past. It was the first real test the acolytes were faced with during their training. He'd heard the connection points referred to once by one of the Guild Masters as chakras, but never again. With care and precision, he placed each cup in its spot. Keegan watched, looking between him and the body, his mouth opening as though he wished to speak, only to close without giving his question voice.

Once everything was set, Emmet sat back on his heels and cast a cold eye to his handiwork. "It's ready."

The sound of the revolver being cocked by his ear should have frightened him more than it did. "I believe you're missing something."

For a fleeting moment, he thought his secret had been discovered. His body tensed and Emmet was ready to turn and fight, when a thin glass vial was held out for him to take. Relief eased some of the tension in his chest. They still had a chance. He slipped it into place on the panel and flicked the switch for the power.

"Thank you, Mr. Dennison. Please move away from it now."

"Pardon?" The muzzle of the revolver bit sharply into the back of his neck. "It's difficult to perform an extraction without being near the machine."

"Which would be a concern if it were you performing the extraction. Move."

Edison led him over to the workbench and quickly secured him with his shackles. "Nicola, as much as I'd love to allow you free rein, I suggest you come here as well. I'd hate for you to wander off before we test the quality of your work." She did as asked, and within moments they were secured.

"What are you doing, Edison?" Emmet struggled against the chains. "You can't be thinking to perform the extraction yourself?" The man clearly had no understanding of the task if that was his intention.

Edison's laugh quickly chased that thought away. "Oh, no. While I believe in taking risks to get ahead, I'm no fool. No, my young friend here will be my assistant. Wouldn't you like to try Miss Tesla's machine, Keegan?"

The boy's eyes lit up. "Can I? That would be amazing, sir."

"Of course you can. You've proven more than capable to run

a device such as this. Consider it an extra treat for the exemplary work you've done on your automaton."

Keegan picked up the goggles, his fingers flexing against the casing. "What do I do?"

"Please Thomas, don't do this." Nicola tugged at the cuffs around her wrists. "He's just a boy."

"Mr. Dennison, explain to Keegan what he needs to do." The revolver was now pointed directly at Nicola's chest. "If you please."

"When I get free from here, I swear to whatever gods exist that I will rip your body apart, limb by bloody limb."

Thomas smiled and shifted the revolver so it now pressed over her heart.

Fucking bastard. "Keegan, I need you to place the goggles on your head, but don't push them in front of your eyes yet. Just get them into position." He did as Emmet said and waited. "Good. Now the glass vial that's in the top of the panel, I need you to press down on it to activate the machine. Wait for the indicator light to change from red to green, then you are ready to begin." Keegan did as he was told, finally slipping the blacked-out goggles down his face.

In the real world, this would be performed under the watchful gaze of a Guild Master. They would know what to look for, signs of distress or fault with the machine. Emmet wouldn't know what to expect, having only been witness to a few extractions, and never focused on the part leading up to the actual start of the process. He should have known—another mark against him.

This time it didn't matter. Keegan stared out into the room and waited, leads running across his body, the goggles making him look smaller than his slight frame really was. Thomas held the revolver steady, the muzzle pointing at Nicola, and waited.

Emmet stared at the cooling body of Jonas, former guard and hooligan.

"The machine isn't talking to me." Keegan's voice was swallowed up by the vastness of the room. "It's not alive."

"What?" Nicola's voice rose and she twisted to face Emmet. "What did you do?"

Edison growled, turned fully to face Nicola, and fired.

Chapter 14

A scream ripped from her chest and exploded out from her mouth. She wanted to hide, find a way to escape this painful death, but her chains held fast. When the ringing in her ears subsided and there was no blast of pain in her chest, or anywhere else for that matter, Nicola knew she'd been granted another chance.

Most likely her last.

"I know you take me for an arrogant fool, Dennison, but I'm not." Thomas recocked the revolver and adjusted his aim. "That was your one warning. What is the extractor missing?"

Goddammit, she should have suspected Emmet would try something like this. Here she thought they'd come to an understanding, had formed a partnership where they actually trusted one another. She'd actually been slipping out of her self-imposed solitude and let him slip in, wrap himself around her heart. All along he'd been playing her the fool.

"Why?" She didn't bother to keep the hurt from her voice. They'd run out of time for games. "Why didn't you trust me?"

His jaw was clenched as were his hands. "You know why."

"No, I honestly do not. Are the secrets of your precious guild so important that you'd risk the lives of others?"

Emmet stiffened and turned his attention solely to her. In that moment there was no gun, no threat of death, only him and her, their souls laid bare. "I was doing it to save you."

Guilt welled up and washed away her anger. "What?"

"I knew if the extractor was functional, you were his target. I wasn't about to put your soul at risk. I couldn't do that to you."

Nicola's stomach turned. There was a part of her that had wanted to see the extractor finished and working. That insatiable scientific curiosity that never gave her brain a moment's peace.

She'd been wanting to know.

He'd been worried about something greater.

"I often wonder if I have a soul," she whispered.

"While this is all very touching," Thomas moved in closer, gun pointed once more at her chest, "I want my extractor to work."

This was their last barricade to stop Thomas, and they'd failed. Beyond this point lay death for one of them.

"Tell him," she said in a soft voice, wishing they'd had more time to get to know each other. "It will be fine."

"No one should have access to this technology." Emmet pulled against his chains once more, this time with less effort.

Edison snorted. "No one except your merry guild? Come now, Dennison, that's arrogant even for you."

"Surely you understand why the Guild Masters do what they can to keep this from others. Human life would become a commodity, bought and sold based on the value of information they had stuffed away in their heads. Your own life would be at risk from the people with whom you conduct business. Do you want that, Edison? To fear for your life day in and out?"

"I'll kill her. Then you. And Keegan will still do what I asked."

She'd heard that determination from Thomas before, knew there wasn't anything either of them could say to change his mind.

"Emmet, please. Just tell him."

He growled and jerked against the chains one final time. "It needs to be primed."

"How?" Thomas didn't move, his gaze locked onto hers. "You have five seconds to tell me."

"The extractor needs to know the destination for where to pull the memories to. Like siphoning water from one spot to another."

"Four."

"Blood!" Emmet's body sagged, as though the remaining strings that held his body were cut. "It needs to be primed with the blood of an archivist. There is something...it simply needs to be our blood."

Thomas withdrew a knife from his utility belt. "Blood from an archivist, you say. I wish we had one present. I guess you will have to do."

The blade flicked across Emmet's forearm, cutting through the fabric of his shirt. Within seconds it was saturated with the red. "And where exactly do we place our primer?"

"I think I know, Mr. Edison, sir. I can see the void now that he's told me of it." Keegan's joy would have been better suited to Christmas morning than to a vigil over a corpse.

"He's more of an archivist than you'll ever be." The fabric tore easily, leaving Emmet's cut exposed.

Nicola could only watch helpless as Keegan squeezed the blood from the cloth into the guts of the extractor. He replaced the panel, secured the goggles onto his face, and let out a breath. "Oh."

"Dammit, Edison. He's just a boy. Don't do this to him."

"I don't understand," she didn't bother to keep her voice low, "Keegan hasn't been trained as an archivist. This shouldn't work."

"He's special," was all the answer Emmet would provide. "You'll ruin him," he said to Thomas.

Thomas lowered his weapon and resumed his watch over the boy. "Do you hear it?"

Keegan's body jerked violently, sending him flailing to the floor at the same time Jonas' body jerked.

"Thefuckingbastardisgoingtopaymeingold." The words came from both Keegan and Jonas, their voices melted together in perfect harmony. "Iwantofuckheragainstthewall."

"Oh my God." Nicola's voice shook.

"He's fresh. The closer to the time of death the faster the archivist is able to sync up with the thoughts."

"How long will the process last?" Thomas moved around where Keegan jerked on the floor. "Minutes? Seconds?"

"Minutes. If it doesn't kill him."

No, Keegan didn't deserve to die this way, cold and scared on a dirty floor. She wanted to take him away, take him back to Canada and keep him under her watchful eye. She wanted to give him a life of comfort, give him projects that would challenge him. She wanted him for her own.

"Make it stop, Thomas. You know it works now."

"Mummyyou'reaslutandIhateyou."

Emmet's face had paled. "He can't stop it. Once the connection has been made it needs to run its course."

If Nicola had felt helpless before, now she was so emotionally stripped, she was certain her soul was exposed for the world to see. Tears streaked her face, but she refused to look away from the torment Keegan was undergoing. Emmet's arm around her shoulder, pulling her close to the warmth of his body, did little to ease the ache in her heart.

Time stretched on as they bore witness to the life of Jonas Weatherly. Hate and fear spewed forth until finally, blessedly, both boy and body dropped to the floor, silent.

No one moved. Even Thomas, the instrument of the event, didn't say anything for several long minutes. When he cleared his throat and moved to pull the goggles from Keegan's face, Nicola could see that the boy was as pale as Emmet.

"The vial should be full." Emmet's voice shook as he spoke. "It will be red."

"Why red?" Thomas pulled the vial free and held it up.

"Violent death. They're always red."

Thomas stepped over Keegan's prone body and made his way to the automaton. He withdrew a key from his pocket and slipped it into the side of the chest. The chest plate sprung open, revealing a mechanical heart and the Parkesine orb. The blue light changed to purple as the memory vial was slipped into a slot.

Nicola held her breath as the automaton shifted, the head lifting from its prone position to face Thomas.

"Hello, boss." The voice echoed from the metal lips, tinny.

"Do you know who I am?" There it was again, that note of hopeful desperation in his voice. "Do you know who you are?"

"You're Mr. Edison. Hello, boss."

As quickly as he'd placed the vial into the orb, Thomas yanked it free. The automaton sputtered and jerked, falling to its knees in a single fast motion. Thomas stepped away, clutching the vial in his hands. "It worked."

"Congratulations." Emmet pulled her closer to him. "You're a monster."

The vial fell to the floor, shattering against the stone. Thomas drove his heel into it, obliterating any chance of saving the remnants of Jonas' life.

Rest in peace, you fool.

"Sir?" Keegan was still on the floor, his eyes peeking out from over top the goggles. "Did I do good, sir?"

"Yes, my boy."

"Can you get him out now?"

Thomas frowned down at him. "Get who out? I removed the vial from the automaton. It is pure once more."

"No, sir. From my head. Can you get him out now? He's scaring me."

"Who is?"

But Keegan lost consciousness.

"That will kill him, having Jonas stuck in his head."

"It doesn't matter. None of you do, now that I have what I need." Thomas tucked the revolver into his pocket and marched past them.

"Where are you going?" She knew things weren't over. Not by a long shot.

He returned moments later, gun out and key in hand. He tossed it to Emmet. "Undo the cuffs for both of you. Get the extractor and come with me."

"I'll do nothing for you. If you think for a moment I'll allow you to take Miss Tesla's memories—"

Thomas' sharp burst of laugher cut Emmet short. "Nicola? You think this is about her? I should have guessed you'd be that arrogant. No, I have no intention of stripping her memories away. Though if you give me reason to kill her, I might consider it. She owes me payment for more than a few lost patents."

"What?" She'd assumed… "If not me, then who?"

He steadied his aim at her forehead. "Move."

Emmet retrieved the extractor and the two of them preceded Thomas down the hallway, past their cells, and around a corner. This section of the warehouse was in worse condition than where they'd spent their time. The stone in the walls was crumbling, metal was rusted through, and the stench of must and mold was high in the air. There were many rooms, none of which had doors, the guts and remnants of what had once been left to decay.

It wasn't until they neared the end of the hall that there was a door, closing the room beyond from sight. It had been repaired much the same way their cell had, though the quality of the work was far better. Whatever lay beyond was clearly of great import to him.

A key on a chain was held before her face. "Open it."

She didn't want to know what was on the other side. The sickness that had been building in the pit of her stomach had grown to the point where she wasn't certain she'd be able to contain it much longer. But they were long past the point of turning back. Their fates had been set in motion, leaving them with only the aftermath.

The lock clicked easily and the door pushed open with one gentle shove. She braced herself for what she was about to find, but instead was presented with something she couldn't recognize.

A large metal box filled the space, leaving little more than a few feet around the circumference. Light shone up from the far end, casting long shadows against the crumbling walls. Thomas gave her a shove, sending her staggering into the tight space. Emmet didn't follow directly, needing an extra shove.

"I've seen one of these before. Not functioning, though." Emmet set the extractor down on the small table near the door. "Who is in there?"

Who? Without thinking, she stepped to the side of the box and looked down through the clear cover of the top into the lifeless face of a young woman. "Mary?"

It explained so much about what had transpired in the past two weeks. Her friend appeared frozen, her skin having taken on a blue hue and her hair appearing lighter than it would have in life. "How?"

Thomas' aim slipped for a moment before he righted it. "She often complained of headaches."

"I remember. They made it difficult for her to concentrate."

He nodded. "They got worse as the years went on. The doctors prescribed her morphine, and it helped for a time. But eventually the pain returned and the morphine did little. No matter how much they gave her, it was never enough. She died one evening after being in great pain. It was a blessing. And unacceptable."

"She died, Thomas. She wouldn't want you to torture yourself this way. She'd want you to move—"

"Unacceptable!"

Nicola closed her eyes and hoped she hadn't pushed things too far. "I'm sorry for your loss."

"But it's not a loss, is it? I was floundering around in my shops in America, all the while hearing whispers about the disturbing creations that existed in the old land. Machines that could remove a person's very soul, package it up, and tuck it away. What a magnificent invention, with endless applications. But these guild runners didn't go far enough. They didn't see the power and potential of their device. A chance to reunite loved ones. Mothers with children, husbands with wives." His voice cracked on the last word, forcing him to clear his throat.

Thomas turned to Emmet, the gun falling to his side. "You'll bring my Mary back to me. You'll bring her back and I'll put her in that body. I'll have her with me until the day I die. You'll do it right now or I'll kill Nicola as surely as the doctors killed my wife."

Nicola didn't want to see Emmet, see the pain he must be feeling then. She knew this was the last thing he ever wanted to do. Still, she had to look, needed to be there for him through all of this. He stood in a patch of light cast from the metal casket, his face a mask. Without a word, he picked up the extractor, carefully pulled the lid back, and removed the goggles.

"Emmet, you can't do this." She looked from Mary to where he worked, for the first time in forever at a loss for what to do.

"She'll need to be removed from the machine. We'll need to warm her up before the cups will connect to her skin."

Thomas moved with precise motions, disengaging the locks on the casket and shutting down what appeared to be a motor beneath. Air hissed loudly as the cover was released, sending the scent of roses through the room.

"Help me to lift her out."

Nicola didn't move, but Emmet came to Thomas' aid. "What are you doing?"

"Helping." Together they hefted her free and carried her to the small space between the end of the casket and the door. "Lay her flat."

"If you do anything to hurt her—"

"She's dead," Emmet said simply. "She won't feel a thing."

He placed the extractor on the floor directly beside Mary. Nicola couldn't get too close, unable to bear being next to the woman she'd once considered friend, but she wanted to be there to support Emmet. Still, she couldn't look as he began to place the connectors against Mary's skin.

"I trust you have a second memory vial for us to use." He held out his hand and waited for Thomas, who hesitated for a moment before handing it over.

Emmet pushed the vial into the waiting slot on the panel, picked up the goggles, and pressed them down over his eyes. He sighed as he adjusted himself to be closer to Mary.

"Time to grow up." He slipped the dead woman's hand into his own before he pressed the switch to engage the extractor.

* * *

Keegan woke slowly. His head ached and his body throbbed, making it difficult for him to pull himself into an upright position. He couldn't make his brain work, the haze of his thoughts clouded, preventing him from remembering what had happened to put him in this position.

Get up, ye fuckin' little bastard. You can't laze about all day when there's work te do.

He blinked his eyes, the voice of the man sounding surprisingly close. "Hullo?"

I said get up. You don't want him finding you laying down on the job.

Yes, Mr. Edison wouldn't appreciate him resting when he should be working. Though, Keegan was certain there was something he'd forgotten. The brush of something cold against his arm finally had him turn his face.

His robot.

And she was beautiful.

The automaton had fallen to her knees beside him, her long arm stretched out so it brushed against him. He could almost imagine she was alive, seeking to offer him comfort in his time of need.

It's a bloody machine, not yer fuckin' mother. Now, get up!

Knowing the voice was right, he pushed himself to a sitting position, doing his best to ignore the pain in his head. It was then that he saw the body lying not far from where he was.

"Oh."

Oh? I get a bullet to the bloody neck and bleed out across the stones and all you can manage is "oh"? Are you a daft child, or has the poppy finally eaten the last bit of your brain?

"You're Jonas."

Yes, I'm Jonas. Idiot.

"How can I hear you in my head if you're dead?"

I don't rightly know. Something to do with that blasted machine of theirs.

"I'm sorry you're dead."

Images raced through his mind of people and places Keegan hadn't known nor had ever been. Burly men coming home covered in soot and sweat. Old men, wearing the wounds of a battle Keegan hadn't been alive for, picking him up and spinning him around before settling him on their shoulders. The sharp bite of a birch switch cutting across his back, punishment for some crime he hadn't committed. Cruel hunger gnawing at his gut, the soft buzz of alcohol making his head swim.

Don't be.

"What do we do now?" This automaton was completed, the test was successful, and Jonas was in his head. He'd done everything that had been asked of him and more, and now Keegan felt he'd earned his reward.

You're a bigger fool than I thought if you think he's going to give you anything. He's going to kill you as surely as he killed me.

"No." He'd been good. That wasn't fair.

Life isn't fair. Get used to it.

Keegan looked down to where his automaton's hand rested in perfect beauty on the floor. If there was one thing he'd learned during his time with the Underlings, it was that the only person who was willing to look out for you was yourself.

"I'll wait for Mr. Edison. I'll give him the chance to give me what he promised first."

And what if he proves me right? What will ye do then?

Keegan looked up at the automaton, smiling as the light in her eyes intensified. "I'll make him pay."

Chapter 15

Emmet's heart raced as silence blanketed his head. He'd lied to Nicola back in the alley about his fear of small spaces. It had taken him years to adjust to the Archives, keeping to the large rooms and meeting areas and avoiding the many corridors the others had played in. It wasn't until much later, when Samuel had given him an extensive tour, teaching him the various pathways, that he'd grown comfortable enough to go exploring on his own.

But there were still moments, like the time in the alley, crawling through the machine to find Nicola, when the closeness pressed down on him, when his instinct to run overwhelmed his reason and ability to calm himself and it all became too much. In the blackness of the goggles was such a moment, the darkness compounded by the close space of the room, the nearness of Nicola, Edison, the corpse. He thought he might be consumed.

The unexpected gentleness of a hand to his shoulder stemmed the panic. He knew it was Nicola from the gentle caress of her fingers against his skin, into his hair. He would have reached up himself to return the gesture in silent thanks, but it was in that moment that a bright rush of light slammed into him.

He was standing in a field, spinning around and around in the tall grass. The smell of fresh ground filled his senses. It had rained recently, so she needed to be careful not to get mud on her skirts or mummy would be so mad at her.

Running as fast as she could through the narrow streets. She couldn't afford to be late on her first day. What a terrible impression she'd make on her new employer. She'd heard Mr. Edison was a tough man, who expected everything a person could give. Maybe she'd make some friends here, learn from those who were smarter than she was.

Pain in her head. Lord, if the children would be quiet everything would be so much better. But they were outside and she couldn't tell them they weren't allowed to play at all. What kind of mother would that make her?

Thomas would be home soon. She was still so nervous about running the house full time instead of working at the factory. She would have preferred to stay with him all day and work on the projects. She missed the challenge of solving the puzzles with him, the look of triumph on his face and the elation she always felt when they succeeded.

"Emmet?"

Pain tearing through her body as the baby refused to come. Dear God, can't you just pull the bloody thing free? Christ, it hurts! Thomas, help me!

"Emmet, you need to calm down and breathe."

More pain, so much it hurt to sit up. She didn't feel the needle as he pushed into her veins, but the blessed rush of relief as the morphine flooded her body. For the first time in ages, peace. Sleep, she needed to sleep.

The light began to fade as the rush of images petered out into nothingness. What little strength Emmet had disappeared, and he was no longer able to keep his body upright. The stones were cool against his heated skin, encouraging him to turn and press his cheek to them. Hands fumbled at his body, pulling and turning him. The pressure around his face was suddenly gone, leaving him to look up into a woman's face.

She was beautiful.

"Emmet? Please say something to me."

Emmet. And she was—

"Nikki, what happened?"

"Well, isn't that cute. He has a pet name for you."

His mind was still muddled, but with each passing moment things grew clearer. "Edison."

"You best pray this works." He was holding a vial, though unlike every extraction he'd seen in recent years, the color of this one was purple. "Why is this different from Jonas? Did you do something to make this wrong?"

The last moments of Mary Edison's life became crystal clear to him. The feeling of utter relief as the morphine dose washed through her stronger than before. The strange feelings as her body no longer did as she wanted, the weakness that overcame her and the brief worry for her husband and children when she realized she wouldn't live through the night.

"Her death wasn't violent. She was happy in her final moments."

"No. I can't accept that she was pleased to be leaving us behind." Thomas got to his feet, the vial in his hands, and strode from the room.

Nicola's hands cupped his cheeks, forcing her to look him in the eye. "Oh, Lord. What the hell did this do to you?"

She loves you.

For a moment, he thought the voice was his own. Yet the sentiment was too honest to be his. With a shake of his head, he tried to push Nicola away and give himself room to move. "Help me up."

Clearly worried for him, she did as he asked and continued to pat his body down, looking for wounds that didn't exist. "Go slow. You've been through an ordeal."

Not an ordeal. He was now officially an archivist.

He'd officially lost his soul.

Don't say that. You did what you had to do. Thank you for that.

"We need to stop Edison."

"Thomas can wait. We need to make sure you're okay."

Ignoring her protests, he stumbled to his feet. "He's going to put her into the automaton. We have no idea what he'll do after that."

Please help him. I know you think he can't be trusted, but he's a good man at heart.

"Your eyes—"

"Have changed. You saw the same thing with Jones and said nothing. We don't have time to worry about what might happen to me."

Nicola narrowed her gaze for a moment before she took him by the hand. "Come on then."

His body hadn't fully recovered from the extraction, and didn't move as gracefully as he would have liked. Stumbling along behind her, he paid a passing thought to the other guards and what might have happened to them before they saw Edison standing in front of the automaton pointing a gun at Keegan.

"I said get the hell away from her."

If Keegan was afraid, he didn't show it. "I will, Mr. Edison, as soon as I receive my payment for the completion of my task. I did everything you asked as quickly as you wanted."

"I don't have time for this. Don't you understand, we have the memories. I need to know, to hear her again. Now move!"

Keegan held his ground. "I'll make sure she doesn't work. I can bend the metal now without even touching it. Use my mind to change the song to a tune you won't know how to play."

Edison's hand that held the gun shook. "You want your payment? Fine."

"No!" Emmet pushed Nicola aside and ran toward them. "Don't you dare shoot him, Tom. He's just a boy."

Edison's head snapped around and he stared at him wide-eyed. "What? What did you say?"

He'd given voice to the words before they'd fully taken thought in his mind. Mary was in his head and there her memory echo would stay until the archivists removed her. "Don't do it."

"You called me Tom." He licked his lips and looked back toward where Keegan stood. "Fine. You want your payment. You can have it."

A small bag landed on the floor, skittering across to stop by Keegan's feet. He stared at it before hesitantly picking up the offerings. "More sweets?"

"Here's a silver as well." The metal made a loud clinking noise as it landed. "There's all I offered you, so that's all you get."

Keegan pushed two of the sweets into his mouth before reaching for the money. "Ta."

Edison waited for him to step away before approaching the automaton. Perhaps he should stop the man from taking this final step, but his body refused to move.

He loves me and is scared. I promise you he can be reasoned with.

"Emmet?" Nicola took his hand in hers.

"Wait." Emmet's voice echoed in room, but it went ignored.

Edison unlocked the chest piece with the key, the plate sliding open far more smoothly than it had before. With three quick movements, the vial was placed into the Parkesine orb, changing the light to indigo.

Thomas stepped back as the automaton lifted its head and slowly rose to its feet. The machine's eyes flashed bright and she awkwardly turned her head to inspect the room. Her unnatural gaze landed on each person in the room, pausing in her inspection until she saw Thomas.

Nicola squeezed his hand and held her breath as the automaton reached out and cupped Edison's face. "Hello, Tom." The voice was most definitely feminine and had lost Jonas' edge.

He loves me. That's why he's doing this.

"Hello, my darling."

"I'm cold."

"I'll make sure to warm you up. You'll never feel anything but happiness again."

"I'm cold."

"The children are looking forward to seeing you. Dot hasn't been sleeping well and William wants to visit your grave constantly. I didn't have the heart to tell him you weren't buried in the ground."

The robot Mary turned her head and looked at Keegan. He smiled at her when she gave him a stilted little wave.

"Mary?" Edison followed as she rose to her feet and moved to where the boy stood. "Let me help you. We can visit the children together."

"I'm cold." She said to Keegan and held out her hand.

"I can fix you up, Miss Mary." He slid his fingers into the much larger metal ones until they were laced together. "You won't be cold no more."

The metal of the automaton's hand began to glow as Keegan closed his eyes. Thomas moved to pull the boy away, but Mary swung out her arm, connecting with Edison's chest.

"Thomas!" Nicola raced to the fallen man's side, checking his head and neck.

He loves me. But I hate him.

The automaton reached down and lifted Keegan up, placing him on her shoulder. "I'm not cold."

"Keegan, where are you going?" Emmet ignored Mary's giggle in his head. "You need to get help so we can get Jonas out of your head."

"I don't need to worry about Jonas no more either. Mary here can get him out of my head." Mary turned him to face Nicola. "Thank you for everything you've done. You're a nice woman."

"Mary—" Nicola tried to get up, but Thomas held her fast.

"Don't go," Thomas pleaded with Mary.

"No. We need to go," said Keegan. "She's going to help get Jonas out and I want to show her our city."

Mary moved to the wall and set Keegan down. She pulled back her fist and began to pummel the stones, shaking the wall. Dust rained down, covering them all. With one final blow she knocked a hole through to the outside. Emmet was frozen.

He loves me. But I hate him. He took advantage of me from the beginning. My projects, ideas, he gushed over them. Over me. When he'd touch me, caress my cheek, it made me feel special. There was a time when I thought I was the most important person in his life. More important than his work. Oh, how wrong I was.

I think Tom loved me in his own way, but it was never about me. He loved my ideas and where they could get him. He loved taking credit for them, basking in the accolades that should have been mine. I confronted him about it once, before I got sick, and he laughed. "We're married. Everything about you belongs to me now."

I needed to get away, as far away as I could, so he wouldn't touch me. My head screamed with pain and he never did anything to

help. Take your drugs, stop your whining, he always said. I hated
him for that. As long as I could still work, fix his broken ideas, that
was all he cared about. I never left the house, he wouldn't let me.
Raise the children. Spread my legs for him. Do what he wanted.

I took more and more of the medicine. It let me forget. It gave
me a way out.

I wanted to die to escape him.

Keegan stepped carefully over the rubble, disappearing into
the bitter night air. Mary followed behind, leaving them alone.

"Emmet, help me."

As quickly as he'd frozen, Emmet could move. With a shake
of his head, he jolted himself into action and turned to Nicola
and Thomas. "What's wrong?"

"He hit his head and is bleeding."

"We need to stop her," Thomas muttered and attempted to
rise, but quickly slumped back to the floor.

"We need to get to the Archives first." Emmet looked toward
the broken wall. "Will you be fine if I see where we are?"

"Go. He won't be going anywhere." She withdrew Edison's
revolver and stood above him. "Hurry, before I'm tempted to
shoot."

Knowing time was of the essence, he bolted off in search of
help.

* * *

The air was cool, but Mary's body gave off a pleasant heat that
warmed his body. Keegan clutched the hand that held him in
place on her shoulder, enjoying the gentle sway as she walked. It
was dark, leaving the streets nearly abandoned. There was no one
to see him and his beautiful creation.

What the hell did you mean she'd git rid of me? You little bas-tard! I'm here and I ain't going nowhere.

Even as Jonas spoke in his head, Keegan could feel Mary's presence infiltrating alongside him. He wasn't sure how he knew, but Mary would be able to crush Jonas under the weight of her personality, filling the void he left behind.

"What do you want to do, Mary? Would you like to see the city?" She said nothing in response. "I would. No one pays much mind to an Underling in this place. They'd just as soon run me over as look at me."

"Home?"

He didn't have a home to speak of. No family anymore to go to, to be greeted with open arms and kisses. The Underlings were there, though he doubted he was missed much by that lot. Still, it was a place to go with a bed and a meal.

"We could go there. Bet Glyn would like to catch a glimpse of you."

Her metallic voice reverberated from the mouth hole as she hummed.

"Do you miss him? Mr. Edison?" he asked. "We could go back and get him if you'd like?"

"No." She turned the corner to the alley that would lead them down to the Thames. "Home."

"I'm not sure if the Underlings will be able to keep you a secret for long. You're too big for our place."

The rest of yer little pack will destroy you, boy. I-I-I can't w-w-w-wait-t-t to see.

"Home." Her robotic voice now reverberated inside his head. Somewhere deep in his mind he could feel Jonas scrambling, looking for a way out.

W-w-what's h-happening t-t-to me-e-e-?

"You're dying." Keegan patted Mary's shoulder. "We'll be fine with the Underlings." It would be good to see the others, even if he knew they wouldn't care for what he'd created. "I'll take you home tonight and we can rest. Then I'll show you the city."

That would be wonderful.

Keegan reached out with his mind and gave her cogs another little nudge. There was something in her voice, something wonderful now that he could hear her in his mind. The tune had changed, and for once Keegan thought he actually knew the steps to the dance.

As they continued along the river, he popped the last sweet into his mouth, savoring the sugary rush while he heard Jonas scream for the last time.

Chapter 16

It took Emmet some time to locate a Bow Street runner. "You there!"

The lad, who was clearly a new recruit, took one look into his eyes and nearly fainted. He'd been forced to grab him by the shoulders to keep him from bolting.

"Cole, sir."

"Cole, do you know Sergeant Hawkins?"

"Yes, sir."

"Do you know who I am?"

He shook his head, but answered, "You're an archivist, sir."

"Yes, I am. And if you don't fetch Sergeant Hawkins and bring him to the abandoned warehouse closest to the river from here, I'll be certain to make mention of your name to the Guild Masters."

The boy swallowed hard, turned, and bolted. Emmet used the time to do battle with the growing consciousness that was Mary Edison. With each passing moment, her voice grew in strength, her suggestions becoming more demanding. She seemed to be able to paralyze him, holding him captive as she bombarded his mind with sensations.

By the maker, how had Piper survived with the thoughts of a prostitute in her head for as long as she had? It was so easy to let himself slip away, dive beneath the surface of her presence and drown. When the sound of carriages and footfalls reached him, he barely had the strength to silence her.

You men are all the same. You put yourselves before us, shove us away unless it's to breed, fix your meals, or satisfy your desires. I hate you all.

"Dennison!" He looked up to see Samuel and his man Timmons jump from the carriage. Samuel quickly closed the distance between them, frowning all the way. "What the hell sort of mess did you get into?"

"One that didn't require him to bathe." Timmons stood behind Samuel, the moonlight glinting off his metal hand. "You look like shit, man."

"Fuck off. We've been held captive."

"I'm aware. The guild has been combing the streets for you for well more than two weeks now." Samuel took him by the shoulder, stopping short when he caught sight of his eyes. He opened his mouth twice before he managed a soft, "Bloody hell."

"Don't." He didn't need an interrogation by his friend. "Nicola needs help."

Timmons barked orders to the men, sending them off down the alley. "She's in the warehouse?"

"With our captor, Edison."

"David will be happy to hear she's unharmed. I haven't seen him that unnerved by news since Aiko insisted he stop experimenting for a month. Let's move, boys. Get the lead out."

Emmet waited until Timmons was gone before cocking an eyebrow at Samuel.

"David was a Company man. Rory won't go into details, but I suspect he's a specialist of sorts."

"We might need him to help us clean up this mess." He wanted to continue, but Mary chose that moment to scream as loud as she could. The pain dropped him to his knees, clutching his head.

"Emmet, what's—"

"She won't stop."

Evil bastards! You take and take, use and use, without caring about the results. I hurt all the time, my head nearly split open with pain, and no one cared. The doctors pumped me full of medicine that didn't help. Thomas left me alone to deal with it on my own. Bastards, every single one of you!

"You mean you haven't had your memory wiped?" Samuel grabbed him once more by the face to look into his eyes. "There's someone still in there?"

"Yes. It was done tonight."

"We need to get you to the Archives before there is damage done."

"Not until Nicola is safe. Not until you know everything."

"You and Piper." Samuel growled. "Did they teach you both how to become extra stubborn after my departure, or had I always been blind to your pigheadedness?"

"The boy built an automaton. A giant metal woman. Edison had us build an extractor and pull the memories of his dead wife to plant into the robot. They're out there now doing who knows what." Samuel stared at him for so long, Emmet grew concerned. "What?"

"You built an extractor yourself? That explains it."

"Explains what?"

Samuel's mouth tightened and he squeezed his arms hard. "Your eyes have gone white."

"That's normal, Sam."

"Not as much as this. It's nearly half your irises."

If he'd had the time to think about it, he might have panicked. But given everything else that had happened, his changed eye color was the least of his concerns. "Remind me how calm I currently am when I revisit this at a later time."

"I will. Let's find your charge and get you both to safety."

Emmet drew what little strength he had left and followed Samuel. It gave him a sense of rightness as he fell into step behind his friend just like when they were kids. He'd have never admitted it, but Emmet had hated Samuel for a long time when he'd left them behind, fleeing from the Archives. Emmet had hated him for not only what it did to Piper, the woman who now shared Samuel's home, but for leaving him to fill the void as leader of their little group.

"I want to see him, now." Nicola stood in the center of the room, looking tired and dirty, a force to be reckoned with. She turned as they slipped through the wall, smiling when she saw him. "I should kick your ass, Dennison."

The men in the room chuckled as they went about their business. If it had been any other night, he would have sparred with her. But seeing her safe and Edison in custody of the King's Sentry, Emmet gave himself permission to give up the fight. He smiled briefly before he let unconsciousness win.

* * *

Nicola was moving toward him the moment she saw his too pale eyes roll back into his head and his knees buckle. Their time together in captivity had forged a bond she hadn't expected. She could feel the duress he was under from across the room, knew he was barely holding on, despite the brave front he tried to project. With them now safe and Thomas in custody of the King's Sentry, it was clear that he could hold on no longer.

Samuel was already on the floor at his side by the time she dove into place. He cast her a curious glance when she ran her hands across his cheeks and neck, reassuring herself that he had no additional external wounds.

"Miss Tesla, I presume?"

"He's performed an extraction tonight. He tried to explain it to me, about her thoughts being in his head until they are removed." Despite her understanding of the process and what she'd learned about the Archives, Nicola couldn't assume to know what that entailed. "Do we need to get him to a physician?"

"No, the Archives themselves have the tools required to help him." The man swore none too quietly. "I'll escort you back there myself."

She wasn't certain, but he seemed less than pleased by the idea. "If you're one of these people who have issues with the guild, or are scared of what they stand for, I'm certain we will be fine on our own."

"I was a part of the guild until I...left. My relationship with the Guild Masters is strained at best and my presence might cause more issues than Emmet would appreciate."

Nicola would have to ask Emmet about this sergeant once he regained consciousness. "The HBC would be forever in your debt for helping a member of her company."

"The HBC are a collection of thieves and villains who'd as soon stab their members in the back as help them in a moment of crisis."

She looked up to see another man, far larger than the sergeant beside her, his artificial hand wrapped around a pistol. There was something in his tone that would brook no argument. She promptly ignored it.

"And pray, how would you know what the Company would or would not do?"

"Because they used my brother to clean up their mess in the Orient and then left him to die." The words were spat with a bitterness that seemed to surprise his companion.

The sergeant waved him away. "Rory, why don't you make sure the men have secured the perimeter and ensure they've spoken to all potential witnesses."

Rory Timmons. The constable Simon mentioned in his letter.

"Samuel—"

"That's an order, constable."

"Yes, sir." Rory turned sharply and marched away.

"Not a fan, I see."

"He's rather protective of his brother. I'm sure you can appreciate that."

"My brothers think I'm odd and better suited to live in the wilds of Canada than in civilized society." She ran a hand down Emmet's chest, pausing when she detected his heartbeat strong beneath her touch. "We should move him."

"The carriage is on the way. I'll send word ahead to have the doctors ready."

When his pause stretched on too long, she finally looked away from Emmet. "What?"

"Do you understand what happens when his memory is wiped?"

"They remove traces of the extraction. Mary Edison is removed from his thoughts."

"Not just Mary. All traces of his time while he had her thoughts in his head. He won't remember anything from the moment of the extraction until she's gone. No thoughts, no conversations," he looked away, "nothing intimate. He'll be blank."

She remembered the brief conversation she'd had with Emmet regarding Jones all those days earlier. The fear and confusion the man had reflecting in his eyes. The trepidation with which Emmet had dealt with him. Then her mind turned to all that had happened this evening. The fear, the connection they'd had while standing over Mary's cold body. She didn't want to sacrifice even a moment of those memories.

"My wife performed several extractions before she removed herself from the guild." The sergeant's voice had grown soft, but the steel remained in his eyes. "Even months later, she'll wake in a panic, struggling to remember what had transpired. The human mind isn't designed to forget such things. Isn't meant to store information only to have it stripped bare."

"Is your wife...will she be okay?" Somehow the thought of Emmet waking all alone in the night, forced to deal with the disconcerting notion that his mind had been altered, while left to ponder the state of his soul, felt wrong. "I've only known Emmet for a short time, but I worry for him."

"She'll be fine. My Piper is a strong one." Samuel smiled, the light igniting in his eyes. "And don't worry about Emmet. The bastard is far too strong to let something like this destroy him. He's the third son of the Duke of Bedford, after all."

"Let's get him to the Archives before he does any more damage to his upper-class head."

The entire trip back, Emmet remained unconscious. She wasn't sure if it was a blessing or not. She had no means to relate to what he was going through, no way to help beyond listening to the advice of those around him. When the Guild Masters swooped in upon their arrival at the Archives, she nearly lost him.

If Sergeant Hawkins hadn't intervened with the Masters, she wasn't certain she'd have seen Emmet again. "He'll wake in a panic if she isn't present. You know what he's like, especially if there is someone under his protection. Let her stay to reassure him when he wakes."

That's how she found herself sitting by his bedside once the Archives physicians had completed the wiping of his memory. Emmet hadn't regained consciousness throughout the process, something she was told was quite uncommon. Of course he'd need to be difficult about the thing. She sat there, afraid to hold his hand even though that's what she wanted, wishing she could do more. Until she saw the flutter of his eyes moments before they slipped open, she'd begun to doubt that he was going to wake.

"Hey. It's okay, we're safe now." She smiled, trying to put on her best performance of reassuring confidence. "We're okay."

He swallowed as he looked around the room. "The Archives?"

"Yes." She wasn't used to the idea that he'd have lost his memories of the event. The doctors had told her it was possible for him to have lost more due to the unpredictable craftsmanship of the extractor that he'd used. "What's the last thing you remember?"

Emmet was cute when he frowned. The lines around his mouth and in the corner of his eyes crinkled. His lips turned in such a way that she wanted to kiss him instantly. Instead, she leaned in a bit closer and waited.

"He, Edison, he killed…someone." He groaned and pressed the heel of his hands to his eyes. "I can't get my brain to work."

"You're doing great. Yes, he killed Jonas. Then he forced Keegan to perform an extraction as a test."

"They wiped my head." He didn't quite manage to hide his muttered *fuck*. "It's not supposed to be this bad."

"The doctors said it had something to do with the nature of the extractor we made. We were good, but not precise."

He nodded, grimacing almost as soon as he did. "Did they mention anything about headaches?"

"No. Should I fetch someone? Is it bad?"

"Don't. I'll be—"

"Doctor, can I get some help? He's awake."

When she opened the door the only person on the other side was the young man she'd met briefly all those days before. "Mr. Jones, it's you."

"Just Jones is fine." He smiled and stepped closer. "Is he up for visitors?"

"Get that idiot out of here."

"Of course he is. Come in."

Emmet turned his face to the side so his friend wouldn't be able to see. "I said, get him out of here."

"Don't be such a child." There was no heat to his words. Jones looked at her and cocked an eyebrow. "They won't tell me a bloody thing."

"Got kidnapped, built an extractor, took memories from a frozen body, and now a giant robot is on the loose. Oh, and apparently Emmet here is grumpy when he's had his memory wiped."

"He's like that on a good day. At least nothing serious happened." Nicola could tell that Jones wasn't discounting a single thing. "So, we need to catch a giant robot. Better than what I had planned for the day. Count me in on the adventure."

"Excellent!" Now that they were safe, that she knew Emmet would be fine, Nicola finally started to relax. "But I suggest we start our search in the morning. We both need to bathe and a chance to rest."

"I'll make sure that you have a room prepared, Miss Tesla. While I'm sure you'd be perfectly safe in your hotel room, I know I'd rest easier knowing you were here under the Guild's protection."

"Believe it or not, for once I won't argue. Thank you, Jones." The simple though of a bath and a comfortable bed was heavenly.

"I'll have the apprentices get one for you as well, old man." Jones squeezed his shoulder. "Trust me when I say it helps."

Emmet rolled his head and slowly opened his eyes. It was strange to see the two of them, their eyes a pale reflection of the damage done to them both. Brothers, not by blood, but through circumstances and mutual admiration.

Jones let out a soft hiss and squeezed Emmet's shoulder once more. "They'll be forced to leave you alone now."

"I have no more excuses for not going."

Jones held his gaze a bit longer, before lowering his head and moving away. "I'll get those baths."

Nicola walked him out to the hallway, not certain what else she could do to help. "Thanks. I don't think everything has sunk in for him yet."

"It hasn't." Jones looked past her briefly before meeting her gaze. "Knowing him as I do, knowing what I went through, he's going to panic. The hole in our minds... it's disconcerting to say the least."

"I'll stay with him."

"He'll push you away. Emmet isn't the easiest man to deal with."

"I'll stay with him."

There were many times over the course of their captivity when he could have shut her out and didn't, when she'd tried to block him, but he refused to give quarter and back away. He'd been her silent support throughout the building of the extractor; the least she could do was be here for him now.

"He's stuck with me, whether he wants me or not."

* * *

Keegan loved the moments before sunrise. It was the only time when New London held the feeling of promise. The air was crisp against his skin as a light breeze blew across the courtyard. He should want to get inside, find a steam room to warm up, get a hot meal. Instead, he was content to sit on Mary's shoulder and watch the sun rise above the peaked roofs of the city.

"Hullo?"

He twisted his body around to see a group of five boys standing behind them. They were all small and scrawny, and looked terrified. He didn't recognize any of the faces, which meant Glyn sent out the new recruits to face the unknown.

Typical.

"Tell Glyn that Keegan's back."

One of the boys peeled away and raced toward the house. The leader of the group edged closer, his gaze roaming over Mary's body. "What's this, eh? Bloody big robot?"

"She's an automaton." Was this how Mr. Edison had seen him? A small, frightened child putting on airs to protect himself? "And she'll kill you if I ask."

The group stepped back several paces. "Glyn won't let you hurt me."

"Glyn doesn't give a rat's arse about ye. Better get used te that idea."

A door slammed open and a large boy stepped out. Glyn was easily as tall as Mr. Edison, though not as broad. Keegan knew from personal experience that Glyn's body was as strong as he was slippery. He'd used that deceptive strength on more than one occasion to get exactly what he wanted.

The older boy strode across the broken cobblestone yard and shoved his way through the group of boys to stand before him. Hands on his hips, he ignored Mary and narrowed his attack on Keegan.

The best defense is a good offense. He tightened his grip on Mary. "I've come back."

"Where the hell were you then? Gerry told me he saw you a few weeks back and you ran away." If he was intimidated by the automaton, he gave no indication. "I've a good mind to thrash you within an inch and toss your ass out from Underling protection."

Keegan tapped Mary's arm and she plucked him from her shoulder to set him on the ground. Glyn was older than he by many years and far stronger. There was a time when Keegan would have feared for himself, feared for the boys around them. But not any longer. Mr. Edison had taught him that he had skills, could defeat someone stronger than himself. He simply needed to reach out and take what he wanted.

"I don't think so." With a little mental nudge, Mary reached out and took Glyn by the shirt collar, lifting him from the ground. "In fact, I don't think you'll be handing out any more thrashings at all."

"Put me the fuck down!"

Ignoring him, Keegan looked for a familiar face. "Russ, come 'eer."

They'd turned up around the same time and had remained friends of sorts since then. The boy stepped up, though not close enough to put him into Mary's range. "Yeah?"

"Is my bed roll still free?"

He looked at one of the new boys and grinned. "Sure is."

"Good. Glyn will be sleeping there. Someone move his shite from his room. I'm moving in."

Russ looked up to where Glyn dangled from Mary's grasp. "Ye got it, boss."

Boss. Yes, that was another lesson he'd take from Mr. Edison. He'd be their boss, not their oppressor. "And make sure that everyone has food in their bellies tonight."

The chatter started up and more boys filtered out into the yard. This was his chance to right all the wrongs that had been done to them over the years. They could be a unit, a team, and together they'd do great things.

"Listen to me." The voices died down as Keegan walked around. They formed a loose circle, all eyes on him.

"Most of you know me. I've been with you for a while now. You know I'm clever. You know I can do things. Well, this is Mary and she's mine. She does what I want, when I want it."

Mutters started up, a rising buzz of excitement and trepidation.

"I've learned a lot in the little bit I was away. I learned that boys like us are stronger when we work together. Not just running around doing what Glyn wants, but what's good for all of us. I built Mary. I can control her. Make her do what I want. We can take food, money, clothing, anything that them muckety-mucks didn't want us to have. It's time we showed this city that there are more people than the ton and the guilds. Normal people live here too. We have lives, and they need to respect that."

Several boys shouted their agreement, while a few more whistled. A fire ignited deep inside Keegan's chest, fueling his rage.

"I've had enough of others shoving us down into the mud."

"Yeah!"

"I've had enough of being hungry. And cold."

"Fuck yeah!"

"Let's show 'em. Let's show 'em all what happens when you piss the Underlings off!"

The boys roared their support, cheering and clapping. Keegan grinned, knew this was the right thing, what he'd been meant to do. In the back of his mind he heard Mary's voice whisper as the metal continued to spin.

That's right. No one deserves to live this way. Thomas tried to keep me down, shoved me aside until I was little more than a shell. I won't let them do that to you. Together we'll show this city. We'll make the sky burn.

And it would be a beautiful sight.

Chapter 17

The water had grown cool by the time Emmet had finished soaking. He'd lost track of the time he'd spent in the water, his mind preoccupied by other matters, specifically the giant hole in his mind. Finally, he'd grown uncomfortable and hefted his mass from the large copper tub. It should feel wonderful to finally have the dirt and grime washed from his skin, to have washed his hair. The relief should be palpable to him, with their freedom having been secured with far less damage than he would have thought possible.

And all he wanted to do was scratch at his brain.

Looking in the mirror did little to improve his mood. Jones had told him that they'd been missing for two weeks, and the beard on his face confirmed as much. But it wasn't the growth of hair that soured him, but the thick rings of white that now circled the blacks of his pupils.

He picked up the shaving pot and pressed the brush filled with cream to his cheek. He should be able to feel it, the silkiness as he spread it across his skin. It was as white as his eyes.

"I'm a zombie now."

He'd sucked out the soul of a dead woman. He didn't remember now, but apparently her memories had been implanted into the automaton that the boy had built and subsequently stolen. Even the Administrators hadn't learned of their location yet, an impressive feat of deception.

The straight razor was heavy in his hand. Emmet turned his face, pulled back his cheek to tighten the skin, and slowly dragged the blade across the fair hair. Freed, it dropped in giant plops to the water basin below. He watched it fall, fascinated by the void left behind.

I've a hole in my mind. Memories gone that I'll never get again.

The blade cut into the skin and the blood soiled the white cream. "Shit."

He didn't move immediately to wipe it away, letting the pain soak into his body in the hopes of shaking him free from this funk he'd fallen into. He was alone, broken, and once again questioning his decision to have chosen life in the guild over what his father had offered.

A knock at the door had him blinking at the sound. He wasn't alone, for good or ill. Archivists before him had passed through this cave of darkness and emerged through the other side. Both Piper and Jones had survived their ordeals, more or less intact.

A second knock, louder more insistent this time. "Emmet?"

Why did it have to be her? "One moment, Miss Tesla."

Ignoring the cream on his face, he slipped into his dressing gown and tied it tight around his waist before flinging the door open.

Nicola had bathed recently as well. Her hair was still damp from the water, her skin was flushed, and the fresh scent of lavender soap clung to her. Someone must have fetched her clothing, for she was wearing a fresh shirt, her doeskin trousers, and a corset he recognized from her first few days of working on the machine.

She looked as though she meant to say something, but when her gaze landed on his cheek, she frowned. "You're bleeding."

"Yes. That happens when one is startled while shaving with a blade. What can I do for you, Miss Tesla?"

"What happened to being Nicola? Or Nikki?" Her blush deepened.

"We were rescued. That would no longer be appropriate." He stepped back into his room and started to shut his door. "If it's not pressing, I'd prefer to finish cleaning up."

She pushed past him and strode into his room. "The poor acolyte who ran your bath was convinced you'd drowned. No one wanted to check on you."

"Apprentice." Why he'd felt the need to correct her, he hadn't a clue. "The acolytes are younger and aren't allowed into this area until they pass into the next phase of their training. He would have been an apprentice."

Shutting the door and locking the two of them away from the rest of the world shouldn't feel normal. But as the handle clicked into place and they were alone, some of the tension in his body eased. "What do you want?"

"To check on you. Once the doctors kicked me out, no one would tell me anything. I needed to see you with my own eyes and make sure they'd looked after you properly."

Her skin still being damp from her bath made her white shirt cling to her upper body in places that weren't entirely decent. The tops of her breasts were pressed up in an enticing manner, spilling over her corset. Memories of seeing her naked flesh, touching her, kissing her were a balm to his wounded mind. He shouldn't want her again, shouldn't give in to the temptation that was Nicola Tesla, for nothing good came from getting what one wanted.

"Let me finish shaving you."

The suggestion made his cock swell. "I don't believe that's a good idea."

"Of course it is. Clearly, you're having difficulty completing the task on your own, and I think the apprentices are terrified to hell of you. Sit and I'll clean you up."

She didn't wait for him to comply and made her way over to the wash basin to gather the implements of his demise. Whether he was more affected by the memory wipe than he wanted to admit, or he simply didn't have the strength to argue with her just then, Emmet did as she asked, grabbed his stool, and sat upon it.

When she turned to face him, she chuckled. "I was expecting at least a token argument."

"Sorry to disappoint you. Do you even know how to use such a thing?" A foolish question, as he'd seen firsthand how capable she was with every tool she ever attempted.

"I have two brothers and a father who are lazy and a mother who prefers a clean face. I learned how to shave a man at an early age." She rearranged everything on the table before she flipped a towel across her shoulder. "Head back, please, Mr. Dennison."

Emmet did as she asked, closing his eyes as well. There was a pause before her sure fingers touched his cheek and gently tugged the skin. "I'll go slow."

"I trust you."

The blade moved with ease over the planes of his face. He could feel her breath coming out in short bursts, chasing each pass of the blade. After a few minutes, her confidence grew and she relaxed into a steady rhythm. "It seems I won't kill you today."

A flash of red filled his mind; the sound of a gunshot and the dull thud of a body hitting the floor made him jump.

"Emmet?" Hands cupped his face, tilting his head forward. He opened his eyes to look into hers. "What?"

He licked his lips, wishing he had asked for a glass of water before they'd begun. "I don't have a clear memory about things surrounding the extraction. I've started to have...flashes. They catch me off guard."

"Do you want me to—"

"No. Please continue. I'm finding it calming."

Whether she believed him or not, Nicola did as he asked. This time, he kept his eyes opened and locked onto her. "Are you close? To your brothers, I mean."

Her lips twitched. "We were when I was growing up. They had no choice but to let me follow along on whatever adventure they were embarking on. Which is fine when you are a rambunctious girl of six, but when I was still insisting on following when I was sixteen, they started to get frustrated with me."

"A hoyden then."

"Did you expect anything less?" She finished one cheek and quickly lathered up the second. "How about you? Are you close to your family?"

"Not close. There was a time when we could have been, but Father demanded that each of his sons take up his expected role in the family. Anything less than that was seen as failure on our part."

"He didn't approve of you joining the Archives?"

"No." If only there was a way for the doctors to remove those parts of his memory. "Not at all."

They passed the remainder of their time in silence, until Nicola finally patted his skin down with the warm, damp towel. "There we go. You look human once again."

She leaned in and pressed a kiss to his forehead, gathered the towel, and proceeded to clean up. That quick press of skin on skin broke what little restraint he had remaining. He stood in one quick jerk and stepped behind her so her back was flush to his chest. She stopped moving, stopped breathing, as he leaned in and pressed his mouth to her ear.

"Do you remember what I said to you back in our cell?"

A sigh followed by a soft, "Yes."

His fingers itched to touch skin, but he wouldn't do anything to jeopardize her reputation. Still, he couldn't resist licking the shell of her ear. "I said I would take the first opportunity I had to throw you into my bed and keep you there."

She shuddered. "I remember."

"Did you lock the door?" He pressed his hips forward so his erection was hard against her ass. She shook her head. "Well then, we better hope that the apprentices are as terrified of me as you claimed."

He stepped away from the basin, taking her with him until they stood in the middle of the room. With his hands on her hips, he closed his eyes and began to suck the skin of her throat, nipping at the spot just below her ear. For a moment, he wasn't certain she wanted this, wanted him. Her body was stiff beneath him, though she made no move to pull away.

With his lips on her skin, he nipped at her. "If you don't want this, you need to leave. I won't take advantage of you, but I don't want your pity, either. Stay or go, but do it for you."

Nicola turned in his arms, her hands still by her sides. "I'm still a virgin. Is that a problem?"

"Only if I don't take my time." He moved in for a kiss, but stopped short. "It will hurt."

"Life hurts. That's how we know it's real."

They met each other in the kiss. He cupped her face, pressing his thumbs against her cheeks, loving the way her skin felt beneath his touch. She looped her hands around his neck and dug her fingers into his hair. The kiss deepened, became something urgent, necessary, and Emmet felt his mind sink lower into a place of rightness.

His cock ached, and for the first time in months he knew the only way he'd be able to soothe himself was through physical contact. It was selfish, but he didn't think Nicola would mind.

"Nikki." He reached behind her and frantically pulled at the bindings that held her corset in place. "I need you."

"Yes. Please." She pushed her fingers beneath his robe and tugged it open. "I want to feel you."

Her nails scratched down his chest, catching in his hairs as she went. He stumbled when she connected with his nipple, sending a jolt of pleasure through his body. "Minx."

"Get this off me."

"Trying."

Somehow they'd made their way over to his bed. Nicola stumbled and fell so she was seated on the mattress, her face close to his hard, exposed cock. Her eyes widened and she licked her lips, a gesture that was far more erotic than he suspected she knew.

"I didn't get to see you properly last time." She tentatively reached out and circled the tip of his shaft with her forefinger. "So hard, yet soft."

He moaned when she gripped him, circling his girth with her hand. "You're killing me."

"I wonder." She leaned in and flicked the end of her tongue across his cock. "Salty."

Emmet grabbed her head and pulled her away. "You lied to me about being a virgin."

"What? No, I swear—"

"Then you are the most talented amateur in the history of sex."

"I'm a scientist. I believe in experimentation and exploring all boundaries."

"Using all tools available to you."

"Of course. Different tools may elicit different responses."

He didn't hold her back when she leaned in a second time and sucked the entire head into her mouth. Her tongue flicked across the tip, sending a pulse of blood through his shaft. He tried to hold back, to resist the temptation of her innocence, but within moments of her starting, his hips set a rhythm in and out of her mouth.

It was a bliss he'd never experienced before. His previous fumblings had been quick, filled with the sole purpose of finding physical relief. He'd never had this connection before with a woman, this innate understanding of the other that gave him peace. Not even his friendship with Piper offered what he'd gained in his short acquaintance with Nicola.

"You've such a wicked mouth, Nikki."

As good as it felt, it wasn't enough. He wanted everything she was willing to give, wanted to give her so much more in return. His body protested with a shudder as he pulled away, the cold air assaulting his cock. He pulled her to her feet once more, spun her around, and yanked open the bindings of her corset.

"I wanted to strip this from you last time. I wanted to feel your skin on mine, taste every inch of it." The stiff fabric opened enough to allow the corset to fall free. Nicola stepped out and turned. Emmet could clearly see her hard nipples through the shirt. "Oh, I remember these."

Taking them between his forefingers and thumbs, he rolled them through the fabric of her shirt. Nicola moaned, her head tipping back to expose her throat. They were both well past the point of teasing. He took the hem of her shirt and pulled it over her head. Now clothed only in her breeches and boots, Emmet took a moment to admire the sight before him.

"Gorgeous." He ran his hands down the sides of her breasts, reveling in the softness of the skin. "You're unlike any woman I've ever known. So strong, but every inch a woman."

Emmet dropped to his knees, the fabric of his dressing gown pooling around him as he lifted one of her feet to work her boot free. Nicola sat and together they made short work of the remainder of her clothing. Before her breeches landed on the floor, she stretched back on his bed, spread out for him to admire.

No, she wasn't like any other woman of his acquaintance. There was no fear in her, no shame in her actions. If she was shy or nervous about what they were going to do, she didn't show it. Shrugging free from his robe, Emmet bracketed her legs with his knees and held himself above her. So close, their bodies were mere inches apart, the inevitable pleasure only a short move for him to take. Memories from their first time together, alone in the dark, dirty cell, were there as well. He wanted to do things properly this time. Wanted to claim her as his, so if circumstances parted them, she'd never forget.

The same way he'd never forget her.

He lowered his head to her throat to lick the skin. He kept his body from touching hers, wanting to draw the experience out as long as he possibly could. Every sigh, every twitch was labeled, categorized, and placed next to the sounds in his mind that were now associated with her. He moved slowly down her body, licking and sucking her skin, wanting to see if he could pull a different response from her. She was ticklish close to her armpit. Touching the dip of her waist would cause her to squirm away. Running his tongue around her toes had her moan and spread her thighs.

For her part, Nicola watched him intently. He could tell she was learning as well, deciding what she'd try on him when the time came. When he'd do something unexpected, surprise would flash across her face, before her eyes would roll back into her head. Her dark hair was a stark contrast on the pale cream of his sheets, the short strands spread out this way and that in an odd sort of halo.

"Emmet." She reached for his head, pulling at him. "I need... something."

"I know what." He'd been dreaming of doing this very thing ever since he'd touched her back in the cell. "Relax."

He pushed her thighs apart, opening her up to him. She blushed, but didn't look away from what he was doing. *Always the curious one.* So he held her gaze as he lowered his face to her pussy, stuck out his tongue, and licked a long, slow swipe up her clit.

If he thought she'd been responsive before, that touch set her on fire. Her hips bucked and she squeezed her fingers into his hair, hard. Emmet leaned in and sucked hard on the swollen clit, torturing her with his tongue until her hips matched the punishing pace he set. It was only then that he pulled back and licked around the soft curls that covered her mound.

When he brushed a finger along her entrance, Nicola's back bowed off the bed. "God!"

She was wet, ready for him to push into her and give her the pleasure they both wanted. But he wanted this to be a memory she'd never forget, needed to create something in his mind that would fill the gnawing void that now lived there, not a quick fuck. She was worth so much more than that.

He pressed his finger in, felt the proof of her virginity before pushing past. He suckled her clit once more, this time moving his hand in rhythm to the beat. On and on he went until her moans stopped, her back bowed, and her muscles twitched madly around him. One moment she was silent, the next she cried out as her body spasmed around him. Her essence wet his hand, and he continued to pump her body until she collapsed to the bed.

"No more." And she jerked when his tongue touched her clit one last time.

Emmet drew himself up and positioned himself between her thighs. He opened his mouth to ask her permission, to make sure that everything was still good, when she hooked her legs around his waist and tugged him forward. He lined himself up and with a slow, steady thrust forward, he filled her.

If Nicola was in discomfort, she didn't show it. Still, he held back as long as he could manage, giving her body a chance to adjust to him. He closed his eyes and let the sensations wash through him. This was Nicola's body, holding him. Her sweat-soaked skin sliding against his. Her encouraging noises and gentle tugs wordlessly begged him to move. Sliding back, he thrust forward with more strength, filling her completely.

"Fuck, Nikki." He slipped his arms under her shoulders and pressed his face to the side of her neck. He wanted to remember this moment forever, but his mind couldn't settle, couldn't focus on one particular thing.

"Yes." She cupped the back of his head with her hand, her nails teasing the sensitive skin of his scalp.

It was too much for him to hold back. The telltale tingle of pleasure began to build in his balls, and it wouldn't be long before his orgasm came. He didn't want to leave her, break the close connection and pull away. But if he didn't the consequences could be more than either of them was prepared to deal with.

Holding off as long as he could, Emmet pushed himself from her, took his cock in his hand, and spent himself on the sheets as a long moan ripped from him. When he finally opened his eyes, it was to come face to face with a confused Nicola. Her skin was flushed from where his body had rubbed against hers, her hair tussled, and she looked quite thoroughly fucked.

"Why did you pull away?" With one simple question she'd gone back to being the scientist.

The twinge of pain deep in his chest was easily ignored as he got up and cleaned himself off. "I didn't think you'd want to bear my children. Always a possibility, you know."

"I'm not an idiot. I know how children are made." She grabbed the sheet and tugged it over to cover her body. "I just…it seems a shame we had to end things that way."

"Practical." He didn't want to tell her what would happen if the Archives discovered one of their own had sired a child. The memories of Master Ryerson and the consequences of his actions were still too fresh to discuss. "You'll be on your way back to Canada when this is all said and done. If you were with child, I wouldn't be there to assist."

He should go back to the bed, pull her into his arms, and reassure her that everything was fine. They could spend the night in his bed, make love until dawn, and forget about everything.

Instead, he retrieved a blanket from his cupboard, turned up the steam heat, and sat down beside her.

Shoulder to shoulder, thigh to thigh they stayed until Emmet took her hand in his. "I've never been very good with people. My friend Piper once called me a hedgehog, prickly and defensive. I… I try to be better. To let people in. But it's hard. I'm sorry for that."

She gave his hand a squeeze. "I'm not the easiest woman in the world to get along with. I'm too fixated on my projects to see the world around me sometimes. Thomas once called me selfish." She smiled, but looked away. "What will they do with him?"

"Keep him in custody for the time being. We might need him to find Keegan and his automaton."

Nodding, she finally turned back to face him. There was something in her eyes, an emotion he didn't want to name, that same flicker he'd catch from her when she thought he wasn't looking. He ignored it now they way he had before.

"What about us?" Her voice was soft, but strong. "What do we do about this thing between us?"

For the first time in a long while, Emmet was torn between his heart and his duty. He knew what he wanted more than anything, but this wasn't the right time. It might never be. "For now, I suggest we keep things as they were. Once we've found the boy, then perhaps."

"Yes. Perhaps."

She leaned her head on his shoulder and for a while, Emmet relaxed and prayed the world could take care of itself.

* * *

Keegan woke up coated in sweat. Swallowing the air in large gulps, he frantically looked around the room. Nothing. There was nothing there. Ignoring the chill in the air, he stumbled from the cot and made his way to the window. Mary had stayed out in the courtyard while the boys had come back into the building. She was too large and heavy to be adequately supported by the worn floorboards. It hadn't felt right to keep her apart, but he wouldn't risk her being close either. Glyn had wanted to take Mary apart, to sell her for scrap, but Keegan had quickly put an end to that line of thinking when Mary lifted Glyn once more from the ground and gave him a shake.

Oh, Glyn had been downright terrified at the abrupt shift in his position with the Underlings. It wasn't all fear in his demeanor when Mary had finally set him down and the boys had in no uncertain terms made Keegan their new leader. Glyn wasn't fool enough to argue with them, but Keegan knew well enough to keep his eyes open, certain there would be eventual retribution.

It was full day now, and sunlight washed the courtyard. Mary wasn't immediately visible, and for a moment he thought Glyn had somehow managed to get rid of her. But before he could move away to find out what had happened, a glint from the far corner caught his attention.

There she was, hiding from sight behind a mountain of scrap. He smiled when she looked up and gave him a little wave. Everything was fine. She'd still be there to help him take his retribution, unleash the payment for every wrong this city had put against him. It was going to be fine.

If he could simply get rested enough to make things better. With shaking hands he pushed his hair from his face, surprised by the sweat that came away on his fingers. Maybe he was getting sick? It was possible, though Mr. Edison had taken good care of him, providing decent food and water. Keegan missed his sweets, though. He would need to send one of the boys out to discover where he could get more. He should do that now. Yes, he'd get his own sweets, then they'd finalize their plan to use Mary against New London. Today, everything would finally come together. He'd get his revenge.

Chapter 18

The room was a hive of activity around Nicola as members of the King's Sentry and the Archives buzzed around her. She'd had little to add to the conversations, though she had no choice but to listen having been christened the official representative of the Hudson's Bay Company in this crisis.

The focus had been to track where Keegan had gone and disable the automaton before something terrible happened. While some of the Sentry dismissed how much trouble one boy and a robot could get into, the rest of them knew that given the condition Keegan was in when he left, things had the opportunity to go poorly before any of them could stop it. Currently, Emmet was arguing with the lone government official about the idiocy of sweeping the streets collecting every waif of a boy they could find.

"Do you honestly think for a moment you'll be able to find a boy who's successfully lived on the streets for years?"

The man, rail thin and pinched nosed, snorted dismissively. "Do you think so little of the Sentry? Unlike your *guild*, they know their duties and perform them admirably."

Sergeant Hawkins was leaning against the wall beside Timmons. They were a veritable human wall, one merely large in stature, the other even more so. The sergeant had allowed the bickering to go on, but at the mention of his men, he cleared his throat. "I've sent the runners out to look for the boy, but most of the Underlings have gone into hiding."

"That's bad news." Emmet held on to the edge of the table, his fingers growing white from the force of his grip. "Keegan had been fed opium-laced sweets the entire time he was with Edison. No one knows the full extent of his addiction or what it will drive him to do. If the other boys have started to follow him—"

"Then the city is at great risk of falling into chaos." Sergeant Hawkins pushed away from the wall and strode across the room to a large map on the wall. "Timmons and I marked out where the Underlings normally work. There are pockets in the city, neighborhoods where the runners will occasionally pick them up."

"It's completely random. We'll never find him that way, especially if they move around from site to site." Emmet moved to the map and Nicola couldn't help but compare him to the sergeant. While both men were handsome, there was something about Hawkins that struck her as *dark*. Strange, given he'd been nothing but forthright and kind to her since her arrival.

"No, it's not." All eyes turned to her, some questioning, some with a degree of hostility, but all curious. "It's quite clear from where I'm sitting."

"Miss Tesla," the government man—she couldn't have been bothered to remember his name—waved his hand dismissively, "you're not even from our city. I doubt any insights you could provide would be helpful."

Emmet's gaze narrowed on the oaf of a man, and she could see he would have made a move for the man if it weren't for Hawkins' hand on his shoulder and his easy, "Steady now."

It had been a great many years since she'd been dismissed so easily by anyone. Crossing her arms, she lifted her feet so they rested on the edge of the table. "Well, then I'd hate to waste your time, sir. Sorry for the interruption, sergeant."

"Miss Tesla, we would appreciate your assistance. Sometimes a fresh perspective is the very best kind." He released Emmet and stepped in front of the man. "Isn't that right, Mr. Clements?"

Rather than be cowed, Clements snorted. "I shouldn't be surprised you'd take her side, Hawkins."

The tension in the air was thick enough to snap. Nicola caught Emmet's gaze and nodded toward the map. "I'm surprised you don't see it."

"See what?" He turned and she saw the tension bleed out of him. "All I see are circles where they are known to…oh. Of course. You really are quite brilliant, Miss Tesla."

"I know." Hearing him say as much in a room full of strangers gave her a pleasant tingle. "But it's nice of you to acknowledge the fact."

The room once again filled with mutters as everyone tried to see what was so obvious to her without admitting they couldn't. It was a game she knew would drive the pompous of their gathering to distraction. As she looked around, she noticed a tall man standing outside in the hallway. He was slighter in frame than Emmet, and had a striking resemblance to Timmons.

The man held up his hand in greeting, allowing his unbuttoned shirtsleeve to flap open. Her smile froze on her face when she caught sight of a tattoo, a stag's head, done in heavy black lines on the pale skin. He didn't move for a moment, ensuring she saw it, before letting his hand fall to his side.

He was with the Company.

"Excuse me, gentlemen." She got to her feet, never breaking eye contact with the newcomer. "I need a moment of privacy."

"Where the bloody hell do you think you're going, girl?" Clements got to his feet. "You expect us to believe you, then have you walk away when you don't tell us what you know?"

"The Underlings are somewhere in the void." She nodded toward the map. "Mr. Dennison sees it as well as I do. I'm sure these men are more than capable of moving forward from here. I'm only an engineer, after all."

She ignored any further comments and the stares that followed her from the room, intent on meeting the onlooker. He was grinning as he rocked up onto the tips of his toes before landing flat once more. There weren't many Company people out and around New London, which was the reason she'd been sent here in the first place to help repair the Archives. Which means, this could only be—

"David Timmons, at your service." He stuck out his hand and gave her a hearty shake. "Pleased to meet you, Miss Tesla."

"Timmons?"

"Rory's my brother. He normally likes to keep me as far away from the Tower as possible, but there was no way he could keep me from meeting you." A burst of voices erupted from the room, drawing David's attention. "We should find someplace more comfortable to talk. This really doesn't have anything to do with that lot."

In other words, Company business. "Lead the way."

"I don't think Samuel will mind if we borrow his office for a time. It's just this way."

David walked with a spring in his step that was contagious. His excitement was palpable, as though he were some kind of mischief maker who'd been given free rein to create as much havoc as possible. Of course, Nicola instantly liked him for it.

The office was simple, if not a bit cluttered. The large desk took up a generous portion of the room. It was close to the message tubes that ran throughout the city, connecting important government agencies with each other and their staff.

David sat down on the desk and let his feet swing several times. "So. Giant robot running around New London?'

She couldn't help but chuckle. "Yes, it appears so."

"With the memories of a dead woman tumbling about inside the works?"

"Yes, indeed."

"You didn't build it?"

"No, but I did build the extractor."

David hummed. "Life and death I assume?"

"Naturally."

"Well then, that's all the official stuff they told me I had to say." He grinned, making his eyes sparkle. "Now the good stuff. The boy built it, eh?"

The last thing she wanted to do was cause more trouble for Keegan than he was already in. "Unofficially?"

David's grin slipped. "I spent the better part of three years trapped in a slave camp following my duty for the Company. They decided it wasn't good business to get me out, might damage their working relationships. I might still be there if it wasn't for the assistance of a friend."

She'd heard rumors about a Company man who'd been taken back when she'd first joined and arrived in Canada. The idea of being held in such a place, something far more deadly than her own recent ordeal, terrified her.

"But you got out."

"I did, and I left the official employment of the HBC. I would never, *never* do anything to put another soul through what I did. But I need to know the extent of risk that this city is under. The risk that my brother might be facing out there, and if there's anything I can do to help him."

It was strange, she hadn't noticed the mask he wore right away. David was the type of man who used the force of his personality to hide what he was really thinking and feeling. He was a bit like Emmet then. She moved the chair that had been set to the side so it was directly in front of him and sat down.

"The boy seems to have the ability to, well, talk to the metal. He is able to bend things internally, small pieces that would click into place without him touching. I only got to see him work closely a few times."

"Have you told anyone that? At the Company?" All traces of humor were gone. "If you haven't, for the sake of the boy, don't."

"My report to Simon is already late. I can delay things longer, leave out a few key bits of information." Not that it would do them a lot of good. Simon had a way of discovering information hidden or otherwise. "Do you think they'll take him?"

"Take him and put him to work. A skill like that is worth more than any automaton he could have built. But I want to make sure he's fine before something like that happens. See if alternatives are needed."

"You can do that?"

"I can do a great many things, Miss Tesla." This time when David smiled, there was no mistaking the metal behind his personality.

The Company had been good to her over the years, and she'd had no reason to think they'd mistreat Keegan in the least. The thought of turning him over to this man who she'd only just met and didn't know, let alone trust, didn't sit well. David clapped his hands and jumped to the floor, the abrupt change in his personality making her head spin.

"Nothing quite matters until we catch the boy and shut his automaton down." With his hands laced behind his back, he begun to rock on his feet once more. "Need some help? Because I'm happy to enlist for the task."

"Oh, God, who let you in?" Nicola turned to see Timmons, Emmet, and Sergeant Hawkins standing in the doorway. Timmons pushed the others aside to advance on his brother, finger pointed. "I told you this is not your concern."

"Giant robot wandering around New London? You honestly thought I'd stay away?"

"Where's Aiko?"

"She had errands to complete."

Timmons rolled his eyes. "She'll be furious."

"I'll make it up to her. Plus she'll understand. Giant robot, Rory. It's brilliant!"

Sergeant Hawkins snorted on his way to his desk. "Only if we get to the boy first. That fool Clements will see to it that Keegan and the rest of the Underlings are thrown in shackles and put to work on the first airship heading to the Americas. Right now, we have time to set things right."

The men continued to chat, planning out strategies on the best way not only to stop Keegan, but also to ensure no one was hurt in the process. Her opinion was consulted more than once, and the annoyance she'd experienced earlier vanished as they listened and incorporated her ideas. Everything was going well until a new arrival appeared at the door. The men all stopped talking, their gazes snapping to the small brunette woman who entered.

"No one told me we were having a party. I would have brought cake."

"Piper." Emmet's smile melted the ice in his eyes. "You look well."

They embraced, a hug that went on for several heartbeats longer than Nicola cared for. She wasn't the only one, as Sergeant Hawkins was standing stiff as a board, not once looking away from them until Emmet finally released her.

Piper was beautiful in the classic sense. She had fine features and a sense of style Nicola nearly envied. Unlike her own practical attire, Piper carried herself in full skirts and a silken corset, her hair stylishly piled atop her head. The white rings around Piper's eyes did nothing to detract from her appearance. Nicola shouldn't be jealous of Emmet's friendship with her—they'd known each other for years—but she couldn't stop the small twist in her gut the longer she stared at the other woman.

"You look very well." But as soon as she said it, Piper reached up and cupped his face. "When did you perform an extraction?"

"Two days ago." He stepped back, breaking the contact. "It's a long tale."

"One relevant to our case." Hawkins crossed his arms, but let his gaze slip from Emmet's. "Sorry, I'd forgotten."

"You're not given to gazing into my eyes to be constantly reminded. Bastard." They all chuckled, even as Emmet retreated further away from where the couple stood. "Besides, my memories have been wiped. And my recollection of the events surrounding the extraction is spotty at best."

They took a moment to bring the rest up to speed on the details of their time held hostage. Emmet's description was clinical, as emotionally detached as she'd ever heard him. He went through the details of what Edison had done, his ability to control the mechanical horses from their carriage, the boy's abilities to manipulate and build the automaton, their attempts at delaying their progress with the extractor. But as he got further into the story, she could see him begin to struggle with the details. Missing bits that were relevant, if not critical. Soon she was filling the gaps, and before long she'd taken over the rest.

"Mary is…was, Thomas' wife. She worked for him, which is how they got familiar with each other. She was every bit as brilliant as he was, more so in many respects. When they got married and she retired from works, I was surprised. It didn't seem right for her to give everything up to raise her family."

"Some still believe that a woman can only hold one role in her life." Piper shook her head as she bumped shoulders with Hawkins. "We do our best to correct them."

"I'm not certain if the decision was hers or Thomas', but in either regard, her memories, once transplanted into the automaton, appeared angry. Mary was sweet natured and even tempered, but I can imagine death would have changed that."

"You'd be surprised." Piper and Hawkins shared a look, but said nothing further.

She was surprised when Emmet moved to stand beside her. "We know where to start our search for the boy." He brushed his hand along the side of her shoulder. "Can you send men out?"

"Already done." Hawkins turned and took Piper by the shoulders. "Timmons and I will lead the search. Mind running things from here?"

"You're going to have me stay off the street and away from all the action?" Piper looked over at Nicola once more. "See what I have to put up with?"

"You're in no condition to be out there yet and you know it."

Nicola cocked an eyebrow, but Piper said nothing further to

her. "I'm aware. Fine. I'll run the lads from here and get them where you need them to go. But you better keep me informed, or else I'll come looking for you."

"Nicola and I will also continue the search. Give me some men, Samuel, and we'll head straight out to—"

"No."

Emmet stiffened beside her. "What do you mean, 'no'?"

"The two of you are not members of the Sentry. You have no place out on the streets chasing this thing down. We'll let you know when we find her."

Nicola crossed her arms and kicked her hip out to the side. "We're not going to abandon this now. Keegan needs our help."

The sergeant looked between them, but she could already tell he had no intention of relenting. "You'll have your chance to help. After we catch him. For the time being I believe you've earned a reprieve. Dennison, be a good host and take her out. Show her the sights. And if you happen to come across a giant rampaging robot, please let me know."

"I believe that's our cue to clear the office." Timmons pushed his brother out the door. "You and I need to speak."

"Come now, Rory. I'm a grown man and more than capable of looking after myself."

"Move."

Nicola found herself being tugged as Hawkins and Piper turned toward one another. Emmet held his hand out for her to take. "Would you like a fresh tour of New London, Miss Tesla?"

"Most definitely. I do believe you were going to show me Big Ben. We might have a good view of the city from there. See if there are any rampaging robots."

"Indeed. Exactly what I was thinking."

As they left, Nicola turned her head in time to see Hawkins

lean in and place a kiss on Piper's forehead. The coil of jealousy wound tight in her chest loosened.

"The sergeant seems rather possessive of Piper." In Nicola's experience, that never turned out to be a positive trait in the men she'd known.

"He has good reason to be. Not that long ago she was almost killed by Jack the Ripper."

"Oh. Right."

"She's only been back on her feet for a short time and insisted on starting her position far sooner than Samuel would have cared for. Not that anyone can stop Piper from doing what she wants."

Perhaps Nicola could take the time to get to know her. She seemed a woman after her own heart. Then again...

"You two seem rather close?" There it was again. She had no reason to be jealous of a woman who was clearly in love with another, and yet her rational mind wouldn't let her pull away from the memory of how Emmet looked at her. "You spent a lot of time together?"

Emmet nodded. "Samuel left us behind, myself, Piper, and Jones. She took it rather hard."

"And you were there to offer comfort?"

"It wasn't like that."

"But you wouldn't have minded if it was." He stopped walking, forcing her to slow and turn around. "What?"

"You're jealous?" It wasn't so much accusatory as curiosity. "Why?"

"I'm not. I have no reason to be. We've only shared—" She stopped herself short, looking around to ensure they didn't have an audience. She lowered her voice as her gaze slipped to the floor. "We've only shared physical intimacies in times of stress. I never assumed any emotional connections would develop between us."

No, she hadn't assumed, but recently she'd started wishing that it might come to pass. That in itself was an odd turn of affairs for her; never once had she been even the slightest bit interested in forming a permanent relationship of any kind. So why she'd spent the better part of the night after leaving Emmet thinking about what might be, she hadn't a clue.

"As an archivist, I can't. You know that."

"Piper and Samuel are together."

"Piper is no longer an archivist. She resigned her position after Jack had…after Jack. She's now a resident of New London, free to be with whomever she chooses."

"And that's not something you'd want for yourself? To be free to choose?"

"No." He said that single word with such certainty, she was left with no doubt of his sincerity.

"I see. Then I shall simply enjoy our time together before circumstances part us." Smiling, she pushed away all future thoughts of relationships to focus on what was truly important—her work. "If you think we still have time, I would love to see Big Ben in his tower."

If Emmet questioned her change of attitude, he didn't mention it. Instead, he held out his arm for her to take. "I'll have a carriage brought around."

It was for the best, to keep things between them light, casual. She'd worked too hard to simply throw everything away for a man who'd committed himself to an order. In time, she'd come to resent him, especially if she was forced to give up her ability to work, as Mary had been with Thomas. And she'd never ask Emmet to do the same.

She'd treat her time here as a break and a chance to test her theories. Sex was wonderful, but the opportunity to discover if her theory about electrical currents was correct would prove far more lasting.

* * *

The ground shook beneath them as Keegan rode upon Mary's shoulder. Even in full daylight, few people spent time in this section of the city. Unsavory people. These were the men and women who used the Underlings to perform their dirty work, to do such tasks they deemed beneath even them. One such man, who went by the name of the Baron, would hire the smallest of their group to climb deep inside the steam engines to clean out the works.

If the boys were lucky enough to survive the task, they were then left to defend themselves against the advances of the Baron himself.

Keegan had been one of the lucky few to have barely escaped both the machine and the odious man's touch. But many of his friends hadn't been as fortunate, something he wished to address.

Yes, we will have a conversation with him. Nice and long and pointed. Keegan smiled and patted Mary's shoulder.

The building was one of many in this part of the city, covered in pipes that carried the steam heat to places other than where it was needed most. Dirt and soot from a bygone time when they used such crude materials as coal to heat and drive the power New London consumed was still caked to the stones, forever stained. The warehouse was smaller than where Mr. Edison had kept him, but was large enough for the Baron's business. The machine fashioned large metal ribs that were critical in the manufacturing of the king's airships. That was all he made, one single part on the backs of those who never shared in his fortunes.

Keegan patted Mary's shoulder once again. "Stop here."

The metal creaked as she slowed, coming to a rest before the warehouse door. It only took a moment for him to slide down Mary's tall body to land firmly on the cobblestones.

"Baron!"

He had no doubt the man had already been informed of his approach long before Keegan had rounded the corner of this courtyard. Like many others who lived on in these parts of the city, his network of spies was always on the watch. So when the Baron stepped out of his building, three of his enforcers in tow, Keegan wasn't the least bit surprised.

"Well, now, what's this we have here?"

"Greetings from the Underlings." Keegan laced his hands behind his back to hide the fact they were shaking. He didn't want to give the impression of being scared; he was far from that.

"What happened to Glyn?" The Baron stepped closer, ignoring Keegan in favor of staring at Mary. "And what the bloody hell is that?"

"Glyn isn't in charge anymore." He stepped closer. "I am."

"You don't say?" The Baron chuckled and pointed the club he'd been carrying at him. "I remember you."

"And I remember you." Keegan's stomach threatened to spill its contents. He hadn't been right since leaving Mr. Edison's care. He needed to find more of those sweets. "I'm here to tell you that the terms of your arrangement with the Underlings have changed."

"Oh? And what are your new terms, little master?"

"No boys will work for you unless payment is received in advance. We expect thirty percent of what you make." That had been Mary's idea. Keegan wasn't certain how much thirty percent was, but she insisted on it. *You need to get what you are due. And if he won't, then take it.*

"Are you out of your fucking mind?"

"And no boys will ever be alone with you again."

The Baron stared at him long and hard before he spit on the ground between them. "Fuck you. Boys."

The three men advanced as one, clubs raised high as they rushed at Keegan. He knew he should be afraid for his life. These men didn't care if he was a boy, unarmed and defenseless. They would kill him where he stood, disposing of his body without a second thought. He should be running for shelter, lifting his arm to protect his face from the inevitable blow of wood against flesh. Keegan simply stared at the Baron and grinned.

Before the first one got within striking distance, Mary stepped forward and swung her giant hand. The unfortunate man was sent flying high, his body landing with a sickening thud against the side of the stone wall. His lifeless corpse landed in a heap on the stones.

The other two men stopped short, their full attention now focused on Mary. They circled around them, trying to attack from both sides simultaneously. A noise bubbled from her voice speaker that sounded like little more than a screech, but Keegan suspected it was a sound of pleasure, if such a thing were possible.

Mary reached out and grabbed the larger of the two men by the front of his shirt. The second seized the opportunity to launch his attack, slamming the club against her side. The blow was strong enough to dent her casing near where the lock was housed. A few more like that and there was a possibility of her getting hurt. Not that she gave them the chance. With a simple move she swung her captive around and slammed the two men together. They knocked heads, sending a spray of blood across the stones. Then she simply stepped on their unmoving bodies, ending any further assaults.

Now defenseless, the Baron edged backward toward the safety of his warehouse. "You're fucking mad."

"No, I'm tired of others being in control of my life." With a silent command, he sent Mary after the Baron. The man was too fat to escape and was soon dangling from her metal grasp. "I'm tired of men like you and your abuse. Taking what you want, never caring about the consequences."

"Put me down! I'll fucking kill you!"

"I'm tired of the guilds taking who they want to live and work within their buildings. I'm tired of not knowing what happened to my parents. Of trying to survive on my own." His hands shook to the point of no longer remaining clasped behind his back, so he let them fall to his sides.

Keegan knew she was toying with him, a cat playing with her prey before moving in for the kill. Maybe he could rework her face and mold a metal smile on her lips. She seemed the sort who would like that, to be always smiling.

"Get this metal bitch away from me."

"I don't think so. She's my friend and she's here to help me fix things. See, this city is broken from the inside out. Them muckety-mucks don't see it. They're not down here in the dirt with the rest of us. They let the guilds do what they want and they let strangers come and do what they want and no one cares about us. Well, I care, and I'm going to make things right!"

Keegan gave Mary a mental push. The sound of metal gears grinding against each other filled the air, masking the screeches from the Baron himself.

"I think it's time you have a closer look at your machine, Baron. I think it might need a cleaning."

"No. *No!*" He struggled uselessly as Mary carried him into the warehouse toward the giant pipes of the machine.

The few workers present fled from the place without so much as a backward glance at their employer. Keegan struggled to keep pace with her, his head spinning from the exertion. Mary waited for him before the giant boiler, steam hissing through the pipes and heating the small space to a nearly unbearable temperature, even in the cold winter.

"Put me down and I'll give you whatever you want. Gold, money, *anything*."

That's what they all say. They promise and promise to give you everything, but in the end they only take and take and take and take. The sound of Mary's voice in his head sent another wave of pain through his body. *Let me do this for you. I'll give and it will be wonderful.*

"Please, boy."

"Can you give me back my old life? Can you find my parents and have them walk through that door to take me back to our home that no longer exists?" Tears came from nowhere, streaming down his cheeks. "Can you make up for all the cold nights I spent alone? Hungry and scared?" When the Baron said nothing, Keegan shook his head. "I thought not."

Without Keegan telling her to do so, Mary turned and began to climb up onto the boiler, the Baron still struggling in her grasp. When she got to the top of the closest steam pipe, she opened the maintenance hatch and shoved him inside. With a *clang* she shut the door on his screams, bending the handle so it would never be opened again.

Chapter 19

There were 334 limestone stairs to the top of the Clock Tower, and Nicola counted every single one as they climbed the winding staircase. The air around them grew colder the higher they rose, making her wish that she'd retrieved her thicker wool coat from the inn before making this journey. Despite the dropping temperature, sweat trickled down between her breasts as they continued on their steady pace. It was far from pleasant, and she couldn't be happier.

After having spent their days cooped up in captivity, it was amazing to find freedom as she climbed. Emmet had retreated into his shell, leaving her with only her thoughts. The engineer in her was ecstatic at the opportunity to see firsthand the craftsmanship of the double three-legged gravity escapement she'd previously only heard about. More so, she wanted to set eyes upon the cast iron spire to inspect the handiwork.

Back in Canada, she'd been toying with the idea of building a metal structure herself, a means to generate and conduct electric currents. Simon had teased her about the idea and the practicality of the applications, but she knew the idea held potential. Her plan was to construct a top terminal consisting of a metal frame in the shape of an oval, though the exact structure of the frame wasn't working in her experiments. She hoped to glean some ideas from the metal cage and spire that housed the giant bells.

"Your mind is surprisingly loud when you're thinking."

She stumbled on the next step, shocked by the sound of Emmet's voice. "I've heard that complaint more than once. Little I can do to stop it, I'm afraid."

"The clockwork mechanism is in a room above the pendulum. Uncle Edmund took great pride in building it. Says there isn't a thing that can ruin the accuracy of his work."

"From what I've heard, his pride isn't misplaced." It was difficult to talk and climb stairs without sounding completely winded. But she wanted to keep him engaged now that the silence between them had finally been broken. "You seem rather familiar with this. Did you visit often?"

"Before I joined the Archives, Uncle Edmund would let me tag along when they were constructing it. I often act as liaison between the guild and the king as well. I stop by and visit, enjoy the view whenever I'm at the castle."

"You're most fortunate to have access to such an amazing piece of engineering."

"Here we are." Emmet pushed the door open and allowed Nicola to go first.

The clockworks were massive and took up much of the room. Unlike in the stairwell, the room itself was bright as sunlight spilled across the clock mechanism and the floor. The ticking of the machine filled the space as much as the machinery did. Like a moth to a flame, Nicola moved in for a closer look.

The simple beauty of the clicking cogs was matched by the swinging pendulum below. Something glinted in the light from the steam lamps that dotted the walls, pulling her closer still. "Pennies?"

"I asked about that as well. Uncle Edmund said they are used to adjust the speed of the clock. They do so to ensure the accuracy of the time."

"Amazing."

Emmet gave her space to climb around the works, though he'd tense whenever it appeared she were to touch something she shouldn't. After the second time he did it, she treated it like a game, counting how many times he'd flinch.

"You're doing that on purpose." He finally said, leaning back against the wall. "I swear you've come to this country simply to torture me."

This was the first time since their return to freedom and Emmet's memory wipe that he'd started to act more himself. She'd grown ever more aware of his changing moods, wishing she could do something to fill the void that now filled his mind. She could only imagine the pain and frustration it would cause him, knowing that his flawless memory would never be the same again.

Ignoring the long rods that stuck out from machinery, she turned toward where he stood. "And what if I have? What would you do about it?"

He didn't move, but she could tell he'd gone on alert. "What would you have me do?"

"Well it wouldn't be very gentlemanly for you to fight back, though you are more than capable of sparring with me verbally. You're certainly not the type to whine, a fact I'm forever grateful for, if you must know."

"You're welcome."

"That only leaves seduction. It would be the best way to distract me while not causing yourself harm."

"I'm not going to seduce you in the machine room of a clock."

"Why not? I'm a clockwerker, after all. There isn't a better place for a seduction in my opinion."

"Miss Tesla—"

"Ah, ah! None of that now."

He huffed. "Nikki, we can't do this here."

"Why not? Are you scared we'll be discovered and you'll be forced to make an honest woman of me?" She would be concerned about that herself, if she thought society would care one wit about the state of her virginity and propriety.

Emmet's gaze never wavered as she moved closer. This seemed to be a natural thing between them, this need to attract and repel each other constantly. Their lovemaking and awkward parting was still fresh between them, a reminder that neither of them was as adept at relationships as they might like.

Surprisingly, she'd grown comfortable in his presence, even if she still didn't understand her kaleidoscope of emotions. Much as she'd become with Simon and the other men of the Company, Emmet was a presence she'd begun to take for granted, the difference being that she wanted more from him than she ever did the others.

"Nikki?" His voice had grown quiet and was nearly drowned out by the machines.

"Kiss me." She didn't stop moving until their bodies were pressed together. "Please."

"We shouldn't."

"Don't you want to?"

"Of course, but—"

"Then kiss me."

With his hands at his sides, he bent forward and pressed his open mouth to hers. There wasn't the desperation as when they'd come together previously. This was softer, more exploratory than possessive. She held her arms at her sides as well, allowing her mind to drift and her body to enjoy the brief touches of contact between them.

This was what she'd wanted, passion and companionship. Despite his harsh nature, Emmet treated her as an equal in ways that even her colleagues at the Company didn't. He also treated her as a woman, something she hadn't realized she'd wanted before now.

The kiss went on and her body relaxed into his. The feel of him hard beneath her, still obvious despite the layers of clothing between them, betrayed his desire. They both finally slowed the kiss, coming to a stop together. She opened her eyes and looked into his. The thick white bands that now circled his irises were a reminder of what he'd given up to help keep her safe, of what he'd lost in the process.

She pressed her hand to his face, letting her fingers linger near his eye. "If anything, it makes you look dangerous."

"It brands me forever as what I am."

"And what's that?"

He swallowed. "A man who steals souls."

"That's not what your guild believes."

"No, but it's what I believe now. I've seen so much, heard too much from others to believe otherwise."

She knew it was a dangerous admission for him to make, putting him at great risk with the guild. "What will you do?"

"Whatever I have to. I volunteered to join the archivists, unlike so many others. I can't walk away from this now."

"Your family?"

"Wouldn't have me even if I wanted them."

Being abandoned by her parents, her brothers, she couldn't

imagine the heartache that would bring. They'd accommodated each of her odd requests as a child and into her womanhood, she knew they would never turn their backs on her. The Archives had become Emmet's family by proxy. No wonder he clung to the life he'd chosen.

The clock mechanism wound up, and the sudden loud clanging pulled a startled yelp from her that she couldn't help but giggle at. The clock chimed, the loud noise making her ears ring from its suddenness. *Da, de da, da de de dum.* As quickly as it started, the chimes stopped.

"Three o'clock," she said with a smile.

The sound of the door opening had her take a step away. While she didn't care about what others thought of her, she wouldn't put Emmet in an uncomfortable position. A man stood in the doorway dressed in a long black coat and bowler, staring at Emmet. He wasn't the clock minder they'd met upon being granted access, but there was something familiar about him.

"Mr. Dennison."

Emmet pushed away from the wall and stepped between her and the man. It only rankled a little that he felt the need to protect her in such a way, especially after all they'd been through. But as she looked closer at the man and took notice of his white eyes, she understood.

"Administrator. What can I do for you?"

She'd of course, heard tell of the Administrators. They were the enforcers of the Archives, and less than savory sorts, if Simon's reports were to be believed. They were the men and women who would get their hands dirty completing the tasks others were unlikely to hear about, let alone wish to do. As she looked closer at the man, she realized she'd spotted him on a number of occasions before their abduction, passing through the areas she'd been in. She needed to develop a better sense of awareness if so many people had been following her since her arrival in this blasted city.

"We have a situation. One that will require your presence as well, Miss Tesla."

It shouldn't bother her as much as it did that he knew her identity. "Anything that I can do to assist, I shall."

"What's wrong? Did they find Keegan?"

The Administrator looked between them, and Nicola couldn't stop from shivering. "No. But he's begun to cause…difficulties. Your presence is required down at the Baron's."

She leaned in and whispered in Emmet's ear. "Who?"

"He makes airship components for the King's Navy. What did Keegan do?"

"Killed the Baron and destroyed his warehouse."

"Shit," Emmet muttered and reached back for her hand. "That means we'll need to cut short our tour once again, Miss Tesla."

"Someday I shall see the bells. And the clock face. I hear it's quite beautiful."

The Administrator didn't move away to give them any privacy, instead watching them intently as they approached. He only gave them the barest of room to pass and start back down the massive staircase.

"I believe I've gotten a sufficient amount of exercise for the month now." She grabbed the railing and set a steady pace down.

Upon their exit, they were met by a second man, clearly another Administrator, based on the way Emmet tensed. They were guided toward one of the guild carriages, with little choice but to follow. If she was meant to be intimidated, it wasn't going to work. She'd come face to face with polar bears and manic scientists with home constructed weapons, and she'd been stuck onboard an airship with faulty ballasts. A bunch of dour-faced men weren't going to set her nerves off.

Grinning, she jumped into the carriage, taking the forward-facing seat and made just enough room for Emmet to join her. "I don't normally have this sort of excitement working for the Company. It's all gadgets and profit margins. Boring most days."

"Come to New London for the sights." Emmet bumped her shoulder as the Administrators took the seats opposite. "Stay for the murders."

"Rather catchy."

The trip from the castle across town took a surprisingly little amount of time. Nicola was amazed at how the crowds on the streets would simply part, allowing the Archives carriage to pass. She'd catch the faces of the people as they passed—disgust, fear, awe—before they'd moved from sight.

"They don't want to catch the eye of the zombies within," Emmet said softly into her ear. "Scared we'll take their souls from them where they stand."

"Better they fear us than get in our way." She looked at the Administrator. His unblinking gaze would have unnerved most. Thankfully, she wasn't most people.

"I've often learned that people will do more to help a friend than they would to punish an enemy. It's a shame things don't work that way for your guild."

"Yes, it is." His lips twitched into a smirk.

"Why do you need us here?" Emmet leaned forward, pulling the Administrator's attention to himself. "Surely you don't need me to conduct an extraction?"

"You are both to offer insight into the state of the boy's mind and his capabilities in controlling his automaton."

Frustrated, she mirrored Emmet's pose and looked the

Administrator straight in the eyes. "We don't know the full extent of what he can do. We only had limited contact with Keegan at best. Just enough to realize Thomas was drugging him. What insights do you expect us to be able to give?"

"Enough to continue to make your presence in our city necessary, Miss Tesla. I'm certain your employer will want you back as soon as possible."

"Are you threatening me?" While, yes, she suspected Simon was anxious to have her back, she knew him well enough that he'd allow her a grace period before yanking her chains to return.

The Administrator's face remained glacial. "Threats are for those who lack the resolve or capability to follow through with action."

"Enough." Emmet straightened, pulled Nicola with him. "We are working together in this matter. Miss Tesla and I will inspect the scene and provide what we can to the King's Sentry."

When they finally turned the corner and slowed their approach, she was more than ready to be once again out in the open. That was until she set foot onto the cobblestones and the stench of cooked meat assaulted her nose.

Emmet jumped down beside her and pressed the back of his hand to his nose. "What the hell is that?"

"That would be the Baron." The Administrators stayed in the carriage. "I expect you'll find passage back from here. Please make a report to the Guild Masters immediately upon your return, Dennison. Good day, Miss Tesla."

The scene was full of men from the King's Sentry and several who bore the marks of other guilds. The Baron must have had wide-reaching connections for his death to garner this much attention. The largest cluster of men was near a machine, and they set off in that direction as one. The group parted on their approach, revealing the burned body of a large man. His face was contorted from the heat, rivets burned into the skin.

"Have the archivists been dispatched?" Emmet crouched down to inspect the body. "Has Sergeant Hawkins been notified?"

"Yes, sir. We just got here ourselves."

"You Administrators are efficient." She kept her distance from the body. While she might have a great deal of experience in the world, the dead were not her area of expertise, nor was she comfortable being so close. The reminder of how frail humanity truly was disturbed her on a deep level.

"They would have been watching the Baron. They tend to have eyes on the more colorful figures of our fair city."

Why would Keegan do this? His rage against Thomas made sense, given what he'd done to him and Mary. But why this man? With her stomach threatening to cast up its contents, she moved away from the group and allowed Emmet space to work. It was strange how he didn't even notice the fact the man was roasted as one would a pig on a spit, turning the body this way and that to mentally record the details. For all his talk of hating the extractions, of regretting his joining of the guild, Emmet seemed most at ease while dealing with the dead.

In time, the crime scene swelled with people. Runners from the King's Sentry came and went, preparing the site for the inevitable arrival of the archivists. The atmosphere changed once more when the guild's carriage appeared and the door swung open. What she wasn't expecting was to see the tall frame of Jones jumping to the cobblestones. She gave him a little wave, which got her a small smile in return.

"Miss Tesla." Jones leaned in and placed a soft peck on her cheek. "You were the last person I expected to see."

"The Administrators pulled Emmet and myself in. They

wanted insight into why the boy attacked the Baron. You're here to do the extraction?"

He nodded, little joy in his eyes. "I am. Seems the Baron had considerable information that the Guild Masters want to ensure we capture. I have the freshest mind for such a task."

The single ring of white around his eyes would grow once this extraction was complete, stretching the hole even wider in his mind. Bit by bit they gave themselves in service of their city, and they were treated horribly in return. Nicola couldn't imagine living such a life.

"I'm afraid an extraction will be impossible." Emmet strode up behind her and placed a hand on her shoulder. "It's a bit too soon for you to be out again."

Jones looked at Emmet's hand and couldn't quite contain a smirk. "Well, you know the Guild Masters. Once you're on the list…"

"You're never off."

"Why can't we extract?"

"Head trauma. Seems when Mary shoved him into the pipe, she wasn't exactly careful. The rivets tore the skull and damaged the brain and a spike pierced the top of his head."

"You know I have to try." Neither man looked pleased by the prospect.

"Take care." Emmet clapped him on the back as Jones passed by. To Nicola he said, "You and I will need to do some old-fashioned digging around."

"Isn't that what the Sentry is for?"

"The Administrators don't want the Sentry; they want me." He leaned in and pressed his lips to her ears. "You can't tell me you don't want to be involved with this."

The shiver that raced through her had nothing to do with the excitement of the chase and everything to do with wanting to feel his lips on her flesh. "You know I do."

They stood that way—front to back—while the crowds moved around them. It would be so easy for her to simply close her eyes and picture them somewhere else, someplace far away from the city where they could enjoy the luxury of each other's company. "Come to Canada with me."

He stiffened behind her. "What?"

"When this is all said and done, you should come back to Canada with me. There's lots to keep you busy. I know Simon would love to have another able body who can take care of himself and others around."

"I—"

She spun around and pressed her hand to his mouth. "Promise to think about it."

It was then she caught a flash of movement from the corner of the courtyard. They were being watched. She stiffened.

"What's wrong?" He whispered once more into her ear.

"I believe I might have found a witness."

Nicola stepped past Emmet toward where the young girl was hidden. A small head poked around the corner of the crate, her eyes widening when she saw Nicola's approach. Scared the girl would bolt, Nicola held up her hands and smiled.

"Hullo there. That's a rather cleaver hiding spot. No one would think to look inside a crate. Good for you."

The girl said nothing, but nor did she run. That was something at least.

"There are a lot of strangers here now. A lot of mad goings on today." She edged herself closer to the side of the box. The girl had pried off two large planks, making a space only large enough for her to crawl into. "I bet you were quite scared."

The girl sucked on her bottom lip and tears welled in her eyes. "The monster killed the Baron."

"Yes, she did. What's your name?"

"Cat."

"What a pretty name. Well, Cat, I'm Nicola, and I'm trying to stop the monster."

Cat flexed her fingers around the wood, and looked around at the people. "I wanta go home."

"And I'll make sure you get there. But I need to know one little thing first. Do you think you can tell me? One tiny thing?"

"Can I go home?"

"Yes, of course. Right to your mum and your dad."

"Just me mum. Da's gone off on them ships. The ones the Baron makes."

"So he's a brave man, then. Flying in the King's Navy. I bet a brave man like that has a brave girl for a daughter."

Cat inched her way from the box. "I'm brave."

"I can see that." Nicola smiled and held out her hand. "Why don't you come out here now? I promise the monster is gone and it's safe." With another tentative step, Cat emerged from her hiding spot. Nicola let out a breath and gave the girl's hand a squeeze. "See, you really are quite brave."

"Ta." She sucked on her bottom lip once more. "The monster took the boy. I was scared she'd take me."

Nicola looked around for Emmet, but he was keeping his distance, ensuring no others would approach. "Did you know the boy?"

She shook her head. "Mum only sent me here to work for the Baron a bit ago. I don't know them all."

"That's quite all right, Cat. Did you see where the monster went? Which direction?"

Cat pointed in the direction from which she and Emmet had come. "The boy spoke to the monster."

"Did you hear what he said?"

"He wanted to make them pay." Cat buried her face against Nicola's chest. "I want my mummy."

"Okay, sweetheart. I'll get someone to take you."

"No, you!"

Nicola dropped to a squat and brushed the tears from Cat's cheek. "But I need to go find the monster. I need to make sure everyone is safe."

Cat sniffed, but said nothing else. Nicola quickly found a runner to take the girl home and then shared what information she had with Emmet. "Shouldn't we have seen them? I mean, Mary isn't exactly something easily missed."

"Not if they kept to the alleys. But it's daytime. Someone must have seen."

"Or else they're still close." The thought didn't bear repeating. If Keegan and Mary were backed into a corner, she could only imagine the chaos that would ensue. "We need to find them before they kill someone else."

* * *

Mary set Keegan on the ground moments before he was violently ill. Sweat covered his skin, his body shook, and his head throbbed. They'd gone farther into the city, hiding in the slums as best they could. But as the day drew on, more and more people saw them. Thankfully, most turned and fled.

Hurry. We must go. Find them all. Kill them all.

Keegan spit, wiping his mouth with the back of his hand. "I need rest."

No. No rest. They won't stop. We can't stop. We must find him and end this.

"I don't know where they took Mr. Edison." Why had he grown ill now? He never got sick, and the few times he had it wasn't this bad. "I need water."

I helped you. Killed the man. It's your turn to help me.

Mary reached down and picked Keegan up by the back of his collar. He was too sick and too tired to put up a struggle. Instead he hung limp, knowing if she wanted to take his life there was nothing he could do to stop her.

"And I will. But I'm sick."

Thomas did this. We will make him pay.

If it was true, that Mr. Edison had somehow made him ill, then they really did need to find him. Keegan would need to know how to get better. "I don't know where he is. But I think I know who will."

Mary lifted him back onto her shoulder. He was so far up, it would be easy to slip to the ground, smash his head and end it all.

Oh no. You won't get to do that, little man. I'll keep you safe until we both have our revenge. Now, how to locate Thomas.

"We need to find someone who knows where they would keep him. We need an archivist."

Mary's laugher echoed in his head. *I know just the one.*

Chapter 20

Exhaustion gnawed at Emmet as the day wore on. Jones had attempted the extraction, even though the brain damage was obvious, and had no luck. At least his friend was spared the horrors of seeing what sick things the Baron had done in his life. If even half the tales Emmet had heard were true, Jones was lucky indeed.

With the Archives being able to offer little insight, the bulk of the investigation fell on traditional investigative tactics. Emmet wasn't used to being shoved aside or having his opinion ignored. He continued to be a thorn in the side of Timmons, who'd taken the lead in the Baron's case.

"Hawkins was put in charge of handling Edison, while I get to clean up the mess," the constable groaned. "While trying to keep my brother from getting involved."

"We can pair him up with Miss Tesla." Emmet wanted to keep her as far away from this place and the insanity of Mary as possible.

"Are you insane? You don't put two Company people together and expect the city to remain safe." Timmons was then hauled away by one of his men.

Nicola looked as tired as he felt when he next laid eyes on her. After she'd sent the young girl home to her mother, she'd gotten her hands dirty inspecting the machine the Baron had once used. Occasionally, she'd pick up a cog or gear and slip it into the pocket of her now recovered leather greatcoat. She'd never look, as though she wasn't even aware of the action.

"Bloody magpie."

The sun was falling toward the horizon when the body was finally taken and the scene cleared of any remaining evidence. The temperature had dropped with the sun, increasing the chances of frostbite the longer they stayed here to work. Sauntering over to where she was currently reconstructing a motor, he held out a mug for her.

She gave it a passing glance, but didn't stop working. "What's that?"

"Soup. One of the fair folk from this area decided to feed the coppers. I took some for us to help warm up."

"Thanks." She set the mug on the ground by her knees. "I nearly have this up and running again. Your king won't be without his new airships for long."

He dropped to a squat and picked the mug up again. "You need to eat."

"Later. When I'm done."

"Nikki—"

She took the soup and swallowed it down so quickly he cringed. The liquid was still scalding. "There we go."

"What the hell's the matter with you?" He thought he'd grown to know all her moods during their short acquaintance. Apparently, she was far more emotionally diverse than he'd first assumed. "And don't say *nothing,* because clearly it's something."

The spanner fell to the ground with a clang, drawing the

attention of several men walking past. She opened her mouth to speak, but clamped it shut just as quickly before getting to her feet and walking away. Emmet followed, but wasn't fool enough to ask her what was going on a second time.

Once they'd gone a short distance from the others, she spun on him. "Do you know what I don't understand?"

"What?"

"Why your guilds are so busy taking children from the streets to do their bidding, but leave more of them to suffer the fates of men like the Baron. Do you know what Cat told me?" Her nostrils flared and her cheeks had reddened. "The Baron didn't want her around because she was a girl."

"There are some men who don't feel the girls are strong enough to do the work—"

"Because he *preferred* little boys! He used their bodies in the most despicable way. I'm glad the bastard's dead."

Her shoulders slumped forward and she swayed. Between their kidnapping, rescue, climbing the Clock Tower to Big Ben, and now working all day, he wasn't surprised her exhaustion was catching up to her.

"Let me take you back to the inn. You need to sleep."

"I need to find Keegan and stop him before someone else gets hurt."

"Perhaps he's only going after the unsavory types. We could let him continue on a bit longer."

She blew a strand of hair from her face. "I'm sure it's only a matter of time before an innocent gets in the way and is hurt. Enough have suffered already. Keegan included."

So there was a wide strip of empathy to go along with her sharp mind and sharper tongue. He wasn't really surprised; if anything, it endeared her to him even more. "Timmons has his best men out looking for them. I'm surprised they haven't been found, given the nature of what we're looking for."

"Giant man-killing robot and her pet boy." She rolled her eyes.

Emmet grabbed a passing officer and gave him a message to give to Timmons. "We'll check back in the morning. If the boy is found before then, send word to the George Inn."

"Yes, sir."

"This is a waste of time. I don't need sleep. I've gone for days without it, especially when I've caught onto a thread of a new discovery."

He'd heard Timmons complain about the same thing in regard to his brother. Perhaps it was a trait of a clockwerker, this intense focus that overrode all else. Emmet hadn't been that driven, not even when on the trail of Jack the Ripper. He'd always taken the time for himself, hadn't pushed things that bit farther that the others seemed to have. It wasn't due to laziness or a lack of desire to see things resolved, but he'd simply been brought up to take time for himself. A fault from his upper-class upbringing? Maybe the Administrators and the Guild Masters were right in their lack of faith in him.

Emmet reached down and took Nicola's hand in his. Her entire body relaxed, and for a moment he knew they'd forged a connection, one that ran far deeper than either of them was likely to admit.

"I'll take you back to the inn and you can get some rest. We can take the irons from here. It will be fun moving in and out of the fog banks."

"Emmet—"

"I'm not like you. I need food and sleep." He tugged on her hand, bringing her closer a few inches. "I'd rather share a bed than return to the Archives and sleep alone."

"I don't want to stop." Her pout was childlike, projecting an innocence he knew she didn't have.

"Tomorrow. At first light."

After that, it was easy to move Nicola along. They didn't need to say much as they made their way toward the irons, though he'd occasionally let slip something designed to pull a smile from her. When he'd become a flirt, Emmet wasn't certain. Most likely around the time Nicola had crashed into his life.

They hadn't gotten far from what remained of the Baron's when a breathless Bow Street runner emerged from the fog. "There's been a sighting!"

Emmet cast a quick look at Nicola before they both moved as one toward the boy. "Where?"

"Sir. The boy and the automaton were seen leaving the market down near the Thames. They…" He gave his head a shake and looked away for a moment. "There's not much left."

The carriages would take too long to come and Emmet didn't want to delay for even a moment. "Take us."

"Sir, I need to report this to Constable Timmons—"

Emmet grabbed another one of the officers who'd come to see the commotion. "Tell Timmons what he needs to know. Let him know we're already on our way."

"Sir?"

"Do it!"

Nicola turned the runner and encouraged him forward. "Show us. We have no time to lose."

Samuel would have his head later. It would all be worth it if they were able to put a stop to this now. Nicola's face had grown pale, but there was no mistaking the determined look in her eyes. He knew she felt responsible for the destruction that was now befalling the city, and he'd do whatever he could to remove that burden from her soul.

They took the irons toward the marketplace alongside the

river. The path Keegan had taken was nearly a straight line from the Baron's to the market. It was strange. The merchants who peddled their wares here weren't known for being the most honest of the trades, and yet it made little sense why he'd take out his frustrations on them. Was this simply a crime of convenience, or was there some deeper meaning Emmet had yet to discover?

As they hopped off the irons and made their way toward the market, the echo of voices grew in volume. The normal smells of fresh market animals, metal and sulfur, flowers and dirt weren't there. Instead the stench of blood and burned flesh turned his stomach long before he witnessed the destruction with his eyes.

"Oh, God," Nicola whispered and fumbled for his hand. "What have they done?"

Overturned carts spilled across the cobblestones, the remains of chickens and pigs spread this way and that. Radiation goggles were smashed, the darkened glass scattered and reflecting the falling sun at odd angles. The cries of men and women, shouting at anyone who came close, begging them for help, overwhelmed all other sounds.

"There've been a few deaths, sir." The runner, no more than a boy, stopped moving forward. "I've seen all I want. Don't make me go any farther."

"We won't." Emmet cast an appraising eye across the scene. "Wait for the constable and the other men. Lead them in as soon as they arrive."

They needed to discover all they could, learn what madness had overcome Keegan so they could stop him. Emmet caught sight of a man standing in an alleyway. Far calmer than the others around him, he stood removed from the chaos. A latecomer like themselves, or someone with a far stronger constitution than the rest of the victims.

Emmet approached him, surprised when the man didn't move away. "Did you see what happened here?"

"Aye." His accent was thick, not from New London, but not instantly recognizable as one from any specific place. "Mad boy and his machine."

"Did you hear what they were after? Was it something specific, or were they simply out to cause destruction?"

The man turned his crystal blue gaze onto him, and Emmet got the impression his worth was being measured. "I did."

Emmet said nothing else. This man would either share the information with him, or he'd withhold it. And there was one thing that the third son of the Duke of Bedford never did: beg.

The man turned his attention to Nicola, his lips parting as his gaze traveled down her body. "What will ya give me for it?"

"I'll ensure you're not thrown into the Tower. Or worse."

He winked at Nicola before looking back at Emmet. "The boy was in need of the poppy. His little toy tore the place apart lookin' for it."

"Poppy?" Nicola frowned. "Why would he think he could find opium here?"

"Ye can find everything here."

Emmet had listened to Samuel complain about the nefarious nature of the markets the last time they'd had a pint together. It was growing to become quite a thorn in the side of the King's Sentry. "Did you give him what he wanted?"

The man chuckled. "No. He didn't look good for me business."

"If he doesn't get more of the drug, he'll grow ill." Nicola said once they'd moved from the man. "He'll become more irrational, which will make his behavior more erratic."

"And more difficult for us to stop him." There were a great many places around New London where Keegan would be able to find the opium that he needed. The question was, which one of them would he go to next? "We're not going to be able to cover all possible locations."

Nicola knelt down and retrieved a spool of wire from the ground and slipped it into her pocket. "He won't go to all possible locations. He's still just a boy. He'll stick to the areas of the city that he knows and is comfortable with."

The point was valid and would help them narrow things down considerably. "He got the opium in the sweets that Edison gave him. It seems logical that he'd want to find the same sweets."

Nicola's eyes widened. "You think he'll go after Thomas?"

"It would make sense."

"Where is he?"

Samuel had taken custody of Edison, and Emmet could only imagine where he would have been taken before a trial was conducted. But it didn't matter where Samuel had put him. Keegan was like every other citizen of the city. As far as they were concerned, criminals were taken to the Tower. He turned and looked behind them, then looked ahead. Following a straight line from the Baron's workhouse through where they stood led to the Tower.

"We need to warn the others."

"Do you know where he's going?"

"He'll want to get to Edison for the sweets. I suspect Mary will want to get to Edison as well, but for a much different reason. The Tower is where criminals are kept."

"It would be too dangerous for them to hit the King's Sentry directly. They'd never get close enough."

Nicola had barely said the words when Timmons and a fresh complement of men arrived on the scene. They fanned out and started to help the victims, thinning their numbers to the point of barely being visible. A woman screamed, drawing everyone's attention to another building up ahead. An eruption of steam shot high above the rooftops, sending with it a blast of clay shingles.

Keegan.

"He's heading toward the Tower, causing as much destruction as he can along the way so the Sentry is thinned out. The Tower will be minimally defended by the time they reach it."

"Thomas." Nicola yanked on his hand. "We need to warn them."

"Timmons!"

The constable was helping lift a fallen cart off a trapped woman, freeing her legs. His metal hand squeezed around the wood, holding it still as though it weighed nothing. "A bit busy here."

"Is Hawkins at the Tower?"

"Yes, though I told him he needed to rest. Why?"

"I think that's where the boy is off to." Emmet quickly laid out his logic, leaving the other man frowning.

"Bloody smart little shit."

"I don't think it's him." Nicola wrapped a blanket around the crying woman before turning her over to the care of another. "Mary was as smart as Thomas. With her memories in the automaton, she would be the one telling Keegan what to do. The boy is suffering, and she is offering a way to ease it."

"We need to get over there and warn Samuel."

Timmons left one of the other officers in charge of the scene, sending a second over to evaluate the destruction of the other building. "If there aren't lives in danger, leave it for now and get back to headquarters."

The three of them then turned and raced for the Tower.

* * *

Keegan could barely keep his eyes open. He wanted to rest, crawl into a cot, put a thin blanket across his body, close his eyes, and forget everything for a little while. But every time he'd try to let his mind go, Mary would be there, screaming inside his head.

No, no, no, no, no you can't leave me. Everyone always leaves me. Thomas left me and I died. My children are gone and I can't have them anymore. You're mine. You'll always be mine, and I'll take care of you.

Once I take care of Thomas.

He'd barely been aware as they'd marched through the front doors of one of the Clockwerker Guild's factories. The screams sounded as though they came through mounds of cotton, shoved deep into his ears. He'd nearly slipped from Mary's shoulders to the ground when she'd smashed through the place, pulling the steam lines from the walls, crippling the facility and sending billows of scalding water through the place. The explosion through the ceiling jolted him enough to bring him back to the present. "Mary?"

You need the sweets, my love. The sweets will make you feel all better. You'll be smart once again, be able to make the metal dance and sing, do what you want it to do and how you want to do it. We only need to find Thomas.

"I'm tired. I want to sleep."

No, you promised me. You'd stay with me. You'd help me kill Thomas.

"I'll get some of the Underlings to help. They'll do what I say now. I'm their boss."

I don't want them! You're mine. Just you. You need your sweets. Thomas has them. If we stick together we'll both get what we want. What we need.

"But—"

I promise you can rest when we're done. Promise.

"Fine. Then we should go to the Tower now."

Yes. The sooner we go the sooner you get your treats. And we'll smash and crash everything we can as we go. They'll be running this way and that, never knowing where we are. Then we'll pluck him away.

"Then I'll be myself once again."

Oh yes, love. You will.

He knew her plan. Even though she wasn't speaking to him directly, all her thoughts echoed through his brain. The force of them hurt nearly as much as his want for the sweets. With each passing moment, he could feel his mind slipping, being siphoned from him and pulled into Mary. She grew stronger to the point where he knew she was no longer his. There would come a point where Mary would have no need for him, and Keegan would be cast aside.

Never, love. I'll always keep you close.

If only he could believe her. "Let's go get your Thomas."

The laugher in his head echoed louder with each step closer they took.

Chapter 21

Nicola had moved beyond a state of fear into a realm of calm. Her heart should be beating madly in her chest as they jumped from the iron walk and raced toward the Tower. Her hands should be shaking and her gut sick from the memories of the chaos and destruction she'd been witness to in her time since their escape.

Instead she'd slipped past it into a state of intense focus.

She'd been here before, many times, when she'd been following the thread of a particularly important discovery. But her life had never been in danger then, she'd never thrown herself headfirst into madness. Simon would kill her if she managed to survive her adventures and return home.

Now, she raced alongside Emmet, determined to put an end to things before Keegan was past the point of assistance. He was a child, one who'd never asked for any of this to befall him, and she'd be damned if she'd simply stand idle and watch him be destroyed. The others wouldn't understand that he wasn't to blame for all that had happened. The victims would want their vengeance, and the authorities would have little choice but to offer him up as tribute.

Timmons skidded to a halt, sending them all crashing together. "Shit, we're too late."

Nicola didn't see what had caught his attention immediately, not until she realized that the people around them were running away from the Tower, running away from the giant automaton. "Oh, no."

Timmons turned to Emmet. "Do what you can to distract her. I'll find Hawkins."

In that moment she saw Emmet hesitate, his gaze snapping to her before sliding away. It was a given that she'd follow where he went, and for whatever reason he didn't want that. Well, that wouldn't do. Grabbing him by the hand, she set off toward the Tower.

The closer they got, the easier it was for her to see Mary. Her metal gleamed in the sunset, revealing every pit and dent of her casing. Her hull seemed to lack the shine it had the first time Nicola had laid eyes on her. Keegan was sitting on her shoulder, his body slumped against her head and neck. She couldn't see his face from this distance, but there was something wrong with the way his body rested against her.

"We need to get Keegan to safety." She let go of Emmet's hand, ignoring him as he called out after her. "Hey! Mary!"

The automaton turned her head toward Nicola, even as she swung her massive arm, knocking aside the two King's Sentry men who charged her. The light source in Mary's eyes flared too bright as she turned her body to face Nicola.

Okay, that's not good. "Mary, what are you doing?"

The automaton moved across the cobblestones toward the main entrance to the Tower. Emmet came up behind Nicola, gun at the ready, and placed a hand on her shoulder. She wasn't used to relying on anyone other than herself, but there was something comforting in knowing he was there, ready to assist. "Mary, you need to stop this. Innocent people are getting hurt."

A loud metallic screech echoed from the small mouth hole. Keegan slowly lifted his head. Closer now, she was able to see how sick he'd grown, how small and frail his body was.

"I don't want to."

"He's lost his mind," Emmet muttered and cocked his pistol.

There was something in the way the boy spoke. This wasn't the excited young man who had said he could make the metal dance. This wasn't even the boy who'd taken great pride in making his automaton a woman. Nicola was no longer convinced this was Keegan at all.

"Mary?"

"I don't want to," Keegan said again, but this time there was something else in his voice, a familiar cadence Nicola finally recognized as Mary. "I want Thomas. He needs to pay."

"Why? What did Thomas do to you?"

Keegan cocked his head and licked his lips in a slow exaggerated manner. "He needs to pay."

"Why does he need to pay, Mary? Did he do something to you before? Did he hurt you in any way? If he did, we can make sure that he is held accountable. He's in the custody of the Sentry as we speak. He'll go to trial."

Out of the corner of her eye, Nicola saw Sergeant Hawkins and Timmons emerge from the building. Emmet circled to a point between her and them, putting himself in line with the building group of officers emerging from the Tower. If there was a fight, they would be ready.

Mary stepped forward toward the bridge to the Tower. "Give me Thomas."

"You can't have him unless you talk to me." Ignoring Emmet's hushed, hurried words to move away, Nicola came closer to the automaton. "They need to understand."

Keegan groaned, his grip slipping. "She's screaming."

"Keegan, sweetie, can you come down? Mary will be okay if you leave her."

He opened his eyes and slowly shook her head. "I can't. She won't let me."

To further the point, Mary's grip on Keegan's small body tightened. He was bound to her metal frame with a single unmovable arm.

"Mary, Keegan is sick. He needs to see a physician so we can help him get better. You want him to be better, don't you?

"Nooooooooo." The word seemed forced from his mouth. "Give me Thomas."

"Not until you let the boy go. It's a fair trade."

In the next moment, it felt as though every person standing there watching held their breath. Nicola's heart pounded, and she was ready to run away if need be. But when Mary straightened her arm and held Keegan away from her, high up in the air, Nicola moved to catch him.

The boy weighed far less than she would have suspected. Her arms easily absorbed his body as she let him rest on the ground. She was able to give him a quick look to satisfy herself that he wasn't about to die before Mary's heavy hand clamped down onto her shoulder, preventing her from moving.

Emmet broke his position, skidding to a halt mere inches from where she now stood trapped. "Nikki!" He picked up the boy as one would a baby. "Let her go."

"She's so angry," Keegan whispered, his voice raw. "She wants revenge."

"Revenge for what?" Nicola wished she could brush his fringe from his eyes, make sure he would be okay. "What did Thomas do to her?"

"He lived. She was sick and in pain. He got her help but they couldn't do anything. He lived and she died and she hates him for that."

Mary's metallic voice screamed once more, and Emmet pulled Keegan closer to him. "I need to get him to safety."

They shared a look, one that told her Emmet wanted nothing more than for her to be the one he was taking far from here, even as he took Keegan away. With her interpreter now gone, Nicola was left with little to go on. She craned her head around and did her best to maintain her façade of calm.

"Thank you, Mary. The boy didn't deserve to pay for Thomas' misdeeds."

Sergeant Hawkins, Timmons, and several of their men moved closer now that Keegan was gone. The sergeant's brow furrowed as though he were concentrating on something immensely complex. It was then she remembered Emmet's comment about his friend's ability to have automatons do what he wanted and she silently wished the sergeant luck.

"Miss Tesla, are you able to get free?" Hawkins waved some of his men to circle around behind Mary. "I'm unable to do anything to slow her down. It's as though she's somehow able to block me."

"She might stop if you bring Thomas out for her to at least see." The painful grasp of metal fingers against her shoulder bit harder. "I don't think she's able to see reason, and I suspect she is quite mad."

"It's a fucking machine," one of the men called out. "It can't *see* anything."

"It has the extracted memories of a bitter, hurt woman in

there." Emmet had rejoined them. He started to come close, but Hawkins held him back. "We need to get her out of there."

"We will." But there was something in the way Hawkins spoke, in the quick look he shared with Timmons, that told her there was more to this situation than they knew. "Mary, we need you to let Miss Tesla go."

Instead of complying, Nicola felt her feet leave the ground. Much as Keegan had been, she now hung dangling. Pain lanced through her body, ripping a cry from her as the metal fingers tightened into her flesh. Everything was too much, too bright and painful for her to process. Unconsciousness threatened to overtake her.

Hawkins staggered back from where he'd moved closer, his hands pressed to his temples. "Shit."

"What?" Emmet's gun was up, but he looked hesitant to shoot. "What's wrong?"

"She's screaming at me."

"Then give her what she wants and get Nikki free."

"I *can't*." Hawkins dropped to his knees, groaning loudly. "Get out of my head!"

The metallic screech this time turned Nicola's blood cold. Whatever humanity Mary once had had been lost upon her death and rebirth. She knew those were the sounds of pure hate and rage, neither of which would be quelled until Mary got what she wanted.

Hawkins met her gaze and she somehow knew what he was going to say before he did.

"Edison's not here."

Another screech, this one accompanied with a tightening of her hand around Nicola's body.

"The Administrators wanted to conduct their own questioning. They needed to know about the extractor and who Edison's connections were in France. They were fearful of the machine falling into the wrong hands, or someone being able to build it again. They took him to the prison in the base of the Clock Tower."

She had a vague memory of the clock minder mentioning the cells, though now that she thought about it, he discouraged any questions on the topic. She'd been so close to Thomas and hadn't even realized, as though the connection, the camaraderie she'd once shared with him, had been completely obliterated. Now, both their lives would be in danger, and there was nothing either of them could do to stop it.

Mary moved Nicola to her shoulder, pressing her belly against the metal and leaving her head hanging down her back. Dented metal, battered into a rough shape with the love and caring of a boy who had no idea of the monster he would create. The seams were tight and secure, and would make it difficult to break through. From this angle she was able to see the hinges Keegan had installed that would allow the metal chest plate to swing open and reveal Mary's core.

The core that held the heart.

"The key!" She shouted as loudly as she could while Mary started to move her away from the group. Emmet dodged into sight, reaching for her as he moved. Mary swung her away, but not before their fingertips brushed. "Emmet!"

He moved around again, this time not bothering to reach. "What key?"

"Keegan has one for the chest plate. We can use it to get inside, pull her heart out. It's her power source."

"I'll find it."

Mary's grasp tightened further, the pain spreading like quicksilver down Nicola's spine. Nicola stilled as much as she could, trying to breathe through the pain. Much more pressure and her back would snap like a twig, leaving her little good to anyone. The men of the King's Sentry circled around them, each with a weapon in hand. Guns, nets, ropes, anything they could find she suspected that was close at hand. It would do little good. The heart needed to be removed, or shorted out, something to interrupt the flow of power to her brain.

"Hold your fire!" Hawkins shouted at his men, causing Mary to spin around once more. She was a cornered animal and it was only a matter of time before she struck out. "We don't want to hurt Miss Tesla." *Yes, please don't hurt Miss Tesla.*

But she could tell with every spin Mary made that the men were growing more restless, more nervous about the outcome. They wanted action, wanted to put the rabid dog down, as it were, and Nicola had no doubt they would sacrifice her if that meant destroying Mary. With the blood rushing to her head, she started to feel nauseous. Her vision swam and the idea of losing consciousness was fast becoming a real possibility. She needed to keep her wits if she was to survive.

The tense silence was cut with the bang of a pistol being discharged. The vibration of the bullet slamming into Mary's metal chest reverberated through Nicola's body. Mary roared, swinging her large arm into the group of men, sending their bodies flying. Screams of pain competed with shouts of orders to stand down as chaos erupted. Nicola covered her head as Mary continued to mow through the men, snapping through their ropes and tearing their nets.

Another metallic roar and Mary strode away. Nicola looked up and caught sight of the bloody remains of the Sentry.

"Oh, God."

Bodies lay broken and twisted, silent and unmoving. Blood

seeped across the stones, tracked this way and that as people rushed to aid the injured. She caught sight of Hawkins and Timmons as they assisted their men. She couldn't see Emmet.

Her throat tightened as the tears dropped from her eyes to land on the rough metal below her. No, no, he couldn't have fallen. She would have felt it in her gut if he was injured. *Like you knew Thomas was there?* That was different. Her relationship with Thomas was one of professional courtesy.

She'd fallen in love with Emmet.

The last thing she saw was Hawkins moving to a pile of bodies. "Dennison!"

No. No he couldn't be dead. The idea was unfathomable.

"You better not have hurt him." She spoke the words, no longer shocked by the venom they held. "Pray I'll go back and find him alive and unharmed or I swear to every god and the universe that I will tear you apart cog by cog." Mary's grip tightened. "Oh, yes, you understand me. There was a time you would have understood."

Rage fueled by unexpressed love filled her very being. The time for kindness was over. Nicola would stop Mary once and for all.

* * *

Emmet lay still on the ground, his head throbbing from where it had connected with stone. He'd been trying to see Nicola once more when Mary's swing had sent the bodies of two men slamming into him. He'd been unable to move from the weight of the men, his breathing shallow from the pressure. Blood had dropped onto his face from above, so when Samuel pulled him free he could only imagine the sight he appeared.

"Are you hurt?" Samuel shouted for a doctor, even while he

dropped to his knees to check for a pulse on the clearly dead men. "Fuck."

"I'm fine. Banged my head. Where's Nicola?"

When Mary had lifted her from the ground, Emmet thought his heart would never start beating again. The woman was mad, infuriating, and if she got herself killed, he'd never forgive her.

"That metal monster is heading toward the Clock Tower. I've sent word ahead to the men stationed at the castle. They will build a barrier and hopefully that will slow her down enough for us to make it there in time to take her down."

"We'll need bigger weapons than what we have here."

"What we need is a clockwerker." Samuel spun until he spotted Timmons. "Where's David?"

"I had one of the lads fetch him when I heard that thing was coming. I'm surprised he isn't here already."

David was mad, but both Samuel and Timmons trusted him. Emmet didn't much care for the man one way or the other, but he'd offer him every bit of wealth he had stashed away if he could help stop Mary and save Nicola.

The sight of her hanging limp against the metal made his heart ache. She was in pain, and there had been nothing he could do to help. While he was good with a pistol, the Sentry men wouldn't have allowed him to stand in their way. His authority with the Archives meant nothing here. His standing as the third son of the Duke of Bedford meant nothing here.

Standing there, forced to do little more than look at the woman who'd captured his heart be held hostage, made him sick. What kind of man was he if he was not able to protect the ones he loved? Pitiful. Exactly what his father had always accused him of being.

"I'm going after them." He snatched a pistol from the ground as he passed by, shoving it into his waistband.

"Like hell." Samuel tried to stop him, but Emmet spun, landing the unseen punch square on his friend's jaw.

"Not this time." Emmet shook his hand, glaring at the men who stopped to stare. "If you think I'm going to sit by while others flounder around, you're as much of an idiot as they were for shooting at that thing."

Emmet turned and broke out into a run. Mary was heading toward the Clock Tower. The city itself, with its twists and turns, would slow her down, as would the terrified citizens who would no doubt get in her way. He'd be able to take a more direct path to the Clock Tower and would be able to get word to the men there about what they were facing. With luck, they'd be able to set a trap.

He'd made it nearly to the iron walk when the sound of a dirigible engine echoed off the buildings. Looking up, he briefly saw a dark head poke over the side of the hull before it disappeared. The ship itself was a smaller version of what the King's Navy used, with only one smaller balloon and an engine fan that would have been used as a secondary propeller on a normal ship. A long rope ladder dropped to the ground a few feet away from him, which was soon followed by the dark head poking over the side again.

"Hurry up!" David Timmons sounded very much like a man on his way to a carnival—excited and eager. "This is faster."

He must be mad to even consider boarding a ship that could easily slam into the side of a building, be torn to shreds, or explode if they got too close to a steam vent. Emmet shoved his pistol back into his pocket and leapt onto the ladder. David didn't wait for him to reach the top before he began to retract the ladder into the ship. He barely managed to throw his leg over the side before landing in a heap on the deck.

"You're fucking insane."

David chuckled. "I believe the saying is, it takes one to know one." He spun the ship's wheel and turned the direction of the ship toward Big Ben, clearly seen now that they were in the air.

Emmet got to his feet. "How fast does this thing fly?"

"Well, I haven't finished conducting all my tests, but the last time I had it out—"

"That metal fiend is taking Nikki to Big Ben. If she is hurt or, God forbid, dies, I will tear this city apart to punish everyone who had a hand in it. How fast?"

David's jovial mask dropped and coldness filled his brown eyes. "I, too, would kill to protect someone I love."

"Then you understand."

"I do." David stepped onto a pedal near his foot, which sent a blast of steam pounding through the engines. The ship lurched forward and he smiled. "Let's go save your lady love."

Chapter 22

Nicola had closed her eyes as Mary lurched through the guts of the city, sending her citizens running this way and that. Men would sometimes try to stop her, or children would throw bottles, but each time Mary would cast them aside. Nicola was helpless, unable to do anything but bear witness to the destruction, until it became unbearable. She had to close her eyes, leaving her little to do but pray to a god she didn't believe in and plot a means of stopping her.

They'd turned along the side of the Thames and Mary now followed it. Nicola recognized the path from her earlier trip with Emmet. It wouldn't be long before they reached the Clock Tower and the prison cell that held Thomas.

Despite his failings, his crimes, she didn't want to see him hurt. Not like this. What he'd done by stealing her ideas was unforgivable, but it wasn't worth the price of his life. Even his crimes since arriving in New London could be understood as those of a grief-mad husband, unable to cope with the loss of his beloved wife. He'd pay for his crimes, but in a court of law, not at the end of a metal fist.

The automaton wasn't Mary Edison. It might contain her memories, but the kind soul of the woman Nicola had worked side by side with wasn't present. With luck, it had passed on to the heaven she and others believed in so much and she was truly at rest. This was little more than a perverted echo of the woman, a thing that needed to be put out of its misery.

Mary's steady progress came to a lurching stop. Nicola barely had enough time to brace herself and stop her face from slamming against the metal. She couldn't hear anything at first, and being unable to see left her more frustrated than before.

"Mary, what's going on?"

She didn't think the automaton would respond, but was shocked when the metal hand that had held her fast in place moved, lifting her up once more. With a jolt, she was perched unceremoniously on top of Mary's shoulder. The sudden change in position had her head spinning and her vision blacking out. She had to shake her head to try to clear it, though she wished she hadn't the moment her vision cleared.

The King's Sentry was ready for them. A barrier had been erected with overturned carriages, merchant carts, and heaps of scrap metal. Resting on top the haphazard pile were two large cannons. It was hard to tell, but they appeared to be quite old and covered in rust. While there were newer machines available to them, these would be sufficient to blast a hole into Mary. The impact would have the unfortunate side effect of killing Nicola.

"Stop where you are!" The voice was tinny, amplified so as to reach them. "We won't allow you to come closer."

She cupped her hands before her mouth and shouted as best she could. "I have no control over this creature."

"You need to. The king is in residence and we cannot allow any harm to come to him."

Wonderful. "I can't. She won't be satisfied until she has what she's come for. She's not listening to me."

"Then you'd best get yourself away."

Mary began her approach once more, though slower and more deliberately than earlier. The unmistakable sound of weapons being prepared to be fired reached her as a whisper would into her ear. This was it then. Her life was forfeit so they could save their precious monarch. Not that she suspected it would be as easy as they thought. But she was far too exposed to stay safe for long, which meant she needed to find a way to get free.

"Mary, please put me down. They're going to fire upon you and I will only get in your way." The metal fingers held fast. "I'm no good to you any longer. They're just as likely to put a bullet in my brain as they are to try to rescue me."

Several of the Sentry men emerged from around the side of the barricade and opened fire on them. Bullets ricocheted off Mary's body and flew off in alternative directions. When one of them lifted the barrel of his rifle higher than the others, she knew he was aiming at her on purpose.

I'm so sorry, Emmet. Sorry I never had the chance to tell you how I feel.

The crack of a shot letting loose rang in her ears, though the flesh-rending impact never came as Mary jerked her from her perch, moving her from the bullet's path before it connected. Nicola stared at the automaton's head in shock. "Thank you." Perhaps there was a small part of the real Mary buried in there after all.

The infantry and their barrage had distracted Mary enough for the cannons to be prepared. A flash of fire being pressed to a fuse drew Nicola's attention long enough for her to brace for the inevitable blow. The twin explosions were quickly chased by the cannonball itself, which slammed into Mary's chest and right shoulder.

Her world turned upside down as Mary screamed and they were both launched into the air, only to come crashing down on the frozen banks of the Thames. Nicola had gone deaf, her brain slowed and body numb. It hurt to turn her head, but she did so, seeking out what had become of the automaton.

Mary lay a few feet from her, a jet of steam exploding upward from the joint of her arm. She didn't appear to be moving. Nicola forced herself to move, pushing the ground so she could roll onto her stomach and crawl toward what remained of the automaton. The stench of burned wires, melted metal, and sulfur were the first indication that her senses were slowly beginning to right themselves. Her fingers dug into the frozen soil as she pulled herself along.

Steam hissed as the frozen ground melted from the superheated metal. Nicola pushed herself to her knees in the hopes of getting a good look at the damage, to confirm that this nightmare was in fact over.

The chest plate was dented inward, but miraculously had stayed together. The cannonball wasn't as large as some she'd seen, only ten inches in diameter and nowhere near enough to obliterate an automaton of Mary's size. Keegan had done an admirable job at reinforcing the metal, give how her hull had survived. The right arm was another matter, having been blown completely off. The eyes were no longer illuminated, and there were no sounds indicating that Mary's internal systems were still functioning.

With a groan, Nicola sat down on the ground and let relief wash over her. It was over.

As her hearing improved, she could make out the sounds of shouts and something far stranger—a dirigible engine. She shielded her eyes with her hand and looked up, trying to catch a glimpse of what manner of airship could fly so close to the buildings. The setting sun made it difficult at first, but finally she saw it circling high above her. Two dark-haired heads poked over the side of the hull, and one of the men waved.

"Hullo, Miss Tesla," David called down to her. "Did we miss all the fun?"

"Are you hurt?" Emmet's voice had her laughing.

"You're alive!"

"Of course I'm bloody well alive." She didn't need to see his frown to know it was there. "I'm coming down."

A long rope ladder was cast over the side of the ship and left to dangle many feet from her current position. Emmet swung himself over the side of the ship and began to descend. The moment he was safely on the ground, she was going to kiss him. She didn't care who saw, if it got reported back to Simon, the Archives, or anyplace else. Somehow, without her realizing it, she'd grown to love this man, and there was nothing to stop her from telling him.

Before Emmet got a quarter of the way down, David began to shout. "Tesla! Move!"

She couldn't imagine why she would need to move, if there was a problem with the airship and he needed to land it, or what, but she knew better than to not listen. Emmet froze on the ladder, only to fumble for his pistol inside his greatcoat. "Nikki, get out of there!"

Hearing her pet name spoken with such frantic fear served as more of a motivator than anything. She struggled to her feet at the same time that she looked over to where Mary lay. The eyes were black no longer, the twin orbs now growing brighter as the soft whirl of a motor deep inside her started back to life. The metal squealed as the automaton sat itself up, a low buzzing noise spilling out from the mouth.

Nicola backed away as slowly as she could. The earlier shouts started again as several of the Sentry started to come down the riverbank to where they were. They opened fire, forcing Nicola to jump out of the way of the stray bullets. Pressed flush to the ground once more, she watched in horror as Mary got back to her feet, her head no longer sitting straight upon the constructed neck. She turned and snatched the closest attacker from the ground. Using him as a child would a bat, Mary swung him at the others, striking them down as she went.

The Sentry weren't ready for a second attack, most having come out to inspect the destruction and congratulate themselves on their easy victory. They now were left unprotected, easy targets for Mary to pick off a few at a time. Nicola wanted to rush to their defense, somehow find a way to stop the monster, but she was hurt and without resources. If a cannonball couldn't damage the clockwerk heart within, then there was little chance the Sentry would easily be able to stop her.

What they needed to do was short-circuit the creature, overrun her heart to force it to not work. She immediately wished there was a way she could use one of her inventions to stop the thing, but even the best of her ideas would require months to construct. Her energy coil would be the perfect thing, generating and forcing electricity into Mary's heart.

Nicola sucked in a breath and spun to face the Clock Tower that housed Big Ben. The tower that was crowned with an iron top, giving her both the metal and the structure she needed. It wouldn't be perfect, but if she were very lucky it would give them a chance.

One single opportunity.

"Emmet!" He was still hanging from the ladder and craned his head around to find her. "I'm coming up."

Nicola was fearless when it came to heights, throwing herself onto the rope ladder and dashing up the swaying rungs. It was slightly terrifying as the bitter winter wind began to blow off the river, tossing them both and forcing them to cling to the rungs. David shifted the position of the dirigible, bringing it closer to the nearest building, allowing it to act as a shield from the wind, giving them the ability to make their way to the top. Emmet was waiting for her, hands outstretched to assist. Slapping her hand to his wrist, they clung to one another for a moment before he helped her climb the side of the ship and set foot on the deck.

She'd no sooner managed her footing than she was pressed against the rail and engulfed by the man she thought she'd lost.

"Don't you ever scare me like that again." He spoke the words against her temple, kissing her skin between each one. "From now on you stay safe in a lab somewhere."

"Me, stay safe?" She pulled back and punched him in the shoulder, enjoying the way he grimaced. "I thought you'd been killed."

She shouldn't be this close to tears. The burning in the back of her throat should be easily swallowed down, pushed aside, but it refused to move. Emmet gently pulled her in once more and cupped her cheek with his hand.

"Let's take care of Mary, then you and I need to have a talk."

"No."

His frown pulled at his bottom lip, begging her to lean in and suck on it. Giving in to temptation, she kissed his mouth until he gave in with a groan and returned it. Their tongues sought and found each other, caressing until Nicola moaned with want. She pushed her hand beneath his greatcoat and waistcoat, until she could feel his beating heart against her frozen fingers. They broke apart at the same time, and Nicola knew she couldn't wait a single moment more.

"I love you." They weren't her words, but his. Cupping her face, he kissed each eyebrow then the tip of her nose before ending with a chaste kiss on her lips. "I love you more than I can express. I want to spend hours telling you, showing you how deep my feelings run, but I can't. We can't. Mary is down there and people are dying."

Shit. Nicola blushed as she stepped back. "You're right. David?"

"Hullo." She hadn't seen him standing the short distance away in front of the large wooden wheel. "I hate to rush your reunion, but it appears my brother has arrived with reinforcements. If you have a plan, I say now is the time to enact it. I'd prefer Rory is alive when this is all said and done, despite him being a massive pain in my side."

With one final look at Emmet, Nicola shoved all her tender feelings aside for the time being. "Don't think we are done with this."

His smile, one of the few genuine one's she'd seen from him, had his eyes sparkling. "I wouldn't assume otherwise."

"David, can you bring me close to Big Ben's tower?" With Emmet at her side, she strode the length of the dirigible up to the bow of the compact ship. "I think the only way we'll be able to stop Mary is to overload her power source. It's well protected in the casing, so we'll need a strong blast of electricity."

Emmet shouted above the increasing wind. "How will you do that?"

It would have taken her too long to explain, and as much as she loved Emmet, his wasn't a mechanically oriented mind. Rather than waste any more of their rapidly decreasing time, she dropped to her knees and began to empty her pockets of the items she'd been collecting over the course of the day.

"I have this...device that I've been experimenting with. It's the aether, you see. The atmosphere generated by tiny, energetic particles as they jump between copper. I can generate a path for the electricity to move. Simon had me working on a way to generate light and heat back at the Company."

"The Clock Tower is made of iron. Uncle Edmund said as much."

"Yes, but the steam pipes." She stopped with two glass tubes clutched tightly in her hands. "The steam pipes are made of copper. They're supposed to be coiled around the inside of the spire, used to heat the building. They'll be my primary coil."

Emmet stared at her and finally gave his lips a lick. "You don't need me for this. You need another clockwerker." He went to where David held the steering wheel and shoved him out of the way. "Help her."

David didn't leap at the opportunity to assist, something she knew went against his very nature. Any man who could build his own personal dirigible wouldn't hesitate to play with electricity. There was something holding him back, and it didn't take a genius to figure out what it was.

"I promise you I won't breathe a word of this to the Company. They will know you were here as support, but not to the extent. I won't let them pull you back in, if that's what you're concerned with."

As the seconds ticked on, Nicola couldn't afford to wait for his response. She begun to build the capacitor, though with the supplies she had, the size wouldn't allow for much of a charge. She'd need to find more, or a bigger jar.

David squatted beside her. "What do you need?"

"A Leyden jar would be ideal, though something larger will allow for a stronger charge."

"I have just the thing." And he disappeared below deck.

Emmet was steering the ship closer to the clock face, now fully lit in the night. It was beautiful and an impressive display of engineering ingenuity. She prayed it wouldn't be damaged as a result of what they were about to do.

"Is this going to work?" Emmet's voice was nearly swallowed up in the rising wind.

"It better." She didn't know how, but Nicola suspected Mary wouldn't stop once she'd exacted her revenge on Thomas. They were all in danger.

* * *

Cold. It took greater effort to move now. One step. Another. Slow and steady. But it was now so cold. She didn't feel pain any longer. She couldn't because she was dead. Was this hell then? She looked at her arm, no longer attached where it should be, lying silent on the ground. She didn't need it. There was nothing for her to hold on to any longer.

The boy, Keegan.

She'd grown used to his company. It wasn't love she felt for him. Could she feel anything? Not possible to love when one died. How long had it been? How long had Thomas kept her cold, lifeless body?

There was a time when Mary knew he'd loved her. In the beginning, when she was young and pretty. She'd never questioned it. Others thought Thomas had been sweet on Nicola, but Mary knew different. He saw her for what he could take, use, monetize. Money. Fame. Notoriety.

Mary was different. She'd seen a different side of him. The way he'd dote on their children. Dot. Dash. Will. He'd cared for her as well. Even when the pain had come, grown into something neither of them understood.

Men were around her now. Shouting. She turned and their images filled her mind, allowing her to see everything. They tried to stop her. Wanted to keep her from getting to him. To stop her from snapping his neck.

She hated Thomas.

She wanted him to die.

Why couldn't he have left her to rot, to move on to heaven, where she'd have found her rest? She'd escaped the pain, finally able to close her eyes and not feel as though her head would split wide. No, he couldn't give her the gift of peace because he was selfish. He didn't want to face life without her.

Not fair. Stay with me, love.

No.

"Load the cannon again! Fire when ready!"

The cannon. She'd forgotten the name. There were giant gaps in her mind where things should live. Words. Thoughts. Feelings. Yes, a cannon. It would need to be destroyed, lest it take her other arm.

More men swarmed around her. New arrivals from the Tower. There was the one whose mind was like Keegan's. She could reach out and talk to him. Did so now. Buzzing in his mind as she scratched around, learning his secrets.

He could make the metal do things, too, would try to harm her if possible. Mary increased the buzzing, knowing it would hurt him. Keep him from hurting her. His friend came to his side, a man with a metal hand. Mary looked down once more at where her arm should be. Yes, when she destroyed them all she'd find a replacement.

Maybe Keegan would build her another.

If he lived.

Thomas would pay for what he'd done to the boy. It had made it easier for Mary to talk to him, but Thomas didn't know that. He thought the boy was expendable, an acceptable loss if it got him his Mary back.

But she wasn't back. She was living in a cold shell. Only a shadow of her former self. She'd never feel the warmth of skin on skin or enjoy the wet kisses of her children. She'd be forced to live a life of torture, all so Thomas wouldn't be alone. The bastard.

If he wanted to be with her, then that's what he'd get. She'd tear his body bit by bit until he was only a head. They'd do to him what they did to her. Pull her back from the doorstep of paradise as she was about to cross. Maybe they'd put him in an automaton as well. Then they could stare at each other through dead eyes for all eternity.

Chapter 23

Emmet was left to watch as Nicola and David worked on constructing the strangest device he'd ever laid eyes on. They'd stopped talking in complete sentences, somehow understanding what each other intended to do without speech. It was the sort of symbiotic relationship Samuel shared with Piper. It was what he wanted for himself, the only thing worth his sacrificing all he'd had.

A large copper circle now filled the majority of the dirigible's deck. David apparently had a plethora of odds and ends below deck, giving them what they needed to construct a rudimentary coil. He could tell by the way Nicola was fussing with it that she wasn't pleased with the result. The clockwerker in her wanted to continue to poke and prod, tweak until the end result was fascinatingly perfect. But as the screams from the dying men below reached them, they all knew that time was quickly running out.

"What do you need to do with that thing?" The wind has increasingly picked up as the night wore on, making it difficult to keep the dirigible steady.

David was sealing off the top of the largest glass bottle Emmet had ever laid eyes on. The scent of alcohol was no doubt burned into his nose, as David had poured the wine he'd been fermenting across the floorboards. "It's going to store the electricity until we can discharge it."

"How will you do that?"

"Don't know yet." Nicola looked up at him and grinned. "Can you bring the ship to the top of the spire? We're almost ready to do this."

Finally, a task to distract him. "Hold on."

* * *

Mary stumbled as another blast from the cannon flew past her. The rush of air sent her stumbling, nearly crashing to the ground. They weren't able to aim to hit her if she continued to move. The cannon was slower than she.

"Fire all you've got at her! Take the bitch down!"

She laughed. The sound erupted from her as she swung her arm wide, connecting with an unfortunate group of soldiers who thought they were being clever as they tried to outflank her. They were fools. And now they were dead.

She looked down and saw a man writhing on the ground. He had the same brown hair as Thomas, though worn longer. Mary stepped on him and crushed him into the ground with her heel.

Thomas.

The man who's head she invaded stepped out in front of the barrier, his hands held up. "Mary, stop!"

No. Never stop.

"I know what you want. You want us to bring Thomas out to you."

The man's name was Samuel. His wife called him Sam. She was with child. He'd only just learned of it and wanted to go to her now. All this rushed through her mind in a flash as he pushed the information out to her.

Dot. Dash. Will.

She stopped.

"These men are scared. You've terrified them, but I know you don't want anyone else to get hurt."

"What the bloody hell are you doing, Hawkins? Get back here," the man with the metal hand shouted, but Samuel didn't retreat.

"I'm ending this before anyone else dies." Samuel stepped closer, but still remained out of the reach of her arm. "I'm giving her what she wants."

* * *

The wind made the short distance to the Clock Tower challenging, and more than once Emmet had to fight to keep the wheel steady and prevent them from slamming into the building. Steadily, he managed to circle the tower as they rose, until they hovered near the very tip.

"Get beside it. We need to place this over the top." Nicola's short brown hair whipped around her face as she shouted. "We have no time to spare."

The muscles in his arms strained, but he was able to maneuver the ship exactly where they wanted. Then he was forced to watch the two clockwerkers struggle to lift the large copper ring and toss it over the side. For one breathless moment, he was certain the ring would be caught by a gust and blown off course, but then it hooked around the center and wobbled its way down in a lazy circle.

Nicola whooped her delight. "Now to connect the top to the copper steam pipes."

It was easier to release the air from the dirigible's balloon and allow the ship to sink quickly. Within seconds they were hovering in front of the clock face, and Nicola was retrieving her harpoon gun.

"Where did you get that?"

"Believe it or not, it's standard issue from the Company. It's David's."

Another mystery for another day.

Emmet held his breath as she fired the gun, the blade from the harpoon piercing the stone beside the clock. Without hesitation, Nicola jumped free of the ship and swung across to a small balcony used for repairs to the exterior. God, how he loved this woman.

"The capacitor!"

David had secured the glass jar into thick rope netting. He clearly intended to drop it over for Nicola, though the ways in which the glass could smash to shards far outnumbered its ability to get there safely.

"Wait!" With some coaxing, he was able to turn the airship to the side, and brought the ship up enough that the jar would be on level with Nicola on the balcony.

She cut the jar free and carefully took it inside. Now gone from sight, Emmet could only pray everything would fall into place.

"Once she connects the primary and secondary coils and installs the capacitor, it will only take a short time for the electrical buildup to occur. We'll simply need a way to direct the current."

*　*　*

Mary dug around inside Samuel's head, looking for the deception she had no doubt was lurking within. He'd either grown accustomed to her prodding, or she was losing some of her strength. Neither possibility was good.

If it was a lie, she could find no trace of it. Samuel would bring her Thomas. She knew the others wouldn't understand her words—her voice box must have been damaged in the blast—but she let loose a loud roar, the speaker Keegan had used for her voice box echoing through her metal.

She wanted to cry, but was not capable. The other emotions she knew she should have—fear, frustration, loneliness—none of it resonated. They were only words. Empty as her shell. She had only her anger.

Keegan had told her he'd put great love into the crafting of her heart, the power source that forced her to move on. She wished he hadn't, that it would wind down and stop working. That she could die.

"Mary, I need you to promise me that you won't move." Samuel's voice rang clear. "Don't hurt anyone else while I have Thomas fetched or they'll think you can't be trusted. Then you'll never get what you want."

She would. If she had to tear the city apart brick by brick, she'd get her prize in the end. For now she'd wait. Lowering her arm to her side, she continued to scan the group of soldiers, watching for any sign of betrayal. They were nervous. Scared. Wanted to fight her, but not sure how to win. She could tell they trusted Samuel, but they wanted vengeance for the blood she'd spilled.

It was something she understood.

Samuel nodded and shouted for someone to come. "Fetch Edison. Quickly."

"Sergeant?"

"I gave you an order. Now move!"

The man scurried away, leaving her standing face to face with the man who could talk to machines. Curious, she pushed a thought out to him much the same way she had with Keegan.

You know what I will do to him.

Samuel stiffened, stumbled back slightly. His mind was too bright, where Keegan's had been dulled by the drugs. But something must have come through, for the next thing she knew he crept closer. Nearly into range of her arm.

"Are you trying to speak to me?"

* * *

Nicola's hands shook as she quickly installed the large Leyden jar in place. It wasn't ideal, still damp from David's wine and not nearly big enough to contain the electricity she hoped would be created. It was possible that the electricity would be too much for it and the glass would shatter, cutting through the skin and bone of anyone unfortunate enough to be standing in the way.

Her final task was to find an adequate power supply.

The clock minder had explained to them on their abbreviated tour that castle and Clock Tower were self-contained when it came to power. Their steam generators were housed beneath the ground in a tunnel, though the energy created was pushed into where it needed to go. It had been installed by the Hudson's Bay Company, which meant the technology would be familiar to her.

She simply needed to find a way to plug in.

The clock mechanism had originally been intended to be wound daily as a means of keeping time. The clock minder had been quite put out when an electric power source had been installed the previous year. The energy flowed from the base of the tower through a hollowed out core and into the bottom of the machine. Nicola dropped to her hands and knees, frantically searching for the copper wiring that would grant her the power she needed to make her electricity coil function.

The thick bundle of cabling was visible running through the bottom on the far left side. Stretched out as far as she could go, she pulled on the bundle with all her might. For a moment, she wasn't certain it would come free. But bit by bit she worked it loose, until she jerked it from its mooring with a thud. The pulse of live electricity hummed between her hands as she carefully slid it free from the metal clock mechanism.

One wrong touch and she'd be burned to a crisp. She'd been witness to the end result of a Company man's experiment gone wrong, and had no intention of ending up in the same manner. With exacting moves, she put the live power source in place and backed away from the capacitor.

The air in the small room hummed, and the hair on her arms and the back of her neck stood straight up. The lights in the room flared bright, several of them exploding from the rush of electricity. Strange, she hadn't considered that all devices might be impacted. She'd simply hoped to generate a strong enough blast of power to stop Mary.

Think about this later!

It would only be a matter of minutes for everything to be ready. She needed to get to the ground for the final piece to be fitted, or all her work would be for nothing.

* * *

Time held little meaning to Mary. It was only a means by which those who had life measured the ticking down of it. An hour in the presence of a person you respected. Five minutes while a man thrust into your body. Days where pain continuously throbbed through your body. None of that mattered to her.

She was dead.

She was infinite.

She was immortal.

"They're getting him, Mary." Samuel didn't once look away from her. Whether he was looking for some sign of betrayal on her part, or simply did not want the distraction his men provided, she did not care. "Thank you for trusting me."

Trust?

Did she trust any longer? Was that something she could do, existing inside a metal shell? No, this wasn't trust. This was nothing more than the inevitable turn of events. They'd bring Thomas to her. She'd kill him. They'd try to kill her.

And time would tick on.

A rush of voices behind her. Shouting and orders, though not directed at her. It was then that she felt the soft rush against her mind, the gentle caress of the one person who cared for her in her current state.

Keegan?

"Mary." He stumbled into sight, slipping past the guards, who wouldn't get closer. "Mary, what are you doing?"

I'm getting my revenge.

"But they're going to kill you."

They can try.

"Boy, you need to move back." Samuel was faster and far stronger than the boy, snatching him up in his arms. "She'll kill you."

Keegan struggled to get free. "No, she won't!"

Yes, I will.

He stilled and looked up. "What?"

"Are you talking to her? Can you hear what she's saying?"

Samuel set Keegan down, but held him by the shoulders to speak to him. "I think she's been trying with me, but I can't make out the words."

"Aye." Keegan licked his lips and looked over to her. "She talks in me head."

"We need to get her to stop. To stand down. Do you think you can convince her?"

You know what I want. They will bring him to me and I will make him pay.

"No. She'll never stop. Not until Mr. Edison's dead."

Mary's ears easily picked up Samuel's muttered curse. "There has to be another way."

"Make way!"

The moment Thomas emerged from behind the barrier, hands shackled in front of him, guards on either side, she knew this was the end. He'd refused to let her go into death. She refused to be stuck in this hell alone.

Have them send him to me.

Keegan looked between her and Thomas. She knew the boy felt a connection to her husband, despite what he'd done to him. When one has known nothing but hardship, it was easy to appreciate the glow of respect when given by another. Even if the motivation behind it is less than pure.

Send him to me.

"Mary—"

NOW!

Keegan's legs buckled and he would have fallen had it not been for Samuel. "She wants him sent to her."

Samuel looked at his men and nodded. They pushed Thomas forward and withdrew their pistols, discouraging him from turning back. Thomas' snarl was familiar, as was the proud tilt of his head as he walked straight past Samuel and the boy, out into the open center.

"I'm here."

If Mary's heart were capable, it would be racing in her chest. This was it. Her moment of revenge. Something that no one would take from her.

It was then that everything went to hell.

Chapter 24

Nicola raced to the outside of the Clock Tower, relieved to see Emmet and David still holding the ship strong in the wind. She would have shouted to them, but David waved his hands and pointed down. From this distance with only lamps as light, she couldn't make out faces below. Not that she needed to. Mary was clearly visible, as was a lone man walking toward her, the crowd parting to give him room.

Thomas.

"Shit." The stairs would take her far too long to descend and her grappling gun didn't have a cord long enough to get her safely to the ground. That left only one option. "I need to jump back!"

"Are you out of your mind?" Emmet's voice was carried away on the wind. "You'll die."

She didn't wait for him to approve and stepped onto the thin railing. "Move closer!"

The two men spoke to each other and in a flash David took control of the dirigible while Emmet leaned over the side, arms outstretched. "Get ready."

Another gust pushed the ship away, forcing David to fight the wheel and pull it back on course. Nicola counted to five and stepped up another rung. She'd have to launch herself without hesitation and pray that it would be enough to see her to safety. The ship drew closer, Emmet stretched out, and Nicola took the final step, only to have the dirigible come too close.

Now unbalanced, Nicola pinwheeled her arms, trying to prevent the inevitable fall. Backward and she'd crack her skull. Forward and she'd die. Eyes wide, she looked up in time to see Emmet's hands reach for her, and she grabbed on.

The ship's stern slammed into the face of Big Ben and the silk from the balloon caught on the minute hand. There was the sickening sound of fabric rending as the ship lost buoyancy and began to fall from the sky. Emmet's grasp on her wrists was solid, and the position gave her room to mirror the hold. She would be crushed if she couldn't get back onboard, smashed between the hull and the stones of the tower.

For an instant, she pictured this as the end of her life. There would be many who'd mourn her passing. Colleagues and employers, customers who would always be left to wonder what new trinket or machine she'd come up with next. Simon might even shed a tear, though that particular image didn't seem right at all.

Other than her parents and her brothers, she wouldn't leave many loved ones behind. She'd never wanted a family of her own, not even a partner with whom to share a bed on the cold winter's evenings. With her gaze locked onto Emmet's, the fear and love she saw staring back at her told her how wrong it would be for her life to be over without know what it was like to be forever in the company of someone who owned her heart.

"I love you." The words were blown away by the wind, but she knew he'd heard them all the same from the softening of his eyes. "I love you."

With a growl, he pulled her hard, dragging her halfway into the ship. "Use your feet to find purchase!"

Now ignited into action, she kicked at the hull until she found footing on a groove. On the next pull, she was able to kick off, forcing her body the rest of the way onto the deck. There was no time to celebrate their triumph as David wrestled with the ship's wheel. "Hang on!"

The hull landed hard on the ground, sending wood flying as it crushed against the frozen ground. Nicola screamed as they were cast about until, as suddenly as the world erupted, it went silent once more.

Voices below them, calling to them, a stark reminder than their task was far from completed. Shaken, but not broken, Nicola got to her feet and held out her hand for Emmet to take. "Work to do."

He took hold of her wrist and pulled himself up. "And don't think we won't discuss your revelation later."

Blushing, she ignored him and jumped over the side of the ship to the ground.

Their unexpected landing had been a surprise to all, including Mary, from the look of events. Thomas was lying on the ground, crawling back toward the barricade that appeared to have absorbed a great deal of punishment from the automaton. Mary's attention had been drawn by their crash, as she now approached them with long, steady strides.

"What do we need to do?" Emmet's breath came out in hard pants and he squeezed her hand. "I'm no scientist, but I can follow directions."

She looked up in time to see the first bolt of electricity shoot out into the night's sky from the spire of the Clock Tower. They would lose the opportunity to use the aether discharge if she couldn't get the copper in place.

"I need her chest plate opened up and this put on." She pulled the copper brick from her deep jacket pocket. "It will draw the electricity from the tower and overload her heart."

Emmet scanned the crowd as a grin slipped onto his face. "I'll get it opened. You do what you need to so we can end this." And he was gone in a flash.

She wouldn't be able to place the brick from close range, which meant she'd need to throw it. Her aim had always been good, but there was too much of a margin of error to go simply on trust. She needed a guarantee.

* * *

Emmet gave Mary a wide berth, circling around until he reached Samuel. "We need to get her chest plate open."

"Why?"

"Nikki has a plan, but we need that thing's heart exposed." Turning to his friend, Emmet dropped all pretenses he normally wore around Samuel. "I know you can make metal do things. Can you do it?"

Samuel looked between him and Mary before closing his eyes. Emmet couldn't pretend to understand his friend's gift, but if this worked he would be forever grateful to him for it. He needed this nightmare to be over before anyone else got hurt.

A flash of Nicola hanging from the side of the dirigible slammed into him, forcing a shudder. So many times he could have lost her over the past few weeks, gone before he'd gotten up the courage to make things right. He loved her, and now he knew that she loved him back. She'd given him a gift he had no intention of squandering.

Samuel huffed before he swayed to the point of falling. Emmet caught him, but not before he dropped to his knees.

"Every time I try, she feels it. She gets in my head and screams, pushes back. I can't get close enough to make it work."

"I can try."

The two men looked up to where Keegan stood, pale and shaking. He barely looked to have the strength to stand, let alone be able to take on the metal monster. Emmet reached out and put a hand on the boy's shoulder. "It could be that the lock is damaged and cannot be opened."

"It's not. There's a trick to it." He pulled a large key from his trouser's pocket. "I can distract her so you can use the key."

"Keegan—"

"This is all my fault. I built her. I chose each part of her with care. Loved her. Then she turned wrong." Tears welled up in his eyes, but they stubbornly remained where they were. "I need te help fix this."

Oh, Emmet understood that feeling. He'd been left on the outside his entire life, wanting to do something, be a key part to *anything* that would make a difference. It's why he'd tried to impress his father by partaking in so many wild adventures as a child. Why he'd chosen to walk away from his privilege and wealth to join the Archives. But through every adventure, every case, he'd been left a little bit hollow. He'd been wrong in chasing status. He should have followed his heart.

It was the last time he'd make that mistake.

Getting to his feet, he took Keegan by the shoulders and moved closer to Mary. "What do you need to do?"

"I can get her to stop, force her to listen to me. I won't be able to give you much time, but it should be enough for you to use the key and get her chest plate open."

Mary was outright attacking the remnants of David's dirigible, sending splinters flying through the air. "Let's do this now."

* * *

Nicola stood in the base of the Clock Tower looking once more for an energy source. She'd managed to find a steel pipe from the barricade and a strip of cloth. While it wasn't possible to magnetize copper, the steel would work perfectly. Bound together, it would keep the copper in place to draw the power directly into Mary's heart.

If she could manage to get it magnetized.

The power running up to her coil was creating a magnetic field that filled the air. Her hair rose and her skin tingled from the power. Streaks of lightning shot from the top of the tower, arcing through the sky. It would start to jump to other buildings, rods, and roofs, anywhere but where she needed it to be. She needed to hurry.

There!

Dropping to the ground, she pulled out the cable that ran into the small secondary machine that appeared to shunt any excessive energy away from the Clock Tower. The bars clanged onto the floor where she dropped them. Splitting the wires, she pressed one to each side, ignoring the sparks and the pain as the energy flowed through the steel. The magnetic field wouldn't last long, but it should be enough.

It was time to end this.

* * *

Keegan stood directly behind Mary, his eyes closed and hands at his side as Emmet looked on. The key was warm in Emmet's hand, making his palm sweat. Another explosion of electricity shot from the top of Big Ben, this time connecting with the flagpole onto the castle. The flag burst into flames before disintegrating into ash.

They were out of time.

"Come on, boy."

Mary lifted her arm, but froze before her metal hand connected with the group of Sentry men who'd come around the corner, rifles out. He managed to wave them off in time, preventing a deadly distraction. The automaton turned to face the boy, stepping closer to him. Keegan's body began to shake, sweat clearly visible on his skin despite the cool winter air. Mary stilled and the light in her eyes dimmed.

Now.

Key in hand, Emmet raced toward the metal monster and climbed up the side of her body that lacked an arm. The metal was hot beneath his hands, burning his skin and forcing him to shove the key into his mouth. Falling and breaking his neck was a death he didn't particularly want, far from the heroic passing he'd often envisioned as a child.

The chest plate was damaged, dented inward to the point where the seams were strained. The keyhole was undamaged, giving him the first rays of hope that the outcome might play to their advantage. He shoved the key into the lock, prayed silently to the God he wanted so much to believe in, and turned it hard.

Nothing happened.

"Shit." He slipped his fingers into the seam and tugged, but the metal refused to budge. Risking a look at Keegan, he could see the boy's body vibrating now. It was only a matter of time before he'd lose his control over Mary and Emmet's life would be over.

Another bolt from the Clock Tower struck out, this time connecting with the barricade, sending the metal and wood exploding out. Men screamed as they ran, several falling from the impact of the shrapnel. If he didn't hurry, they were all going to die.

* * *

Keegan's stomach soured, his chest ached, and his brain throbbed. He could feel Mary pressing against his mind, trying to break through the cage he'd wrapped around her.

Why are you doing this? Let me have my vengeance!

"I can't."

You of all people must understand. They took your mother, your father. You were cast to the streets, left to fend for yourself with boys who cared nothing for you.

"I know."

Then let me free! I shall destroy Thomas. I'll make the others pay. You and I will be free to go where we want.

"I can't."

Traitor! You'll die with the others. I have no feelings. I'm incapable of caring for you. Your life will be snuffed out as easily as the others.

"I know. I'm sorry."

He closed his eyes as her screams filled his head.

* * *

"Emmet!" Nicola's voice was directly below him. "Can you manage?"

He ignored her in favor of pulling harder on the chest plate. The metal gave a little, reigniting the flame of hope. He needed to put a bit more muscle behind it and...

The chest plate popped open, sending him off balance and nearly crashing to the ground. Breaking his neck in full sight of the woman he loved was low on his list of how he wanted his life to end.

A glowing light shining down from the head casing illuminated the chest cavity. The heart was still contained within its metal cage, ticking softly in the night. Emmet held on with one hand and reached down with the other.

"Throw it up."

Nicola grinned and climbed Mary's leg high enough to be able to slap the metal rods into his waiting grasp. "It's magnetized. Place it anywhere near the heart and get the hell out of there."

The sky cracked once more as an explosion of lightning bolts shot from the face of Big Ben. Emmet did not want to be on the receiving end and burned to a crisp, so he turned and slapped the steel bar to the heart's casing, leaving the copper side out. Another explosion—one, two, five bolts all touched down on the ground, each strike drawing closer to Mary's unmoving body.

The air around them suddenly grew heavy, as though the energy was being drawn from all around them. Nicola had already turned and ran toward the safety of the Clock Tower. The rest of the Sentry had done so as well, Samuel dragging Edison along with him. Only Emmet and Keegan remained in harm's path.

* * *

Keegan knew his control over Mary was nearly over. His body and mind were too weak, too damaged from the drugs, to be able to stand against her any longer. He prayed it had given the man and Miss Tesla enough time to do what they needed.

"I'm going to miss you," he whispered into the night.

I will not.

Then his world went black.

* * *

Emmet jumped free from Mary's body as a sky-rending crack boomed through the air. The force of the lightning bolt striking the automaton pushed him higher and farther than he would have managed on his own. As the ground rushed at him, Emmet had barely enough time to tuck his body into a ball and roll, delaying his death and serious injury to another day.

When he looked up, Mary stood rigid. The beams of electricity continued to pound into her metal frame in wave after wave, like water upon a beach during a storm. The stench of melting metal permeated the air. The frozen ground around her feet melted, leaving a puddle of muck and burned grass. Another crack filled the air, this time accompanied by an explosion of glass. He had just enough time to see the clock faces of Big Ben rupture out into the dark night, illuminated by lightning.

"Fuck!"

He scrambled to his feet and grabbed Keegan. They would be cut to shreds if they didn't reach shelter. The Sentry had all crowded into the base of the Clock Tower. Samuel and Nicola stood in the doorway, yelling and waving for him to move.

They'd never make it in time.

Emmet pulled the boy as far as the barrier before the first shards began to rain down onto their heads. Dropping beside one of the cannons, he pulled a piece of metal from the barricade, held it above their heads, and prayed.

The glass beat over them for several long seconds, reminding him of being trapped outside in a hailstorm. He counted the time down in his head, needing a distraction. By the time he got to twenty, the noises had ended and everything was disturbingly still.

"Sir?" Keegan's weak voice sounded loud in the small space. "Is it over?"

Pressing the boy tighter against his chest, safe beneath the metal, Emmet looked around the edge. Mary was laying flat on the ground, her metal blackened and smoldering. The sky was presently clear of any lightning bolts, though he couldn't be certain more weren't possible.

"Emmet!"

Nicola bolted from the Clock Tower directly for them. He tossed the metal aside and picked Keegan up in his arms. When she reached them, she wrapped her arms around them both, kissing their cheeks and checking their bodies for injury. "Are you hurt? Let me see."

"We're fine. What about your machine? Are we still in danger?"

"I think the capacitor has blown. I'll need to disconnect the power source to be sure it's off but—"

"I'll do it." Emmet looked over to where David stood beside his brother. Both men looked relived, if not exhausted. "I think you've worked your fair share today, Miss Telsa."

"Thank you." She clung a bit tighter.

Samuel shouted directions at his men, though they all kept a wide berth around Mary's remains. "Edison is back in his cell.

I suggest once we ensure your machine is turned off and the wounded have been cared for, we all retire for the evening."

Rest. Yes, sleep and recovery. Then he'd determine what his next course of action would be. Give up the life he'd sacrificed everything to have, or give up the woman who'd taken his heart.

Chapter 25

Nicola stretched out across the length of her bed, reveling in the feel of the fresh cotton against her bare skin. Her body still ached. The muscles in her arms and back caused her to twinge whenever she'd turn in just the wrong way, reminding her of her adventures along the wrong side of the dirigible's hull. Her feet throbbed only when she walked, an improvement over her hobbled state when she'd first entered her bedchamber after the incident with Mary.

But it was the ache between her thighs that currently held her attention.

She turned her face so her nose was now pressed to the sheets. The scent of sex clung to them, a reminder of her recent activities. Sweat had transferred from their skin to the fabric; it made her hair stick to the side of her face and sent a chill through her body. She wouldn't change a thing. Though the bed was now cold from the absence of his body heat, the mattress still held the impression of Emmet's body.

Emmet.

Grinning as a debutante would, Nicola closed her eyes and

ran her fingers down the side of her throat, wishing he was here. They'd spent the better part of two days in this room, eating, bathing, sleeping, making love, learning each other. They didn't speak of the future, of what they would do now that the danger had passed. Hell, she hadn't even inquired about Thomas and what his fate would entail. She wasn't foolish enough to believe he'd pay for his sins. The owner of the Illuminating Company had more money and influence than the common man, and would never be subjected to a common fate. She had no doubt their paths would cross again.

Only next time, she'd be ready for him.

Nicola closed her eyes, her thoughts going back to the man who'd unexpectedly shown her what true love was. Emmet had been pulled away from their bed by a summons from the Guild Masters. They demanded their report, and nothing Emmet could say to their representative would deter them. His last kiss still lingered on her lips, his deep rumbling words of love in her ears. This was worth letting her barriers fall, worth any potential heartache because for the first time in her life, she felt electrified.

There was a time when she'd believed that forging intense personal relationships would hinder her creativity, would cloud her ability to remain objective and clear-minded when it came to her inventions and scientific discovery. Pleasures of the body would interrupt the logical flow of the mind.

What a fool she'd been.

This wasn't the same rush she got when an experiment went right. While her heart would race with excitement and she'd rattle off her findings to her closes colleagues, it never gave her the same sense of satisfaction. Simon had often denied it, but she knew the others were jealous of her creations. Jealous that a woman was outperforming them and had gained high praise from the Company. There was none of that with Emmet, and not because they were from different professional backgrounds and he didn't care. He did care, quite a bit. She could see the pride shinning at her when she'd spoken to Sergeant Hawkins and Constable Timmons. No, he saw her as equal parts the woman he cared for and a brilliant scientist.

And that was the reason she loved him.

She must have drifted off, for the knock on the door had her sitting bolt upright and sent her heart racing. Damn, she was going to miss the leisure that privacy provided her. "Who is it?"

"A message for you, miss." She slipped on her robe and opened the door enough to catch sight of the blushing maid, a message tube in her hand. "This arrived this morning. We didn't think you and your, ah...friend would want to be disturbed."

This morning she'd tied his hands to the headboard while she climbed on top of his body to ride his cock. That had been a pleasant distraction. "Thank you. Your discretion is appreciated."

The maid scurried away the moment Nicola took possession of the tube. She'd have to remember to leave a little extra something for the poor girl. Closing the door, she carried the message tube over to the chair closest to the fireplace. The wood cracked and snapped. Heat from the fire wasn't necessary as the room had been fitted with steam pipes, but she preferred the ambiance.

Yellowed paper slid from the tube, sporting the seal of the Hudson's Bay Company. She'd been expecting a message from Simon for some time now. She had no doubt he'd been told of her misadventures and most likely was going to admonish her for not heeding his advice sooner. But as she broke through the stag's head and unrolled the scroll, Nicola was surprised at what she saw.

Hello, Nikki.

I would normally start with a lecture on how you need to listen to me better as it will save you a great deal of heartache in the future, but I won't. It's come to my attention that you have formed a bit of an attachment to one of the zombies since your arrival. You know we don't care about what you do in your personal life as long as it doesn't impact your work. Well, I care, but I've accepted long ago that ours will always be a professional relationship.

My sources are quite good, as you are aware. I've heard things that have caused me concern. All I can say is that you have my blessing. I trust you to know what you're doing. You might be a bit mad, Nikki, but you've got a good heart. It's a good thing that you've finally started listening to it.

And for the record, you were right. Turning the Clock Tower into an energy coil that way. Brilliant. Simply brilliant. I expect you to work on the plans when you get back. The opportunities to expand on what you've done are endless. Though we'll have to refer to it as a Tesla Coil, because Jacobs has his sonar coil contraption that he's been working on. We'll need to keep it straight.

I'll book your passage home for three days' time. I'll book extra space in case you need it for equipment, trunks... other important things.

Come home. The frozen North isn't the same without you.

Simon

How the hell had Simon known that much about Emmet? And what the hell had he meant by she had his blessing? One of these days, she was going to have a long chat with him about the idiocy of speaking in riddles to a woman of science.

More footsteps approached, only this time there was no knock chasing it. She tucked the note away and listened as the person paced outside her doorway for several minutes, before her frustration got the better of her.

"Emmet, if you don't come in you're going to traumatize the maid." She didn't need to hear his huff to know he'd blown one out.

He stepped through the door, closing it with a quiet precision she'd come to recognize as his nature. He continued to stand by the door, his hand holding the handle and his gaze locked on the window. Since they'd taken up residence in her bed after Mary's destruction, Emmet had been far more relaxed in his manner. This wasn't the man she'd grown accustomed to.

"What's wrong?" She pulled her robe tighter around her and started to her feet.

"Don't get up."

"All right." The cushion swallowed her bottom and legs as she relaxed once more. "Are you going to tell me what the matter is?"

"Yes." He finally released the handle and stepped a few paces more into the room. "I don't know quite how to put it."

"Will it help or hinder if I'm naked?" Flipping one side of her robe over the chair, she enjoyed the rush of air against her naked breast. "I'm open to discussing options."

Emmet's gaze traveled down her exposed side, lingering on her thigh. "You don't play fair, do you, Nikki?"

"Not if I can help it."

"The Administrators wanted to congratulate me on not only

seeing to the repairs of the Archives central machine, your safety, the destruction of Mary, and the continued safety of New London, but also for undergoing an extraction under less than pleasant circumstances."

"That's good, right?"

"Yes." He patted the side of his thigh. She could smell the cold outside air that he'd brought in on his clothing. It was fresh and brought life to the room. Perhaps she could convince him to go for a walk after they made love again. "They've offered me a position of Administrator."

The idea of stripping him of his clothing quickly left her. "What?"

"It's an honor. I'm the youngest archivist to ever receive the appointment, which the Guild Masters stressed several times. It's the very thing I've worked toward, a position of status within the guild. Something even my father would be proud of."

She hadn't considered the thought that their time together would be coming to an end. Not a permanent one. But she had Simon's summons, and Emmet had finally found the position he'd always wanted. The outside world had come crashing down upon them, raining shards far sharper than the glass from the Clock Tower.

"When do you begin?" The pain in her throat and chest was entirely unexpected. She should make note of it, a detached observation on how the body responds to soul-wrenching grief.

Emmet slipped his greatcoat off, letting it fall to the floor without care. He held her gaze as he crossed the room, the white rings around his irises becoming more prominent with each step. The moment he reached her, he dropped to his knees and placed his head in her lap. The ragged roll of his breath across her naked thigh sent a shiver through her.

"It's the one thing I've always wanted. Position and status to make my father proud. Since I was a child, I was made to feel less worthy of his attentions than my brothers. He'd forbid me to join the Archives, but I forced his hand. I needed him to know I was my own man, capable of accomplishing my own feats of wonder."

She should be trying to distance herself, to keep what little dignity she had by not dissolving into a mess of tears. Her life had been complete before Emmet had crawled into her life inside the guts of a machine, it would be as complete when he crawled away.

It would be simply a little *less*.

"I should be ecstatic that I finally have what I want." He gripped her thigh with his hand.

She in return carded her fingers through his hair. "You're not?"

Neither of them spoke for a time. The snap and crackle of the fire slowed in frequency. The hiss of the steam through the pipes increased. A rush of pattering against the window pane drew her attention. It was snowing. That was something she did miss about her home in Canada. The quiet that would descend upon the land when the snow would come, giant flakes falling from the sky as one would drape a blanket upon the bed. She'd change the date of her return trip to tomorrow, if possible. There was no way her heart could bear it to stay in New London, knowing Emmet would be gone from her.

All I can say is that you have my blessing.

Nicola stilled her hand, her fingers buried deep in his fair locks. "Emmet?"

"Hmm?"

"Have you already accepted the position?"

"Not yet. I asked the Guild Masters for a day to collect my

thoughts. Used the excuse that I've only completed one extraction and might wish to continue on as an archivist for a bit longer. They were surprised, but agreed to the time."

The idea was more than a little mad. There were many things she hadn't considered, implications and fallout. If she gave herself more than a moment, she would realize that this was a terrible idea indeed.

You might be a bit mad, Nikki, but you're got a good heart. It's a good thing that you've finally started listening to it.

Tugging on his head, she couldn't stop herself from laughing at the confused look on his face. "Why are you looking at me as though I'm one of your experiments?"

"How do you feel about secondment?"

Even his frown appeared cute to her now. "What do you mean?"

"I think you should accept the role. It's critically important and one you've worked quite hard to obtain. You'd be a fool to cast it aside."

"Nikki—"

"And then they will receive a message from the Company thanking them for taking such good care of me. Management would like to offer their congratulations and thanks in person. It would be a way to further the good relations between the archivists and our own interests."

"You want me to give up my life and come to Canada?"

"No, I want to you take charge of your chosen profession and see it expanded. There is a lot the Guild Masters could learn from us about their central machine. This is critical information and would require extended study. Not the sort of thing an archivist could do, given the nature of their role."

She watched as his mind turned the idea over and over, looking for the flaw in her logic. She knew Simon would support her, would go to whatever lengths needed to help her bring Emmet home with her. They would then have the time away from the prying eyes of his overlords to see if this thing between them was as strong as she suspected.

Emmet slowly began to smile and rose to his knees. "You really are brilliant."

"I know." She leaned in and kissed him.

Their mouths opened as they deepened the kiss. Her tongue sought its mate, teasing the moist flesh with her tip. Her mind slowed and her senses picked up, reinforcing that this was exactly the right thing. They needed this, balanced each other. Nicola wrapped her arms around him and promised herself that she'd never let go.

"Nikki…" He sucked the side of her throat, pulling a gasp from her. "I love you."

"I love you, too." Tears filled her eyes as emotions overwhelmed her. "Come with me."

He chuckled, his mouth pressed to the skin below her ear. "How could I refuse?"

"Quite easily, I suspect. You would simply tell me that the third son of the Duke of Bedford would never subject himself—"

Emmet growled and yanked her from the chair so she landed hard on her ass on the floor. "Bastard!"

He pushed her robe aside, fully exposing her body. "You have no idea."

Nicola took hedonistic pleasure in watching him remove his clothing. First the boots went flying across the room, landing who knew where. Then the layers of the archivist's uniform fell bit by bit—black waistcoat, crisp white shirt, black pants—

until there was nothing left but Emmet the man, standing bared before her.

"You're the first person to see beyond and really notice me." He stood straight and proud, his cock already hard and thrusting toward the sky. "I never felt like a third son of a duke, or a zombie, or an outsider. You teased me. Spoke to me, in a way even my friends never quite managed."

Emmet dropped to his knees and placed a hand on each of her knees. They'd been here enough over the past three days that she knew what to expect from him now. He was a man who preferred to make the most of what he was given. Leaning forward, he hooked his hands beneath her thighs and lowered his face to her pussy.

Oh, she could spend a lifetime with him and never grow tired of this. The press of his tongue around her clit had her moaning in pleasure and anticipation. He'd somehow trained her to crave his touch, her body growing wet from the closeness of his body to hers. She could only imagine it would get worse the longer they were together, and relished finding out for certain.

Sucking her clit into his mouth, Emmet pushed two fingers into her waiting body. He'd taken to fanning them out, stretching and teasing her, touching deep inside her in a place that made her see stars. All she could do was hold on and let the sensations wash over her. She'd tried to stop them, to hold the pleasure back until she was ready for the mind-blowing rush. All pointless. He was relentless, sucking and coaxing her body to give up what he wanted from her. So she lifted her legs so they rested upon his shoulders, held his head tight and closed her eyes.

He circled her clit with his tongue before lowering his mouth and licking the skin around where his fingers lay. With his free hand, he reached up and found one of her hard nipples, squeezing the tip in time with the flick of his tongue. Her body responded, her hips bucking gently to the pace he set.

"Killing me," she whispered and turned her head to the side. Heat from the fireplace washed over her skin, adding to the torrent of sensations racing through her.

He chuckled again, this time with his mouth against her thigh. "You want me to end it all?"

"Please."

"You want me to make you scream?"

"God, yes."

This was it. He pinched her nipple and sucked her clit hard. His fingers continued to thrust into her the way she wanted his cock to. Her body was an instrument he'd mastered, he a maestro and she his faithful follower. But as wonderful as this was, she wanted more from him. As the first tingling of her orgasm approached, she tugged at his head.

"Not like this. I want to feel you inside me."

His lips were wet from her and glowed in the firelight as he smiled. "Ah, sweet Nikki. Whatever you wish."

The floor was far from comfortable for either of them, but she was past caring. Bracing her feet she waited for him to position his cock between her legs and thrust hard into her pussy. They held still in that moment, staring at each other, their breathing falling into a rhythm. Her mind latched onto the idea that together they were as cog and gear, working as one to move the world around them. But in her heart she knew it was far simpler than that.

This was love.

Nicola bucked her hips again, encouraging him to move. She then tightened the muscles of her pussy, squeezing his cock as hard as she could manage. She'd discovered that little trick quite by accident during one of their previous lovemaking sessions. Emmet clearly appreciated it. His eyes rolled into the back of his head and he thrust into her without mercy.

Yes!

Her body had been primed for release before this, and it took little time for her to feel the return of the now familiar tingle of pleasure. Her breasts grew heavy and her nipples sent pleasing jolts down to her clit. Stars appeared in her vision and she knew she was racing toward the edge. She curled her body around Emmet's, pulling him as close as she could until the first waves of her orgasm slammed into her. She tensed, screamed, and writhed beneath him.

With his face pressed to her shoulder, he continued to pound into her. She turned her face, nearly breathless from the strength of her release, and kissed the shell of his ear. "I love you. I need you. Come for me."

Emmet growled before throwing his head back to cry out. The rush of his seed spilled into her pussy, giving her a sense of rightness. They hadn't done anything to prevent the possibility of children since their return. The idea of children no longer terrified her the way it once had, as long as they were with him.

Panting, their skin cooling and her back aching, Nicola placed a final kiss on his cheek. "So, will you do it?"

"Huh?"

"Come with me? I'll have Simon send the Guild Masters an official request. And by request I mean order. No one says no to Simon."

With his forehead pressed to her shoulder, he started laughing. "Does your brain ever shut off?"

What an odd question. "I don't believe so."

"Then I better get used to these non sequiturs if I'm to come with you."

She didn't bother to try to hold back the grin. "Most definitely you will."

"I'll endeavor to improve and keep up with your conversations. Oh, and Nikki?"

"Yes?"

"I love you, too."

Epilogue

Keegan stood in front of a large door of a house on Regent Street. This wasn't a part of town he was familiar with. The Underlings didn't work these parts and his family certainly wasn't of means. The card with the address printed on the front with an elegant script was now damp as he crushed it in his grasp. Nerves. The man wouldn't have given him the card in the first place if he hadn't wanted him to come.

That had been a strange visit itself. Not many nobs would come to see a sick street rat in the hospital. Not many would even pay attention enough to know he'd been sick. But he'd had a wide smile and eyes that danced when he spoke. It wasn't as though Keegan had anything to lose. With Glyn back in charge of the Underlings, he'd made it clear that Keegan was no longer welcome. Not that there was any way he'd be able to return there after what had happened to him.

The door knocker was a brass stag head, the antlers twisting up and embedding into the wood of the door. He'd never seen its like before. Before he lost his nerve, Keegan reached up and banged on the door twice before stepping away. If this turned out to be another thing like what Mr. Edison had pulled him into, Keegan intended to run as far and as fast as he could manage.

He counted to five in his head before the door was jerked open by the most beautiful woman he'd ever seen. Her long black hair was twisted up into a bun atop her head, with strands of hair having escaped to lay along the top of her shoulders. Her eyes were dark and her skin smooth and white. He'd seen plenty of Asian women before, but not one like her.

She wore a black corset with red dragons embroidered across the fabric. Her skirts were also black, but pulled up at the front to reveal black riding boots. Keegan wasn't sure how he knew, but this woman was dangerous.

"Well, now. It took you long enough." She put her hands on her waist and kicked her hips out to the side. "We've been in there watching you. You just cost me five pounds."

"Pardon, miss?" His voice was sore, and came out as an embarrassing croak. "I—I'm supposed te meet a man 'ear."

"Keegan, my boy!" The man with the dark hair and smiling eyes poked his head over her shoulder. "Aiko, you're scaring the lad."

"He should be scared." She lifted an elegant eyebrow. "Though of what is still up for debate."

"Oh, don't mind her. She's simply grouchy because Rory wouldn't let her share his bed with her last night." Aiko shoved her elbow into his stomach. "What, it's true!"

"And not for a child's ears."

"That's all right, miss. I've seen and heard plenty worse than that. Why there was that time when Glyn had two of them whores from down the road in his bed and they was—"

Aiko growled and hauled him into the foyer and slammed the door closed behind him. "That will be enough of that."

The man rocked onto the balls of his feet, still grinning. "Aiko, darling. Would you be a dear and fetch us some tea and biscuits? I do love your biscuits, especially the chocolate ones."

She narrowed her gaze and lowered her chin. "What are you up to?"

"Me? Not a thing." He turned and stuck out his hand for Keegan to take. "I'm David, by the way. I don't remember actually telling you my name when I saw you last."

He hadn't, but the nurses had muttered about him once he'd gone. *Quite handsome for a lunatic.* "Nice te meet ya, sir."

"Let's conduct our business in the study. I've always wanted to say that. Conduct business in the study." David chuckled, turned and strode away.

Keegan stared after him. "Is he always like that, miss?"

"No. He's not normally this well behaved."

Still, Keegan couldn't bring himself to follow. Aiko placed a gentle hand on his shoulder and bent forward to look him in the eyes. "I've heard what you've been through. I know you have no reason to trust me, but please do. David is brilliant, a touch mad, and one of the most loyal men I know. If he went to the trouble of inviting you here, then you can believe what he says as truth." She released him and left.

Now alone in the hallway, Keegan had two options—to follow David and see what he had to say, or leave. He knew neither of them would follow him, nor would they come looking for him. Stay or go, the choice was his.

The first step forward was the hardest, but a weight lifted with each continued one toward the study. The door had been left open and Keegan easily slipped inside. David sat on the desk, a glass of alcohol in his hand. He took a sip and waited to speak until Keegan was standing before him.

"Good lad. I knew you had a will of iron in that body of yours."

He downed the glass in one large gulp. "Now, you're wondering why I asked you here."

Keegan nodded. He was nervous, but no longer because he was scared of what David might do to him. No, he was nervous that he wouldn't be able to live up to the expectations.

"I saw what you did at the Clock Tower. You'd been wronged, were ill, and could have easily slipped away to care for your wounds. You didn't owe any of those people a thing, and yet you put your life on the line to save others. An admirable trait in one so young."

His face flushed and he found he couldn't meet David's gaze any longer. "Ta."

"You see, I'm always on the lookout for people such as yourself. Boys with special abilities and the strength of character to know how best to use them."

"But I didn't, sir." He bit down on his lip, but the words had already escaped him. "I mean, I made Mary for Mr. Edison. I should have known he was up te no good."

"Pish posh, never mind him. Edison fell off our radar for a while, but that won't happen again."

Keegan watched the happy-go-lucky man fade away and be slowly replaced by a different David. This man was as dangerous as Aiko, as strong and sure in his actions as Sergeant Hawkins. Keegan's heart raced and he began to question if he had in fact made a mistake. "No, sir."

"You see, there are many people out there who want to disrupt the lives we have here and in the new country. They want to tear us down after we've clawed our way back from the brink of destruction after the war with France. Those people, friends of men like Mr. Edison, are the real villains in this game we play."

Oh. Keegan had heard whispers in the night about this.

French and Spanish men turning up dead on the shores of the Thames. Fleets of airships flying off silently in the night, heading to destinations unknown. "And you stop them?"

"Well, we play our games, back and forth. It can be quite entertaining when we're not trying to kill each other." David stood up and placed a hand on Keegan's shoulder. "When you stepped in front of the automaton when men twice your age and experience went running away, I knew you were the exact sort I need to help me. You're brave and smart. The perfect combination."

"I am?"

"You are." David let him go once more and filled his glass once again with alcohol, Scotch from the smell of it. He then filled a second glass, taking it up in his hand when done. "Keegan, my boy, how you would like to be a spy?"

"For the king?" He didn't even think there really were such things as spies. Only tales told to keep the wee ones in line.

"No, His Majesty isn't exactly aware of our comings and goings. Though quite often our objectives line up." Keegan took the second tumbler from him and watched as he rolled up his shirt sleeve, revealing a tattoo of a stag's head.

It was exactly like the door knocker. "Yer with the Company?"

"Think of it more as a consortium. A brotherhood of spies, if you will." He let the fabric fall and reclaimed his own drink. "So, what do you say? What to join up?"

Keegan took a drink of the amber liquid, enjoying the way it burned on the way down. It was the furthest thing away from working for one of the Guilds, or being under the *protection* of the Underlings. Finishing his sip, Keegan stuck out his hand. "Aye."

David laughed and shook his hand in return. "Welcome to the Shadow Guild."

Please see the next page for an excerpt from

Gilded Hearts,

book one in the Shadow Guild series.

Chapter 1

The cold bite of the late fall air against Samuel Hawkins' cheek had long since caused it to go numb. Frost covered the ground and crawled up the sides of the surrounding buildings, making New London's Whitechapel district sparkle from the muted glow of the sulfur lamps lining the cobbled road. Samuel's shadow stretched across the stones, reaching out like a dark sentry alone in the night. His men had wandered a short distance away to take shelter beside the vacant remains of a clockwerker's factory, laughing quietly as they made plans to venture out to one of the local gambling hells afterward. He was the only holdout, standing guard over the corpse.

It had been hours since death had claimed the victim. The torn flesh and exposed organs, having crystallized, were now luminous upon inspection in the light. The body had bloated and twisted the gashed skin, making it impossible for Samuel to discern the identity of the victim. He'd given up trying to determine any distinguishing features almost immediately and instead took what comfort he could with his greatcoat fastened securely around him against the wind.

The damned archivists better hurry up before he joined this latest victim in death.

"Sergeant," Constable Rory Timmons called out. "Care to join us?"

"Someone needs to follow protocol, seeing as you lazy bastards won't." The men laughed even as Samuel stamped his feet, willing some of the feeling to return. Truth was, he never liked being in a crowd, even one as small as this group. "As I'm doing your jobs for you, having something to fight off the chill wouldn't go amiss right now."

With his back turned to them, he focused on the lamplit road ahead. It was a breach of protocol to have alcohol on duty, but he wasn't about to pass up the warming benefits of a drink.

A muted sloshing and clunk sounded behind him as a metal tin landed hard against the ground, quickly followed by the renewed chatter of the men. The flask was a pleasant weight in his hands as he fumbled with cold fingers to get it open. Shit, that was damned good. His body had reacted unfavorably the first few times he'd imbibed. Thankfully, he'd had five years of lonely nights to adjust to the alcohol's effects.

Tucking the flask in his pocket, Samuel turned toward the road, where a distant mechanical thumping was getting louder. His wrist strap buzzed, confirming the identification of the approaching carriage. "About bloody time."

The men rejoined him by the time the simple black carriage turned the street corner to begin its final leg of the journey. The glow of the horse's red eyes cast two pools of light as it pulled alongside the walking path, increasing the demonic appearance of the automaton. No one spoke until the carriage came to rest opposite them. A burst of steam shot from the leg joints of the mechanical horse as it settled into a resting stance. Its massive black metal head turned, and for a moment it appeared to be staring directly at Samuel. Someone behind him gasped as several more shuffled their feet.

"Go to sleep now," he whispered. The horse held his gaze a moment longer before another burst of steam blasted through its nose and it lowered its head.

His gift, the ability to manipulate machines with his will alone, was one few knew of. The Clockwerker Guild would have swallowed him whole had they known he could nudge and bend the metal to his desires. Still, being able to *speak* to the various automatons had been a comfort to him growing up, filling the void when he'd been alone.

"God, I hate this," one of the men muttered. "Fucking zombies and their creepy faces."

There was a time when the slur would have cut deep and Samuel would have grabbed the man by the throat in retribution. Thankfully, that time had long passed. The archivists weren't his family anymore, not his concern. He'd begun to replace them over the years, swapping the shadows for the light.

"Shut it, man. They have their job to do, same as us." Timmons' sharp bark was enough to silence further comment. He was a bear of a man who stood a full head taller than Samuel and generally terrified the newer recruits to the King's Sentry with his size, demeanor, and iron hand. "Sorry, sergeant."

A rush of frustrated embarrassment rolled off Timmons and through Samuel. Timmons had become quite protective of him over the years since Samuel had joined the King's Sentry. He'd been surprised by the steadfast relationship, but had few enough friends to question Timmons' motives and welcomed the brotherhood. "It's fine."

He had to consciously stop himself from holding his breath when the carriage door hissed open. This wasn't anything new; it shouldn't still bother him. But every time he came face to face with the archivists, he once again became a scared nineteen-year-old wandering the streets of New London, driven forward by the need to rise from the ashes of his old life, instead of the twenty-four-year-old man who'd fought the odds to earn a post with the King's Sentry.

And every time that carriage door opened, he was still looking for *her*.

Clenching his jaw, Samuel took his hands out of his pockets and straightened.

An old man emerged first, white head bobbing as he stepped down onto the stones. He was clad in typical archivist attire—black pants, waistcoat, and overcoat that highlighted a stark white dress shirt. The man was without a top hat, despite the chill in the air. His gaze roamed over the scene, pausing on Samuel.

Master Ryerson.

Blast it boy, again. Again! Until you get it correct you won't leave this room.

Of course it would be him.

Ryerson's gaze was as cold as the night air and cut as deep as the bitter wind. The old man's lips turned up in a sneer even as his gaze roamed over Samuel, no doubt cataloguing his appearance for future reference. Another set of data gathered and stored in that cold, clockwerk mind. Hate coursed through Samuel, though for once he didn't know if the emotion came from Ryerson or himself.

Empathic, that had been the term Ryerson spat at him when

Samuel was barely old enough to understand the meaning. A curse Samuel was constantly punished for possessing, despite not being able to prevent it from happening. It took him years of practice, of shutting everyone out, before he'd been able to function in the Archives as a member. Not that Ryerson ever gave him credit for his accomplishments, instead radiating disgust as he beat Samuel for his faults.

Since joining the King's Sentry four years ago, Samuel had managed to avoid seeing the Guild Master. The halls of the Tower were a safe haven for him, one where he could burrow deep, far away from the prying eyes of the Archives and the Masters who ran it. Of course now that he had risen to the rank of sergeant and was the lead investigator on many cases, a meeting had become inevitable.

You'll never make apprentice if you don't listen. Now stop crying, boy. Do it again. Properly this time.

Ryerson deserved no reaction from him. Samuel wasn't a child to be bullied any longer.

He should have suspected that fate was working against him when Ryerson's sneer turned into a smirk. With his gaze still fixed on Samuel, he stepped to the side and held out his hand. Samuel's heart rate increased as Piper Smith slipped her fingers into Ryerson's waiting grasp and gracefully stepped from the carriage. Looking up, Piper observed the scene, her gaze landing immediately on the corpse.

She'd grown even more beautiful than the last time he'd seen her. And this time she wasn't crying.

Those tears were one of the few things he could clearly remember from that night five years ago. Her thick brown hair unbound and blowing around her, and tears that streaked her cheeks. Blinding panic had muted him of his words, robbed him of his reason and eventually sealed his memories away behind a silent chant of *run, run, run.*

"Pip." He shouldn't have spoken, it went against protocol, but he needed her to see him.

Sam, don't leave me.

Her body stiffened and her lips parted as her gaze snapped up to his. Her surprise was easy for him to feel, the warmth of her shock and pleasure stretched out to fire every fiber within him. He'd missed that, the brush of her emotions against his mind. She'd been one of the few who'd always been able to soothe him, her kindness a balm against his battered soul.

His Piper.

But the forgotten warmth brought with it a pressure against the numb spot of his memories. The dark place he'd long given up trying to penetrate. The monster in the shadows, locked away in the box within his mind. *Run, run, run!*

No. That was the past. *She* was his past. Samuel hadn't left everything he'd ever known, created a new life, begun to explore the potential to start a family, only to step back so willingly into the darkness.

Piper's mouth had fallen open as she took a step forward, despite the way Ryerson held her back. A flash crossed her face, echoed by her emotions. Excitement bubbled inside her; the urge to leap appeared as a bright warmth in her mind.

Ryerson stepped past Piper and strode forward with a long, even gait. "Who is the sergeant in charge?"

"That would be me." Samuel gave the customary bow stiffly, knowing his men would be watching the exchange with interest. "Sergeant Hawkins." Adding his name was only a formality.

Ryerson stopped on the far side of the body across from Samuel. His eyes were pale, the irises nearly white with only an edge of blue rimming the outside. His skin stretched tight across his face, marred by only the occasional wrinkle.

"*But, sir, see it's better. The machine spoke to me and I listened.*"

"*You little fool. They aren't alive.*"

Samuel held up the tiny motor, allowing the cables to drape across his arms. "This one is. Look, I made its heart beat. And I can hear it talking to me when I plug it in. It's lonely."

The motor shattered as it landed on the floor, his cheek stinging from the slap he'd sustained.

Ryerson cleared his throat. Samuel had been staring too long. *Shit.* "The victim is female, but given the state of her body we cannot determine an age. Based on her attire I'd guess she is a prostitute. My men will ask our normal contacts to confirm this. We have collected what evidence we could and have taken a few photographs, though given the lack of light, I'm not sure we will get much detail from them. Obvious signs of a struggle. Her body was cut open and her face slashed. There is a distinct lack of blood on the scene, indicating that the body may have been moved."

Ryerson nodded. "We will make a note in the Archives once we have processed the information."

Piper stepped up beside the old man, but she wouldn't meet Samuel's gaze. He was hyperaware of every ripple of her emotions—hurt, excitement, relief. The scent clinging to her skin. How the warmth from her body seemed to beckon him closer. She'd managed to clamp down her impulsive urges to speak to him, to chat, and instead had slipped into a calmer space. Of course they would have drilled away the one thing about her he'd always loved before they would have allowed her to become an archivist.

Dammit, this wasn't how things were supposed to have gone for them.

She'd brought light to his life with her arrival at the Archives all those years earlier. He'd been relegated to the shadows, pushed aside and ground down until he was nothing. Piper saw him, forced friendship on him with her bubble and charm, and refused to let him fade further. She arrived as a child of five, but she'd somehow known how to save him.

Tonight her hair was pulled back into a simple bun. Errant strands curled across her cheeks, kissing the skin. Like Ryerson's, her attire was standard issue for their guild, plain and service-able with no ornament—full skirts, blouse, jacket, simple black boots. The lamp cast a glow across the fabric of her bodice, making it impossible to tell if it was green or blue.

"Sam. Please, don't go."

"Pip...I..."

Piper carried a large black box around her neck—the extractor. The shadows box. A thick leather strap was bolted to each side of the thing to support its bulk. Her muscles and skin pulled with the weight of the machine, and she fought to stay upright. Samuel had never held the contraption, but he knew it weighed more than thirty pounds. The Hudson's Bay Company had designed the extractor to be rugged, capable of withstanding any climate or landscape from the damp of New London springs to bitter Canadian winters. It was far too heavy a burden for such a slip of a woman to carry.

Piper let out a soft huff. "I'm ready, sir."

Christ, he'd missed that beautiful Welsh lilt. "You're running the machine tonight, Miss Smith?"

Piper's gaze finally returned to his. The dark brown of her eyes hadn't yet faded. In fact, they hardly looked touched. Samuel swallowed his sorrow that one day her eyes would become a shallow reflection of their current state. White, lifeless in their gaze.

"I am." A wave of regret flowed from her, a palpable press of emotion against Sam's oversensitive mind. They both knew he didn't want to watch what was about to happen. "Sergeant, am I clear to begin?" Piper's face went blank and the flow of her emotions stemmed. She was the only one who could do that for him. The only one who'd ever cared enough to try.

Don't do this to yourself, Pip. You deserve more. But he'd run and she'd stayed, and this was where they were now. "Yes, Miss Smith. Gentlemen, step back and give the lady room to work."

Samuel waved his men away, and all but Timmons scurried back to the shelter of the clockwerk factory. The weight of their emotions lifted enough to help Samuel focus.

Coiled hate…it was the only description he had for the emotions emanating from Ryerson. The tendrils licked out at Samuel, courting his repressed anger, luring it out to the surface. He'd learned to deal with this years ago, keeping the impact of others' emotions at bay. And yet here he stood, hands shaking and jaw clenched as Ryerson's white gaze flicked up and away repeatedly. *Goddammit, no.*

Piper eased down to her knees beside the frozen body. She freed herself from the weighted box, setting it on the ground to her left. With a brief look at Ryerson, she set to work straightening the body.

"Set the extractor beside the body close to you and get her in position," the Guild Master snapped. Piper hesitated, her fingers wrapping around the straps. "Quickly, Miss Smith."

"Let me help." Falling to his knees beside her, Samuel stretched out the dead woman's limbs and pushed aside the tattered remains of her shirt. "You need the chest exposed, yes?"

Piper nodded, a quick grin curling her lips for a moment before disappearing. Her hands shook as she fiddled with the straps of the machine, shifting the box close to the body. "And flat on her back, if possible."

Samuel bullied the corpse into the requested pose. He leaned against the body's shoulders, shivering as the cold seeped into his hands. The body protested the change in position, but eventually stayed where he wanted it to.

"Make sure she's flat. Push the organs back in if you need to, sergeant." Ryerson couldn't even bother to keep the disdain from his tone.

Samuel should have moved away then and rejoined his men. Instead, he rubbed his hands along the tops of his thighs and waited. Timmons frowned, but Samuel waved him off. There was no sense in both of them being face to face with the horrors to come. Not that Timmons listened. Stubborn bastard stayed put.

Piper cocked an eyebrow at him before turning her attention to the machine. The lid was locked, the key on a chain around her neck. He knew the metal would be warm when she pulled it from between her breasts. Unable to tear his gaze away, he watched as she did just that and leaned forward to release the lock. The hinges were silent as she carefully pushed the lid back, exposing the guts of the box.

This could have been his life.

Nothing but wires and bodies, stretching on forever and ever. Not that he'd remember any of the encounters. They'd take even the most basic of experiences from him, the sole purpose of being an archivist. Madness or memories—not much of a choice.

Piper pressed one of the leads into a small suction cup, then dipped the cup into a foul-smelling liquid kept in a pot she'd also brought with her. With the cups, she mapped out a path across the victim's chest, securing each one to the dead flesh. The stomach and chest had been slashed, but enough skin and bone remained where it was needed to make the necessary connections. Samuel watched in morbid fascination as she repeated this action—one to each temple, across the jugular, over the left eye and several spots around the neck and torso where the killer hadn't sliced. The free ends of the wires were then wrapped around contacts on the box. The moment Piper completed each circuit, a small light engaged on the control board. Soon, red, blue, and amber lights cast sparkling patterns up into the night.

Piper double checked her placements, muttering. "Base, solar plexus, heart, crown..."

"Check the ninth." Ryerson stepped closer, nodding as she made the adjustment. "That's good, child."

Samuel watched as the old man pulled a large glass cathode from his inside coat pocket. It looked like a thin glass vial, but Samuel knew it was more than that. It had to be, considering what they were about to cram into it.

"You know what to do next," the old man said with pride.

Piper full-out grinned and the sight took Samuel's breath away even at such an inappropriate moment. She was no longer an impulsive child or even the crying girl he'd left behind. No, she'd matured into a woman of twenty-one years of age, one who possessed the knowledge and confidence to face the darkness of her trade.

She took the cathode with sure fingers. The glass slipped easily into the slot made specifically for the container. Several of the men shuffled behind him, but he was too engaged watching Piper to care if they were trying to get closer or run away.

Piper put on a pair of goggles and pressed the final wire into a small notch in the frame. The lenses were blackened so it would be impossible to see the images that would be shown to her through them. Not that Samuel had any desire to witness such horrors.

"Sergeant, you might wish to move back a bit," she said in a hushed voice. "I wouldn't want you to get hurt."

"Please. You're here, I'm here," he muttered. This was old ground for them. An argument that had a much different outcome the last time they had it. "Continue, Miss Smith."

Samuel wasn't sure if she sighed, or if it was a trick of the wind, but Piper leaned forward and pressed a small button along the top of the circuit board. He counted three heartbeats before the quiet of their surroundings erupted into chaos.

Piper gasped, back arching like a current was going through her. It took every bit of his self-control to stop from reaching out and holding her tight. Instead he watched as the corpse also jumped, mimicking her with a ghoulish gasp.

Then it began to speak.

"HolyGodwhat'shappeningtomepleasedon'tithurts." The corpse's voice lacked emotion or syntax. Simply one long mess of words, pulled from memory by the archivists' bloody machine.

"Workstoomanyhours. Beautifulskinshitwanttofuckyou. Please MumcanIgoandplaynow."

Somewhere along the way, Piper began to say the words half a beat behind the reanimated corpse. Samuel ignored it, watching the lower half of Piper's face twist with emotions that weren't hers. What feeling the corpse lacked, she more than made up for.

"IhatethatbastardsomuchIwanttokillhim."

"I hate that bastard...soooo much I want to kill him."

Ryerson stood over her shoulder, watching but doing nothing to stop her from twisting and turning, and scratching at her hair. The cathode in the box glowed red. As it filled with the too-bright liquid, the corpse began to lose its voice. Piper continued the litany, speaking words of the dead.

"I don't like the dark. Why the hell am I here? Mum's solstice pudding makes me sick, but that's because she puts too much rum in it. If he's not careful, they're going to find out and then everything will go to shit."

Time ticked on for God only knew how long, as she spewed forth string after string of information in no semblance of order. Finally, she let loose a long shuddering sigh. Her body slumped forward, as if someone had pulled a lever and shut off the steam. He barely had time to react, catching her before she landed across the bloody body.

"Are you all right?" He chanced a quick press of his lips to the shell of her ear, memorizing the smell and taste of her before setting her right.

Piper's hands shook as she pulled the goggles from her face. "Not exactly what I was expecting." Tears now streaked her cheeks as she stared at him wide-eyed. They were still brown in color.

Thank God.

And yet…

"Sam, you're crying." She reached out to touch him, but stopped herself short as someone cleared his throat.

Sam brushed away the wet trail and pulled back to glance at his damp fingertips. Strange, he hadn't even realized.

"Did you gather all of the data, Miss Smith?"

Samuel jumped, having forgotten that Ryerson stood over them. "Give her a minute to catch her breath."

"She knows her duty, even if you do not." The words were bitten off, sharp and painful.

"I am well aware of my duty. I serve as a bastion of the law." Samuel spat the words, no longer caring if everyone saw his disdain. "My life to protect and serve the citizens of New London."

"I have no doubt you'll betray them too. Run away when they need you most."

The comment stung. "You never needed me."

Piper cleared her throat. "Master Ryerson, Sergeant Hawkins, I have captured all of the data—"

"Memories, Piper. They're her memories." The cold couldn't chill him as much as her words. With so little effort the archivists had begun to strip away her humanity.

"I've collected her *memories*," she rephrased, but still not sounding like the girl he remembered. "We will review them." She smiled at him, far from the professional detached manner that all the archivists used. "I'll let you know if we learn anything that will help catch her killer, sergeant."

"So it was premeditated murder?" Given the state of the body, he'd been nearly certain.

"I'm not…" She shook her head and snapped her mouth shut. He didn't need to be able to sense emotions to know Piper was frustrated. She'd always struggled between doing what she wanted and what she knew others expected. "I'll require the use of the equipment in the Archives to give you a full report, but I believe so."

"God rest her soul."

"There is no such thing. We collect only the shadow of who they were." The old man's voice was too loud in the silent evening. "I hadn't realized you believed in that superstition, sergeant. Are you finished yet, Miss Smith?"

"Yes, sir."

"Come along then. We must return." Ryerson turned on his heels and strode back to the carriage.

Not wanting it to end like this, Samuel helped Piper lift the machine, giving her room to pull the heavy strap around her neck. "Thank you," she muttered.

"You're welcome." She started to turn away from him, but he caught her by the arm, stopping her. "It's been far too long."

Piper looked up, so close he could see the light dusting of freckles across her nose. "Then you shouldn't have left."

Sam, please don't leave me.

"I had no choice. You know that."

"I know, but—" She cast a quick glance at Ryerson before leaning in and whispering. "I…there's…"

"What?" He squeezed her arm.

"I shouldn't say." She closed her eyes for a moment. "There is a procedure to follow."

"Since when did you start worrying about proper procedure?"

"Since I turned sixteen and had no choice but to play the part of an adult."

He was dancing too close with the past, but if there was something he needed to know about the victim, the sooner he uncovered the truth the better. Bending down, so his face was close to hers, Samuel rubbed his nose against her cheek. "Pip, this is me. Please."

"Damn you." He felt her shiver before she stepped back, once more meeting his gaze. "I think this murder is connected to the Archives."

Crying in the dark.

"Sammy, where are you? I'm scared."

"What? How—"

"She called the killer a zombie."

"Come now, Miss Smith!"

Piper turned and waved to Ryerson, before giving Samuel one final small smile. "I miss you still, Sam. Even if I think you were wrong to leave." She strode away without another look back.

He was forced to watch her disappear inside the carriage until the door closed. The mechanical horse roared back to life with a hissing cloud of steam, the sound drowning out the cries of a nearby child.

A killer from the Archives. Dear God.

"Are we ready to take her now, sergeant?" Timmons' voice was its normal steady self, reminding Samuel that they still had a duty to perform here.

"Yes, let's finish this up quickly and get inside where it's warm."

"You heard the sergeant, boys. Move your arses! I want to be in bed before morning."

Samuel didn't need to supervise his men, so he stepped closer to the road to give them room. The lamplight still burned bright and strong, aiding the men in their work. There were no shadows in the spot where Piper had stood. No way for the light to have fooled him into seeing something that wasn't there.

No way had he imagined the thin rings of white around the center of Piper's irises.

About the Author

Christine d'Abo is hooked on romance and, as a novelist and short story writer with more than thirty publications, her imagination is always flowing. She loves to exercise and stops writing just long enough to keep in shape. When she's not pretending to be a ninja in her basement, she's most likely spending time with her husband, her daughters, and her dogs, Jack and Jill.

CPSIA information can be obtained at www.ICGtesting.com
Printed in the USA
LVOW06s1521040414

380378LV00001B/81/P